A NOVEL

I0630394

GARY WENKLE SMITH

STORY MERCHANT BOOKS
LOS ANGELES
2018

STORY MERCHANT BOOKS

Story Merchant Books
400 S. Burnside Avenue #11B
Los Angeles, CA 90036

www.storymerchantbooks.com
www.thestorymerchant.com

ISBN: 978-1-7323411-6-6

Cover & interior design by IndieDesignz.com

DEDICATION

To quote a song from my generation: "This is dedicated to the one I love."

My wife, Pat Rearic Smith, has been my best friend, lover and wife for forty-six years. It hasn't been easy being married to me, I assure you. Not all have been blissful years, and I am responsible for most of the unpleasantness. Yet, the good times have put those other days in the distant fog, and we have a great life today, without remorse or recriminations.

During these past several years while I have become serious about my writings, she has been the one person who has steadfastly stuck with me. She has been unbending in her desire to guide me past my many faults, as a writer and a man. When I tried to mold myself into the stories I wished to tell, she removed the frill and repetition written by someone who really hadn't a clue about half the time. When I did know what I was doing, I still needed to ask her to help me do it much more simply.

Having trained to write as a lawyer made writing for enjoyment an onerous task. Lawyer's are repetitive in our legal briefs. We are taught: tell them what you are going to tell them; then tell them; then tell them what you have told them. The best legal story tellers repeat themselves with eloquence.

My first editing with Pat was a war. I had asked her to help me with *The Last Midnight*, my first published novel. Then I rejected her many suggestions to the point of turning her away. After begging her to give me a second chance, I wasn't much better at accepting her proposals that I give up significant amounts of my writing and live without it. I remember feeling betrayed at her intimation that she declared such a large amount of my precious words unworthy of publication. I confess to being burdensome and defensive.

I praise her for her amazing patience, and love. She has stuck with me in editing all that I have written. She can take long paragraphs I have labored over for hours and turn them into three sentences that say everything I was trying to convey. She can read an entire novel in a few days and make all the necessary corrections. It took a while, but now I don't ask that she edit it so that I can see what she has changed. I accept her work without question and move forward with completion of whatever I have in progress.

So, to you my dear, love of my life, best friend, my Woman-Girl, I thank you for staying with a guy like me. I am truly grateful.

INSIDE THE LIE

It is as though
the stories
never cease.
And the truth,
mixed within
the lies
is so easy
yet so painful,
that we often live
Inside the Lie
rather than searching
for that
which is just
and true.

GARY WENKLE SMITH

1.

THE COURTROOM REEKED OF FEAR. The hushed conversations halted, and all eyes turned toward the entrance each time the handle was cranked. The old hinges whined and shrieked as the ancient oak door was pulled outward. Everything in the Historic Courthouse needed restoration. In fact, the courtroom was in the same condition as all the others in the building, which was constructed in 1934 and had had little maintenance since the new courthouse was erected almost thirty years ago. It was serving as a processing center, where among other lightweight matters, misdemeanors motions were heard on Fridays, and always in that courtroom.

It was nearing 1:30 p.m., the time when all defendants were told to be present. Few of the lawyers were ever on time. Regardless, everyone with business before the court still hoped to see the face of his or her attorney coming through the doorway.

The jury box was filled with law enforcement officers, while several other cops were scattered about the room. Most were seated close to one another, speaking in confidential tones. They looked grim and fearless, but underneath that cover they were part of the atmosphere that was full of anxiety and trepidation. Each of them awaited the assault upon their integrity by one of the defense lawyers soon to show.

When Rex McKinley made his entrance at 1:22 p.m., he was the only defense lawyer present. Everyone watched him as he scanned the courtroom looking for his client, Albert Rodriguez. He saw him across the room and nodded. Albert smiled and waved, proud to have Rex McKinley as his lawyer. They had already discussed his case at length, and he knew what was going to happen. Because his case was a misdemeanor, he didn't need to be present—per the Penal Code. The judge, however, had a different idea how things worked, and always demanded the presence of each defendant. Regardless, Albert had come for the show.

Rex usually didn't handle misdemeanors except on a rare occasion like that day. Albert Rodriguez was the brother of one Rex's high school friends, Sonny Rodriguez, sports editor of the Danbrier Sun newspaper.

Rex was forty-one years old and had been a lawyer since he was twenty-five. Known as T-Rex to his friends and foes alike, he did all could to create an atmosphere of mystery and excitement as he strolled with purpose toward the defense side of the long oak wood counsel table. He did not set his briefcase on the table; not because of the sign prohibiting such conduct. It already had too many years of scarring and abuse. It was a shame to see such fine wood damaged and neglected. The four matching oak wood chairs at the counsel table had brown leather backing which was cracked and faded, and when Rex sat in one and leaned back the chair creaked. Like the door, it was in desperate need of oiling.

He was dressed exceptionally well, always better than most of his colleagues. His black wool suit was expertly tailored and appeared to have been freshly pressed. The pale mint cotton shirt he wore set off the teal green in his silken paisley tie. His shoes were glossy black, thin soled, and obviously very expensive. He was of medium height, but stood straight and tough, as though he were a giant.

As the clock ticked toward 1:30 p.m., Rex looked over at Bailiff Jimmy Vanterwellen, a good 'ol boy with over thirty years of service. Van, as he was called, had always been loyal to his judges, even though this one was a drunk.

That day Rex was moving to suppress the evidence of his client's blood—and the alcohol level thereof, and the cop he was after was Victor G. Gehrig.

2.

VICTOR GEHRIG WAS SIX FEET TWO INCHES TALL, with closely cropped white hair and steaming black eyes. He hated people, especially drunk drivers, and was known to commit some serious brutality on many of his arrestees. He scared everyone out on the street.

There was no doubt about who was the boss when he pulled over a car. If his authority was challenged, he was happy. He'd do a toe dance on a man's head and only worry about scuffing his spit-shined shoes. Women got frisked roughly, and there was an unwanted intimacy in his handling of some. That day his eyes showed distance. There was steam leaving through his brow in the form of sweat. His appearance was of a cornered grizzly.

Officer Gehrig was wearing a tan sport coat with a darker squared weave. His dark slacks sat below his large gut.

Rex swiveled to the left in his chair and looked over the courtroom. He gazed upon Victor Gehrig, Danbrier Police Officer, downtown Patrol.

Today, Gehrig was going to lie, and Rex was going to prove it—with a packed courtroom and a newspaper reporter ready to print the vivid details. Rex had a friend in the media, whom he kept abreast of courthouse news, especially his own. It didn't hurt that his client was the brother of a reporter with the same newspaper.

Van stood and loudly demanded: "All rise and come to order. Before the flags of the United States of America and the State of California, this court is now in session. The Honorable Reynold Alterman, Judge Presiding."

Judge Alterman stepped up onto the Bench with his usual bloodshot eyes and sagging face. His hair was sparse, yet he slickered the little bit that he had across his oily dome. His face was red at the cheeks and neck. He looked unhealthy and seemed very uncomfortable that day.

After settling himself in his high-backed swivel chair, which was black leather, and had been his throne since he took over in Department E, he addressed the courtroom.

"Good afternoon, ladies and gentlemen. You may be seated. Do we have anything ready?"

Rex gave the only audible response:

"We are ready on the Rodriguez case, your Honor."

"Very well. The Court calls People v. Albert Rodriguez. Please proceed, Mr. McKinley."

3.

REX WAITED FOR THE JUDGE TO FOCUS HIS ATTENTION upon him, smiling all the while. Then, he fired his first arrow, saying:

"Your Honor knows that it is the People's burden to justify a warrantless search, so I expect that Mr. Donner will be calling the arresting officer, Mr. Gehrig."

Judge Alterman did not respond, other than with glowing eyes that could easily be read as angry. It was no secret there was an on-going grudge between Rex and Judge Alterman.

Bruce Donner, a seasoned prosecutor who preferred the less serious misdemeanor calendar that usually allowed him afternoons off, excepting Fridays, took the cue and stated: "People call Officer Gehrig."

Gehrig was huge as he stood and made it a point to stare hard at Rex as he walked behind him, then past Bruce Donner as he turned right toward the witness stand. Rex watched him peripherally. The Clerk, Betty Gartner, stood across the room and from memory recited the oath to Officer Gehrig.

"I do," he swore, then slowly sat in the chair on the witness stand. It creaked loudly as he got comfortable. He reached out to the microphone and adjusted it, a task usually performed by Van, but for some reason skipped by him that day.

Judge Alterman looked over at Officer Gehrig and said: "Good afternoon, Officer."

"Good afternoon, your Honor."

There was a smile between them. Rex knew that Judge Alterman would go against him no matter what happened with Gehrig. He was a cop lover, and they would always support him in his re-election campaigns, and Rex had always opposed him.

"Mr. Donner, you may proceed," said Judge Alterman.

Staring at the report in a file before him, Bruce Donner began:

"Officer Gehrig, did you have occasion to make a traffic stop of the defendant's vehicle on June 13th of this year?"

"I did."

"And why did you detain the defendant?"

"I observed him driving northbound on Main Street swerving across the double yellow lines into the oncoming traffic lane. I activated my emergency lights and siren, and conducted a traffic stop on Main Street, just below Central Avenue. When I approached the defendant, I observed that he had bloodshot eyes, slurred speech, and a strong odor of alcohol on his breath."

"Thank you, Officer. Nothing further."

Bruce Donner never looked up from the report.

Rex had a plan for Victor Gehrig. It wasn't a trial, but a motion to suppress evidence. If he won, there would be no admissible evidence. Moreover, he'd have a written record of the lies of Victor Gehrig.

Rex stood slowly while looking at Gehrig, and inquired:

"Officer Gehrig, when was it that you first observed my client's vehicle?"

Rex seemed calm, his face blank.

"When he turned left, or northbound from Park Lane onto Main Street."

"And did the defendant give a proper signal before his turn?"

"I really don't recall. I assume so, or I would have written him for failure to signal."

"Did you notice any construction work in the area?"

"No."

"And was your vision good that night?"

"I have excellent vision. I still do not wear glasses." Gehrig leaned forward as he spoke, resting his huge arms on the counter of the witness stand. His large hairy hands were clenched.

"And were you familiar with that area prior to the evening in question?"

"Of course! It's been part of my patrol area for ten years. I know it like the back of my hand." His eyes had become beady as he glared at Rex.

"Like the back of your hand?"

Bruce Donner did not object to his quip. Rex continued.

"So, Officer, is it your testimony that after my client turned northbound onto Main Street from Park Lane that he began swerving across the double yellow lines into oncoming traffic? Is that what you have told us?"

"Yes, that is my testimony." His voice was hard, a finality in his statement.

"And can you tell the Court the approximate distance between Main Street and Central Avenue?"

"Approximately two miles."

"And how many times did the defendant's vehicle swerve across the double yellow lines before you stopped him just below Central Avenue?"

"Oh, at least ten times. I was really worried that he was going to have a head-on with someone travelling south."

That testimony was what probable cause was all about. There was a dangerous drunk driver crossing into oncoming traffic.

"I imagine you were. Do you happen to have any photographs of the area in question?"

Rex lowered his voice. Everyone was listening, except maybe the Judge, who did not seem to be paying attention. He was sitting back in his seat, eyes almost closed.

"Photographs? Why would I have those? I know the area in vivid detail. I can tell you where the trees are planted along the side of the road. I can tell you where the birds land in the spring time. I've been there for ten years, counselor."

Gehrig had raised his voice, expressing himself with righteous indignation. Rex casually crossed the room as he walked over to the Clerk, who handed him a stack of photos that been marked as exhibits that morning. He walked back to the counsel table and showed them to Bruce Donner who glanced at them and said: "Fine."

"So, Officer Gehrig, would you mind looking at some photographs that I had my investigator provide? I'll have a few questions afterward. For the record, I'm showing you exhibits one through ten."

Rex asked the Court for permission to approach the witness, even though he knew that the Judge wasn't listening. He hesitated, and then asked again, in a much louder voice, which got Judge Alterman's attention.

"You may, counsel," he said with a bit of a slur as he turned toward Officer Gehrig.

Rex handed the exhibits to Gehrig and stood close to him while he looked at them. There was no sign of recognition on his face.

"Have you had a chance to review those exhibits, officer?"

"Yes, I've looked at them. Did you have some questions, counselor?" He leaned toward Rex as he spoke.

Rex smiled but moved away from him.

"Might I show you blow-ups of those exhibits?"

Rex nodded toward an extremely muscular and tattooed man sitting in the audience, who crisply stood and walked to the wall near his seat. As he did so his image drew the attention of everyone. Eddie Logan, Rex's best friend and private investigator, had shown himself. Everyone was looking at him at that moment—the entire courtroom watching his every move, except Gehrig, who did not seem to acknowledge him. Eddie Logan wore a tiny smile at the corners of his mouth as he reached for some poster sized items—also exhibits marked that morning—and picked them up and walked forward, setting them down in front of the jury box, close to the witness stand. They were two feet wide and three feet in height. They were white in color, and as Rex turned them around it became apparent they were blow-ups of photographs. Eddie Logan walked slowly to back to his seat. Rex waited for him to sit and blend with the audience so that he had the full attention of the courtroom.

"Officer Gehrig, I am showing you what has been marked as exhibit eleven. Does that exhibit appear to be an enlargement of exhibit one?"

Rex held the enlargement up so that Gehrig could see it.

Gehrig shuffled through the exhibits, flipping them over to read the exhibit labels. "It does."

He did the same with each enlargement, getting Gehrig to agree that they matched each of the remaining exhibits, two through ten. Rex put each exhibit on the easel as Gehrig agreed that they were an accurate depiction of the area in question. After showing each of them, Rex set them on the floor in front of the jury box, except the last one, exhibit twenty, which he left on the easel.

4.

THE EASEL WAS THE NEWEST ITEM IN THE COURTROOM. It was made of lightweight aluminum framing and would hold exhibits or huge paper pads.

"Officer Gehrig, would you mind telling the court whether exhibit eleven depicts Main Street looking north from Park Lane?"

"It does."

"And would it be your testimony that each of these exhibits and the enlarged photographs, depicts Main Street and the path of travel of my client's vehicle on the night in question, as well as your path of travel as you followed him, including exhibit twenty?"

Gehrig hesitated but answered:

"Yes, counselor, I believe these photographs accurately depict the path of travel of both the defendant and me." He glared at Rex as he answered.

Rex turned his back on Gehrig and looked out over the crowded courtroom. He shook his head slightly from right to left. He drew in a deep breath then sighed as he released it. He paused for what seemed like a full minute, then asked:

"So, Officer Gehrig, would you mind telling the court what that gray thing is in the middle of the road there in Exhibit twenty?"

He looked at the photos on the witness stand railing, then at the enlargement on the easel a couple of times. He turned beet red and gritted his teeth. His jaw muscles bulged, as did the muscles over his temples.

"Your answer, sir?"

Gehrig remained silent. Bruce Donner raised his head and looked at Gehrig.

"No answer, sir? Perhaps I can help you. Isn't it in fact true that the gray thing in the middle of the road, from Main Street to Central Avenue, is a fourteen-foot-wide, nine-inch-high center divider? Isn't in fact true, sir, that there are no double yellow lines on Main Street in the area in question?"

The courtroom was completely silent, except for the heavy breathing of Gehrig. Rex let the silence settle over the courtroom for a minute, then he said:

"Your Honor, it appears as though I am going to have to ask the Court to intervene and instruct the witness to answer the question."

Judge Alterman turned deep red, his eyes glowing.

"Well, Mr. McKinley, I think you have made your point. You did a fine job. Motion denied."

"Oh, not so fast your Honor," Rex said while raising his voice. "I'm not through. I still have a witness, Mr. Logan, my investigator, who will testify that he took these photographs, and that the probable cause for the stop, crossing the double yellow lines into oncoming traffic is a factual impossibility, as your Honor can already see. So, if the court is not inclined to grant my motion, then I will continue with my witness so that I have my record for appeal."

The judge's eyes were bulging when he said: "Mr. McKinley, I have ruled. You have your record."

There was noise and murmuring in the courtroom. Rex turned his back on the court, and facing the people in the gallery he said:

"I appreciate your time and consideration, your Honor," and then muffling the rest with a cough, he said:

"Fuck you very much." Rex turned and faced the Judge.

Judge Alterman looked over to Van who was sitting at his desk. Van looked at Rex with the slightest hint of amusement in his eyes, but quickly became serious. He turned his eyes back to Judge Alterman. He shook his head in the negative, and the judge smiled.

"You're very welcome, Mr. McKinley."

The gallery roared. Judge Alterman hurriedly left the bench.

Rex turned to Donner, and quietly asked: "Dismissed, Bruce?"

Bruce nodded his head affirmatively.

Gehrig remained on the witness stand, hanging his head, hiding his red face and bloodshot eyes.

Rex looked his way and as smoothly as he could, said:

"Oh, you're excused Victor."

5.

REX LEFT THE COURTROOM, AND ALBERT RODRIGUEZ followed him into the hallway.

"Thanks, Rex. That was worth the beating he gave me. Is the case over?"

"It's over, Albert. I'll get a dismissal filed within a week or two. Don't worry. Judge Alterman didn't even set another date. I'll take it from here. I'll order a transcript and include it with the complaint." They shook hands and Albert walked off a happy man.

While smiling to himself, Rex walked back toward his office. Eddie Logan appeared at his side and joined him.

"Did you enjoy the show?"

"Most of it," Eddie paused, then said: "I hope you keep your wits about you. Gehrig hates you more than ever. The judge does, too."

"I know."

They walked in silence. It was a hot day in August. Rex removed his coat and carried it over his left arm. Then it hit him.

"Okay, come out with it. You have something on your mind, and I don't seem to be hearing you."

They continued walking. The sidewalk was radiating the volcanic energy of the summer through the soles of their shoes, or boots in Eddie's case. He always wore cowboy boots. Rex had seen him wear at least a hundred different pairs over the years.

"I think you're heading for a wreck. This thing with Gehrig today was a work of art. But did you need to do that to the judge? You're still going after Judge Alterman and that's personal, not professional."

"And?"

"And you're making up for some shit you're not dealing with."

"Wow. That hurts."

"Then don't ask."

Rex stopped in his tracks. He saw the blue sky lit by the violent sun. The trees lining the sidewalk were a sharp contrast of greens and browns against the grey concrete and black asphalt of the street. He watched the traffic on Main Street pass. People always took the time to look at Eddie Logan, female and male alike. He was a stunning figure in any place, and downtown Danbrier was no exception. He was about the same height as Rex, his arms were huge, and his shirt fit tight, always custom tailored. His ink work was the most unusual anyone had ever seen.

"Would you treat him any differently?"

"Need you ask? Did I tell you I thought you were being unprofessional? Do I have to repeat myself? What the fuck, Rex!"

They started walking toward the office, Rex consumed by the emotions of the moment, no longer feeling the heat, or seeing the street and the people rushing by in either direction. Before they reached the office, Eddie said:

"Call me when you need me. Later." He turned and walked away. Rex had a moment of regret, a hollow feeling in his gut as he watched his friend walk away. He continued the rest of the block alone, the door to his office soon coming into sight.

When he got inside the office, Gail, his ever-faithful secretary and office manager, inquired about the motion. Rex offered: "Alterman; the usual." Gail sighed.

"Bruce Donner will dismiss at the next Pre-Trial. Alterman got so upset that he forgot to calendar anything. If you call his department tomorrow, I'm sure that Betty Gartner will accommodate us and get a Pre-Trial set."

Gail was quiet. Rex thought he was king of the world about twenty minutes before but had begun was feeling like it was all in vain. He wanted to go home and call it quits for the day.

When it was late enough that he felt he wasn't being a slacker, he told Gail goodnight, and have a nice weekend. He didn't notice any response, but instead went out to his car and drove home. When he got there, he went to his study and sat at his desk, gazing off at nothing; doing nothing.

He left his study and went to his bedroom and shed his lawyer attire and put on some warm ups and a t-shirt. He laid on his bed and watched the evanescence of the sun. His body sunk into the mattress as his vision faded. At some point, he fell asleep.

6.

IT HAD BEEN DARK FOR LESS THAN AN HOUR when the driver shut off the headlights and drove to the end of the road. He parked behind some bushes. The dark man was his passenger.

The two men left the truck and began moving toward the house. The dark man gave all the instructions. He crept forward slowly and using the long wooden club he carried in his right hand, walked around the house and broke the outside lights.

"C'mon, get in there. He won't hear you," he spoke above a whisper.

The driver crept forward and reached for the door. It was unlocked. He turned the knob slowly, pushed the door open, and stepped inside.

The dark man followed him. He had a knife in a sheath on his hip and the club in his right hand. Both men wore black leather gloves.

The driver hesitated.

"C'mon, do it. Get him," growled the dark man. He urged him forward, pushing him from behind.

In a voice, far too weak and soft, the driver said:

"All right motherfucker get up."

The big man sleeping in the bed did not move.

The dark man moved forward and pulled the covers off his body. He yelled at him: "GET UP, BITCH! NOW!"

The big man's eyes opened. They were clouded. He reached for the covers, but the dark man pulled them off the bed.

The driver was pointing a gun in his face.

"GET UP MOTHERFUCKER!" The driver yelled at him, now encouraged by the ready violence of the dark man.

The big man tried to stand.

"On your knees, motherfucker!" The driver took charge. "Now, motherfucker, or I'll blow your fuckin' head off! Do it!"

As the big man rolled out of the bed and put his feet onto the floor, he tried to stand, but the dark man hit him behind his left knee with the club. He fell with a groan.

"What the fuck! Waddaya guys want?"

"You ain't such a badass now, are ya motherfucker?" The driver raged.

"C'mon man, cut this shit out. Put that fuckin' gun away."

The driver squatted down on his haunches in front of the big man yelled: "Scared now, ain't ya, bitch? How's it feel? You ain't shit, motherfucker!"

As the driver was yelling at the big man, he lost his balance and began to fall backward. His reflex to grab onto something made him squeeze the trigger of the gun. It went off, and the gun jerked back in his hand. There was very loud explosion. He looked on as everything went into slow motion.

There was a hole in the big man's forehead, with blackness around it. A spray of mist blew back into the driver's face, stinging his eyes. The big man's eyes vibrated, and then looked back at him before they began to roll upward. Red stuff blew out the back of his skull. He heard a thud as the bullet hit the wall behind him, and his body began to crumble to the floor, twisted to one side.

The driver stayed in the squatted position while it happened.

"All fuckin' right! You did him! About fuckin' time. This piece of shit had it comin'. You did him in the fuckin' head." The dark man leaned forward and looked carefully at the big man on the floor.

"Fuck! He's still breathing," said the dark man.

He dropped the club and pulled his knife from its sheath. He raised it in his right hand and struck the big man in the neck once, and then again. The blade sunk to the hilt both times with the sound of bone cracking.

The driver was still seeing it in slow motion. The large man's body jerked both times he was struck with the knife. Blood was already flowing from the wound to his head, and now his neck; it was pooling on the floor.

"Get some fuckin' towels. We're gonna clean this up and dump this piece of shit out where they'll never find him. Go! Get some stuff!" The dark man had taken over, giving orders. He wiped the blade of his knife in the hair of the dead man and grinned. He looked huge to the driver, who was looking out from the darkness that had engulfed him.

The driver stood and went to the bathroom. When he got there, he leaned over the toilet and vomited. When he was through, he retched for a few moments. He turned on the faucet, bent down and sucked in water. He spat it out, and put his gloved hands under the water, and rinsed his face and eyes. He grabbed a robe and a couple of towels, and after wiping his face he threw them toward the dark man.

"Let's go. I can't stay here," he said.

He ran out of the house, jumped in the vehicle and started the engine. The dark man jumped into the passenger side and said nothing.

The driver revved the engine, put the vehicle in gear, and raced down the dirt road to Highway 26, turning south into the night of the desert.

7.

IT WAS STILL OVER A HUNDRED DEGREES in the Basin. Flies had made their way into the house at the end of the dirt road. Although all the lights were on inside, the outside lights had been broken. The waning moon was of no help.

The call went out at around 0914 hours, but it was just past 0100 hours when he arrived. Lieutenant Russ Walden lived in Danbrier Heights, and his drive was smooth but long; it was one he did not favor. He knew the area he had come to and had investigated several killings there during his tenure with homicide. It was desert, and evidence was difficult to preserve. Heat and wind-driven sand was the enemy of any crime scene.

He parked on Highway 26, got out of his unit, and walked toward the house at the end of the dirt road called Little Basin Road, about a quarter mile in length. Upon entering the scene, his initial observation was that there were two sets of footprints leading to the house, and away from a single set of tire tracks. There were some other prints crossing some of the tracks; there were too many sets of tire tracks on the scene.

There was a set of footprints traveling around the house, with deeper impressions below each of the outside lights that had been broken. Although in sand, those prints seemed to match one of the sets of prints leading away from the tire tracks.

After entering the house and based upon the time of the call and the indications of rigor mortis, Russ Walden surmised the man had been dead for at least a few hours. His name was Steve Michaelson.

His huge body, weighing at least three hundred fifty pounds, was sprawled out on the floor, eyes open but clouded, and without a stitch of clothing. "Fuck the World" was tattooed on his left shoulder in bold black lettering and was surrounded by what seemed to be a mass of ink, which was the way most of his upper body and arms appeared. His hair was dark and long, as was his full beard.

The pooled blood that drained from his head and neck was crusty and solid around the edges, and where it had once flowed away from the body, it had congealed and dried. The killers used a towel and terry cloth robe to dam up the blood that drained away the life of the man on the floor. The blood spatters and brain matter on the wall had been dry and caked for some time. There were empty beer bottles on the nightstand, and an ashtray full of filtered cigarette butts, some white, some brown.

There was no evidence of the firearm, except a bullet that had come to rest in the wall. The height of the bullet hole was odd, but the likely trajectory indicated that perhaps the shooter had been squatting and the victim had been on his knees just before the bullet ripped through his left frontal lobe, exiting to the rear, and removing a significant amount of brain matter and skull as it spattered on the wall. By then, the bullet had been flattened from its entry into the skull, then its exit, with its final damage coming upon impact with the wall. The path of destruction was large, and although a good deal of the brain had been destroyed, the killers seemed to find it necessary to stab the man in the neck twice as he lay on the floor.

The smell in the air was one never forgotten. It was a pungent odor from the presence of death, decomposing flesh, and a large amount of blood. Every person who entered the scene of a murder perceived it, and that sensory impression made a major impact on their life.

A seasoned veteran was reminded of every dead body ever found. It was oppressive and dominated the senses and was present whether it was a fresh kill or a day's old find. If a person was around it frequently, it never left their senses. It was in their food; on their clothes; in their sinuses and embedded on their taste buds.

8.

RUSS WALDEN HAD BEEN A DEPUTY SHERIFF for twenty-nine years.
He was a Lieutenant in the Homicide Division, known by the men and women
as the L.T. He was fifty-years old, very fit. He wore close cropped hair, still
somewhat reddish, with dark blue eyes, and tanned but freckled skin. His
forearms were muscular, his hands large for a man his size. His stomach was flat,
and his chest and arms showed definition through his shirt. He was five feet ten
inches tall, stood straight and true as he walked. He had been with the homicide
division for fifteen years.

He carried a Glock .45 on his hip, and his gold badge was clipped to his belt
in front. He was wearing a short sleeved white dress shirt with a button-down
collar and the traditional black tie with black slacks and black rubber soled
shoes, which were well polished when he arrived at the scene.

Everyone there either knew him or had heard of him. Russ Walden had
come up through the ranks in a carefully paced process. His career had taken
precedence over all other aspects of his life. Loyal to the Sheriff, and to the
Department, he did what he should, with or without an order. He always
protected his team and would never undermine a fellow deputy under any
circumstances—even if it meant he had to fabricate a story; to lie if necessary.
There were those times it was for the greater good.

He was a man who would stop at nothing once he got the scent of a killer.
He was seen by some as a man who would do anything it took to secure a
conviction, regardless of whether it was within the bounds of the law, but none
in his department ever openly found fault with his ways. Russ Walden was
exceptional in many ways, but human, and had his share of character defects,
most of which were very well hidden.

During his review of the scene inside the house, Lt. Walden realized that while outside he'd observed something that troubled him and conflicted with the briefing he had received when he arrived on the scene. In fact, it tended to negate information imparted to him. He would think about it and address it later. He knew he must govern the flow of information. He made the rules on the scene. The deputy who did the briefing, Larry Wear, had come in first, and was carrying a camera. Russ Walden ordered it collected but did not want it processed as part of the crime scene evidence. He lost contact with Deputy Wear early in his investigation. He would later discover that Wear's camera was never seized.

His report would read that the crime scene needed to be carefully examined, processed and photographed. *He* would direct the photography. In Russ Walden's world, the control of evidence was always the key to a conviction.

He took photographs of the house and surrounding area and kept the forensics team out of the scene. He wanted all tire tracks photographed, but a serious problem resulted from the first deputy on the scene driving to the house on the dirt road, and then several other units followed suit when they heard the radio transmissions. There simply wasn't that much excitement in the Basin; mostly drug busts and DUI cases from people driving out that way to party. Thus, the call of a 187 got everyone excited, and careless. There was also evidence that would not fit in with his presentation. Ignoring evidence was a dangerous proposition, but there were ways to deal with conflicts.

Lt. Walden would later summarize in his notes that: "Overall, there was nothing particularly special about this killing, but for the fact that the man who had once resided in the body on the floor was the brother of a fellow deputy, Detective Donny Michaelson."

9.

DONNY MICHAELSON DIDN'T LIKE HIS BROTHER STEVE, but he loved him, or so he said when he found out about his murder. Steve had gone the opposite direction of him—at least in Donny's mind—but he was still his brother. In truth, Donny Michaelson was simply on the other side of a badge.

Donny was not huge like Steve, but older, and a whole lot meaner. He reported that he was six feet tall but was just under five-ten. He pumped iron a minimum of four days a week at the Danbrier Detention Center gymnasium, which was available to all deputies. There were clear indications that he was a steroid user. His twenty-two-inch arms were the first sign; his red face and ill temper were further evidence of his addiction to the drug. He had massive shoulders, a very small waist, and a washboard stomach.

His dark brown eyes—framed in a squared face set by black hair and eyebrows—seemed to see everything. The way he looked at people was a challenge. If a man stared back at him he was likely to make something of it. He had been known to say: "What the fuck are you lookin' at?" Sometimes he called names; he challenged every man who was not his superior at work.

His physical appearance was threatening of itself, and the rest came from a well-practiced routine of dominance and intimidation. If he were not a cop he could have been a very successful thug—some considered he was both. On the street, he was a very dangerous man, more than willing to do whatever was necessary to perform what he had defined were his duties as a law enforcement officer.

He had shot two men in the line of duty, killing them both, and never had any bad feelings about it. Administration sent him to the shrink, whom he threatened to beat senseless if he didn't give him a ready to work order. He was a master of the strong-arm tactic. He had beaten countless suspects, most of whom confessed afterward. Those who did not were isolated in custody until their injuries healed. They were usually accused of resisting arrest and assaulting an officer.

He had sworn an oath of vengeance upon whomever murdered his little brother, and he would not be stopped. The homicide team knew they must find the killers quickly, or they would be lucky to bring them in alive.

10.

THE FIRST HOUSE OFF HIGHWAY 26 was lit up, and there were two Sheriff's units parked off to the side. The occupants, Ron and Cheryl Porter, were home and they had provided information about the killing.

When interviewed, Ron Porter presented a short fat scruffy looking man who smelled like he hadn't bathed in a week and didn't use deodorant; he hadn't shaved in several days, either. A strong odor of alcohol emanated from his breath and person. His dark squinted eyes were blood shot and he swayed as he stood in the living room of the small brick house. The room was appointed with old furniture including a worn-out couch and a rocker made of dark wood.

Cheryl Porter was strikingly the opposite of her husband both in appearance, and grooming. She was tall with long bleached-blond hair, dark blue eyes, and a nice smile. The two did not seem well matched. She was too cheerful and did not look at her husband at any time during the conversation that ensued with Russ Walden.

"So, it's my understanding that you two had some contact with two men sometime yesterday? You think they might be the killers?"

Lt. Walden was standing with his notepad in hand, trying to be unobtrusive. He was conscious of how attractive Cheryl Porter was, freshly made up at almost three in the morning.

It was Cheryl who responded.

"It was Scooter Billy and some guy. They came by around four or five. They were driving Billy's old black pick up and stopped by for a beer. We heard them drive by the house, then we heard some noise, and they showed up here." She smiled at Russ Walden, and he detected suggestiveness in her eyes.

"What you're telling me is that you think those two men committed the murder next door? Is that correct?"

Russ had not looked up while asking the question but held his pen as though ready to write her answer. He was, however, watching her carefully.

Ron Porter interjected a response at that point.

"So, you think it's them that kil't Steve? Hell, hon, that ain't when they came by. It was way after dark, after the bitch went to work. She went to work, and those guys showed up way after. I heard some stuff, but I don't know what they done."

Although appearing to be a drunk, it became apparent that Ron was calling the shots in the Porter house. He was glaring at Russ when he spoke.

"Alright, Mr. Porter. Have a seat, please. I need to get some personal information from you. Do you have a driver's license?"

But he didn't sit. Instead he moved a bit closer to Russ Walden.

"I don't have to give you shit, mister. You ain't nobody. I live here. I ain't done nuthin', and I ain't sayin' nuthin' more."

Russ Walden hit the button on his hand-held twice, and the door opened. Two uniformed deputies entered the room. They immediately charged Ron Porter and shoved him onto the couch. One said:

"Sit, motherfucker, or we'll make it so you can't stand again. Got it?"

Ron Porter remained seated and said nothing. His face was red, his eyes glowing, but he didn't move.

"Can we try this again, Mr. Porter? Do you have some ID?" Russ Walden's voice had not changed. He was being courteous and polite but had not wavered in his demand for compliance. He had shown a use of force, and it worked.

Some people took a bit more assertion of authority than Ron Porter, but almost everyone complied sooner or later. It was just a matter of how much pain they could endure. From Ron Porter's easy compliance, as well as the nature of his tattoos on his arms, Russ Walden knew that he had been in prison and therefore knew how rough it could get.

"When did you do your last stretch, Mr. Porter?"

"I'm on parole. I don't want no shit, man. It ain't my fault that motherfucker got hisself kilt. Fuck him, man. I never did like him. Waddaya wanna know?"

"First, Ron—may I call you Ron? Tell me how you know *who* was killed next door.

11.

MICHAEL MOSELY WAS TIRED THAT NIGHT. He had strained his patience hours before as he had struggled with a report on a domestic violence case involving one of their own. The repeat offender was also the Sheriff's nephew. His wife wanted blood, and the Sheriff wanted her silenced.

Mosely was one of two African-American detectives in the Danbrier County Sheriff's Department. He was six feet four inches in height and weighed one hundred ninety-five pounds. He was medium dark complexioned, his hair closely cropped, high and tight on the sides. He'd never stopped wearing a Marine haircut, even though he'd been out of the Corps for sixteen years.

He got the call from Central to roll on a homicide in the Basin as back up at 0949 hours, and immediately called Rick Gutierrez, his latest partner. They arrived at the scene on the dirt road at 1157 hours, and were briefed by the patrol deputy, Larry Wear. As others in the homicide division had arrived, Detective Phil Bellgram directed Mosely and Gutierrez to find the owner of the house, one Mary Jane Rankin. They were given her work number, and Mike Mosely called her.

Mary Jane was tending bar at the Steel Spur Lounge on Highway 26 on the outskirts of town when she got the call. After Tony the bouncer told her about the call, she walked to the register behind the bar and picked up the phone.

"Yeah?"

"Ma'am, this is Detective Mosely with the Sheriff's department. We need you to come home right away."

The pause was deafening. Finally, Mary Jane had said:

"Is there a problem, officer? I'm kind of busy now. Can't it wait?"

"No, ma'am. There has been a homicide at your home, and we need you here right away. We can send a unit out to pick you up."

"A homicide? You mean, like a killing? Oh, goodness, what happened? Who got themselves killed?"

Mosely decided to hit a little harder.

"It's your boyfriend, Steve. He's been murdered."

Another long pause.

"Steve? I haven't seen him in two weeks. We're broke up. He can't be at my house. He's not welcome there."

"Ms. Rankin pack your purse, I'm coming to get you."

Mosely hung up and walked to his unmarked detective unit.

"Motherfucker. This one takes it all," he steamed. He got in and began driving to the bar.

When Mosely and Gutierrez arrived at the Steel Spur it was 0114 hours. There were a couple of vehicles in the parking lot. They walked through the front door to find the bar all but empty. Rick Gutierrez moved to the side of the room and guarded his partner as he approached the one man remaining in the bar who was busy emptying a trash can. Mary Jane Rankin did not appear to be inside.

"Sir, can you tell us where Ms. Rankin went?"

Mosely tried his best to be polite, but he was fuming.

"Who? Oh, you mean M.J? I think she split with some dude on his motorcycle. Old guy, dirty jeans. Comes around sometimes. They call him Pappy; somethin' like that."

"Do you have any idea where we might find this Pappy fellow?" Mosely was still trying to be polite and patient.

"Ya know, I don't get into people's business, mister. He could live anywhere or nowhere. I really don't give a shit. Now if you don't mind, I got work to do, and you're just in the way."

The man turned and walked into the room behind the bar and began making rattling noises as though he were emptying trash. Mosely and Gutierrez looked at each other and headed for the door.

12.

SHERIFF'S DISPATCH SENT THE ALL-POINTS BULLETIN, or BOLO—be on the lookout—over the air at 0524. It was the standard stuff when killers were sought. A very detailed description went out and was discussed in the briefing room.

"Be on the look-out for one Billy West, blond hair, five feet ten to six feet, one hundred thirty to one hundred fifty pounds, Caucasian; and another male, name unknown, generally described as six feet tall, long dark hair and a full black beard, two hundred fifty pounds, Caucasian. Subjects were last seen driving a faded black pick-up truck, nineteen seventies model, and may still be in the area. Billy West is known to have friends in the area. Proceed with caution, they are armed and dangerous."

The armed and dangerous message meant you may have to shoot the bastards. Do not let them reach for anything.

At 0949 that morning, the truck was spotted.

"There they are; the black truck. Go, go, go," California Highway Patrol Officer Jim Fairfield was commanding from the passenger seat. Dale Rider was driving. The suspects in the killing of Steve Michaelson just fell into their lap. It would be a CHP collar, and they would get the recognition. They did have to put it out on the air, and make sure that the Sheriff's people were notified.

They hit the lights and siren as they got in behind the truck. The driver looked in the rearview mirror; he was scared. The passenger had long black bushy hair but did not show his face.

As the truck pulled over, Dale Rider called out through the PA:

"Keep your hands where we can see them; put them up above your heads. Driver, put your arms out the window, open the door, and step out."

Jim Fairfield had already stepped out of the unit, shotgun in hands, with his door opened as a shield. He moved the barrel back and forth from driver to passenger. At that range, he could hit them both with a single blast.

The arrest of the suspects was without incident. Both complied with all orders, and no one was roughed up. Before they left the scene, they waited for Sheriff's patrol to secure the suspects, and make a call for the homicide team to take over the scene. Dale Rider searched the truck for weapons but found none. He looked in the bed of the truck and saw dark cloth. He retrieved two black t-shirts that appeared to have blood on them. He bagged and tagged them separately, marking the date, location of the find, and signing each with his name and badge number, with CHP as the last lettering on each baggie.

One of the deputies who had arrived at the stop said he would take the suspects to the Danbrier Basin Jail, part of the Sheriff's substation in the desert. Dale Rider had heard that the victim in the 187 was the brother of a Sheriff's deputy. He let the deputy know that the two suspects were cooperative and had no injuries.

After Billy West and Erich Trotter were in custody, and on their way to the jail, the forensics team arrived and began processing the contents of the truck. No weapons, neither gun nor knife, were found in the vehicle. There was a briefcase with dozens of traffic citations—all made out to William John West, some of them several years old. There was a lot of junk in the bed of the truck, but the find of the day was the two black T-shirts that Dale Rider had given them.

When Russ Walden heard the news, he ordered DNA testing. It would take several weeks to get the results, but most murder cases were not rushed.

It was reported that both suspects had refused to make statements.

13.

AT BOOKING, BILLY WEST WEIGHED ONE hundred twenty-four pounds and was six feet one half inch tall. His dirty, scraggly blond hair hung in his face. Instead of combing it, he ran his dirty fingers through it. His Fu Man Chu mustache was reddish blond, and he had a cracked front tooth, and two more decaying on the upper right side. He had not shaved in a few days. At 29-years old he looked aged. His faded blue eyes seemed to be out of focus. He never looked directly at anyone or anything, including the camera until ordered.

In his cell, he was listening to the music playing in his head. He passed a lot of boring times that way. He was a drug addict who preferred methamphetamine but would use whatever he could get. He sold small amounts of meth to support his habit whenever he could get someone to front him an amount larger than what he usually bought for himself. His health was poor, his mind fragmented. He really didn't have much to say about anything, but he would try to talk cool whenever he was around others who were sharing their experiences.

When Ronald Paul Maddux walked into his cell he was a real badass looking guy, with lots of tattoos on his arms. He was probably forty-years-old and had the look of a man who had spent a lot of time in prison. In fact, he was released just a few days before, but Billy didn't know it.

Maddux was big, but not tall; chunky, weighing around two hundred fifty pounds. His arms were large, and he wore a T-shirt that was too tight, and old blue jeans, and worn canvas shoes. He had yet to be processed into an orange jumpsuit, a fact that Billy did not notice.

Maddux displayed the look of a predator, but Billy didn't notice. He sized up Billy in two seconds and began to make his moves.

"Hey, youngster, what's up? Call me Big Daddy."

Maddux sat beside Billy on the concrete bench that was secured as part of the wall, and had a matching bench above it, both of which served as beds, with two-inch-thick dark green mattresses. Billy had already claimed the lower bunk. Being disrespectful to territorial rules would have caused a fight in most instances. Maddux had Billy figured for a wimp, or he would have moved more slowly.

His freshly shaved head shined with natural oils, and his dark eyes were small and close together, but penetrating. Maddux put his hand on Billy's shoulder, and gave him an encouraging squeeze.

"Looks like we're gonna to do some time together, youngster."

He released Billy's shoulder, and leaned forward with his elbows on his knees.

"What're ya in for, kid? I hear you wasted some dude. That true?"

Maddux was staring at the wall across the five-foot span to the other side of the cell. Counting the bunk built into the wall, the cell was only eight feet across.

Billy hadn't been able to speak quite yet but began to feel like that guy with some experience was being friendly.

"I shouldn't say, but he had it comin'. Fuck him!"

"No shit, huh? Are you just talkin' smack, kid?"

Billy wasn't looking at Maddux, but staring straight ahead, but didn't answer.

"I guess it's a good idea to clam up, kid. I always like this bunk, so you gotta move your shit, now."

Although Maddux had not raised his voice, Billy moved fast. While moving his stuff, Billy spoke: "Do any ridin'? My brother has a Harley."

He moved his meager belongings, which included a blanket, bed sheet, piece of paper, golf pencil, and about a third of a roll of toilet paper he would use as a pillow.

"Yeah, I ride. I was out with my 'ol lady all day yesterday. We got it on twice on the roadside. She can't get enough of me. But I'm not getting any of that for a while. I'm gonna be here with you for a bit. What'd you say they call you?"

"I'm Billy," he said, and offered his hand.

Maddux smiled, accepted Billy's hand, and squeezed real hard. Billy grimaced. Maddux smiled to himself.

"All right, kid. Don't be fartin' in here. I use the toilet first. If you gotta shit, don't let it stink. The smell of shit makes me horny, and I might just forget you ain't a real blond."

He paused. A full minute passed.

"Don't sweat it, kid. I ain't no fuckin' fag. I'll take care of ya in here."

As Billy climbed to the top bunk, Maddux said: "Let's keep down the noise for a while, youngster. Your daddy's gonna take a nap."

"Okay," Billy squeaked.

14.

"MY LITTLE BROTHER'S BEEN ARRESTED FOR MURDER."

Sitting across the desk from Rex McKinley was Doug West. Rex had become friends with Doug and his fellow motorcycle enthusiasts, known as Blood Oath Motorcycle Club, for a few years. Rex had always been aware of them because they were a motorcycle club unique to Danbrier. Although they had been around for over forty years, they never attempted to spread themselves past the Danbrier County line. No other motorcycle club had tried to claim territory in Danbrier, either.

Although there were other larger and very fierce clubs out there, no one ever picked a fight with Blood Oath. Everyone knew to challenge them meant a fight to the death.

After defending one of their members to a not guilty verdict in a murder case, they had remained friendly with Rex. Doug was in his forties and had been a member of Blood Oath since he was twenty-one-years old. His dad was a member. His brother, Dennis, had been a member, but was killed in an accident on a run to Las Vegas. Doug was the current President of Blood Oath and had been for several years.

He was large, with a very long beard he wore braided, his hair even longer. He sported skin illustrations—tattoos—all over his arms. Rex knew that tattoos covered his entire upper body, as well. The image of Doug was a scary and serious fellow.

According to the information given to Doug through a source in the Danbrier County Sheriff's Department, Billy West and another man, unknown to Doug, a fellow named Erich Trotter, were accused of murdering Steve Michaelson, the brother of a local Sheriff's detective. Doug could gather only basic information. They were being held in Danbrier Basin Jail and were going to be arraigned the following morning.

Doug was adamant as he told Rex that Billy was probably dumb enough to try to impress people in the jail, even if he didn't do it. Rex promised to visit Billy that night. Billy was arrested in the Basin, and he was being held out there to be arraigned at the Danbrier Desert Division Courthouse, a small facility with two courtrooms, a sixty-mile drive from downtown Danbrier.

Doug wanted the visit immediately and was not the kind of person you told to wait. He stood and as he made his point, gripping the back of the chair, it broke in his hands, an expensive antique. He didn't mean to break the chair, but was upset, and when he grabbed things when he was agitated, those things were likely to break, including other people's body parts.

After he promised to either fix or replace the chair, and laid a stack of cash on the desk, Rex agreed to go visit Billy as requested. It was a long drive to the other end of Danbrier County, but he went. Gail had made the call for him, and his appointment was secured.

15.

IT WAS WELL OVER THREE HOURS BEFORE Big Daddy Maddux woke. Somehow his steady snoring had calmed Billy.

"So, kid, let's talk. Ya know, when I was in the joint, my favorite time was when we got to see a movie. We won't be getting that kind of stuff here. Talkin' shit is 'bout all we have, 'cept beatin' on people, and you 'n me don't need to go there."

There was a clanking of the gates, and a uniformed deputy came to the cell door.

"West, you've got a visitor. Get your ass up and out here, now!"

Billy jumped off the bunk and walked to the cell door as it began to open.

"Careful what you say out there, kid. I'll be waitin' for ya."

Billy was led through a short maze of halls until told to stop in front of a door. The deputy used a key to open it and ordered him to enter.

The room was about four feet wide, and the same in depth. There was a mesh screen, a stool on a pipe coming out of the wall, and a very professional looking man in suit and tie with a beard on the other side of the mesh.

"Billy, sit down, please. I'm Rex McKinley. I'm a lawyer. Your brother Doug hired me."

Billy smiled.

"Have you spoken to anyone about what happened, Billy?" That was always Rex's first question to anyone in custody.

He nodded his head. "Just the guy in my cell. But he's cool. He's been in prison."

That was the easiest way to get a confession—a jailhouse rat. Billy seemed to be as simple as his brother thought.

"Don't speak about your case to anyone, ever again. Okay, Billy?"

The smile left Billy's face and turned into a whipped puppy look.

"Billy, this guy in your cell is probably going to tell the cops everything you have said to him, and stuff you didn't say. He probably won't be there when you get back. Instead, they'll put your co-defendant in there with you and record everything you two discuss. So, please, Billy, make my job easier and don't say another word. Not even a whisper. Okay, Billy?"

Billy nodded as the look of a lost soul crept over his face. His shoulders slumped, his eyes faded away to some other place.

Rex explained how the court system worked. Billy would be arraigned the following day and Rex would be there for him. It was a short jail visit. Rex wished he had gotten there earlier before Billy had blabbed to his cell mate.

When Rex returned to the office, Doug was still there, talking to his secretary, Gail. When he looked Rex in the eyes, he misread his expression.

"That dumb son of a bitch. What're you gonna do, Rex?"

"It's not what you think. Let's talk." He walked into his office, and waited for Doug to follow, and closed the door.

16.

WILLIAM JOHN WEST AND ERIC HAMNER TROTTER were arraigned the following day on one count of murder, with the enhancements related to the use of a firearm, and death resulting from the use of a firearm, which, in California, added additional twenty-five years, allowing for a possible sentence of fifty years to life, as well as the use of a deadly weapon, the knife.

Rex was given an envelope containing the basic discovery, reports on what happened, where, when, and who, and an autopsy report by Lieutenant Russ Walden. The report, written following Walden's observations of the autopsy, indicated the time of death was around nine o'clock in the evening. His recitation of facts was derived by listening to the pathologist during the autopsy. There were also two CD's, which were labeled as containing photos. There was a report of blood found on the clothing in the bed of pick-up truck.

Erich Trotter's family hired Mark Mundo, and unknown to Rex. At arraignment Rex told him:

"Mark, let me do the talking. Okay?"

Doug West had already called Mark Mundo to let him know of his concern for his little brother, and that he should follow Rex's lead. Doug asked Mark if he wanted anything mailed to his home address, which he recited for Mark. At arraignment, Doug sat in the back of the courtroom.

17.

THREE DAYS LATER, REX RECEIVED THE FIRST report on the informant—sometimes called a rat report, a jail house rat—Ronald Paul Maddux, who claimed he felt he had to come forward with this information because it just wasn't right what that kid did to that other guy.

Rex called Rick Turner and it went to his voice mail. He left a message.

"Rick, I have your rat report. Where's his rap sheet?"

Rex knew Rick Turner carried his cell phone wherever he went, unless he was with his not-so-secret lover, Stella Mendoza. Rick returned the call within a few minutes.

"His name is Ronald Paul Maddux; has some priors. Did some prison time. I can't remember what for, but I'll get it to you."

"How about now, or are you and Stella too busy?"

"Prick! I'll fax over his rap."

"How about an FBI rap on this guy?"

"Do a motion."

"Is that what keeps you out of the office today? Doing some motions with Stella?"

"Fuck you, Rex. You know I can't get an FBI rap without a court order."

"I'll send over a Stipulation for an Order. Get it back to me right away, please. I hate to make you lose your place."

"Fuck you, asshole." Rick Turner sounded angry, and Rex should have known better. No one liked to be threatened with a violation of their privacy—even joking. That was not the way to deal with a man like Rick Turner. If Rick took to disliking someone, eventually they would know it.

Rex buzzed Gail and let her know what he needed.

"I'm on it, boss."

Just as he had warned Billy West, his cellmate was a rat.

While reading through the report Rex realized that some of this information probably did come from Billy. Snitches were usually very creative. They got a bit of information from their unwary prey and started a good story. In some cases, the cops gave them additional pieces of the story so theirs would fit with the testimony of the cops. Those were dirty tricks.

18.

RICK TURNER TOOK HIS TIME SENDING back the stipulation for the FBI rap sheet on Maddux. Gail took care of getting the order signed by the Pre-Trial Judge. The order was then sent through the proper channels. In a week or so an FBI agent would appear in court with the sealed document to be opened only in the presence of the judge, with an admonishment that the document must not be freely distributed, but only viewed by the judge and lawyers involved.

Gail reported to Rex that the order was signed and delivered. Rex thanked her but was somewhat aloof as he had started thinking he needed some down time. He was a single man; divorced some months ago from a woman he had thought was so attractive. They started dating and having sex. Once that started, Rex could think of nothing else. He reflected on how someone who looked so good at first could look so bad when things turned sour.

When Sondra told him she was pregnant, he did the right thing and married her. When their daughter Ariana was born, Rex thought she was the most beautiful thing he'd ever seen. He did have a question about how she got the dark skin and dark eyes. Sondra was a brunette with hazel eyes, and Rex sandy blond with light green eyes; his beard reddish.

It took only a few weeks after Ariana was born for Rex to realize the magnitude of their problem. He confronted Sandra about the issue, and she responded that she wanted a divorce, and alimony and child support, and already had a lawyer—a guy in the local legal community Rex discovered she had been seeing on the side, a Family Law attorney named Raymundo Sanchez—Ariana's real father.

Eddie Logan had tried to tell Rex about her, but he didn't hear him. Eddie was being polite and indirect, saying things like: "Are you sure you know what you're doing with her, brother?" He even asked: "Have you been checking on where she's going these days?"

That was before she got pregnant. Rex didn't have a clue. He never understood how a person could be so cruel and conniving; so duplicitous.

It was Eddie who told him that he should demand DNA testing. That worked as a re-boot of his brain. When the results came back that he was not Ariana's father, he was relieved, but heart-broken—and still taking it hard.

That was the thing that Eddie said Rex was not dealing with; the thing that motivated him to be so unprofessional with Judge Alterman; the thing that had kept him in a state of anger and resentment, and deep depression at the end of most days.

So, he was still not getting the message. He didn't know why. Maybe because he was a man, and in need of intimacy; maybe because he was arrogant and thought it was all about him. He had, after all, been successful as a criminal defense lawyer, and had made a great deal of money as a personal injury lawyer. He still made a lot of money, and in his profession, that was the true standard of success—at least among most of his colleagues, and a pitch he tried on himself in his times of depression and feelings of failure. He had stuff just like the big players.

It was Friday and Rex didn't expect Rick Turner to give him anything that day. It was close to three o'clock, and the local watering hole, Main Street Bar & Grill, would start filling up soon. He decided he'd go have a drink, or even a few. There would be some single local girls out and about, and with some luck he might just find one.

He met with Gail and made sure she was up to date with what he needed on the West case. If Rick Turner happened to come through before the day was over, she could find him at the bar. If not, okay 'til Monday. He invited her for a drink to end the week. She politely declined.

Although Gail usually went straight home, on occasion she had accepted his invitation, but didn't like crowds, and really didn't like the way men acted toward her when they had been drinking.

The bar was just a bit more than a block away. It was a nice day out, and Rex decided to walk. Although he was generally alert to his environment, that day he was wistful and light-hearted, tuning out his surroundings. Had he been attentive, he would have felt angry eyes watching him.

19.

ONCE INSIDE MAIN STREET HE SEARCHED for anyone he knew, and a place to sit. It was large enough to house about a hundred fifty people comfortably, and two hundred who had been drinking, and no longer had any concern for comfort or privacy.

He saw one of his fellow defense lawyers, Jim Hilfer, who waved him over. Jim was with Susan, his secretary and lover. He joined them, and they exchanged a few pleasantries. Jim had been in the business a bit longer than Rex and had a successful DUI practice. He did it all, from DMV hearings to trials. He kept up with the ever-evolving science in the field. Rex usually referred all the DUI's to Jim because he was honorable and trustworthy.

Jim told Rex his money was no good at his table. Rex accepted his generosity. Jim and Susan had been sitting opposite each other, so Rex ended up sitting beside her. She was attractive, with dark brown hair, big brown eyes, and light complexion. She was in great shape, and ran 10K's somewhat regularly, even did a marathon every year.

Susan had always liked Rex, and it was mutual. He felt good sitting beside her and told her so. Jim chuckled.

While they were chatting, and as Rex was sipping a beer, a young-looking woman seemed to want his attention. He looked at her with a *who me* look; she smiled and walked toward him. As she approached he got a better look at her. She was mid-twenties, long blond hair and brown eyes that were smiling at Rex.

"Are you Rex McKinley?"

"I'm him."

"I'm Mindy Thorn. You know my dad, Frank."

Rex had represented Frank Thorn when he was charged with murder a few years back. He was the owner of a high-performance parts shop on the east side of town. If you wanted to beef up your engine, or buy a tricked out one, or any other kind of thing for a high-performance car, Frank Thorn was the man to see.

One day his wife, Brenda, was parking across the street. She was bringing him lunch. As she backed up her car to park, her bumper touched the front bumper of the vehicle behind her; just a tap, no damage. Regardless, a huge man got out of his car, and rushed to the window of Brenda's car. He hit the window hard with his fist, causing it to shatter. Frank Thorn saw it and was on his way to the rescue. The man punched Brenda through the broken window. He hit her square in the mouth, knocking out her two front teeth. By the time Frank got there, the man was returning to his vehicle.

Frank screamed at the man, who turned to Frank and said:

"You want some too, motherfucker?"

Frank was on him. He hit him once, and the man dropped to the street. Frank rushed to Brenda. He began raging when he saw what had happened to her. An ambulance was called by a passing motorist.

That huge man was Kirk Ruston, and he was drunk that morning. When Frank hit him, it was lights out. Because Frank had a reputation in Danbrier for being one of the old school tough guys, Rodney Gardner, the District Attorney of Danbrier County, decided that it was time to show all the tough guys that this kind of behavior was not acceptable. There was a dead man, and he proclaimed before the media there must be a reckoning.

At trial, the jury disagreed. They thought Frank was a hero and acquitted him on the first vote after picking a foreperson. Rex was careful to make certain there were as many women as possible on the jury—nine women and three men.

The last Rex heard Frank had contracted cancer a couple of years back. He sold the business, and he and Brenda were living in San Clemente.

Rex stood.

"Hello, Mindy. I was just beginning to think it was my lucky day when I saw you looking at me."

"It could be," she said with a smile and promise in her eyes.

Messing around with Frank Thorn's daughter might be a dangerous proposition, but Frank did love Rex, so maybe he would approve. Rex was a man, and when it came to women, he was somewhat typical. He could talk himself into anything to justify his intentions with most women, except the married ones. He knew better. He'd had a couple of cases where the clients took their response to that kind of thing to the extreme. One removed the genitals of the man sleeping with his wife. He did so with a shotgun blast at close range. Besides, Rex wouldn't want someone doing that to him—like his former spouse, Sondra. Her cheating was beyond painful. It still hurt him in ways he didn't understand.

Rex looked to Jim and Susan who both had a blank looks on their faces. He introduced Mindy to them, but neither responded, and Rex didn't think anything of it at the time. She greeted them with a nod and asked if she could have a private moment with him.

He grabbed his beer, and thanked Jim, and told Susan it was always great seeing her. He quickly moved away with Mindy Thorn. They walked until Rex directed her to a seat at a booth. Once she was seated he sat across from her.

"So, is this a business issue, or just casual conversation, Mindy?"

Rex was still reluctant to believe that any woman might be sincere—a left over from Sondra. It seemed all the women he encountered knew it, but Mindy was coming on strong and was starting to look desirable to him. He did have a moment where he really wasn't sure she was attractive. He sensed something was wrong but need made him hopeful and he pushed the thought to the back of his mind. He took a gulp of his beer, then another.

"More like personal. We never really met when you helped my dad. I'm his daughter from his second marriage, and although I have nothing bad to say about Brenda, I never really felt welcome in their home, so I wasn't around much.

"When dad was on trial, I came and watched your closing argument. It's been six years now. I was nineteen, and thought you were exciting. When I had the chance, I called my dad and told him so. He agreed, but thought I was a bit too young for you. What do you think, Rex? Am I too young for you?"

Rex took a deep breath. Things with women hadn't been going that way for him since Sondra. Women sensed his insecurity; he thought it was a turn off to them. There were those women who knew he had money, and came sniffing around, but he was generally good at reading people, and women like that were easy to detect.

This one, however, had his attention. She thought he was a star or something cool. He was thinking. Finally, he responded,

"Not too young, no."

"Is there a problem? Am I not pretty enough? Do I have zits or cooties?"

She had him laughing.

"No zits, but cooties, maybe."

They both laughed.

She was looking better each moment, but she had an edge. He didn't know whether she was wounded like him, or if there was something else going on. He really wanted to believe that it was real but had difficulty with it. Things like that just weren't happening to him those days.

"Do you still live in Danbrier, Mindy?"

"No, I moved to Oakland a long time ago. I'm here on business. I'm a buyer for a department store. We are a chain called Macy's. Ever hear of us?"

They both laughed again. Rex wanted another beer and was beginning to relax with her.

The waitress was near, and he got her attention.

"May I have another beer?" He asked the waitress. "Can I buy you another of whatever you are having, Mindy?"

"How about a shot?" She had a gleam in her eyes. "Just one?"

He was thinking. Maybe it wasn't such a bad idea. He wasn't driving, and he might just get lucky.

"Okay, but just one."

"Two whiskeys and another beer for him," she told the waitress somewhat aggressively. She looked at Rex with a grin, then said:

"This will probably sound corny, but I have thought about this several times. Not this place or this time; but being with you."

"Really?" He was starting to feel anxious.

"Scare you?"

Rex started to vapor lock and couldn't answer. He paused, then he reminded himself that he was a good trial lawyer. He tried a little cross-examination. He drew in a deep breath and began: "What was it you thought about, Mindy?"

"Just being with you."

"As in having a drink?"

"And then some."

"Are you hitting on me, Mindy?"

"Are you kidding? Isn't it obvious? You probably get this all the time."

"Well, I'm generally a shy and withdrawn guy. I don't usually notice when women proposition me."

They laughed. She stared at him some more. He saw something in her eyes but wasn't sure what; it was beginning to bother him.

The waitress arrived with the shots and a beer. Mindy grabbed hers and looked at Rex, waiting. He picked up his and tipped it toward her.

"To us," she said.

He did not respond verbally, but poured the drink into his mouth, and swallowed quickly. It burned and took his breath.

"Whew! Good stuff," he gasped.

"I love whiskey," she said.

"I don't," he said, even though he did.

"One more?"

"No thanks."

She didn't show any response to his refusal; her eyes inscrutable. She was thinking, but he couldn't read it. He was about to say goodnight. She saw it and said: "I have a room at the Radisson. Want to come up for a nightcap?"

There it was, the invitation. It seemed surreal. Something was telling him to go home, but the whiskey and her body were telling him to go with her.

He was thinking. He took a gulp of his beer; then another. The glass was close to empty. He looked at her, trying to get a reading, but the whiskey and the beer and her body were winning.

"Sure. Why not?"

It was all moving so fast he wasn't sure what was happening. He dropped a twenty on the table and got out of the booth, letting go of his hesitation. She extended her hand so he could assist her.

She was of medium build; cute and very sexy. He thought it might be great to be with her—that's what his body was telling him.

20.

THE RADISSON IN DOWNTOWN DANBRIER was four floors with forty rooms per floor. They took the elevator to the fourth floor. They hadn't spoken since leaving Main Street. Rex was uncertain of himself, waiting for her to continue with her role as the aggressor.

Stopping outside room 415, she swiped her card over the electronic lock box and a green light beeped. She opened the door, turned to Rex and offered a wicked smile. He had a fleeting thought that it was his last chance to run.

It was a standard hotel room with two queen size beds, one with some clothing and a suitcase on it. The suitcase was closed.

There was a mini-bar in the corner. Mindy rushed over to it and pulled out two small bottles of liquor.

"I'm betting you won't mind having another one since you're going to stay a while, right Rex?"

Rex looked her over carefully, and for the first time since they met he realized that she was dressed in a very short skirt, dark gray or black; a sheer white blouse, with no bra. She had taken off a gray jacket and tossed it on the bed when the first entered the room. He could see her nipples imprinted into the material. He remembered that the top of her blouse had been buttoned, but he noticed two buttons were undone, and he was seeing skin, and a peek of either well developed or expertly enhanced breasts. She was already pouring the drinks into the stock glasses that come with most hotels rooms.

Because he was watching her so closely, he hadn't seen much of his environment, not his usual style. He always scanned wherever he was, making certain he could recite what he had seen, and of course, whether he was in a safe place. It was a drill from Eddie Logan, and Rex usually was in sync with it.

There was a round table near the window, with the curtains closed. Mindy Thorn took both glasses and sat at the table.

"Come on, don't be shy. I won't bite."

Anxious feelings were flooding over him and he felt he should have been running out the door and never looking back. But, being a man, and seeing what she was presenting: a very fine pair of legs, slightly parted; a nice pair of breasts, slightly exposed; and a very naughty attitude, fully engaged, he couldn't do anything but follow the lead of his beastly desires. He was feeling aroused as he moved toward the chair and accepted the drink she was holding toward him. He sat at the small table.

She lifted her drink, smiled, and said:

"To the most unforgettable night of your life."

The look in her eyes was still confusing to him, but he tipped the drink into his mouth and swallowed. It was easier the second time. It wasn't good whiskey; it might have tasted a bit off, but nothing discernible.

Mindy stood and moved in front of him. She straddled his legs and sat in his lap, then leaned in to kiss him. He responded by attempting to kiss her back. She was holding his face, and said something, but he didn't understand. He thought she said she was sorry.

Then she tore open her blouse and he saw a button flying. He saw her breasts but felt drowsy rather than stimulated. And that was the last thing he remembered before everything turned black.

21.

HE HEARD SOMETHING, BUT COULDN'T BE sure what it was, maybe someone yelling. Then he heard it again:

"McKinley get your ass up!"

He tried to move but was having great difficulty even opening his eyes. His head felt swollen, and his ribs hurt bad; his groin hurt; his whole body hurt. He struggled to open his eyes, but when he finally got them open, he saw only a blur.

After a few moments he saw a pale-yellow wall made of concrete, and then realized he was on a concrete floor. He tried to get up, but there was something hurting him too much to move that way. He tried rolling onto his side, and then he saw it: a wall of bars. His mind was slow to register what was happening, but soon he realized he was in a jail cell.

"What the f...?" He mumbled.

"McKinley get your ass up and out of here. You made bail."

The door began to slide noisily to the left. He still couldn't see very well while struggling to get off the floor.

"Hurry up, or I'll drag your ass outta here."

He still hadn't seen the man with the voice, but he was loud and sounded mean. Rex tried again to get off the floor. He was dizzy and began to vomit. He retched for a minute and the man said:

"I oughtta make you lick that up, motherfucker. Get your ass up and outta here now, McKinley. You ain't shit."

He was so dizzy he didn't know whether he could walk. His hands found the bars and he used all his strength to pull himself up on his feet. He still couldn't see much and was hurting from head to toe. He thought he must have been beaten. He didn't know where he was except it was clearly a jail. He'd only been an official visitor in jails, never an inmate, so he didn't really know what they looked like inside.

Hands grabbed his arms on each side and yanked him around. Pain shot through his brain, he saw bright light and screamed.

The same voice said: "Shut the fuck up, asshole."

Two men were moving him out of the cell and making him walk. They were yanking and jerking him, and every time they did, he screamed in pain. They were enjoying it; every time he yelled that same voice cursed him.

They made a series of stops, the last of which was a door. He knew that because they slammed his face against it and he heard an electronic click and it pushed outward.

Both men pushed him through the door. He was standing in the visitor entranceway to the Danbrier Detention Center—that much he could see even though his vision was still blurred. Something flashed in his eyes, and someone asked something about what had happened to him.

Whoever that person was they sort of shrieked, and he heard a voice say:

"Get the fuck away from him." It was Eddie Logan who grabbed him with his powerful hands, and said:

"Come on, brother, walk with me. We need to get you out of here."

"What's happening, Eddie?"

"We'll talk when I get you home."

He walked with Eddie holding him. He felt the bright sunlight in his eyes. It hurt. He still couldn't see clearly. He realized they were in the parking lot; he saw several vehicles. Eddie guided him to a car and helped him in on the passenger side where he collapsed.

When he woke again he was stumbling from his garage into the back patio at his house. Nothing was clear yet. He hurt all over.

"I'm going to put you in the shower and run some cold water on you for a while. I have a friend coming over to get a urine sample from you. Don't let it go until I say so."

"What?" Rex said. He wasn't sure what was happening but was close to delirium.

He began to regain consciousness when he thought he was starting to drown. There was water in his mouth, too much for him to swallow. He started sputtering and spitting. Eddie said:

"Just relax, brother. I'm taking care of you. Open your eyes."

When he did he discovered he was still wearing the clothing he'd had on Friday night, including an expensive pair of black shoes, now soaking wet.

He looked up toward the voice of Eddie Logan. His vision was still blurry, but he could see enough to detect a look of rage on Eddie's face.

"What happened, Eddie? Did I do something to you?"

"No, brother. You got set up. Do you remember what happened Friday night?"

"What day is this?"

"Sunday morning. You've been in jail since Friday night. We were looking for you. If it hadn't been for Jim Hilfer calling me, I might not have known where to look. I bailed you last night, but they kept you until this morning. Now I see why."

"I saw Jim at Main Street; he and Susan. I met some gal there. Frank Thorn's daughter, Mindy."

Rex wanted to sleep. His eyes rolled back in his head. Eddie helped him out of the shower. Every part of his body hurt, and he moaned in agony.

Rex collapsed into Eddie's arms and blacked out.

When he woke, the room was bright with sunlight. He could see the digital clock, and thought it read 2:28. He tried to get up, but his ribs hurt so much he couldn't move. His head was throbbing, and when he did move he felt the agony in his testicles and screamed in pain.

"He's coming around," said a female voice. It was Gail.

"Gail, what's up?" He looked at her and it was obvious she had been crying. She didn't respond. Eddie came into view with a cup in his hand.

"It's coffee; pretty good stuff. Try to drink some. If you need to pee, do it in this cup."

He set a urine collection cup with a screw on cap on the nightstand.

"What happened to me? I feel like I got beat up."

"You did, and worse. That young lady you were with claims you tried to rape her. We need to do a urine test. You've been drugged."

"What?" He shrieked. "Rape? Drugs?" Rex passed out.

Gail was wiping his brow when he opened his eyes again. It was after three o'clock.

"It's okay, Rex. We're with you," she told him.

Eddie said: "I need you to get up and go pee in this cup. We need proof you've been drugged."

He reached out and gently lifted Rex out of the bed. They moved slowly into the bathroom. Eddie asked if he could stand, and Rex said he thought so.

"Just get some pee into that cup. Leave it on the sink. I have a friend here who will seal it and take it to the lab."

After filling the cup, he put it on the sink and while closing the cap over it, he looked up and saw his face in the mirror. He had a black eye, and it was full of blood completely covering white of his eye—subconjunctival hemorrhage. It was caused in his case by being hit with a fist. Of that he had no doubt. Then he remembered his face being slammed into that steel door after the two men shoved him into it. It was probably a combination of both.

It was then that he realized he was wearing his pajamas. He had no recollection of how that had happened either. Someone had changed him while he slept. He began a careful examination of his body. His ribs had some serious bruising on the left side. His trial lawyer skills set in. He knew whoever did that was right handed. He pulled down his pajama bottoms down and looked. He was bruised all over the area, some of it very close to his penis. His testicles were swollen.

"Jesus, Eddie, help me."

Eddie appeared by his side.

"We're going to need to get some photos, brother. You've been kicked around bad. We'll do it right here. Drop your drawers and take off your shirt. When we're done, Doc Mossman will come by to check you out."

Rex did as he was told.

Eddie used his cellphone to take several shots, and then told Rex to get dressed.

"When you're ready, come out to your study. We need to talk about what happened."

It took Rex a long time to dress again. He was having trouble moving at all, and his testicles hurt so much that he could barely walk. It seemed like the pain intensified with each move.

He made his way out of his bedroom and toward his study, the size of his home now magnified by the difficulty he had walking. As he got near his study he smelled food: eggs and bacon. He was hungry, but the thought of eating made him feel nauseous.

Eddie was waiting for him in the study. Rex took a few more steps and sat in the closest chair in front of his desk.

"You were booked for attempted rape, and possession of an undetermined amount of methamphetamine."

"Speed? Jesus, Eddie, what the fuck happened?"

"According to Jim Hilfer, he and Susan were with you at Main Street when that girl came on to you. Thank God they saw it. She asked to speak with you privately, but they both knew she was hitting on you. Both sensed something bad about her.

"I got Frank Thorn on the phone. He's not doing well. I told him what happened. Mindy *is* his daughter. She's bad news. She has a history. She's probably working off a beef. Frank will get to her for us. He still has a lot of juice around here."

"Rape? You know me better than that, Eddie. Speed? I've never touched that stuff in my life. Who's behind this, Eddie?"

Rex realized he sounded like a whiny child and became angry.

"Fuck!"

The anger was bringing him back to life.

"I remember some of it. We went to her room at the Radisson. I had a second shot of whiskey, and it tasted a bit off. I think we were about to kiss when she ripped her blouse and sat in my lap. That's it. I don't remember anything after it."

"It hit the papers this morning."

"My God," Rex moaned. He looked at Eddie who was stone-faced.

22.

DR. SAGE MOSSMAN HAD BEEN REX'S ONLY physician since he began practicing law. About the same age as Rex, he had moved to the area to complete his residency at the Danbrier County Hospital. He was smart, sensible, not too impressed with his status, and he listened well.

"Well, I don't even have a cute remark for the day. I saw the article, but they didn't report that they beat you. Your face looks bad, but it isn't. It will heal well enough. Your eye is fine, and the hemorrhaging is common, and will go away, too."

"Let's see what else we have here."

He stepped over and closed the door.

"Let's start with your upper body."

Rex removed his pajama top, and Dr. Mossman immediately focused on his ribs.

"Take a deep breath."

As he did Dr. Mossman pushed lightly on his ribs.

"Okay, I don't think anything is broken there. It's a rather professional beating. Whoever hit you probably wrapped their hand in a towel. It hurts deep but doesn't usually break anything."

He told him to turn around slowly, stopping him with his hand on his shoulder and pushed on a spot on his back. Rex groaned.

"You have a rather perfect boot print on your back, I'd say about a size eleven. That is probably the source of some of the pain in your side, but nothing broken back here, either. I think this one came from someone standing there and grinding the boot on your back.

Rex cringed.

"Sorry," he said. "Okay, let's see what's below."

"Yeah, and it feels like someone squeezed my testicles with a nut cracker, too."

He dropped his pajama bottoms.

"Oh, my," he said. "The bruising is from someone squeezing your testicles, maybe with a nut cracker."

"Not funny."

"Sorry. I know Eddie took some photos. I'd like to take some for your medical file. We don't know where this is going, and I want to document your file carefully. Okay?"

"Of course, Doc. I'm sorry for being such a whiner. I'm still in shock."

"I'm giving you a couple of Xanax, so you can relax today. I am also going to order you off work for as long as you would like. A week or two? You say it, you've got it."

"I am not going to hide from this, Doc."

"How about a day or two? You're going to feel even worse tomorrow. By Tuesday, maybe Wednesday, you'll start feeling a little better. But tomorrow is going to be rough. It was a severe beating, Rex."

"Okay, Doc. I hate it when my clients don't take my advice. I'll give it a couple of days and see how I feel."

"Listen, Rex, these guys are playing really nasty. Watch yourself, okay?"

"Thanks, Doc."

"Take one of these now and get some rest."

"Will do."

Dr. Mossman said goodbye to Gail and made his way to the front door and left.

Rex's phone rang, and he reached over to his desk and looked picked it up. It was Jim Hilfer.

"Hey, buddy, I hear you had a rough one. How are you?"

"I'm hurting, Jim, but I'll get over it," Rex said flatly.

"Susan and I felt that woman was bad news. We'll do whatever you need. I don't think this is going anywhere. I spoke with Eddie this morning. I wouldn't want him mad at me. Whoever is behind this had better find another galaxy. You're going to need someone to represent you. I'm available," Jim offered.

"Thanks, Jim. You're a good friend. I'm probably going to take you up on it. I'm going to start kicking some ass just as soon as I get over the ass-kicking they gave me."

He dropped the phone on the desk. As he gazed into nowhere, he had mixed feelings. Anger was keeping him from the feelings the humiliation and shame, but the damage to his body was an intense reminder of the cruelty he had experienced.

23.

DOC MOSSMAN WAS RIGHT, THE SECOND DAY was worse. Monday morning was starting off badly. When Rex tried to get out of bed he could barely move. He had slept hard, probably thanks to the Xanax, but he was in greater pain than the day before. He groaned as he tried to get out of bed. Gail spoke from the doorway of his bedroom.

"I have coffee, and I'll make breakfast. I'm setting up shop here. Anything on calendar this week will be taken care of and you can just rest and work from home. Don't even try to argue with me." She was angry for him; he'd never seen her that way.

As he tried to get up, Gail rushed to his side to help him. She was a big girl, with a full body, and very strong. She took his right arm and gently pulled him up into a sitting position.

"I'm good, Gail. I need to go to the bathroom. I can do it."

He had never felt so much pain as he pushed off the bed and began walking to the bathroom. He washed his face, then brushed his hair and beard as he looked in the mirror.

He was looking bad. His face was swollen and both eyes were black and blue. His left eye still had no sclera, no white of his eye; it was all blood red. He raised his shirt and the area around his ribs was deep purple, and very tender to the touch.

He dropped his pajama bottoms and what he saw scared him. His genitals were bruised a deep purple, his testicles large and swollen. He began to feel anger. He relieved himself and left the bathroom.

He had difficulty walking as he made his way into the kitchen where he found Gail at the stove cooking breakfast. She moved from the stove and helped him get into a chair, and as he groaned she began to cry. She went back to the stove and began filling a plate of food which she put in front of him, eggs and ham and potatoes. It smelled wonderful.

"Am I the only one eating?"

Gail said she would join him and brought a plate of food to the table.

"Have you heard from Eddie?"

"No, not today."

"I don't have any energy today. I'm not planning on doing anything. Maybe you should call it a day and go home. I think I'll take some time off."

Gail had a mouthful of food, but her face scrunched up. She swallowed, then said:

"You need to rise above this, Rex. There are people hoping for you to fail. That's why they did this to you."

Rex got a knot in his stomach, and he thought he was going to lose his food. Gail's words cut to the heart of it all, but he didn't want to hear it. He wanted to crawl inside himself and hide.

24.

HE WAS IN A JAIL CELL, AND THERE were people laughing at him on the other side of the bars. He was naked, and they were pointing at him, making fun of the bruises, one even saying he was missing his penis. He couldn't look at himself for some reason, but he knew that he'd lost his most precious appendage. It was over for him, and he just wanted to die, but they wouldn't let him, and the laughter became so loud that he tried to cover his ears.

Slowly he began to wake to the sound of the mower. It was Wayne, his yard guy, running the tractor-mower past the walkway on his bedroom side. It was Saturday, and he was feeling ugly from the moment he woke. The preceding days had been barely tolerable, even with Gail there to attend to him, until he sent her home on Wednesday. He was miserable, despondent.

But there was no one laughing at him. His house was empty, and he was alone. He got out of bed slowly and made his way to the bathroom. He was still bruised badly, and his ribs and testicles hurt enough to make him groan.

After he finished in the bathroom, he shuffled slowly to the kitchen and began the process of making coffee. While it brewed he went to his study and turned on his computer. He didn't wait for it to boot; instead returned to the kitchen and sat at the dining table. He had no energy and no inclination to do anything that day. As the coffee continued brewing, he heard a familiar sound of Eddie Logan's voice calling his name.

"In here," he replied.

Eddie came into view and asked: "How ya doing?" He stood in front of Rex, sizing him up, then said: "You still look like shit."

Rex didn't respond verbally. He hung his head and listened for the coffee to finish.

"Jesus, Rex, are you giving it up? I heard you lost a couple of clients, serious stuff, too; and no-showed on Billy West. Doug was there, and he gave Jim Hilfer an earful."

Rex felt anger slowly building in him. Finally, he said: "I can't do it yet, Eddie. I'm too fucked up. I'm hurt, man, can't anyone see it?"

"The only thing I'm seeing worth mentioning is you feeling sorry for yourself while everyone else is having a grand time watching you bite the big one. Is this it, man? Are you through that easy? What the fuck, Rex! I'm getting tired of trying to explain for you. You told Gail to stay home. You're not answering calls. People are talkin' and you're not listening."

Rex remained silent, then stood and poured himself a cup of coffee. He didn't offer any to Eddie, who drank it only on rare occasion. He sat at the table and slowly sipped the very hot coffee.

"Got any suggestions?" Rex was half-hearted, at best.

"Billy West needs some attention. Have you looked at the CD with the crime scene photos? There's some interesting stuff in there. I found something that just might blow the lid off it, but I can't do shit without you. How much longer do I have to wait?"

There was scorn in Eddie's voice, but Rex heard something else—a challenge to get with the program and not miss what was being said. Evidence that might make a difference? Until that moment, Rex was convinced that Billy West was going to be convicted and he was going to lose his relationship with Blood Oath. Doug West had already warned him that he wasn't taking care of business. He'd only been down for a couple of days when Doug sent the message that he had better get his ass in gear before the hearing. But Rex didn't show, and he had no intention of it until he could walk without moaning, and he wanted his face healed before he had to suffer the further humiliation of having everyone see how badly he'd been beaten. He knew there would be plenty of people who would enjoy seeing it, and he couldn't bear the thought of it. That kept him hiding, but his honor was being called into question. His duty, too. Yet, if he were to have been asked months later, he would have said it was his curiosity more than anything that brought him out of it.

"What evidence?" He asked finally. Eddie smiled, and said:

"I need your computer," and they both got up and walked into Rex's study.

Eddie pulled a thumb drive from his pocket and inserted it in the USB port. The computer immediately acknowledged the drive. Eddie waited for the files to show and clicked on a jpeg. When it opened, Rex looked at the screen, then said:

"I've seen that one. What is the big deal?"

"Don't get your panties in a bunch. Listen, then look. See the red dot in the lower right-hand corner? Just focus on it for a few seconds. It'll happen."

"Right, Eddie. What'll happen?" And then within seconds, it happened.

"You've got to be shittin' me! That's been there all along?" Rex was beginning to feel life stirring in his body. He was seeing something that he knew was a once-in-a-lifetime event.

"I didn't put it there, they did, and if Walden is the one who took the photos, he's the one who tried to hide it. Do you realize what this does to his crime scene?"

Rex knew, or thought he did, but he still wasn't into the game. He tried, but felt tired, and Eddie saw it.

"Look, brother, I'm not judging you, but you need to get with the program. There are people counting on you. Set a date to be back in the action. Something, man. You're not with it, and I need to be able to speak on your behalf. There are people asking questions, and you're not answering, so I can't answer."

25.

REX SLEPT THROUGH THE WEEKEND. He didn't turn on his cell phone, except to call Gail and leave a message that he would be up and working on Monday.

On Monday, Rex's first order of business was to send an email to Rick Turner. By then it was past noon. He had showered and got into a warm up pants and a t-shirt, no shoes. He was at his desk, and feeling a bit better, so long as he didn't move or laugh. But he was up and at it and wasn't going to give in a minute longer. He had work to do, and there were people counting on him. Eddie's voice rang in his head.

Gail was working at the computer on the long desk built into the wall across from him. His study was designed so they could do just what they were doing: working there as though they were downtown. Nothing was missing, and all their files were scanned and kept in a few different locations.

He wrote an email to Rick Turner about the Billy West case.

Rick,

Maybe you think that bullshit pulled on me was going to stop me. Think again. I want the requested discovery at my office before the day is over. If I don't get it, then I'll just add it to the public statement I intend to issue. Imagine it, falsely accused defense lawyer tells how DA's office is using bogus arrest to stall murder trial.

Maybe you don't know, and maybe you do. Your conduct in response will tell me everything.

Rex

There was absolutely no possibility that Rick Turner didn't know what had been done to Rex, and how it was done.

He sent it, almost slamming the mouse into position over the send button. He was getting angrier by the hour. He called Doc Mossman and told him how he was feeling. Doc said the body heals rapidly, but he might want to do another examination that week, depending upon how Rex felt. He suggested anger was good.

His own arraignment was set for the following Monday. Whenever bail is posted, the bondsman sets the date for arraignment. Eddie had it set soon. He did not want it to drag out. Neither did Rex. However, he wasn't looking forward to the experience of being arraigned on rape and drug charges. He still needed a lawyer, and Jim Hilfer, although a good friend and fine lawyer, was a witness. He didn't know what to do about that problem. Jim could stand in for arraignment, but he needed someone who could come to bat for him, and he hadn't a clue who to call. He believed that most the lawyers he knew would hide from it. Rape and drugs would not be something that his colleagues would want to have their names associated with, especially when it was already getting significant media coverage.

He carried a ridiculous hope that they wouldn't file a case. It lent toward understanding how so many of his clients thought and felt before arraignment. He clearly understood how brutal cops could be, and how down right dirty and deceitful some could be—just like he had been told so many times by clients.

He'd always thought he was on to all the games they played. After his experience, he knew it firsthand. It was always personal to his clients, and now it was personal to him.

Rick Turner replied within minutes.

I have your discovery. Come and get it. I had nothing to do with your Friday night excursion. The word is they're filing on you.

Rick

Rex didn't reply to the email. Instead, he exclaimed: "Fuck!"

Gail came to him and hugged him. She knew.

"We'll get through this, Rex. Don't worry. You have more friends than you know. No one believes this crap."

But Rex knew people would believe it. That was human nature, and he was his own worst enemy when it came to his profession. He'd always been an arrogant unbending prick, and knew he was going to find out just how much his attitude had impacted people's willingness to give him the benefit of the doubt.

"I need you to go to the DA discovery desk and pick up a bunch of stuff. There should be a lab report. I want it copied, and then we'll get it over to Human Tech. There should be a transfer order, authorizing them to send the sample to Human Tech. If there isn't one, which I suspect there won't be, let's take one to Judge Myer.

"There should be rap sheets on three witnesses, the Porters and Mary Jane Rankin."

Still standing by him, she hugged him again.

"We'll get through this together."

Jim Hilfer called, and Gail spoke with him for a couple of minutes, then told Rex he was on line one.

"Hey, Jim."

"How're you feeling?"

"I'm okay. They kicked my ass, but I was unconscious, so I guess that makes them a bunch of pussies."

"That's the right attitude. I took the liberty of notifying the DA that I was your lawyer, and they had a clerk call and say that they are filing, and will be asking for an increase in bail, due to the severity of your alleged crimes. So, they want to play hardball, Rex."

"Increase in bail? How can they do this?" Rex knew he sounded like a wimp. He felt that way, too. Then he got angry.

"Fuck, Jim. Do you think they'll get their way?"

"No, I don't. That's not the biggest problem. I'm trying to figure out my role beyond arraignment. I'm an important witness, and so is Susan. Let's scheme on who we can get to represent you. Got anyone in mind?"

"No. I've never even considered needing a lawyer. Can we think about it, and if you have any ideas let me know?"

"Sure. If anything comes up, call me. You have my cell."

"Thanks, Jim."

Rex was tempted to go back to bed. It hit him hard.

26.

IT WAS LATE MONDAY AFTERNOON WHEN HE HEARD IT. The noise got louder, and then it was in his house. There must have been at least six of them. Nothing sounded better than a Harley-Davidson motorcycle with loud pipes, except several of them. He knew Doug West had come to pay him a visit. Members of Blood Oath had been to his house before, but this was somewhat unexpected. As they drove up his driveway, Rex realized that his breathing was short, and he was feeling flush all over. He was embarrassed and ashamed, and knew he had to face Doug with the truth.

When the front doorbell rang, Gail said she would get it. She got along very well with the Club.

Rex heard the bootsteps before he saw Doug West standing in the doorway to his study. He tried standing, but had difficulty, and instead invited Doug in, offering a seat in front of his desk.

He was such an imposing figure, and he didn't offer a smile. Instead, he said: "You look like shit."

"That's pretty much how I feel, too."

"Well, I came to see if you're going to get over this and take care of my little brother." Doug was not smiling; not kidding. He was in full serious mode.

"It might take me a while to recuperate, Doug. But I'll be in full swing soon."

Rex was anxious, and it was showing. Doug West had come to question his ability to overcome what had happened, maybe even whether Mindy Thorn's story was true. Rex didn't like it, but he was in no position to argue. He hurt too much and was doing his best to hide his shame. The media had run with the story, and now someone in whom he had placed his hope for support was apparently standing back and watching, seeing whether he could handle the pile of shit he'd been thrown into. Being on the outs with Doug West, and therefore Blood Oath, was something Rex deeply feared. Without their support at a time like that, he might not be able to wade through the hell he was in—but he wasn't going to let it show if he could keep it down.

"I'm not one to kick a man while he's down, but I don't have much respect for anyone who stays down and doesn't try to get back up and fight. Which one'r you gonna be, Rex?"

There was menace in his voice. Rex took a deep breath, stood and looked Doug in the eyes.

"I'm no fuckin' pussy, Doug." Rex had raised his voice. "You're the second man pushing on me, and I'm listening. I got my ass kicked but didn't even have a chance to fight back. They drugged me and fucked me up, but I'm coming back. It hasn't been easy, and I could use some help here, like some faith that I've always been at your back when you needed me. Always! I could use some of the same right now."

Rex was angry with his words and his voice. Doug stared long and hard at him. Finally, he replied: "Okay. That's what I wanted to hear. We'll be with you all the way. Nobody'll touch you again. That's our word."

27.

"WE'LL HAVE A PROGRAM UP AND RUNNING BEFORE he knows what hit him."

Junior Garfano was giving the orders. He operated the Eros Club in Danbrier, a strip club. Junior was a high-level gangster, with political connections, and a group of men who followed his lead anywhere he took them. He was a member of the Brotherhood, initially established as a white prison gang, but over the years had developed a quiet but influential presence beyond the walls in many California communities.

If anyone did anything of any significance in underworld activities in Danbrier, they had to clear it with Junior Garfano. Otherwise they might be gone from sight forever. Few knew the power he wielded, and he liked it that way. For those who had reason to know him, or about him, there were rules, and they abided by them, always.

Donny Michaelson had made mistakes, one of which was taking down a drug deal that was part of an operation Junior inherited some months before, and Michaelson stole the cash and the drugs. He was about to experience serious reprisals. Donny Michaelson was going to get hit hard.

"There's a surveillance being set in place as we speak. Michaelson will be there waiting for the big bust. He won't have a clue until he starts checking. He's wired for sound, so we know where he is, and what he's thinking. Ain't modern technology grand?"

28.

IT WAS JUST PAST MIDNIGHT WHEN THEY descended upon the house. If one were wearing night vision goggles they might get a glimpse of something but would dismiss it as some tiny night creature. That was about all the heat emitted through their night suits. The technological development of fabrics that shielded body heat, and therefore infrared detection, had advanced rapidly over the past ten years.

That night members of the Brotherhood were moving through the trees as if invisible. The two dogs had been hit at with tranquilizer darts simultaneously, such that neither was provoked to complain about the other. They were large mastiffs, reportedly very vicious, but would rest peacefully for a couple of hours. The dosage would not hurt them but would keep them down for the count until all activity in the house was completed. The darts were retrieved before entering the house.

The alarm system was expensive, but easily disengaged from the central panel without the alarm company knowing there had been any tampering.

The three men entered. They were armed with Beretta 92fs 9mm hand guns with silencers. They would shoot to kill if interrupted. That was part of the deal. They would never allow themselves to be caught by anyone. They had all been inside and would never go back.

In this instance, there was more to be gained than just money. There was evidence, and Junior Garfano knew of the collection Donny Michaelson had procured over the years. The promise of evidence was the most stimulating part of the venture; the kind that would allow him to play his hand even more heavily in his turf.

One of the three men approached the safe. It sat in a room behind a wall, just as they had been told. It was built by Toledo Safe Manufacturing, a premier safe builder.

Toledo had jumped onto the national stage with high quality safes and vaults, which were impervious to anything but a nuclear blast, or the hands of a highly skilled safe cracker, like the man in the house that night.

The safe before him was an Estate Model 7000. It was seventy-two inches tall by fifty-six inches wide, and twenty-six inches deep and made of ballistic steel. The market price was $25,000.00, which included delivery anywhere in the United States; an impressive investment for a guy on a cop's salary.

The locking system was two traditional dial locks, one on each door. You could not open one without opening the other. That kind of lock had unlimited possible combinations in the three turns necessary to open it, which was multiplied by two for the each of the dial locks.

However, the man about to accomplish the task of opening this safe was careful and patient. A failed effort could result in a lock out if the system sensed that it was tampered with or punched out by an attempt at forced entry.

The man had the skills to open this safe easily and quickly. He was a mature gentleman thief, who became part of the Brotherhood many years past. In this instance, he was brought in for his skillset, and humbly promised there was no safe he could not crack, except maybe the Singapore Vault built for the Deutsche Bank to store billions in gold. He would have loved to try. Although this Toledo Safe was one of the best, but so was he, and his skills went far beyond this kind of crack.

He had the doors open in minutes. One of the other men moved forward with a rolling case from which he withdrew three black duffle bags. The third man stayed on sentry, watching, listening for any activity on his hand-held device. Prior to entry, sensors were set on the perimeter of the property to provide notice of any intrusion, including someone driving into the long driveway.

The initial view of the contents of the safe included a large amount of cash; at least four hundred thousand dollars in banded stacks of twenty-five thousand dollars each—most of which had been recently stolen from the Brotherhood by Donny Michaelson. There were two boxes of loose cash, mostly hundreds, with a lot of twenties; several thousand dollars, minimum. There was a black velvet bag. Inside it they found jewels of various kinds, diamonds, rubies, emeralds, and some other precious gems, some still on finger rings. It weighed at least ten pounds.

There were also what appeared to be a several pounds of drugs. Some white, some brown, indicating methamphetamine and/or cocaine, and probably heroin. It was packaged in kilos. The methamphetamine packaging was clearly from the recent theft. There was a lot of money in that powder. There were also boxes of syringes and bottles of anabolic steroids and testosterone.

There were three highly illegal weapons: An M-4 with a silencer, obviously full auto—a serious federal and state offense to possess the weapon, or the silencer. There were two AK-47's, both full auto, also federal and state crimes to possess.

The weapons were carefully removed and checked to see if they were loaded. The magazines on each were fully loaded, with one in the pipe. They were ready to rock and roll. Each weapon was cleared and then wrapped in a towel taken from the house, so they would make no noise while being carried. The absence of some towels would probably go unnoticed. However, the target, or mark, would undoubtedly check his stash when he came home. At that specific moment in time he was being distracted by a surveillance of what promised to be a huge drug transaction, with a very large amount of cash. Unfortunately for him, the scene was set, but no players would get on that stage. He would wait until the appointed hour. His lair would be empty long before then.

Another door was opened within the safe, and the reason for the burglary showed itself. At least sixty DVD's were carefully stacked on the shelving. Each had a label. On the very top shelf was what Michaelson undoubtedly thought his greatest prize. It was labeled "McKinley."

The safe was carefully emptied, then closed and locked, and the room that housed it was carefully closed and set in place. The single DVD was placed in in a small black nylon bag. It would be handled separately. The others were carefully placed in the rolling case, along with the cash and the drugs. The rifles were carried away in a duffle bag.

The men left the house as quietly as they entered. They had been inside for thirty-one minutes; mission accomplished without error.

The woman who had been their source of information would be given a free pass to anywhere she chose, but first she had a duty to the cause—the complete destruction of Donny Michaelson.

29.

HE CAME INTO THE HOUSE. He had been told the surveillance was a dry run. No one showed; bad Intel. And that bitch was still out of touch. He'd checked everywhere, and no one had any information; none of his informants, and not a single cop.

Because he was a creature of obsession, he checked his property and was stunned to find his dogs suffering from some malady. He didn't really care about them, other than that they were vicious, and that anyone coming near his property heard them. They were the most frightening dogs on earth. Like almost everyone else in his world, he had beaten them into submission, and they wouldn't bite *him*. But this night, they were barely alive, not moving. Something was wrong.

He raced into the house, shutting off the alarm system. That was a good sign. It was still on, but why the dogs?

He removed his gun belt, a Sam Brown with two handcuff pouches; a mace pouch with a full container; an unregistered Taser, which he really enjoyed using. He loved to watch his victims do the chicken as he hit them with darts and dialed the charge up and down. His belt also had an Asp in a pouch—an extendible baton, made of steel, that penetrated to the bone. It was much more effective in causing pain and damage than a standard issue police baton.

He went into the bedroom and pushed the wall. It opened, and he looked at his safe and smiled. He turned the right dial left, then right, then left, and it clicked and the lock on that door receded; he turned the left dial in the same pattern, and the lock clicked and receded. He opened both doors.

His scream was loud and shrill. He opened the door to his DVD's. He screamed again and continued screaming and slamming his fists into a wall until he hit a stud, breaking a knuckle upon impact. He didn't care about the pain. He had broken his rock-like knuckles on lots of heads.

He began panting like a dog when he was through with his screams. Then he began to rage, yelling and cursing threats of murder, but he didn't have a clue who hit him; not until his cell phone rang.

He answered.

"Hey, pig. How's it feel? Don't you wish you could blame this on someone? Maybe some poor guy at the jail? We have it all, and the only safe place for you is far, far away. See you soon." There was laughter before the line went dead.

The voice was one he would never forget. It was soft, yet solid. Whoever it was had no fear. He was not pretending to be tough. He *was* tough. Donny Michaelson became scared.

He stood there with his heart pounding in his chest. *They had it all.* "Fuck! Fuck! Fuck! Fuck! Fuck! FUUUUUUUUCK!" He screamed until his voice stalled.

He wanted to run, but he had nowhere to go.

His family was grateful he was gone so often. He was a horrible husband and father. When he was home, he usually did something mean to his teenaged son, often leaving him with bruises and marks. He made sure that his wife knew who was boss, and that there was no one to tell about the things he had done, including his horrible sexual behavior. He treated her like she was nothing but some cheap whore and told her so. He had infected her with STD's on three separate occasions. She hated him but knew if she complained it would only make him worse. She submitted to his beastly behavior, and told only her sister, who also hated him.

His daughter always ran into her room, then locked herself in the bathroom until he was gone. The little slut acted so righteous. He would love to slap the shit out of her. His wife had always warned him that he had better never touch her. He believed her. He knew that would be the final straw. Why put it to the test? There were plenty of people to beat on.

He knew his family feared him, and hated him, and he knew they were right. He also knew they would not help him in his time of need.

He'd been using the murder of his brother to justify his outrageous behavior of late. He hated his little brother, but he loved him, too—if he really loved at all. His deepest belief was that love was just a bullshit word.

It was times like that when he would have injected a dose of steroids, gone to the gym at Danbrier Detention Center, pumped iron for a couple of hours, and if it wasn't too late, he would find an inmate in holding and beat his ass.

But he had no 'roids. His heart was pumping so hard it felt like it was going to explode. He needed relief, and his bitch wasn't around.

He knew a couple of hookers he allowed to stay on the street for services rendered. It was late, even for them. He knew where to find one, but she was such a skank. *Fuck it.* She owed him.

He dressed, leaving most of his gear at the house, and jumped into his unmarked unit. He was going crazy, his body screaming with need. His face was deep red like he had stayed in the sun all day.

Once on the highway he drove to downtown Danbrier. She lived in an apartment on the southeast side of town. It was a shitty neighborhood, just where she belonged, he thought.

If he didn't know better, he would have thought she was waiting for him. She looked good. She waved. He began to feel aroused. He drove over to her.

"Hi, handsome. Wanna come up for a treat?"

"Don't move."

He parked his car a block away and began walking back to her at a rapid pace; scurrying along. He looked like a speed freak racing to his destination.

As he approached, she reached out and took his hand.

"I've been hoping to see you. You always give it to me so hard."

"You're really gonna get it hard tonight, bitch. You better have some dope, too. I need a bump."

"You'll get everything you need, lover."

They walked to the stairs and climbed. Hers was the first apartment at the top of the stairs, on the right.

"Let's take our time tonight, baby," she said purring.

She called him sweet names because his ego was so fragile with women. But to her he was anything but her baby. He was a mean ugly man who was a rapist and brute.

He was grinding his teeth. He wanted to strangle her while he fucked her. He wanted to make her scream. He wanted to beat her into submission; he could do anything he wanted to her.

She opened the door with her key, and they entered her studio apartment. He'd been there plenty of times in the past. The lighting was subdued, and the room smelled of perfume. He drew in a deep breath. He began smiling to himself.

"Start getting those clothes off for me. Let me go freshen up just a bit."

"You look just fine. Get your fucking ass over here now."

"Be patient, baby."

She went into the bathroom and stayed for a while. When she returned to the living room she had a mirror, with a razor, a straw, and some white powdery substance on it, some of which was in lines ready for ingesting.

He was naked and stroking himself. He was all muscles, but his penis was small, and his testicles were shrunken; the classic steroid user. He stood in front of a mirror hanging on the wall, admiring the muscles he had created while sacrificing his genitals.

Long-term use of anabolic steroids stopped the production of testosterone and male genitals began to shrink while other muscles began to bulge. A steroid user could be spotted on sight: huge shoulders and arms; a small waist; often reddened face, with squared features. Often, the hair started thickening, with some falling out; the voice began to deepen, often developing a scratchy sound; and the eyes began to bulge. Rage was always just below the surface, with high order violence happening instantly when the user determined he was provoked. Cops were some of the most common steroid users. They justified the use by their need to be stronger and meaner than the thugs on the street. They always needed to be ready to show them who the real number one was out there.

She held the mirror up to him, and he took the straw and snorted a line into his left nostril and another into his right. He sniffed in hard sucking it into his sinuses; then he growled as he felt the sting of the drug in his nasal passages.

"Get to it, bitch."

He grabbed her by her hair. She shrieked.

"Don't hurt me, please. I'll do whatever you want. Please don't hurt me. You are way too strong. You always hurt me when you take me. I can't say no, or you'll beat me like before."

It was a script given to her earlier in the evening, and one that she had practiced for this visit—but wasn't hard to remember because it was true.

They knew he would come to her or one other. She was on duty, but not the way Donny Michaelson thought.

"That's right, bitch. I take what I want, and I do what I want. You're mine to use anyway I want, so start sucking, bitch, or I'll fuck you up."

He slapped her face. She tried to scream as he was forcing his penis into her mouth. He slapped her again.

"Bite me bitch, and I'll kill ya."

She withdrew long enough to repeat:

"Please don't hurt me. I'll do whatever you want. Please, don't hurt me."

She was begging just the way he liked it—carefully performing her role.

One of the men monitoring the video feed was becoming concerned that Donny Michaelson would hurt her badly. He suggested they intervene.

"Let it go for now. He won't last another minute," said the man in charge.

He hit her again, but that time he felt weak. He tried to speak, but his tongue felt swollen. He heard her crying and begging him not to hit her again. "Please," she was saying, "don't beat me like you always do," or something like that. Then he saw the floor moving fast toward his face.

Donny Michaelson was going to learn about the word mean from people who knew how to show it. He was going to get a taste of what he so frequently enjoyed meting out to others.

30.

DONNY MICHAELSON HAD SOME PROBLEMS. He was found in the parking lot of the 10-7 Club in Danbrier. It was a cop bar, and Donny had been there dozens of times. Even so, he was not a welcome sight because he was an indiscriminate bully, on occasion knocking around some his brother deputies and officers during many of his rage-filled nights. But, whatever happened at the 10-7 Club stayed at the Club. If you didn't like it, you didn't go there.

When Donny Michaelson was discovered in the early morning hours in his unmarked unit in the parking lot, he was clearly under the influence. A medium-sized baggie with some white powdery substance sat next to a bottle of Jack Daniels that was three quarters empty on the front seat of the vehicle.

The word was that a couple of cops leaving saw him passed out in his unit and decided to call it in—just to make sure that he was not a hazard to himself, and no longer driving in such condition on a public highway. At least that was what they reported. Lots of cops hated Donny Michaelson; some more than others. He was a bad man, and a bad cop; his reputation preceded him wherever he went. Making people afraid did not always have the desired effect.

Coincidentally, the officer who investigated the situation in the parking lot at the 10-7 Club was Carl Wright, an African-American man to whom Donny Michaelson had directed some rather foul racial epithets one night at that same club, including the use of the "N" word several times. That was back when Officer Wright was just a rookie. It must have been karma that Carl Wright was on duty and in the vicinity on the night in question.

Some Sheriff's people came to get Donny, but not before Danbrier City Police Officers, Carl Wright and Bryant Holmes, attempted to have Donny Michaelson perform a Field Sobriety Test. He was so whacked out that he could barely speak. It was reported as DUI, and photographs and video were taken. A formal report would be submitted to the DA for prosecution. But, because no one saw him drive there, no case would be filed for DUI; maybe a possession of methamphetamine case, along with a drunk in public and an under the influence of a controlled substance charge, as well. Probably not, but the reports would exist somewhere.

Donny Michaelson had also been beaten badly. He was found with a broken nose, two black eyes, a couple of broken teeth, and a front tooth missing, some broken ribs, and his testicles had been hurt very badly.

The drugs and alcohol were the kind of stuff that could be discovered by criminal defense lawyers for impeachment. Probably everyone would know about it soon enough. Rumor had it there would be some press coverage, with some of those photos from the scene of Michaelson's arrest leaked to the media and splashed on the front page. No doubt the Danbrier Sentinel would post it.

Copies of a DVD showing him beating the lady of the night, Sarah Flanner, while forcing her to orally copulate him, would be mailed to Sheriff H.J. Martin, and an undisclosed list of others. But no one would see it until Donny was released from the hospital, and had testified—pursuant to a defense subpoena, at Rex McKinley's preliminary hearing. He would be well enough to testify when summoned.

31.

IT WAS EARLY TUESDAY MORNING AND REX woke thinking that there were six more days before he was arraigned on charges of attempted rape and possession of drugs. He didn't know how he was going to stand up to it.

When he got through his morning ministrations, he put on a robe, looked in the mirror and attempted a smile. His face was still tight but was looking better. The swelling had subsided significantly. His ribs still hurt, but not as much. His groin still hurt almost as much. If he walked carefully his swollen testicles didn't bang around. He thought about asking Doc Mossman to come by and make sure that he didn't have a major issue with his testicles.

He made his way into the kitchen and began a pot of coffee. While it brewed he walked into his study and turned on his computer. After he entered his password, he went back into the kitchen to pour a cup. Returning to his study, he decided to perform his daily routine of reading the news online. The Danbrier Sun was his first choice. The front-page headline read:

"McKinley Charged with Rape and Drugs for Sale."

The article read:

Rex McKinley, local lawyer of some fame, has been charged with rape and possession of methamphetamine for sale in what prosecutors and Sheriff's deputies are calling a sting operation.

According to unnamed sources, McKinley solicited a Sheriff's operative posing as a prostitute for sexual purposes last Friday night, and then offered her drugs as payment. When she refused, he forced himself upon her.

Sheriff's deputies in charge of the sting operation were nearby and heard her screams for help.

McKinley is scheduled for arraignment on the charges next Monday. He is currently released on bail.

Rex became nauseous, his stomach churning. He tried breathing so he wouldn't vomit.

He sat alone at his desk. There was no light in the world. He had no one to turn to, and if he did, they would all tell him to man up, which he did not seem to be able to do.

His desk phone rang. It was Gail.

"I'm coming in early this morning. I know you've seen the news. We'll get past this, Rex."

"Stay home, Gail. I've got nothing to do."

"Oh yes you do!" She shouted and hung up.

32.

THE WEEK WAS PASSING QUICKLY. Rex was beginning to feel better. His face had a bit of the yellow and gray tint to it, the last evidence of the bruising. His ribs didn't hurt as much, and the swelling of his testicles had subsided. He still hurt there but could get around.

The lessons of life seemed to be hard and painful for him during that time. He had a vague memory of thinking he was the center of the Universe—at least in a courtroom. He wanted to get that part back, but maybe a bit toned down. He was, after all, an accused rapist. Was there any better way to shame a man and take his power?

Eddie Logan called to check in on him and let him know that he was still on his team; but he was keeping his distance, and Rex didn't understand why.

Doug West and the other members of Blood Oath were keeping their distance, too. It hurt Rex and added to his feeling of emptiness. He had cherished his friendship with the Club, but it seemed one-sided to him as the days progressed. He had felt a deep brotherly love with those men when he represented Carey Sorenson, which was his first real up close and personal experience with the Club. Several Club members were in his office every day of trial, and they threw a party in his honor at the Club House the night the jury acquitted Carey.

To be personally screwed up and weak was not acceptable to anyone in the Club. Doug had promised him protection, but he knew he was safe anyway. No one would dare come after him again, he thought.

33.

EDDIE LOGAN CALLED OUT TO REX through the kitchen door early that next morning. Rex was thrilled to hear his voice and told him he was in the study. Eddie nodded at Rex as he entered. Once there, Eddie broke out with what might have been a smile.

"That look must mean something good is happening, or about to happen," Rex said hopefully. But Eddie turned serious.

"While you've been here suffering, I've been doing what I do. Wanna hear about it?"

Rex waited. His breathing a bit choppy. He knew Eddie Logan better than anyone else in the world. He knew him to be volatile, and that he was unhappy with Rex for being weak and slow to recover. As such, he was careful with any response. He waited for Eddie.

"Do you remember the photo?"

Rex nodded.

"I'll be gone for a few days. I need to find some stuff. Do me a favor and get with the program while I'm gone. Okay?"

Then Eddie told him that the D.A. who would be prosecuting him was Michael Carter, who was probably looking for payback for his loss in the Carey Sorenson trial. Carter had been the prosecutor in that case, and he had obviously thought it was a slam dunk winner until Eddie dug up some conflicting evidence that Carter just happened to forget existed—a second composite drawing by a witness showing the shooter looking exactly like the shooter the first witness described: a tall Hispanic male, slender build, lots of tattoos on his forearms, and brown eyes, only one of which was looking straight ahead, the other cocked to the left.

Carey Sorenson was medium height, light hair, and bright green eyes looking straight forward, and no tattoos on his forearms. You could play down one misidentification, but not two identical drawings by people who had never met, especially when the second such composite drawing was suppressed by the prosecutor. Rex made a big deal of Mike Carter hiding the ball.

After his careful cross-examination of that second witness, the jury was angry. They took minutes to acquit Carey.

Apparently, Michael Carter was still holding a grudge and was taking the opportunity to get back at Rex through the rape and drug possession charges. Rex vowed not to forgive, believing his grudge was justified.

After their conversation, Eddie left as smoothly as he had arrived.

34.

JUNIOR GARFANO AND PATRICK MOYNIHAN were meeting at the home of Junior and his wife, Shelley in San Bernardino. Patrick and Beverly Petrino-Moynihan, his wife and new law partner with the firm of London, Kyle, Smith & Moynihan, were very close friends with Junior and Shelley. In fact, it was Bev who became friends first, several years before, when she was still trying to figure a way to get next to Patrick, a man she had met only momentarily, but could not forget. She pursued him by joining the Danbrier District Attorney to prosecute Martin Van Peltzer, an accused murderer Patrick was defending. Patrick and Bev fell hard for one another and were married shortly after the Van Peltzer case.

Although Patrick and Junior had an understanding that their friendship and business relationships were separate from one another, Patrick would never say no to Junior. He knew Junior would never ask him for anything that would compromise him. And that night Junior began the conversation with a request.

They were in Junior's study with the door closed, while Shelley and Bev were sitting in the living room, quietly enjoying each other's company.

Junior Garfano's physical stature could only be described as huge and imposing. He was not tall, but his body was that of a giant, with large and heavily tattooed arms, and a neck that seemed made of steel girders. He had scarring on his neck and shoulders from his childhood abuse by his mother.

He wore a tattoo on his right arm that was the mark of the Brotherhood. He did not always let it be seen. Letting it show usually had a purpose. The person who saw it always understood. In his position as owner of The Eros Club in Danbrier, he had become the ruler of a domain everyday people would rather not see, much less ever know about: the underworld. From his position, he held a tight grip on the reins of power with the use of information first, and only when ultimately required, force—unrelenting and extremely brutal violence; murder when deemed necessary.

He spoke to Patrick:

"We've come upon some information that will probably help a young lawyer you know. He's about to ride a rape and drugs beef, and thus far it looks like he's going at it alone."

"You've got to be talking about Rex McKinley."

"I am. I know a little about him and hear he's good. They'll destroy him if given the chance." Again, Junior went quiet. His silence could rock the energy of a room, changing the atmosphere as though a storm were brewing. Patrick knew him well enough to let him take the lead.

"Here's what you need to know for purposes of this conversation. The cop, Michaelson, did us dirty," Junior paused. "And he got paid back. In the process, we found something that will clear McKinley—and it will be the death knell to Michaelson, and I want him dead. Figuratively speaking, of course."

Patrick kept a straight face, but he knew what was coming. He waited on Junior. Patrick always knew what he needed to know, and his source was the mystery man himself, Tommy Krumholtz, who always knew, and left it to Rex to inquire.

"I need to ask you for a favor." Junior shared one of his rare smiles. Patrick laughed.

"Junior, you're such a great friend. You know you need only ask." Patrick turned serious. "I've heard about what happened to Rex and I've been worried. Tommy and I met with him and his PI, Eddie Logan during the Van Peltzer case. Eddie's a very good friend of Tommy. I liked Rex a lot. You know how he handled the heavy in Van Peltzer. He never wavered."

Junior nodded. He knew everything about the Van Peltzer case, including the intimate details of the disappearance of Martin Van Peltzer—a closely guarded secret. Patrick had always suspected the truth of it, and knew that Tommy, as his best friend and investigator, was privy to what had happened, but Patrick had never asked. He simply did not need to know. He did know that the world was a better place without the likes of Martin Van Peltzer.

He gazed at Junior as he reflected on those thoughts, and Junior wore a tiny smile, letting Patrick know that he respected his approach to the disappearance of his client. They had never spoken of it, which was the way it should be among two such serious men. Junior said:

"Would it be too much for me to ask you to stand in for him on this case? You can make this case go away at the Prelim. What I have will pay big in civil rights dollars afterward. It's all yours, no strings." He looked at Patrick with his hands held out palms up. His hands were large and hard, and anyone who had the opportunity to shake hands with Junior Garfano was in for a jolting surprise—except Patrick, who had the most firm and powerful handshake even Junior had ever felt.

Junior was more than close with Patrick. Since Bev married him, Patrick and Junior had shared a friendship that was intimate and compelling. They understood each other from the very core of their beings. With Tommy married to Donna Jean, one of Shelley's closest friends, now also very close with Bev, they were all family, and referred to each other as such. It was an unbreakable bond, understood by few.

"Gladly, Junior. I'll call Rex and visit with him." He paused, then showed a bright-toothed grin and said:

"C'mon, what ya got?"

Both men laughed. Junior reached into his desk drawer and pulled out a disk, a DVD. He reached toward his book case and grabbed a remote control. He turned on the DVD player and stood abruptly, and with the smooth movements of a cat reached the DVD player and inserted the disk. He turned on the monitor with the remote, and both men waited for the disk to boot. In a few moments they were taken inside a hotel room with two people. Shortly, the man sitting in a chair by a table was handed a plastic glass by a woman, and he poured its contents into his mouth and swallowed. The woman then sat on his lap. It appeared that the man in the chair, Rex McKinley, passed out within seconds. Only moments later two men entered the room. Patrick was stunned by the remainder of the video. Yes, that case would be dismissed, and there would be a lot of money to be made by suing the two men and their employer, the Sheriff and the County of Danbrier.

Junior looked at Patrick and added:

"Did I neglect to mention that we have the woman? Her," he said pointing to the monitor. "She's all tied up with emotions about the horrible deed she committed. She'll have a new home and a new identity right after she testifies to all she knows, and she knows a lot." Junior chuckled. "My God does this woman know a lot. This Michaelson guy's a really bad boy." Then Junior went silent. He had turned to stone. His revelation to Patrick was out of character for him. Rarely did anyone get inside knowledge about the world of Junior Garfano and associates.

With no regard for the carved in stone look Junior wore, usually a way of warning those around him to tread lightly on what they have seen and/or heard, Patrick responded:

"We have the alleged victim, too? How much better can it get?"

Junior rocketed out of his serious mode with a smile.

"Her name is Mindy Thorn, and Michaelson's had her under his thumb for a couple of years now. She says he rapes and beats her somewhat regularly. She's ready to be interviewed on camera. I have her at a safe location, and she's waiting for me to send someone to liberate her soul. My guess is that'd be Tommy. Yes?"

Patrick was quiet for a while, considering the magnitude of what he had been shown and told. Finally, he smiled and replied:

"Yes, of course. Tommy will take care of Ms. Thorn. He and I will take care of Rex. And, I shall remove Mr. Michaelson's heart and watch it take its last beat." Patrick smiled at Junior, who said:

"Should we rejoin the ladies?"

Both men laughed, then got up and left the room.

35.

HE WOKE BEFORE DAWN, alert and anxious. He was beginning to understand how his clients really felt. He'd been beaten by cops, falsely accused, jailed with no idea how he got there, and today he was going to court as the defendant, an accused rapist and drug dealer.

There was a prosecutor out to get him, and some dirty cops were pushing it with lies and deceit. He had clients tell him the same things over the years, and sometimes he could prove it, other times he wasn't sure he had believed them. He knew he would be more careful and discerning now. Some of his clients appeared to have the same thoughts and feelings Rex had embraced: disbelief in his innocence.

A couple clients had asked for money back and were moving on to other lawyers. It hurt him; a painful education. How he had felt about others was how some people were feeling about him: if there was an accusation, there was probably some truth to it. If it was made against their lawyer, they needed to get away from him and not be taken down with the sinking ship.

The mere accusation of a sex crime was a very hard bell to un-ring. He feared that even when the truth came out, he would still be labeled, and a stigma would attach, and some people would believe the worst. He'd seen it many times.

Were it any other day, without the charges and the shame and guilt he felt, he probably would not have given a thought to how his life was tracking. But there *was* the pending case, and all the feelings that went with, motivating him to try to make himself a better man, a better lawyer. He knew he needed to drop the arrogant attitude—the strutting, the generally disdainful approach toward the opposition in any case—which was driven only by his unacknowledged suffering, just like everyone else.

He had never been a man to consider his shortcomings, his weaknesses, his unwillingness to bend. Those had been the subject of occasional fleeting thoughts. He'd embraced an unrelenting will to stay on top and hold the others with whom he might do battle at the edge of their seats, even though in his heart of hearts he had always known it was just so much bullshit.

Deep inside he was insecure and uncertain of who he really was, and until then he had always been able to shove those feelings into the darkest recesses of his consciousness, showing only that which he knew would count on his behalf. Introspection came hard but was what he needed to survive the assault upon his very being.

It was all at stake now, and he was going to court with a lawyer who was a witness, and with whom he had shared not a minute discussing what was going to happen. How many times had he seen that in court? Some poor soul waiting for his lawyer with whom he had spent no time, and anxiously wondering whatever was yet to come?

He finished dressing and glanced at himself in the mirror in a manner unlike his usual preening and smiling, thinking he was it. That day he felt anything but on top of it all.

He went to the garage and got into his car, opening the roll up door with the clicker on the visor, and backing down the long driveway into the street. He was shaking when he realized that he was truly alone. He knew Jim Hilfer would be there, but they hadn't spoken about anything, and Jim was simply standing in until Rex did something to bring in counsel who did not have a conflict.

The morning sun brought no light to his mind. He drove without seeing anything, following a pathway he had taken so many times before. He was caught inside his pain and fear. He felt dirty, like someone that everyone thought was a rapist.

When he arrived at the courthouse, there were media people from Danbrier, Los Angeles, San Bernardino, Riverside, and Orange County television stations, one of whom he recognized, Shirley Branson from Channel 8 News in L.A.

She stepped forward and said:

"Can I see you later, Rex?"

"Not now, Shirley," was all he could squeeze out. He moved as fast as he could toward the entrance, and got in the line for lawyers, feeling like someone might tell him he didn't belong there, a deep sense of humiliation and embarrassment washing over him. He tried to stand tall like he always did in the courtrooms just past where he waited, but he didn't feel like a lawyer.

He stood there as the accused, and was certain everyone knew, and if they didn't, all the media people trying to get to him made it clear he was the subject an inquiry; he was on the hot seat. He'd already been front page news. How could anyone *not* know?

After clearing security without looking at the faces of those he had come to know as the security team, he checked the electronic docket in the hallway and saw that his arraignment was set in Department 9, which was on the third floor of the Danbrier County Courthouse.

As Rex walked down the hallway he was hoping to see Jim Hilfer and maybe even hide behind him. There were a couple of Sheriff's detectives in the hallway, and he thought they glared at him. He found his way to the elevator and up to Department 9 and stood across the hall from the entrance.

It was 8:17 a.m. when the Bailiff opened the courtroom door and announced all the rules. She knew Rex well; they had always been friendly, but she only called his name like all the others on calendar that morning. She did not look his way when he answered.

Neither the Clerk, nor her assistant looked at him when he entered the courtroom. He tried to avoid looking at them, just so they didn't feel uncomfortable.

The Court Reporter had not made her way in yet, and usually did not until called. When she entered, that meant the Judge was about the take the Bench.

At 8:36 a.m. Michael Carter entered the courtroom. Rex looked his way, but Carter was not engaging anyone with his eyes.

Within minutes, the Honorable Gregory J. Dorsemann, Judge Presiding entered from behind the Bench, and sat down. Judge Dorsemann had been on the Bench for several years, and handled arraignments and preliminary hearings, and when the need arose, he would preside over trials. He was known for his ability to settle tough cases and was considered a fair no-nonsense Judge by all. Rex had known him a very long time and was certain he respected him. "Good morning, ladies and gentlemen. Do we have any requests for priority?"

No one stood. At that same moment, Jim Hilfer walked into the courtroom and scanned the crowd, finding Rex. He walked over and spoke to him.

"I'm going to arraign you this morning Rex, and then we're going to discuss you retaining a lawyer who isn't a witness. Let's get this done and get you out of here. I've got to let the court know we need time. Okay?"

"Jesus, Jim. I don't want this thing to drag on," Rex said firmly. He wanted it over.

"What else can we do? Have you tried finding anyone else?"

Rex had not. He'd been hiding from the world, and now his inability to handle this situation was hitting him in the face. He felt himself begin to perspire and he had a knot in his stomach with a feeling of nausea taking over. Then he felt anger beginning to rise and take him away from the wimpy feelings.

"No. I'll do something." He realized that dragging out a case that would only get worse; more media attention and more gossip.

Jim Hilfer stood and walked through the gate toward the counsel table, and said:

"Good morning, your Honor. Would you call the McKinley case, please?

"The Court calls the case of People v. Rex McKinley, DBF1121769. Please state your appearances for the record."

"Mike Carter for the People."

"Good morning, your Honor, James Hilfer for Mr. McKinley, who is present before the Court, out of custody." Rex had begun walking toward Jim. He stood silently, looking straight ahead. He had seen his clients do the same so many times.

"Good morning, gentlemen. Good morning, Mr. McKinley."

"Good morning, your Honor," Rex said in a firm voice, but looking up only slightly.

"Your Honor, I have received the Complaint, and some discovery. We will enter not guilty pleas to both counts and deny any special allegations. Although Mr. McKinley is going to need to seek other counsel, I'm asking that he Court set a Preliminary Hearing within ten days. Can we set for next Tuesday?"

"Any objections, Mr. Carter?" His Honor inquired.

"None, your Honor," said Mike Carter with what Rex saw as a smirk on his face. It may have been his imagination, but Mike Carter was his enemy at that moment in time.

"Very well, gentlemen. Mr. McKinley your preliminary hearing..." and Rex heard no more. His thoughts faded away to pretending he wasn't there, only to answer "Yes, your Honor," at the appropriate time.

When they were through, Rex left the courtroom. There was a new date set, but he didn't hear it. He just wanted to get away so that he wouldn't have to face anyone—all he could do was go. He left the courtroom and walked as fast as he could out of the building. He ignored the calls from the press, even pushing one reporter who tried to stop him by getting in his way. He got into his car and drove out of the parking lot, taking a deep breath once he was on the road.

He hadn't spoken to Jim Hilfer before he left, didn't even thank him for being there. He would call him later.

When he got to his house, he used the clicker to open his garage door and drove in, closing the door as soon as he stopped the car. Alone again, he got out of the car and walked into the large empty house, his own presence echoing off the walls.

Once in his bedroom he shed his courtroom attire, put on some warm-ups and a t-shirt, and fell onto the bed.

36.

THE POUNDING ON THE FRONT DOOR WOKE HIM. He looked over at the clock on the night stand. It was 9:45 p.m., but he didn't know what day. The pounding became louder and he pushed off the bed, making his way out of the bedroom and through the living room toward the door.

As he drew near the door he yelled:

"Who is it?"

"Rex, open up. It's Doug."

He walked to the door and opened it. He had an anxious feeling growing in his stomach. Doug stepped in, the look on his face made Rex step backward. Big Ron Garrity, the Vice President of Blood Oath followed Doug into the house. He was enormous, and the look on his face was frightening. Before Rex could gauge his feelings, Doug said:

"Eddie's been shot."

"What?" He said it with utter disbelief.

"Let's go. He's at the Medical Center. I don't know much more, except he was shot in the back."

Reflexively, Rex ran into his bedroom to put on clothing. He realized he needed to relieve himself and rushed to the bathroom. A quick look in the mirror reflected a man who had obviously been asleep. He rinsed his face and ran a brush through his hair. He dressed in jeans and a t-shirt, grabbing some running shoes and he made his way back out to the living room.

Doug said:

"I'm going to leave a couple of people here for security reasons." It was not a request for permission. Rex didn't respond, but instead started walking toward the back of the house to the garage. He heard the heavy footsteps of Doug and Ron behind him.

"I'll drive," said Doug.

Rex got into the back seat, while Ron sat up front on the passenger side. He put on his socks and shoes.

As they got into the street Rex heard several motorcycles starting, then riding behind them as they raced to the Danbrier University Medical Center.

Rex was in a daze and did not speak; neither did Doug or Ron.

37.

"HE'S ALIVE AND GOING INTO SURGERY NOW."

The woman speaking to them was a nurse practitioner with a name tag displaying Natalie. She was trying to be completely professional as she faced the grim and angry group, which now had four other Club members, including Carey Sorenson.

Eddie's best gal, Sally, was in the corner, crying her eyes out. Gail was holding her. Then he saw Tommy Krumholtz. If he had ever seen the face of death coming to offer its services, it was approaching him then.

"Come with me," he said as a respectful command.

He was looking at Rex, Doug and Ron. They followed him into a family waiting room. There was a family in there, and Doug spoke quietly to them. They smiled at him and left the room without another word. Tommy closed the door.

"He found the owner of the pick-up truck."

He was looking at Rex, who nodded still not sure what to do. His best friend had been shot in the back.

"Okay," was all Rex could manage.

"He's an ex-con named Samuel James Ellifson. He's a former Marine, Middle East duty. He served time for a home invasion robbery. He went back a second time. While inside the first time, he helped form an organization of ex-military called the Point Men. There are at least five on the outside, including Ellifson."

Doug said: "Motherfuckers!"

"There were about twenty of them in Tracy. They managed to work the system to get housed together; they've been violent and independent. Ellifson's their main man. He's been out a while and has a connection in Danbrier, one of his crew, and they put together a heist. Steve Michaelson was in on it, but he was expendable. He got in the way. Remember the briefcase?"

It was starting to fall into place for Rex, but why shoot Eddie? As if he read his thoughts, Tommy continued,

"Eddie put a word into the prison system, and he was in the process of getting all the information. He was coming out of Sally's house when he took a round to the back. It came out through his sternum. No sound; the rifle had a suppressor. You know who to contact about such things."

The last sentence was directed to Doug. It was not a question. He was referring to Junior Garfano, who would never have let such a thing happen in his territory. That meant there would be another force at work in the resolution of the problem. No one ever came into Junior Garfano's territory without his prior permission—much less use exotic weaponry, a silenced rifle. The only people who claimed equal authority were the members of Blood Oath, and theirs was a different claim; a biker world thing.

"We don't know the extent of the damage, but Sally was coming out of the house with him when it happened. He just dropped. She wasn't sure what happened until she saw the blood on his back."

"What do we do now?" Rex asked.

"You stay here, please." Nodding toward Doug and Ron, Tommy said: "We have some business to attend for now. We'll stay in touch. Put my cell number in your phone," Tommy said as he recited it to Rex.

"Okay. Thanks Tommy." Rex knew that Eddie and Tommy were close friends. Eddie had said that Tommy was his mentor, but Rex always thought a kindred soul thing was going on with them, and that they stayed close always.

Doug pulled Rex aside.

"We know he's your best friend. He's our friend, too. You do what you need to do here, and we'll do our thing. Okay, Rex?"

Again, it wasn't a question. Rex nodded at Doug who said nothing more and left with Big Ron Garrity by his side. Ron took a second to engage Rex, eye-to-eye. The message was clear and hard: get with the program, Rex. He heard it as though Ron had spoken. He nodded and got a small, almost imperceptible nod in return. Then they were gone.

He was called Big Ron Garrity and was six feet seven inches tall. His green eyes had a yellow tinge in the center, making them look like glowing wolf eyes when he was sending a message. He kept his hair closely cropped, but like Doug West, his beard was long and braided. His arms were huge, as was the rest of his body, from a body builder view. His arms were tattooed with Blood on his right arm and Oath on the left. Rex knew that he wore the Blood Oath Patch on his back, a perfect match for the one the public saw on his leather vest. He was buff, with little body fat. He hit the iron regularly, using only the best natural supplements. Blood Oath rules forbade steroids or any other chemicals.

Rex felt relieved to have Big Ron Garrity involved. He also heard his message, even though no words were spoken.

Returning to the group, Rex felt the impact of what had happened. Eddie Logan had been shot and might die. Rex could not fathom the prospect. He joined Gail and Sally. He thanked Gail for coming. He hugged Sally. She was sobbing.

"There, there, Sally. We both know it'll take a whole lot more than some chicken shit sniper to take down Eddie. He's going to be just fine."

Saying those words was allowing him to believe it. There was no way that Eddie Logan was going to die. Half the life force on the planet would disappear. It just couldn't happen.

38.

LAW ENFORCEMENT IN THE FORM OF DANBRIER POLICE were parked outside. They knew Blood Oath and had never had any problem with them. They also knew that the members would not cooperate in any way with their investigation. It was a Sheriff's case anyway.

Time passed very slowly. It was getting light outside; they had been there for a several hours.

Rex began pacing the long hallways. When he made what seemed like his fiftieth pass by the double doors into which the nurse had entered with a pass card, he saw someone coming out. It was Nurse Natalie with a very serious look on her face, but it wasn't the look of death.

When she came through the double doors that opened electronically with a whoosh, they all gathered around her.

"Mr. Logan is going to be fine. He's a rather amazing man."

Sally started crying again.

"How bad is it?" Rex had to ask.

"The doctor will be out soon."

"Thank you, Natalie."

Rex walked outside. Carey Sorenson and a couple of the guys walked over to him. He told them:

"You know Eddie Logan. It'll take a lot more than a back-shooting chicken shit to take him down for long."

They all nodded in response, and Carey said,

"We got your back here, Rex. Like you said, it'll take a lot more than some coward assed punk to take out Eddie."

Rex nodded and excused himself, saying: "I need to pass the word."

39.

IT WAS DAYLIGHT WHEN DR. STERNBERG came through the double doors. He introduced himself to Rex and acknowledged the group that had been increasing in size during the hours of waiting.

Dr. Sternberg appeared to be in his fifties, with a pleasant face that reflected an encouraging smile.

"Your friend is an amazing specimen of mankind. He is already giving orders. When he woke, he tried to leave. Fortunately, I was there, and explained that he needed to rest for a while, or he might bleed to death." There was a group chuckle.

"I don't think I have ever encountered anyone with such a strong will to live. His wounds are severe, but he will recover. It's going to take some time no matter how strong his desire to jump back on his feet. I'll need to find a specialty doctor, one who can handle titanium plating. His sternum was shattered, and when I suggested some chrome he said that was cool."

Again, they laughed. That was Eddie.

"He will probably be trying to check himself out in the next couple of days, so I hope you will all encourage him to settle down. He needs to stay with us for a for quite some time.

"The damage to his lung is repaired. It was a small caliber bullet, probably a .22, and it went in between number three and four ribs shattering number 4 and taking some bone into the lung. It was a close call. A bit more bone and that bullet would have rattled around in him, and he might not be with us today. But it seems your friend has somebody up there looking out for him." He looked to the ceiling when he said it.

"I'm going to let you in, but only one at a time, and only for a minute or two each. He's coming out of a general anesthesia and is a bit groggy."

"Sounds great, Doc" said Rex.

"Who wants to go first?" Dr. Sternberg looked to Rex, who looked at Sally, and she nodded at him.

"Me, Doc," said Rex.

"Follow me, please."

They went through the double doors that whooshed open and then whooshed closed. It felt like a Star Trek adventure until Rex's sense of smell was jolted—typical hospital, with all the unusual smells of alcohol, disinfectant, and human suffering. There was a nurse's station ahead, with people wearing scrubs walking everywhere, some of them wearing white smocks. No one seemed to be paying attention to them as they walked while turning slightly to the right. From what Rex could see, the area was laid out in a circle, with the nurse's station in the center.

They walked around it to an area where there was a large open space, and then a couple of rooms opening off that area. In the middle, there was another nurse's station.

One of the women approached Rex and handed him a robe and a mask. He didn't question her. He put on the robe and fitted the mask around his nose and mouth. She pointed to the hand cleaner dispenser, and he pushed the lever with his hand under the dispenser and rubbed both hands together; he smelled the strong odor of alcohol even with the mask on his face.

They went into a room with only one bed, and there was his best friend. Rex walked over to him, and his eyes opened. Eddie Logan looked at him and said with a very scratchy voice:

"I thought you weren't that kind of doctor."

Rex laughed; an old joke. Rex graduated from law school with a Juris Doctor degree.

"Funny. When 'ya getting' out?"

"Bail me and I'm outta here."

"Bail's too high. I think you need to stay a few days and dry out."

"Everyone else okay?" Eddie asked.

"Yep."

"I can handle this shit."

"I know."

He said: "C'mere."

Rex bent down, and Eddie whispered into his ear. It took a while.

Rex stood back with a somber look.

"Got it." But he hadn't really understood. Eddie was trying to tell him something, but his voice was so weak he seemed to be muttering. He was groggy from the anesthetics. Maybe later, Rex thought.

Rex looked him over. His enormous arms had tubes running into them, with a couple of bags of fluids draining into the tubes. His chest was covered with gauze and tape.

"It went through you. Doc said you need some extra chrome." Rex thought he was being cool.

Eddie smiled. "I'll never make it through the metal detectors now."

Eddie smiled and began closing his eyes.

"I think we should let him rest now," said Dr. Sternberg.

"Okay, Doc. I'll be back later, brother. Try doing what they tell you, okay?"

Eddie nodded slightly and fell sleep.

They walked back out, and everyone was huddling together. Rex smiled at them, and all their faces lit up.

Before Rex could speak, Dr. Sternberg said,

"I think we had better wait for any other visits. He's sleeping."

Rex added:

"He's fine. He was talking, and now he's sleeping. He'll be out of here in no time."

Sally rushed over and hugged Rex. He had forgotten how tall she was until she held him, and he had to crank his neck to look at her.

"He's fine. You know him. He's already talkin' shit."

She sobbed on his shoulder. He held her for a while. She looked at him sweetly.

"He loves you, Rex, and so do I. Thanks for being his friend."

"He's my brother."

She hugged him again.

They discussed taking turns at the hospital. Everyone knew if Eddie was talking, then he was going to be alright. However, there had been an attempt on his life, and Rex needed to make certain he was protected; not Rex's area of expertise. He left that to the brothers in Blood Oath.

It was three days before Rex decided to leave the hospital. There had been several reports on Eddie's progress. Rex had slept in a chair in his room at night, visiting several times each day. He seemed to be healing rapidly, which was no surprise to anyone.

40.

THE MAN SAT BLINDFOLDED WITH A BLACK BAG over his head and was handcuffed hard behind his back. His arms were pulled tight behind the chair with a rope wrapped around his biceps. A little tightening and his shoulders would tear, and if the pressure was applied slowly, the shoulders tore slowly—an extremely painful method of gaining compliance.

The steel chair in which he was strapped was bolted to the floor. He didn't know where he was, but he knew how he got there. He had been cuffed, hooded, and thrown into the trunk of a car that went over some very rough roads, like they were unpaved and full of holes and dips; he had taken a beating.

He felt the presence of someone with him. The black bag was taken off his head. He still could not see. He tried to bend his head backward to see under the blindfold and was slapped by an enormous hand. His head wobbled.

"You know why you're here. You've got nothing to boast about. You're a lousy fucking shot. If you want to live, you'll start talking now."

The man remained silent.

He was slapped on the other side of his face. His head wobbled again and sagged; he'd passed out. Someone put an amyl nitrate snapper under his nose and broke it open.

He sputtered and coughed; his heart raced. He could taste blood in his mouth.

"I'm enjoying this, motherfucker. You sure you want to play this game with us? I think you know who we are, so you might want to give it some thought."

He got slapped again. Another snapper was opened under his nose.

"You don't think fast enough for me. Know this, we're on to you and Ellifson. We know who you're with. Fuckin' Point Men! Couldn't do any better for a name? You're operating in restricted territory. No permission! No green card requested. You people have no respect. We take that kind of violation seriously."

The man seemed startled. His blindfold was removed. The room was dark, except for a very intense light shining in his eyes. It hurt, and he blinked and tried to look away. Someone very powerful grabbed his hair from behind and held his head in place.

"If you're enjoying the beating as much as me, continue to shut the fuck up, asshole."

He was slapped again, this time on the jaw. He went out again. Blood was running from his mouth as well as his nose.

Ammonium carbonate, smelling salts, was waved under his bleeding nose. He sputtered and tried to shake it off.

"I'm enjoying this shit, man, so if you like it, here's some more."

He took one to the ribs. It was a huge fist that hit him. There was a crack. At least one rib was broken, and a couple more had to be fractured.

"It's gonna get hard to breathe motherfucker. In fact, I don't have much more patience. You may just take your last breath if I don't get a response in the next ten seconds."

He got one to the groin. He gagged and moaned. He tried to speak, but his air was gone.

"It looks to me like you're trying to find a voice. I'll give you a minute."

"Okay, okay. I shot him. It was an order. I do what I'm told. We all do what we're told. We're soldiers."

"Not anymore. If you wanna to die easily, tell me more."

"We have a network. We work anywhere we're told. The General, that's what we call him, Sam, he gives the orders. We make good money doin' what we do best."

"Shooting an American in the back?"

"He was the target. I followed orders. He was getting too close."

"Well now *we're* too close. Like about close enough for me to put this pistol up against the side of your head and put a round through it. Here. Have a taste."

The barrel of a gun was pushed into his mouth. There was no doubt about what it was, and the man started to gag. It was shoved a little farther into his mouth, and wiggled up and down, cracking his teeth.

The man tried to nod his head.

"Did you want to say something?" The gun was removed from his mouth.

He spat out a piece of tooth.

"What else do you wanna know?"

"Everything, motherfucker."

Although Junior Garfano did not need to personally involve himself, people had come into his territory and engaged in murderous activity that required exotic weaponry. They shot someone whom he called friend, and was also a very close friend of Tommy, and he was family.

41.

WHEN REX LEFT THE HOSPITAL AND DROVE HOME he had two Blood Oath members on their motorcycles following him.

He parked in the garage and went into the house. As he got near his study he heard a voice in the room. Gail was working in the study. The room was very large, thirty-feet squared, with one side all glass. The walls were ten feet high with open beams and floor to ceiling curtains.

Once in the study, if you looked to your right, you could see Rex's desk with book cases behind it, filled with law books, basically useless since the flourishing of the internet, but they looked good. There were also photographs of Rex and friends at various times covering a couple of the shelves. One was of Blood Oath, their annual Club photo, a gift given to few outside the Club. On the opposite wall there was a built-in desk which was where Gail worked. Supplies were kept in a large walk-in storage room to the left.

The curtains were open, and since the glass was on the east side, the room received all the light necessary during good weather. Otherwise, there were two separate sets of lighting. There was neon, which was recessed into the ceiling and framed out in the wood matching the bookcases and wall desks—black walnut, which was very expensive, but Rex's favorite; and there was spot lighting, also recessed. It was a lower wattage and was used more in the evenings when he worked from home. It could be adjusted up or down for intensity.

On both sides of the door facing the west wall hung his favorite paintings, and all his degrees and licensing documents, including one from the California Supreme Court, and the United States Supreme Court. There were three very expensive chairs covered in antique fabric in front of his desk and brown leather sofas on either side of the doorway into the room.

Gail looked at Rex over her shoulder and said:

"Be with you in a minute, boss."

She could do the work of twenty people. He would be at a total loss without her, a fact he suddenly considered. He paid her well, and never questioned her sick days, which were rare. He gave her time off whenever she asked, and paid for her vacations, wherever she wanted to go. She earned all she received.

He saw a message on his desk from Patrick Moynihan. It said:

"Please call me. I'd like to help you."

Rex was stunned. Patrick Moynihan was a living legend in the legal community. His handling of the Van Peltzer murder case was still a topic of conversation in the legal circles around town.

He drew in a deep breath and called the number. Patrick answered on the second ring.

"Is that you, Rex?"

Rex drew in a deep breath and paused before speaking. "It is."

He was anxious talking to a legend who wanted to help him in his time of need.

"Well, hey there buddy, if you have the time right now I'd like to come over and see if I can help you out."

"That would be most appreciated Patrick."

"Okay. I am on my way."

It wasn't long after Rex had hung up the phone when he heard a car approaching. He had yet to realize that the Blood Oath security team on his property had a program in operation, and Patrick was being directed through the garage to the back entrance of the house. When he made his way into the living room, Rex was waiting for him. Patrick Moynihan greeted Rex with a handshake and thanked him for letting him visit.

"I don't know what to say, Patrick. I'm the one that should be doing the thanking. You've taken me by surprise. Please, come into the study. Would you like something? Coffee, water?"

"If you have some water, please."

Gail appeared and said:

"I'll take care of the water and let you two have some privacy." She moved on toward the kitchen then returned with a bottle of water for Patrick. He and Rex went into the study and sat facing each other at the front of the desk.

Patrick began:

"I know what happened. Tommy's taken the shooting of Eddie personally. He is fully engaged. In the process, a friend of ours has been able to locate the woman who has accused you. It seems she is willing to tell the truth. Presently, she is being kept safely away from her handler, this Donny Michaelson fellow. As of now, she has been professionally interviewed by Tommy, and there is video evidence available. She reported that she'd been working for Michaelson for the past couple of years. He kept her, so to speak, although she fears and hates him. There is also a video of what went on in that hotel room, which we can show in court. I can make this go away, Rex."

Rex was stunned. He felt tears welling up in his eyes. He stopped the display of emotion. Patrick sat calmly and watched.

"Just so you know, Rex, every man I have ever represented who has been treated the way your have—brutalized and lied about—has become so emotional when on the stand, that regardless of how big and tough they might be, the tears flow. It is the natural order of things."

"I'm sorry, Patrick. I've been lost in this, hiding alone, and now here you are…" He drifted off trying to find some emotional balance. "I do want your help, Patrick. I *am* grateful. What do I need to do for you?"

"Be a good client. That's it. I know that will be tough. Around here, everyone thinks you are it, man, and so do I. We'll make this case go away so that you can get your life back, and we'll sue these bastards and make it hurt."

42.

ALTHOUGH HE HAD SEEMED TO BE READY to jump out of the bed and leave the hospital within hours of his surgery, Eddie Logan was now languishing. His recovery seemed slow, and he was suffering from an infection the doctors diagnosed as MRSA (Methicillin-resistant Staphylococcus aureus), a common staph infection that people with weakened immune systems contract from longer stays in hospitals—a very difficult infection to treat, often requiring long-term intra-venous injections of antibiotics. The infection had found its way into the prisons and jails a few years before, and the treatment was difficult and intensive medication was compelled.

In the case of Eddie Logan, when his body temperature took a sudden rise, his turn for the worse had everyone worried. He was quite the celebrity in Danbrier, and in the hospital. He was being fed antibiotics intravenously, but his fever was still reading 104, and had been as high as 106..

Rex visited him every day, often staying into the evenings. The hospital personnel, including Dr. Steinberg, warned him about physical contact with Eddie, as it was one of the methods of contracting the disease. Rex didn't care and made it a point to hug him and tell him he loved him whenever he visited.

Eddie was in and out of delirium with fever, and Rex was becoming afraid for him. Others, like Eddie's good friends in Blood Oath, refused to believe that he would be any worse for the wear. They visited the hospital regularly and kept a vigil on his behalf.

Meanwhile, Rex's next court date was drawing near, and although he had Patrick Moynihan on his side, he was becoming more anxious each day. Patrick had intervened with a substitution of attorneys, and a notice that he would be ready to defend the preliminary hearing on the day calendared by Jim Hilfer, the following Tuesday.

That morning at home, at about ten-thirty Rex got a call from Patrick. He wanted to know if he could come early. He knew he must be there and told him to come on in; then he saw Patrick and Tommy walking toward the garage.

Rex greeted them both as they entered, and they walked to his study. Gail asked if they would like coffee, or brunch, or anything. Tommy said he would love some coffee, but Patrick politely declined, then changed his mind and asked for water.

Patrick was looking solemn, but not too serious.

"Our star witness, the one they are going to claim is unavailable until trial, will be brought in carefully and quietly. I got a sealed *ex parte* order from Judge Dorsemann to keep her on ice with Tommy until we need her. We're having her wait in Judge Dorsemann's Chambers with Tommy until called. Judge Dorsemann granted it after I shared some of our evidence with him; our proof of the need to protect her. He understood that she might be in danger if any deputies know she's there. So, she and Tommy will be there very early, coming in the back way."

Rex had never heard of such a tactic but didn't challenge Patrick.

Patrick continued: "Of course, they'll go for a 115 prelim, and we'll call her as affirmative evidence. This thing will be over on Tuesday, Rex. On Wednesday, I'll have a 1983 action filed in federal court in Riverside. We're splitting that one fifty-fifty, okay?" Patrick was smiling, but he meant it. A 1983 action was a suit filed for a violation of one's civil rights under color of law, meaning a violation of those rights by law enforcement, or someone working for them, and that it was intentional.

"Whatever your say, Patrick," Rex said with enthusiasm. He was feeling good for the first time since his arrest.

In Rex's case, a Prop 115 Prelim meant that Donny Michaelson would be the one to tell it all. It would be his testimony offered to have Rex held to answer for trial. It was the common practice, not calling the actual witnesses for the hearing, but relying upon law enforcement witnesses. That way the actual witness was not exposed to defense cross-examination before trial, thereby depriving the defense of a first chance to question the witness, and a receive a transcript of his or her testimony.

"I'm a bit envious of you, Patrick, getting to have all the fun," Rex offered as a tension breaker. "But, I want you to know how grateful I am for your help; you and Tommy both. I don't know what I would have done without you two. I was so lost in this thing."

"We aim to please," was all he said. Tommy looked at Rex with a sadness that seemed to express his sorrow for the world. Then his dark gray eyes turned lighter and he smiled, then said:

"It'll work out just fine, Rex. That I promise."

43.

IT WAS 3:14 A.M. WHEN REX WOKE. It was Tuesday, the day for his Preliminary Hearing, and although somewhat anxious, he jumped out of bed and made his way into the bathroom, performing his morning ritual. He then found his way into the kitchen and made coffee. After it had brewed, he poured a cup and went into his study. The curtains were shut, and the world was still dark out, as was the room. Sitting in silence he tried to gauge his feelings. Today he needed to pay attention to his champion, Patrick Moynihan.

After coffee he made a light breakfast of boiled eggs and cheese. Then he went to his room to shower and get ready.

He had a suit laid out, with a white shirt and tie. He always wore expensive polished shoes. After he dressed he went into his study and checked his cell for messages. There was only one message. It was from Gail wishing him a most positive day.

At 7:08 a.m. a text message from Tommy arrived:

"The check is in the mail."

How cryptic, Rex thought. That meant Tommy and Mindy Thorn were in Judge Dorsemann's Chambers, and that Patrick Moynihan was there already. He and Tommy never traveled alone. It had been the same with Eddie and Rex, except that day. He would have to be a good client, remaining quiet while Patrick Moynihan saved him from the fires intended by the minions of meanness who had beaten and falsely accused him.

Then he heard them, Harley-Davidson motorcycles. Doug had come to take him to court.

When Doug and Ron came into the study, Doug offered:

"I'm looking forward to this, Rex. You know we think that Danbrier is our town. We play hard, and everyone knows that we won't back down, and we never forget. But we never play dirty. Today, the people of Danbrier will hear about how much they've allowed their community to turn to shit. They'll also see us being the same as always.

"Thomas Jefferson said: 'The tree of liberty must be refreshed from time to time with the blood of patriots and tyrants.' They let a true patriot, Eddie Logan, get shot. They let a true patriot, you Rex, get hurt and wrongfully accused. There will be blood."

He paused for effect,

"Most of it in the spiritual sense." They all laughed.

"So, let's get this show on the road, Rex."

But before they could walk out of his study, Ron stopped Rex and said:

"You know I've been angry with you for being weak. That's just my way of showing that I'm hurt about something. Do you understand?" Ron looked at him long, and hard. His eyes were glowing, the wolf look.

"I do," was all that Rex could manage. And they walked to the garage together, and got into Rex's car, with Doug driving and Ron at the shotgun position. Rex sat in back.

They drove to the Danbrier Courthouse slowly. There was a pack of Blood Oath with them, ten men on motorcycles. They were riding slow; two in front, eight in back. They arrived at the courthouse at 8:04 a.m., and there was already a crowd outside waiting to go through the metal detectors. Rex recognized some as media persons, and there were cameramen standing about. When they drove into the parking lot, the cameras were rolling. There was a Blood Oath member on his motorcycle in a parking space in the front, with another member keeping the area free of other vehicles. No one dared to take any of those spaces.

Doug parked in the first space while the rest parked their bikes two to a space.

Doug said, "Wait a minute, Rex." He and Ron got out of the car.

Ron walked around to Rex's side and opened the door. Rex got out and thanked him. He didn't want anyone to even suggest that he had Ron working for him or was even his chauffer or butler or servant. Ron understood, and said: "My pleasure, brother."

Even if they had been close with a man for many years, most members of Blood Oath would not call a non-member brother. If you were called friend, it was a big deal.

Lawyers don't have to wait in line, and the security people knew Rex, and they knew what was happening, so they cleared him quickly.

Doug, Ron and the other ten men who rode with them that morning stayed outside.

As Rex approached Judge Dorsemann's courtroom, Patrick Moynihan was waiting for them. Rex was glad to see him but contained himself.

"Good morning, Patrick."

"Good morning, Rex."

"Are you ready?"

"I was born ready," Rex said with as much bravado as he could muster.

Patrick smiled, but he was in the zone.

At 8:21 a.m. the courtroom doors opened and the Bailiff, Deputy Alcazar stepped out, and said,

"Good morning, Rex. Mr. Moynihan, how are you, sir? You and Mr. McKinley may enter."

"Thank you, ma'am," Patrick said.

"Good morning, Deputy Alcazar," Rex responded, not wanting to seem too familiar with her in the public eye, even though he knew her well.

She then announced that Department 9 was open for business. She gave her standard admonishment, and the courtroom filled rather quickly, but in an orderly manner. Some members of Blood Oath were in the audience, but they were not wearing their patches. Rex knew they had been allowed to in the past, but for some reason had chosen not to that day. Perhaps they considered they would have taken all the attention away from Patrick, which was where the focus was needed. Members of the media began rushing for seating in the front, where the first two rows on the right were designated for law enforcement, attorneys and the media.

At 8:30 a.m. Judge Dorsemann took the Bench.

"Good morning. Has anyone seen Mr. Carter?"

Patrick offered as he stood: "Good morning, your Honor. I have not, nor have my phone calls to him been returned."

The door opened, and in walked Michael Carter and behind him was Donny Michaelson.

"Just in time, gentlemen. Are you ready to proceed Mr. Carter?"

"Yes, your Honor."

Judge Dorsemann, without giving Michael Carter any time to set up at the counsel table, looked to his Court Reporter, nodded, and asked:

"Gentlemen, please state your appearances for the record."

"Good morning, your Honor. Patrick Moynihan for Mr. McKinley who is present before the Court, out of custody. We are ready."

"Michael Carter, and the People are ready. I call Detective Donny Michaelson."

Donny Michaelson was obviously having difficulty walking, and probably urinating. Rex knew the feeling well. His face was bruised, and there were a couple of cuts healing on his face, one over each eye. He got his butt kicked.

The Bailiff did not walk with him to the witness stand, which was unusual, and it did not go unnoticed by Rex or Patrick.

Rex could feel the intensity of focus of Patrick Moynihan. He was generating a power that was captivating the attention of everyone.

The Clerk, Karin Kornder, stood and administered the oath, to which Donny Michaelson replied,

"Yes."

She told him to state his name and spell it for the record. Rex detected a slight lisp in his speech. He spoke very slowly. Rex looked for a missing front but saw no gap. He probably had a retainer with a false tooth attached. That would explain the lisp.

"You may be seated, Mr. Michaelson," said his Honor.

"Proceed, counsel."

"I would ask that Detective Michaelson be designated as my chief investigating officer," said Michael Carter.

"No objection, your honor," Patrick responded quickly.

"Very well, counsel. You may proceed."

"Mr. Michaelson how are you employed?"

"I am a detective with the Danbrier County Sheriff's Department."

"How long have you been so employed?"

"Eighteen years."

"Were you so employed on October 1ˢᵗ of this year?"

"I was."

Rex looked at Patrick who was not taking notes, but instead watching. Rex again focused on his intense presence.

"Please tell the Court what you were doing on that day."

"We were running a John program out of the Radisson lounge that evening."

"Please explain."

"We had a couple of pretty young women who were working for us, posing as prostitutes."

"Did you at some time contact the defendant, Mr. McKinley?"

"Yes, I did."

"How did that come about?"

"He came into the lounge at around seven forty-five, and immediately solicited one of the women. He was acting strangely, like he was drunk."

"What happened next?"

"After he solicited her services, they went upstairs to one of the rooms, number 415, as I recall."

Michaelson was having a lot of difficulty enunciating his words. Rex remained still, watching Patrick boring in on him.

"What happened next?"

"Me and my partner, Carlos Meza, went up after them and stayed outside the room just in case she needed us."

"And who was she?"

"She is what we call an operative; someone with a desire to help law enforcement, but not a sworn deputy."

"What is her name?"

"Mindy Thorn."

"Does she have a criminal history?"

"She doesn't have any convictions."

"Why did you contact the defendant that night?"

Rex was watching Mike Carter as he read from a script he held tightly.

"We were outside the door to the room, and we heard her scream. We had a pass key and opened the door and entered."

"What did you observe?"

"We saw the defendant on top of Mindy Thorn. Her clothing was torn, and he had his pants down around his ankles."

"What did you do?"

"I yelled at him: 'Sheriff's Department', and then I rushed him and shoved him off the woman."

"What happened then?"

"He tried to get up and fight with me. I subdued him. I told him to pull up his pants, and then I handcuffed him. I patted him down for weapons and felt a large lumpy thing in his left front pocket. I retrieved it."

"What happened next?"

"My partner was assisting Mindy Thorn. She was shook-up. He helped her into the bathroom to clean up. She was hurt, but nothing requiring medical treatment."

Donny Michaelson was clearly experiencing a great deal of pain as he fidgeted in his seat, appearing to be unable to find a comfortable sitting position.

"This lumpy thing you retrieved from the defendant's person, were you able to determine what it was?"

"Yes, it appeared to be methamphetamine in a baggie. I later field tested it with my reagent kit and it was positive for methamphetamine."

For purposes of a 115 Preliminary Hearing in California, that was usually sufficient to establish that it was a controlled substance, unless the defense had demanded a lab person. Patrick didn't object.

"Were you able to determine how much of this methamphetamine was in the baggie?"

"Approximately an ounce. I didn't weigh it myself, but I am very familiar with packaging of this substance, and it was clearly much more than for personal use. It was a quantity sufficient for sales."

Patrick could have objected, but he didn't. No objections meant Michaelson was getting his story told.

"Did you interview Mindy Thorn about what took place?"

"I did. She told me that she had not yet negotiated a price with the defendant and that instead of trying to buy her services, he shoved her on the bed and began pawing her. When she tried to stop him, he slapped her, and then started tearing off her clothes."

"Did she say whether he actually penetrated her vagina?"

"She said that she felt him trying, but she was struggling against him, and he did not actually penetrate her, but did touch her vaginal opening with his penis. She did say he wasn't erect."

He tried to smile just a little, but his jaw was probably too sore, and maybe he did not want to seem like he was being cruel—even though that was the essence of his nature.

"What did you do then?"

"I advised him that he was under arrest. Then I read him his rights. We took him to DDC and had him booked for rape and possession of a controlled substance for sale."

"Nothing further."

"Mr. Moynihan."

"Thank you, your Honor. May I stand."

"Of course."

Patrick stood slowly and began to walk toward the lectern. He moved it slightly as he stood beside it. He had no notes with him.

"How are you this morning Detective?"

"Fine, counselor."

"I believe you testified that you were working a John program on the evening of October 1st of this year. Wasn't it actually Friday, October 2nd?"

"Oh, you may be right."

"Am I?"

Donny Michaelson suddenly tensed.

"Yes, I do believe so. It was a Friday night."

"And this John program, was it something that was planned, briefed, and assigned to you?"

"I am self-assigned in all my work."

"Please tell the court what that means."

Michaelson appeared angry, his beady eyes narrowing. His face tensing, jaws grinding.

"It means that I am an experienced detective, capable of making decisions and directing investigations. I don't need anyone to approve it."

"Are you telling the Court you do not answer to anyone?"

"Of course not!"

"What did you mean?"

"I meant that I conduct investigations, and I report to my Captain with what I have done."

"Before or after?"

"Whenever I think it is necessary."

"Did you report to your Captain before or after this particular investigation, or John program?"

"After."

"Was this woman, Mindy Thorn, working off a beef?"

"What do you mean, counselor?"

Judge Dorsemann intervened. "You know what he means, Detective. Answer the question." Donny Michaelson turned deep red.

"No, she was not. She was simply helping us."

"You knew what I meant?"

"Yeah, I knew."

"Why did you act as though you did not?"

Donny Michaelson paused. He feigned a smile, clamped down on his jaws, his eyes glowing, and said:

"Sorry about that, counselor."

Patrick Moynihan was looking at Donny Michaelson, but he could not look back at him. He averted his eyes to the floor.

"Back to Mindy Thorn, why was she working for you? Just a good citizen helping law enforcement?"

"Something like that."

"Can you be a bit more specific, Detective?"

"She has worked with us in the past. She makes a little money while gets to be with the good guys."

"The good guys?"

"Yeah, us, the cops. The good guys."

"She makes a little money, and enjoys your company, is that what you are saying, detective?"

"Yes."

"Is she available for testimony at trial, detective?"

"Objection. Relevance."

"Overruled."

Judge Dorsemann knew exactly where she was at that very moment.

"Is she, detective?"

"Would you repeat the question?"

That was a standard stall tactic when a witness sensed danger, but Donny Michaelson's default mode was to lie.

Patrick said: "May I ask the reporter to read the question to the witness, your honor?"

"You may. Madam Reporter?"

She read the question.

"Yes, she's available."

"When was the last time you spoke with her about this case?"

"Objection. Discovery."

"Overruled."

"Sir?"

"Last night."

Rex almost smiled but suppressed it.

"And did you write a report about your conversation with her?"

"Not yet."

"Did you discuss her possible testimony with her?"

Mike Carter objected again, and Judge Dorsemann overruled it.

"We might have touched upon it. I think I was more concerned with how she was feeling?"

"You think, or you specifically remember it?"

"That's what we discussed."

"And how was she feeling?"

"She was okay."

"And this was just last night?"

"Yep, last night."

"I didn't see any mention of audio or video recordings in the discovery. Isn't it common practice to have your would-be hookers wear a wire?"

"We do, but hers got damaged when he attacked her."

"Did you write that in your report?"

"I may have forgotten to do that."

"Is Mindy Thorn a drug addict?"

"No. She's as clean as a whistle."

"Have you ever seen her using drugs?"

"Never."

"Have you ever supplied her with drugs?"

Mike Carter stood for his objection. Again, it was overruled.

He complained, and Judge Dorsemann said:

"Counsel, you are prosecuting a very well-respected member of the Bar, on charges including possession of a controlled substance for sale. I am going to allow counsel a good deal of latitude here, especially because the detective has denied any recording, which this Court *takes notice* as being standard operating procedure in the so-called John cases. The detective's failure to explain away the absence of a recording in his reports is significant to this court. I suggest that it should be to you, also."

"Answer the question, Detective." Judge Dorsemann was firm.

"Never. I'm a cop, for god's sake."

"Does that mean that you would never break the law, Detective?"

"Never."

"Is there any video footage of what happened that night?"

Donny Michaelson's face and neck turned deep red and he sucked for air. His breathing was labored.

"Detective, do you need me to repeat the question?"

"No, counselor, I don't need you to repeat the question. I think I already told you her recording device was damaged when he (pointing to Rex) attacked her."

"Was her device a video recorder, or an audio recorder?"

"Audio only. You know that."

"Well, sir, my question was whether there was a video recording of the incident. You hesitated, and I thought perhaps you were remembering something. Was there a video?"

The last sentence was delivered in a raised and demanding voice, but Patrick's body language was very calm.

"I heard you. No there wasn't any video. How many times do I have to tell you."

"Oh, once is enough, Detective.

"Is your statement that there was no video as true as every other part of your testimony?"

"Objection."

Again, Mike Carter jumped out of his seat. His voice was squeaky.

"Overruled, counsel. You know that an objection requires the grounds upon which it is founded."

"Objection, leading."

"Overruled. Counsel, you know that it is appropriate to lead on cross-examination."

Mike Carter sat. He had a deep red tone to his skin and was shaking from head to toe.

Patrick continued: "May I ask the court to instruct the detective to answer my question, your Honor?"

"He will answer, won't you Detective?" Judge Dorsemann said with a slight edge to his voice.

"What was the question, counselor?"

"Is your testimony about the absence of a video as true as every other part of your testimony?"

"Yes. Every word I have spoken is the truth."

"Are you familiar with the provisions of Penal Code, section 118, sir?"

"Clue me, counselor."

Although Judge Dorsemann was about to admonish Michaelson, he looked to Patrick first, and something passed between them. Judge Dorsemann remained silent.

"It defines perjury, sir."

"I just took an oath, I know about perjury."

"Is there anything you wish to change about your testimony, sir?"

"No. I don't want to change anything," said Donny Michaelson. His face was deep red, bordering on purple, and he was shaking. It seemed like he was trying to restrain himself from charging Patrick.

"Thank you, sir. Nothing further at this time, your Honor."

"Mr. Carter, any re-direct?"

"None."

"May this witness be excused?"

Patrick, still standing by the lectern and staring at Donny Michaelson, quickly responded:

"No, your Honor. I may have some further questions after we put on our affirmative evidence."

"Very well, Mr. Moynihan, this witness will not be excused. I don't think it will matter too much, as Mr. Michaelson will be staying with us anyway. True, sir?"

Donny Michaelson ignored Judge Dorsemann.

"Mr. Michaelson, did you hear me?"

"I heard you. I'll be here."

"Now that is an order, detective. You will be here. Do not leave this courtroom until we have spoken. Any further witnesses, Mr. Carter?"

"No. People rest."

"The court will recess for fifteen minutes."

The Bailiff cleared the courtroom of spectators.

When the courtroom was cleared, Judge Dorsemann said:

"We are back on the record in the McKinley matter, all parties and counsel are present.

"Detective Donny Michaelson, if you show one more sign of disrespect to this court, I will have you cited for contempt, and arrested, and you will sit out these proceedings in handcuffs in the jury box. Do you understand me?"

"Yes, I understand."

"Thank you. Anything further?"

Michael Carter jumped out of his seat. "Yes, Judge. Counsel mentioned affirmative defense. I have nothing from him."

"Mr. Moynihan?"

"Your Honor, with all respect to the Court and counsel, I urge Mr. Carter to read the Izazaga case. I have no duty to disclose anything now."

"The Court is familiar with Izazaga. Mr. Carter, you have fifteen minutes. Read it."

Judge Dorsemann stood and stepped down off the Bench and entered his chambers through the door to the immediate right.

Rex told Patrick: "I owe you forever, Patrick."

"With all the fun I'm having? I should be paying you."

Rex excused himself to go to the restroom, and Patrick said he would join him. The hallway was packed with people, and everyone was behaving. They were quiet, and no one attempted to question Rex or Patrick. The brothers of Blood Oath had set the rules without saying a word.

44.

THEY WERE BACK IN THE COURTROOM. Everyone was in place, and Donny Michaelson was sitting closest to Patrick Moynihan, the man who was going to rock his world to its very foundation.

Judge Dorsemann inquired: "Mr. Moynihan, do you have a witness?"

Patrick looked at Donny Michaelson, and said:

"Thank you, your Honor. The defense calls Mindy Thorn."

Mike Carter and Donny Michaelson looked like they were both about to vapor lock and die. Donny Michaelson was flexing his entire body, his face turning deep red, and veins began to show on his forehead. Michael Carter was scanning around the courtroom, eyes squinted, face tight, jaw muscles bulging.

"Your honor, while we wait for the witness, I ask that the record reflect that I am handing Mr. Carter a transcript of an interview with Ms. Thorn, as well as a video of that interview. I am also handing him a transcript of Detective Michaelson and his partner, Carlos Meza, in a room with Ms. Thorn and Mr. McKinley. There is a video to accompany it." Patrick walked behind Donny Michaelson and carefully handed each item to Michael Carter who did not look up, but reached out with his left arm, using only his peripheral vision to take the items offered. He did not look at Patrick.

"The record shall so reflect, Mr. Moynihan." Judge Dorsemann said with a facial expression that could be defined as grim.

Donny Michaelson was frantic; his face had turned purple, with steam and sweat pouring out. His eyes were squinted, and he looked as if he might try to run.

Mindy Thorn was led into the courtroom from the outside. There was an exit from the Judge's Chambers that led through a short private hall to the main hallway that allowed people to come and go without anyone ever knowing.

Tommy stopped at the bar while Mindy Thorn walked forward as instructed by the bailiff. After she stepped up to the witness stand the Clerk administered the oath, and Mindy Thorn said: "I do." She sat and spelled her name for the record.

Judge Dorsemann then turned to Patrick, who was waiting.

"You may proceed, Mr. Moynihan."

"Thank you, your honor."

He stood, but only after asking for permission again. Judge Dorsemann granted his request.

"Thank you, your Honor.

"Good morning, Ms. Thorn."

"Good morning."

"Have we met before this morning?"

"No."

"Do you know a man named Tommy Krumholtz?"

"Yes. I believe he's your investigator."

"How did you meet him?"

"He was introduced to me by a friend. He asked me if I would speak with him."

"And did you?"

"Yes, for a very long time."

"Was that conversation recorded?"

"Yes, we agreed that it would be video recorded."

"Do you know a man named Donny Michaelson?"

She faltered and turned white as a sheet. She gulped some air and calmed herself. She hesitated again, and then looked him straight in the eyes, her gaze steady. He looked down.

"Yes, I know him very well."

"When was the last time you saw him?"

"The night after Rex McKinley was arrested. He told me to get out of town until he needed me for this case."

"You didn't meet with him last night?"

"No."

"How do you know him?"

"It started a couple of years ago when I was working for a general contractor," she paused, but continued: "and was stealing from him. He called the cops, and they started watching me. I needed the money for drugs.

"Donny caught me in a drug deal. He knew about me stealing. He told me if I worked for him that he could make the charges go away."

"Did you agree to work for him?"

"Yes."

"What did that work entail?"

"Lots of things."

"Let's talk about drugs. You said that you were stealing to buy drugs, is that correct?"

She started to tear up but restrained herself. "Yes, to buy drugs."

"So, were you a drug addict at that time?"

"I still am. I've got a few days clean; I'm trying."

"Good for you, Miss Thorn. Did Detective Michaelson know that you were an addict?"

"Of course! That's how he used me."

Donny Michaelson was clenching his fists.

"What do you mean by that, Ms. Thorn?"

"I mean that he gave me drugs when I did what he wanted."

"Do you mean that Detective Michaelson paid you with drugs for working for him?"

"For anything he wanted."

"And what did that include?"

"I have been his slave for over two years. I lived in a house he owns. I 've done everything he's wanted."

"Are you afraid of him?"

"Terrified. He told me he would kill me if I ever told on him. He beat me many times, just to make sure I believed him."

"Did Rex McKinley rape you?"

"No, he did not."

"Did he have drugs on him that night?"

"No. Donny had the drugs. The whole thing was a set up. Rex is a nice guy. I was sent after him. I lured him to the hotel. Donny gave me a drug to put into his drink."

She started crying and looked at Rex.

"I'm so sorry," she said as she sobbed.

Rex smiled.

"Who sent you after him?"

"Donny."

"Detective Michaelson?"

"Yes."

"Did he tell you why he wanted you to do it?"

"Yes, because Rex was representing the man who killed his brother."

"Do you know about a video of that night with Mr. McKinley?"

"Yes. Donny has quite a collection of his conquests; videos of a lot of his busts and beatings, and the rapes. He beat Rex that night when he was unconscious."

"Have you seen that video?"

"Yes. He made me watch it while he raped me."

"He raped you?"

"Many times." She started crying but held it back, apparently more determined than afraid.

"Have you had an opportunity to view what has been marked as Exhibit 1?"

"Yes. It's that video."

"Who is in the video?"

"Me, Donny, Carlos, and Rex, but Rex is unconscious."

At that point, Donny Michaelson pushed his chair back and shouted at Mindy Thorn:

"You lyin' fuckin' whore! I don't have to listen to this shit!"

He started to walk out of the courtroom. He was one crazy looking man, pumped, flexing and acting like he would crush anyone who got in his way.

"Bailiffs!" shouted Judge Dorsemann.

It was then Rex turned around and realized there were several deputies at strategic locations in the courtroom. They had come in quietly. When a Judge hits his panic button, he can send a text with it. He apparently ordered a silent entry.

All the deputies moved toward Donny Michaelson. Two had their Tasers out and ready for action. Donny Michaelson hesitated, and they jumped him. He did something Rex never thought he would see: he surrendered—then he started screaming. No words, just a scream. It was the most horrible sound Rex had ever heard. Other than his screaming, the courtroom was completely silent. Rex watched the scene unfold just a few feet from him.

Donny Michaelson seemed to be possessed by a demon. Everyone watched silently as he was handcuffed and escorted out by a group of deputies, one of whom was instructing him in no uncertain terms that he had better cooperate. They took him past the prosecution side of the counsel table, past the jury box, and to the door that led into the hallway behind the courtroom. He disappeared behind the door. They could all hear him scream again. There were some muffled noise, thudding sounds, and Rex suspected that Donny Michaelson was getting some more of his own medicine.

Rex turned back toward Mindy Thorn. She was obviously just as stunned as everyone else. He looked at Judge Dorsemann. He had a faint smile on his lips. His eyes were glowing.

"Counsel?" Judge Dorsemann was looking at Mike Carter who was hyperventilating; his breathing so out of kilter that he could not speak. He nodded at the judge.

"Mr. Moynihan?"

"Your honor, I think the evidence is clear that the Court must dismiss these charges."

"I quite agree. Mr. Carter, this is your last chance to respond."

Mike Carter tried to look up, but he couldn't. He shook his head from side to side; he was throwing in the towel.

"Mr. McKinley, pursuant to the provisions of Penal Code, section 851.8, I find you factually innocent. I hereby order that all records of your arrest and this prosecution be sealed, and thereafter destroyed so that no evidence of it exists. Sir, this case is dismissed."

He slammed his gavel down.

Rex looked at Mindy Thorn. She was still sitting there. She looked terrified. He got up and walked to her.

"Come on, Mindy. I forgive you. I'm grateful to you for your courage. You did a good thing today, and no one will ever hurt you again."

She stepped down and rushed into his arms. She was crying hysterically. Rex saw a flash and realized that there would be a lot of photos on the news that night, and the hug would be one.

Rex held her for a very long time. Finally, Tommy came over and tapped him on the shoulder. He withdrew from Mindy. She said it again,

"I am so sorry, Rex."

"Don't ever say that again. You are forgiven." He saw another flash.

Tommy led Mindy out of the courtroom toward the hallway, but no one approached her. She was surrounded by members of Blood Oath.

Rex walked over to Patrick, who smiled and said,

"Your suit is soaked."

They laughed, and Rex hugged him.

They walked out of the courtroom together. Once in the hallway, Stanton Sensa, the owner, editor and publisher of the Danbrier Sentinel, asked:

"Have you got a comment, Mr. McKinley?"

"Yes, I do. I stand here a free man because of the greatest lawyer in the world, and the bravest woman on earth." He reached for Mindy Thorn. She came to him. He hugged her and put his arm around her shoulder. He grabbed Patrick Moynihan, and hugged him, too. The cameras were rolling.

45.

DONNY MICHAELSON WAS TERMINATED FROM the Sheriff's department. He was indicted by the Danbrier County Grand Jury for perjury, subornation of perjury, falsification of evidence, and the rape of Mindy Thorn. At his arraignment, he pled guilty to perjury, subornation of perjury, and falsification of evidence. He was granted probation. He had to forfeit his retirement. Donny Michaelson got approval from his probation officer to live with a relative in the State of Arkansas and finish his probation there.

Mindy Thorn was never consulted about the proposed disposition, clearly in contradiction to well-established California law, and policy of the Danbrier District Attorney, especially when there were allegations of sex crimes. Rex heard that Mindy Thorn was given some of the money that Donny Michaelson had stashed—the money that was taken from him—and was told to find a new place, far away. She was given a new identity, but not by the government. He heard that she began a stay at a long-term residential rehab program and was living the life of a clean and sober person, one day at a time.

Carlos Meza was terminated from the Sheriff's Department, but he wasn't prosecuted for anything. He left town quickly, and no one seemed to know where he had gone, except Tommy Krumholtz.

The media went crazy over Rex' case; there were news stories on almost every channel. There were calls from all the top newscasters, asking for interviews with Rex, and Patrick.

They had agreed that neither of them would speak with the media. There certainly was no one in Danbrier who didn't hear about it. It was going to be tough on Rick Turner trying to find a jury that was going to trust anyone from the Sheriff's

Department or the District Attorney's Office in the Billy West case. They should never have allowed a guy like Donny Michaelson to go unsupervised.

That was part of the allegations of the lawsuit Patrick filed on Rex's behalf. It was pending in the United States District Court for the Central District of California, Eastern Division, downtown Riverside.

Patrick did not ask for a dollar amount in those law suits until the case was before the jury. Then he hit hard and won big.

What was done to Rex was undisputed. Mindy Thorn would have to come back for trial. Tommy said he could have her available within twenty-four hours.

Owing to the whole thing being captured on video, as well as Mindy's testimony at the preliminary hearing, there was little to defend.

It was discovered that there had been a rather large file of complaints against Donny Michaelson for various acts of violence, alleged theft of drugs and money, and abuse of women. He even had two complaints by fellow deputies for violent attacks on them. He had been accused of repeated use of racial epithets in front of African-American people, including brother officers and deputies. He had been a train wreck waiting to happen, and it happened in Judge Dorsemann's court.

The house Mindy Thorn testified to living in was searched by members of the Department of Justice of the State of California. The safe was found. No one knew what was in there—at least no one made a public statement. Some said that he cleaned it out before he went berserk; others said he knew something was coming and emptied it and moved it to another location.

His home where his wife and two children lived was also searched. A significant amount of cash, unlikely earnings for a deputy Sheriff, was seized from a hiding place in the floor of his den. His wife denied knowing it was there. She and their children moved from Danbrier. The media tried to chase them around, but they got tired of it. She made it clear that she had nothing to say anyway.

One of the media outlets, the Danbrier Sun, had been trying to do a feature story on Rex since his case was dismissed. Rex wanted out of the headlines. He would resist any temptation to get on stage again with the media and fall victim of his own ego. His next performance would be well planned in the Billy West trial. That case had taken a stall, but he was getting back into the action—but without Eddie.

46.

RUSS WALDEN WAS CHAIRING THE BRIEFING for the Billy West trial. It was only a couple of weeks away, and there was a lot to do. He had a few deputies with him and was reviewing the file.

"We're on a winning streak, and we're not gonna lose this one. It's simple, and it doesn't matter about bad press. People will understand that a man is going to go off the deep end when his brother is murdered. That's not us. He does not define us." He was, of course, referring to Donny Michaelson.

Russ Walden's homicide team had not lost a case twenty-one times in a row, and he was publicly quite certain number twenty-two was on its way. But secretly, he had his doubts. He had cheated, and this time it might come back to bite him.

His three most important witnesses were bad: Mary Jane Rankin, and Ron and Cheryl Porter. He also wasn't sure what might happen to any of them under searing cross-examination. Not knowing was an unsettling feeling. Then, of all the mistakes anyone could make, the lab lost a major piece of evidence. He pondered how that could have happened. *Was there someone in the lab who was disloyal?* That was another reason the case might go bad, and if it was, he would be in serious trouble. Never had he felt that kind of anxiety. If Donny Michaelson hadn't started a shit storm, it might have been different. But now that he had, and that lawyer was looking so angelic, he, Russ Walden, the golden boy, might find himself in deep shit.

"I want all of the witnesses re-interviewed."

Russ Walden did not know a lot about the case, including the whereabouts of Larry Wear and his camera with his early photos of the crime scene. It could become a disastrous find for the defense. He did suspect that Eddie Logan had already acquired the camera, and Rex McKinley would use it at the last minute—not knowing was eating him alive.

He didn't know what Rex McKinley and Eddie Logan knew about other things, and that was wearing on him, as well. He had that running scared feeling he remembered from his early days—like all cops had when they were facing their first five minutes of cross-examination by a skilled defense lawyer. That was the defining moment. If the defense lawyer was any good, that meant trouble for the cop. If the lawyer knew how to play upon that anxiety, even the best cops could get tripped up—even when the cop was being totally righteous, which was not always the case. It took time, training, and self-confidence to withstand relentless cross-examination by a skilled practitioner.

Russ Walden was not without sin in the Billy West case, and he was developing a sense that the other side may have caught a whiff of his deceit. If so, everything he had so carefully built over the years could go up in a puff of smoke in a courtroom. He may have been playing dirty, but he would never try to do anything about it like that fool Michaelson, or like the one that shot Eddie Logan.

47.

IT WAS THE END OF ANOTHER DAY. Rex had had time to think about things. His body was back up and running, and although he was not a super athlete, he had returned to yoga. Stretching made him feel strong and light on his feet. It was still a bit difficult, as the injury to his testicles had been severe.

He meditated each morning, and prayer was part of that ritual. Although not a religious man, he did know there was a Creator, a divine force, a genderless entity that had laid its cosmic hand upon all that was; that everything happened for a reason.

Reflecting how he had been tricked, and drugged, and beaten, he tried to find some reason for what he had gone through. He rationalized that the experience was a necessary part of his growth as a person, and as a lawyer. That was a new part of a philosophy he was embracing.

He felt confident that they would never try anything again, at least not like what had been done. He was further encouraged by the pending civil rights suit, which was still a topic of conversation by the media.

The owner of the Danbrier Sentinel kept track of every event in the case. He wrote an article about it each week. He always began with the same three paragraphs:

The federal civil rights suit filed by attorney Patrick Moynihan of Santa Monica on behalf of Danbrier's own, Rex McKinley, was initiated for the drugging, false arrest, kidnapping, falsification of evidence, and the severe beating of Mr. McKinley, all of which was either told in a courtroom, or captured on video. Mr. Moynihan will continue with his aggressive assault on the defense presented by the Office of the County Counsel for the County of Danbrier, the Danbrier County Sheriff, and two of its deputies, the convicted felon and former detective, Donny Michaelson, and his partner, Carlos Meza. Attorney Patrick Moynihan is well known for his many victories against bad cops.

Michaelson pled guilty early on to charges of perjury, subornation of perjury, and falsification of evidence. He has since left the jurisdiction and resides in Arkansas, but part of the terms of his probation is that he will return to the jurisdiction upon subpoena. He left with cases pending and a lawsuit with his name on it. Michaelson and Meza are the key witnesses in many pending criminal prosecutions filed by the Danbrier County District Attorney. It has been speculated by local attorneys that if neither of the fired cops show, these cases will be dismissed. One cynic has suggested that even if they did show the cases will have to be dismissed, as the credibility of Michaelson and Meza has already been destroyed.

Meza was retired without his pension, in return for his willingness to testify against Michaelson in his criminal proceedings, should the occasion arise. However, it became unnecessary when Michaelson pled guilty.

There was the weekly update:

Carlos Meza has been subpoenaed to testify at his deposition at the law offices of London, Kyle, Smith & Moynihan in Santa Monica this Thursday. It is anticipated that his deposition may be the deciding factor in whether the County will settle this case. This writer has been advised that Beverly Petrino-Moynihan, briefly of the Danbrier County District Attorney's Office, and now partner in the firm of London, Kyle, Smith & Moynihan—and wife of Patrick Moynihan, will be handling the questioning of Meza during his deposition.

The prognosis is this case will cost the County millions. A public apology to Rex McKinley from the Sheriff has been demanded.

Rex was taking great pleasure in reading those articles. They had motivated him to be the best at what he did. Because of them, however, he had some new friends, a new mentor, and a much better understanding of the men who had taken him into their lives, and their hearts, the men of Blood Oath.

He gave one last look around his study, and his box of files full of documents and CD's and DVD's, and he knew he was about to enter a new realm—he was going to step onto the national stage. He was ready; knew his part and his lines, and how to improvise. It was a true-life drama with everything on the line, the life of Billy West in the balance, but unlike the actors, he would get only one take, one chance to do it right.

Friday morning was assignment calendar where he would find out who would hear Billy's trial. Each side had one challenge of a Judge without cause. The prosecutors rarely used such challenges, as the Judges were almost all former prosecutors, and their boss, Rodney Gardner, the District Attorney for the

County of Danbrier, was a political animal. He could not afford to offend
Judges. Absent some rare nutcase judge, Rodney Gardner would never step on
any toes that might kick back.

Getting ready for a trial that was a major event in so many ways, and he
might be doing it without Eddie Logan. He decided to drive to the hospital and
see how he was doing. When he tried to leave, Carey Sorenson came out of
nowhere and told him:

"Not so fast, Rex. There's a system in place. This hasn't been cleared. I need to
call Doug." He pulled out his cell phone and began speaking almost immediately.

"Okay." He finished and told Rex that he was coming with him. He set his
rifle in the back seat of the car and jumped in on the passenger side. He said:
"Let's go. I hear that Eddie is about to leave. I think he's looking pretty good."

"I saw him yesterday," said Rex. "He was talking tough, and I thought he'd
be leaving then, but Doc Sternberg wanted to run a full spectrum of tests before
he let him bail. It was bad, Carey. In my entire life I've never known Eddie to
even get the flu, then this infection damn near killed him."

Rex gazed off through the windshield as they drove toward the hospital. It
was early afternoon, and the day was beautiful. The Danbrier mountain chain
was among the most beautiful anywhere. Thick ancient forests pressed with
shades of emerald velvet, moss and a variety of pine and fir, bringing delight
through the spectrum. The cobalt blue sky was broken by the sun pushing
though a cloud bank to the north bringing joy to Rex's mind.

"It's beautiful, Carey; this world we inhabit. I've been very fortunate. I'm
back on track, and about ready to kick some ass in court. But, I need Eddie.
We've been a team forever."

"Then let's go post his bail," said Carey with a smile. Both men laughed.

When they made their way into the hospital, the amazing Eddie Logan was
standing in his room, wearing warm-ups and greeted them as though he was
expecting them.

"Come to get me outta here, I hope."

"Yep. All charges are dropped and you're free to go," said Rex with a smile.
Eddie had lost a significant amount of weight, maybe twenty pounds. Rex had
never seen him look so lean, almost frail for Eddie.

Noticing his scrutiny, Eddie said: "We're gonna have to stop at the gym. I need to
pump it up a bit." All three men laughed, although Rex wasn't certain if Eddie was
kidding. It would be just like Eddie Logan to pull such a stunt. Carey intervened.

"We have a room for you at the Ranch, Eddie, nurse and girlfriend
included. Doug won't take no for an answer."

"I know. I can spare a couple more days." Eddie was obviously still weak from the long-term fever attendant MRSA. He moved slowly. Rex fought the fear trying to well up in him; he would not show a sorrowful face. Eddie may be in a weakened condition, but he would not tolerate weakness.

48.

THE ROAD TO THE RANCH RAN OFF HIGHWAY 26, and was called Forest Mountain Road, one of the oldest roads in Danbrier. The settlers of Danbrier came to the valley by way of crossing the mountains. They made their way through the forest by cutting lumber for their homes. When they had built all their homes, they had plowed a road down the mountain and through the forest. It seemed they were literal people: Forest Mountain Road.

It was a twenty-minute drive to the Ranch. Once on the Ranch—which required the opening of a huge steel gate with warning signs on each side and passing under an archway made of huge stones from the area, with a massive sign in the center of the archway that read Blood Oath—they drove for another five minutes up a long and winding road that was bordered by pine trees. The road was paved, and very well maintained.

Billy West had lived on the Ranch until he was told to leave. From what Rex had been able to piece together, it was Doug who sent him packing. He had become an embarrassment to his family and friends. He was using drugs and wouldn't work. Therefore, he was not worthy. Knowing that Doug was willing to hire Rex to represent Billy said a lot to everyone. He was still family; he was simply not worthy of Blood Oath status.

The judges of Danbrier County and the politicians knew enough about the Ranch to be impressed, and they didn't want to become the enemies of Blood Oath. There had been a couple of occasions over the years when some of the Sheriff's men decided to try to take down one Club member or another, like the bogus prosecution of Carey Sorenson. They never had any success, and never would. Even if the Club did something that might not fit within the bounds of the written law, they embraced another code, and it would be followed to the death.

Thus, there was an unstated truce. The attack on Rex by Donny Michaelson was not sanctioned by the Sheriff. He would never have been so foolish, or careless—so his messengers reported. But, he had continued to allow a known madman to work under him, just like the Sheriff before him. Everyone knew that Donny Michaelson was a bad cop.

Rex parked near the front of the old house that was the Blood Oath Club House. It was the classic Victorian with alterations, kept in pristine condition by the Club.

Rex drew in a deep breath of the forest air. It smelled clean and rich. On the Ranch, there was no remnant of the outside world; time stopped in the sense that people there lived by their own rules, free of the constraints of society. The land fed them with gardens of vegetables, chickens, rabbits, pigs and cattle.

Eddie got out of the back seat with the help of Carey, although he told him that he could handle it. They walked toward the old house, and Eddie turned back toward Rex and said:

"Hey, I'm in on Billy's case. Get me a couple of days here and I'll be ready." His voice was weak and faded away as he turned back toward the house and entered.

Carey came back to Rex and said: "I've been told to take you home, but there's someone who wants to say hello first."

When she came into view, Rex was stunned. He knew her and had thought of her from time to time. She was Melina Garza, daughter of Doug West. It was a long story, but she had been with Doug since her teen years. The last time Rex saw her was during Carey Sorenson's trial. He thought she was very attractive with her dark complexion, jet black hair and ice blue eyes, but she was the daughter of Doug West, so he tried not to look too hard. That day was an exception. She wanted to speak with him.

As she drew near, Rex appeared a bit nervous. He said: "Hi, Melina. How are you?"

She smiled and stopped a couple of feet in front of him. He looked her over and felt a warm feeling overcome him. She was truly a pleasant sight, and she was smiling up at him.

"Hi, Rex. I wanted to say hello. I've been following what's been going on, first with you, and of course with my Uncle Billy. I'm so grateful you're okay."

Feeling clumsy, Rex offered his hand. She took it and smiled. Very formally and politely, she said: "Would it be alright if I came to watch some of the trial?"

Rex was holding her tiny hand in his, feeling more than a handshake. She was flowing with an energy that rushed into him, examining him, filling him with questions about men and women. Holding her firm but not tight, he looked back at this lovely young woman and became profoundly serious. And, as her scent drifted up to him, he felt deeply drawn to her.

"I would be honored if you would come and watch. It would mean a great deal to Billy, too. He needs all the encouragement he can get."

Melina withdrew her hand, smiled, and turned to walk away. After a few steps, she turned back and looked at Rex. He saw what he thought was an invitation, a hint that she was interested in him. He found his breath hard to come. He smiled at her as she walked off toward the dark dirt road heading toward the cabin where he knew Doug lived. Her hair danced in the breeze as did her dress. She moved as though her feet were not touching the ground, and then she disappeared around a turn in the road. Rex was still looking after her when Carey said:

"It's a beautiful evening, isn't it, Rex?"

Still somewhat dazed by what had just transpired, Rex replied:

"Incredibly so." He turned toward his car. He and Carey got in and began the trip back to his house.

Once there, he thanked Carey and went into the house and began preparing to go to bed. When he finally laid down he slept hard.

He was in the forest, and Melina was there, wearing a sheer dress in varying shades of green, browns and yellow, and no undergarments. He got a glimpse of her naked body beneath. She was dancing like an Elf Queen of the forest, her feet above the ground. She was wearing a crown, and it was glowing. There was a small waterfall behind her that soothed him with its sounds. She smiled at him while she danced. As she moved toward him he anticipated something intimate was about to happen. She reached for him, and he extended his hand. Her scent drifted to him, but it was not at all what he remembered. She smelled like coffee.

He woke realizing that he had set his coffee pot to brew at 3:00 a.m. He smiled. Melina Garza had invaded his dreams.

48.

"WE'RE ALL COMING WITH YOU TODAY, OKAY, REX." It was rarely a question with Doug.

"Good. Is there something specific anyone is worried about?"

"There's one guy we don't know about yet," said Doug with a bit of reluctance.

"Samuel James Ellifson?" Rex asked.

"The same," said Doug with resolve.

"Have you ever wondered why the bad guys always use three names? Or is it just us using his three names? We are secured, right? So, you just want to make sure about him, yes?"

Rex was looking only at Doug when he spoke. Everyone else—Tommy, Ron and Carey—stood quietly during the exchange, as though they hadn't heard a word of it.

"Please strike that last question," Rex offered. No one even smiled. It was more serious than he thought.

"I guess let's go," he said as he walked toward his study to get his appointment book.

They made their way into the garage, and got into Rex's car, chauffer driven by the mighty Doug West. Big Ron Garrity sat shotgun, and the mystical Tommy Krumholtz sitting on the far right. A small pack of motorcycles started as they rolled onto the street. Carey Sorenson was in the front with another member as they took the lead.

The drive was casual, as they had plenty of time to get to the courthouse. It was a beautiful morning, He saw the care with which downtown Danbrier was maintained. The trees were trimmed, the flowers blooming, and the streets were all well paved.

It was about a fifteen-minute drive, with no traffic. If there was traffic in downtown Danbrier, it took a bit longer. It was interesting how cars and people moved out of their way when they entered the parking lot. The motorcycles in front of them may have had something to do with it. The motorcycles in back probably did, too. A pack of members of Blood Oath was a sight to see. In the biker world any well-organized group of bikers caused heads to turn, especially when they were known to the public as fearless and protective of their own. Such as it was, the front row parking was being held by members already on the scene, and once again, no one wanted to interfere.

They parked, and Ron told Rex to wait. Doug opened Rex's door, and Ron opened Tommy's door. Tommy got out, then disappeared into the crowd. He did that kind of thing all the time. It seemed like he passed through people like a mist. They knew he was there, but he was just beyond reach, preternatural.

They went through security as a team, except Tommy. Rex knew he was somewhere ahead of them, scouting the area; the real point man. He joined them at the elevator.

"You've been switched to D-8, Judge Henry Rosen," said Tommy as he approached.

With a curious look on his face, Rex said: "He's not the usual assignment calendar Judge. Maybe someone took a vacation or called in sick. Let's see what happens."

They rode the elevator to the third floor. When the door opened, the four of them, Rex, Doug, Ron and Tommy exited. When the people on the third floor saw Doug and Ron they stepped back. Doug greeted them with "good morning," and "excuse us, please," which dazzled away their fears. Ron offered a smile but said nothing.

They turned right and arrived in front of department D-8. It was 8:12 a.m. and the door was open. Rex nodded to everyone, then entered the courtroom. It was a two-door process. The first door opened to an entryway, with doors on either side, both of which were for attorneys and witnesses. The entryway kept the noise down when court was in session and people were coming and going.

The second door opened to the courtroom. Rex was the first one there, except courtroom personnel. He could not remember the last time he was in Judge Rosen's courtroom, and went about his routine of greeting the bailiff, Deputy Brookings. They shook hands, and Rex felt something in his grip that told him Deputy Brookings was holding something back. Being Rex, he inquired:

"How are you today, Deputy Brookings? Is all well with you?"

"I'm fine, Mr. McKinley."

"Is there something you wanted to share with me?"

Without the slightest hint of surprise, he motioned Rex to step aside, and spoke in a confidential tone.

"I was friends with Donny Michaelson in the early days. Close friends. He turned bad, and I thought maybe you knew that I used to be his friend. I just want you to know that I think what he did was cowardly. That's all."

He offered his hand again, and his grip was different that time; firm and without reservation.

"I appreciate you sharing that with me. I won't forget it. Thank you."

"My first name is Brent."

"Rex. Thanks Brent."

Rex held his gaze another moment, then walked to the clerk's desk. The clerk was Linda Thomas-Miller, who Rex remembered from the early days in the old courthouse. She clerked for one of the Judges who did misdemeanor trials. They had a drink or two together at Main Street. She was a fun gal. He heard that she had married a cop, but didn't know who it was, or if they were still married. He hoped she had no preconceived notions about him from his recent experience.

"Rex! How are you?"

She got up from her seat and came down and gave him a big hug.

She whispered: "I hate what happened to you. I'm so glad that you are okay."

"Thanks, Linda. I'm better than ever."

She turned and went back up to her desk.

"Do we have any courtrooms available today?"

"I think there is one, but I can't say. Judge Rosen gets testy if we start giving out his surprises."

"Surprises? I think I'm going home."

He turned like he was walking away, then looked back and they both laughed.

"It is great to see you, Linda. Is all well on the home front?"

"Yep. We have three children. Two are his; one ours, and life is pretty good."

She held up a photo of her husband. He recognized the face without recalling his name.

"I'm really happy for you," he offered.

He heard the door open and turned to see who had entered. It was Rick Turner. Rex looked at him.

"Good morning, Rick. How are you?" His tone was neutral.

He set his stuff on the counsel table. "Good, Rex. How about you?"

"I'm good," Rex said flatly.

A minute later, Mark Mundo entered. Rex had forgotten him again. He smiled at Rex and said good morning. Rex returned the greeting. He had a gut feeling about Mark that was vague, but troubling. Maybe it was just his general disapproval of how he handled himself as a lawyer, even his appearance.

The bailiff went into the hallway to give his daily announcement of the rules to the public before they were allowed into the courtroom. He let Tommy, Doug and Ron come in while he was giving his speech.

As people were getting seated, Rex watched the Court Reporter come in and set up her machine, which meant Judge Rosen would be out soon. Rex walked around Rick Turner's side, handed her his card then introduced himself. He could not recall having met her before that day. She smiled a big smile, and said:

"Hi, Rex. You're looking good."

"Good morning to you, too. And, thanks." She gave him a thumbs-up.

Billy West was brought in and seated in the jury box, still wearing his orange jail uniform. Billy had not cut his hair or shaved. His hair was long, and as always, a mess. When he sat Rex looked to the deputy and asked for permission to approach Billy. When he got in front of him, it was apparent that Billy had not bathed recently, either. Rex turned and looked at Doug, but he did not return the look. Instead, he was looking at his little brother, undoubtedly trying to make a psychic connection. Sadly, Billy West seemed oblivious to everything around him.

"Billy, what happened to that haircut we discussed? And what about a shower?"

"Sorry, Rex. I had to do my own thing."

"Don't turn and look Billy, because the Bailiff will get upset. If you did you would probably die from the daggers in your brother's eyes. When you come in here on Monday, I expect a clean face, a haircut, and a shower. Do you understand me?"

"Sure, Rex."

Eric Trotter was brought in next, dressed the same as Billy, and chained as well. He was seated next to Billy. Eric had shaved off his very bushy beard and cut his hair very short. He looked good, like a different man. In a coat and tie he would probably be thought of as one of the lawyers, and Mark the defendant. Eric looked at Rex, and he nodded; Rex nodded back at him. Erich did not look at Mark.

Rex looked to the custody deputy who brought Billy in and asked: "Sir, is there some way I can be assured that Mr. West will shower, shave and get a haircut by Monday?"

"I'll see to it personally, Mr. McKinley." Rex was surprised at the encouraging response. He replied:

"I am most grateful, sir." He extended his hand and he and the man who then identified himself and Deputy Crownes, shook hands.

His Honor took the Bench, and the Bailiff, Rex's new friend, Brent

Brookings, announced that Department 8 of the Superior Court of Danbrier County was in session.

His Honor greeted them all with: "Good morning, ladies and gentlemen."

"Good morning your Honor," Rex said.

"Good morning your Honor, repeated Mark.

Rick Turner also offered a morning greeting.

"Good morning, Gentlemen, are you ready for trial?

"The defense is ready on behalf of Mr. West, your Honor."

"As I am on behalf of Mr. Trotter, your Honor."

"People are ready, your Honor."

"Very well, gentlemen, I am going to assign this case to Department 9, Judge Dorsemann. Please report there by 8:15 Monday morning."

"Thank you, your Honor," Rex said, and turned toward his friends.

They were being sent to the man who knew firsthand just how dirty the other side was playing, and it was too late for Rick Turner to do anything about it.

Rex doubted anyone had notice of it, or maybe the D.A. himself might have taken preemptive measure. But he couldn't do it publicly, so they were off to a courtroom where the prosecution did not start with an advantage.

Before he left the courtroom, Rex spoke to Brent Brookings and told him how much he respected him for sharing with him. He thanked Rex and wished him luck, an uncommon encouragement from law enforcement to defense counsel.

He looked to the Court Reporter, realizing he didn't get her name. He smiled at her, and she smiled back. He looked at her name plaque and read Cheryl Hardy. He tried to remember something about her name, but nothing came to mind.

His Honor was engaged in another matter already, but he looked Rex's way and smiled while in the middle of a conversation with a citizen who was before him for some routine matter. Then it dawned on him what might have happened. Judge Rosen didn't assign cases for trial. The usual assignment calendar judge passed the case along to prevent a leak. It was known by the judges where they were going, and the assignment calendar judge had someone who might let it out, thereby giving the D.A. time to file an affidavit of prejudice behind the scenes. To do it then in front of everyone would have cost him.

They left the courthouse as a group, with Rex in the middle, and Doug and Ron taking the lead. Tommy stayed close to Rex, and he could feel his intensity as he waited to speak privately. Rex had developed a sense of Tommy; he could feel him and his intentions, at least to the degree that he understood when he had information to impart.

Doug was the first to speak. "That was a pretty slick move by the judges. Judge Dorsemann won't let any bullshit get in the way of this trial. I'm still watching carefully, Rex, so I hope you're wearing a hat during this trial."

"A hat?" Rex asked with a chuckle.

"Yeah, the kind you pull a rabbit out of…" Doug laughed his deep guttural laugh, and everyone smiled, except Ron. He rarely gave any outward sign of his feelings, especially not in public.

49.

AFTER ARRIVING HOME, REX THOUGHT of Eddie and wanted to see him. He knew he also was hoping to get a chance to see Melina again. He really didn't know what to do about her. He had a stirring feeling and wanted to experience the energy she transmitted to him that last time he saw her at the Ranch. He wanted more.

He asked Doug:

"What's up with Eddie. I haven't received a call. I'd like to visit with him."

"Any maybe see Melina, too?" Doug was serious, but Rex felt his comment to be less than criticism, but a reminder to be up front, always. Doug had sensed his motivation on both levels: Eddie *and* Melina.

"I won't deny that she struck a chord with me the other night. Yes, it would be wonderful to see her again." The direct approach was always the best.

"Eddie isn't any better. He says he'll be there for trial, but he probably won't. Tommy has been keeping him company. I thought you knew that." Doug seemed distant now. He wasn't looking at Rex, but out the window of the study as he spoke. Ron was there, sitting in a chair, quietly absorbing what was happening between Doug and Rex.

"Okay, what am I missing here?" Rex asked forcefully. He was tired of dancing around whatever was going on with the Club and Eddie. Now Doug was telling him that Tommy was in touch, and Rex felt as though there was judgment in Doug's voice.

"Your question says you're not missing it. Eddie hasn't called because he knows you. He's standing back so that you can do your dance, Rex. You should know that by now." Still the cold stare out the window, and Doug's voice was hard, unbending.

"We're starting on Monday, and I want to know about Eddie, from his own lips. Am I being kept from him?" Rex was suddenly bordering on furious. He didn't care who Doug West was in the world. Eddie Logan was his best friend, and something was being kept from him, and he didn't like it.

"Okay. Let's go," said Doug as he started walking out of the study. Ron stood to follow. Rex looked at Ron for any kind of message but got nothing. He only glanced at Rex before he looked away.

They all walked out of the house, into the garage and got into Rex's car, with Doug driving, and Ron sitting in the front shotgun position. Rex did not need to be told to get into the back. As they backed into the street, motorcycles started.

It was a quiet drive, and Rex began to sense that something more was wrong with Eddie. He did not ask, but continued to feel anger, which kept him from speaking. By the time they got to the Ranch he was determined not to engage Doug again until he had spoken with Eddie.

When they parked in front of the clubhouse, Rex got out and waited for Doug to take the lead. They walked up the steps and entered. The entry was large with a living room off to the right. There sat Eddie Logan in a rocker. He looked like he had lost more weight. He had an IV in his arm, and he was dozing. Rex was shocked and scared at the same time. He looked at Doug with angry eyes. Doug turned away and left the room.

As Rex got close to Eddie, he opened his eyes, and with a very weak voice said:

"Hey, brother. How ya doing?"

Still angry, not understanding why at that point, Rex said: "Better than you. What the fuck, Eddie? Why hasn't anyone told me what's going on here?" Rex felt heat flushing over him. Here sat his best friend, obviously worse than he was when Rex last saw him, and no one had mentioned it.

"Easy brother. It seems the infection came back with a vengeance. Doc Sternberg said it would be okay to stay here on IV so long as the fever doesn't get any worse. I have a nurse, and Sally's here."

Rex felt his emotions bubbling over. His best friend looked like a shell of the man he had always known. He was probably thirty pounds down, and even his enormous arms looked small. Rex suddenly feared for Eddie's life.

"Where's this nurse?" Rex said it so forcefully, he surprised himself. Eddie shuddered. He toned it down a bit. "I'm sorry, Eddie. What can I do for you?"

Eddie seemed to be ready to doze off again. He struggled to look at Rex. He was obviously mustering his energy to respond. His voice was weak, but there was determination in his tone, and force in his words.

"Go kick ass in Billy's case, and don't worry about me. I'll beat this thing and be up and running before you know it." He turned his head away, closed his eyes, and seemed to be asleep immediately.

Rex sat and watched him sleep. After a few minutes he stood and reached over and put his hand on his brow, feeling for temperature. He was warm, but not hot. Rex drew a deep breath. Eddie turned and smiled for a brief second, then seemed to be gone into deep sleep.

Rex walked out of the house and stood on the front porch. Doug came out behind him, with Ron following. Not a word was spoken until they returned to Rex's house.

When Rex got out of the car and started back through the house, Doug called to him from behind.

"We'll see you first thing Monday morning."

Rex turned and looked at Doug. He was no longer angry.

"Thanks Doug. I'll see you then. Have a good weekend. Thanks to you, too, Ron."

Both men nodded and walked down the driveway toward their motorcycles. Other members were out there waiting. Soon Rex heard several Harley's start and ride off.

When he got into his study, Gail was still there, obviously waiting for his return. It was Friday night and she should have been gone already, but they had not spoken when he left with Doug and Ron.

"Gail, I'm sorry I didn't say anything before leaving. You should've been on your way home already."

"I couldn't leave without a few words with you. I have all your files in order, and everything copied. But…" She drifted off for affect.

"But what?" He knew he'd said it too forcefully, feeling his anger return. It confused him. He wasn't angry with Gail about anything.

"I wanted to let you know that the anger I saw before you left, and right now, is a dangerous thing for you, Rex. You've been down a long time now, and I'm seeing some of the old Rex coming back, and I like it—at least most of it." She smiled, stood and walked over and hugged him. "Now I'm going home."

Rex told her: "I couldn't do this without you."

She laughed lightly and said: "I know." As she left the room he could hear her walking across the tile toward the front door. The door opened then closed and Gail was gone for the weekend. He was alone, but no longer lonely. He was feeling alive and the anger was turning into a burning desire to be in the courtroom fighting the good fight, doing what he loved best. He had the rest of the weekend to prepare, and to reflect on who he was becoming because of all that had happened to him, and to his best friend Eddie Logan.

His world had changed forever, and so had Eddie's. They would both be different men, wounded warriors. *Was that who he had become?*

50.

HIS HOME WAS MUCH TOO LARGE for a single man. He built it as a show place early in his career. He'd been so proud to display his success to the rest of the legal community. He wanted to feel like he was one of them, although he was not raised as such.

He tried hard to convince those from whom he sought approval that he was a special one. Nonetheless, he knew that it had been his ego that gave birth to his need to seem singular, distinctive. Painfully, he had been shown, along with those watching, that on the surface of it all he was covered with a very thin shell, like an egg, which had been cracked and peeled away, making him vulnerable, just a man, who had been accused of repugnant deeds. And the truth was he had been out lusting after a woman, and got caught with his pants down, literally, or so the story had been told.

He had always been unbending in his desire to win, and was known as a top-flight trial lawyer, the image he wished to project, until he was splayed out before the public as a rapist and drug dealer.

His time with Mindy Thorn was not really something to be ashamed of, a man in need of a woman on a Friday night. Yet, it had become dirty and ugly, and he had been forced to submit to the judicial process, and it still wasn't over. The Billy West trial was going to be part of his vindication; people would see the real Rex in action. Even still, the thought engendered feelings of anger and confusion.

When he wandered through his home that Friday night at the end of a long and strenuous week, he realized an era of T-Rex McKinley, the pompous badass, was over, and he was the one making the decision to change—with, of course, the sordidness from the people he now called enemies. They were deeply flawed people to allow the operation against him to continue into a prosecution. Or, was it just their unfettered quest for power that made them so heartless? Their push for his pain and suffering was cruel, and although they would soon pay big in court, the money wasn't coming out of their pockets. They never had to pay for anything, and thus the anticipation of winning money did not quell his resentment.

His prosecution had to have been approved by Rodney Gardner himself. The District Attorney for the County of Danbrier had to have given his blessing to prosecute a celebrated local lawyer in a case that he knew was bogus. Rex had never been involved with drugs, and everyone knew it. He was a vocal advocate for drug treatment. He had donated generously to a couple of local programs. Gardner had to know about Mindy Thorn, too. He absolutely knew how bad Donny Michaelson was, and still allowed it to proceed.

H. J. Martin, the Danbrier County Sheriff, also had to have given his blessing to the investigation. He knew Donny Michaelson was a psycho, and he *knew* Mindy Thorn was an informant/operative who had been working for Michaelson because she had a criminal history. H.J. knew everything about everyone.

The top dogs of law enforcement, very powerful men in Danbrier County, had colluded to allow their people to attempt to destroy his reputation and convict him for crimes he did not commit, but which would have kept him down forever; ended his career as a lawyer. How could he forgive such conduct? He did not want to forgive or forget. His blood boiled at the thought of it.

Therein he found his anger surging out to cover for his pain. The bitter truth had become a resident in his soul. Wherever he went, whomever he met, any stage that he was upon, Rex McKinley had been accused of rape and drugs, and some people would always believe it.

Then the most important question of the night hit him hard: what about Billy in all of it? Throughout his anguish, he had left Billy to his own world of pain, alone in jail. Rex had given it fleeting moments in his thoughts, but his excuse for not seeing Billy regularly had been that he knew he was not going to testify, and therefore he didn't need to prep him like he would someone who might take the stand. It was an excuse for his disloyalty, and nothing less. It was the measure of his betrayal of his own client.

Billy may have killed Steve Michaelson. It looked bad for him. Yet Rex had no idea what had really happened that night in the Basin that left Steve Michaelson dead on the floor with a bullet through his head and stab wounds through his neck, much less whether Billy had committed the crime for which he was accused. These were things he should have known long before that night.

The thought shuddered through his soul, rocking him to his core. He had abandoned Billy at such an intrinsic level, and although Doug had not addressed it recently, he undoubtedly was hurt that his expectations of Rex had not been met— that Rex had all but forsaken his brother in his most desperate time. He felt gratitude that Doug had not seen fit to throw him over.

He knew that Eddie had information he had yet to impart beyond a few muttered whispers. Rex would be going forward without him for the first time. They had not been able to communicate because Eddie was so ill. And he was experiencing a deep feeling of loss over continuing without Eddie at his side. Bottom line: Rex was afraid to move forward without him.

51.

IT WAS 8:15 A.M. ON SATURDAY MORNING, and that day Rex had taken in the splendor of Danbrier. There was no place more beautiful in his estimation. He had always thought the mountain chain was magnificent. Living at the base of it had always brought him joy. He was surrounded by a forest full of wild life. The valley was laid out with trees and housing that was orderly and well maintained. Although like any place in America, Danbrier had its ugliness and bad neighborhoods, Rex thought only of what was charming and appealing that day. He had embraced the message to his soul, and would let nothing rock his world, including fear of violence from someone trying to prevent him and his best friend, Eddie Logan, from defending Billy West.

The Danbrier Detention Center was a large facility, holding approximately 2500 men and 600 women. It was built with a central admissions structure from which eight separate arms with lengthy hallways running in as many directions. Each had two to four units built off to each side of the arms. From the air, the place looked like a large spider with pods on its legs.

Rex had not wanted to return there since his arrest and beating. Leaving behind his initial joy for the day, he had knots in his stomach as he parked in the lot in front of the facility. Security concerns were still in place, and one of the members of Blood Oath, Carey Sorenson—who now seemed attached to Rex at the hip, for which he was most grateful—waited for him in the parking lot as he approached the building. As he made his way toward the entrance, he heard more Harley-Davidson's, and knew it was backup for Carey. There was still a serious predator out there, one who had the audacity to direct the assassination of Eddie Logan.

After entering the lobby and checking in at the front window, which was covered with inch thick bullet proof glass, Rex was given a visiting slip, and knew the procedure. He approached the visiting entrance. One deputy hit the button that slid the steel door open, so Rex could then walk through a metal detector, and then sign in with another deputy seated behind a desk. He was personable to the man in uniform, who seemed indifferent to him. He was grateful there was nothing said about him or his purpose at the facility. He realized he had never had that concern before that day. It was part of what he carried with him now, an awareness of the potential for bias and prejudice from others because of what he had experienced; something his clients undoubtedly felt all the time.

Moreover, he knew that Captain Russ Walden was commander of the facility, and that he was on duty those nights Rex spent there, drugged and unconscious, beaten severely, and given no care or help for his injuries. Russ Walden was a smart man, but he had made a grievous error. Rex now considered him an enemy, and he knew of Captain Walden's frailties and faults, especially where it counted in Billy's case, and he knew there was more which he intended to get from Eddie Logan that very day. His next visit was going to be at the Ranch. He would visit with Billy, then Eddie.

Billy was in Unit 8, which Rex knew was one of three units housing men the Sheriff presumed were on their way to prison, most being repeat offenders. It was the hard-core men who were kept in Unit 8, and Billy was being treated as though he were already convicted. Perhaps if Rex did not care, he might as well have been. But the housing choices were up to the Sheriff, and no one, not even the judges, tried to tell the Sheriff how and where to house *his* inmates.

It was a fetid smell that assaulted his senses when he stepped into the hallway inside of the facility. The rank odor of hundreds of bodies and their gasses, as well as their inability to shower and change clothing regularly permeated the air. Their fear had its own smell; and the anger and depression brought the senses into conflict, as well. Any jail had its own powerful stench and feelings, and DDC was no exception.

Rex soon adapted to the smell and forgot about it as he kept a steady pace down the long hallway. He turned to his right and followed the hall with bold letters declaring that units 6 through 8 were to be found in that direction. By the time he reached Unit 8, the smell was no longer a conscious sensation.

Inside the visiting area of Unit 8 he found the speaker on the wall with a contact button and pressed it. It beeped for a full minute before a gruff voice asked: "Yes?"

"Official visit for West," Rex replied.

"We'll have him up in a minute," the voice told him.

"Thank you," Rex said, and found his way through the first door into the attorney visiting room. Both that door and the one into the visiting room required the use of the key given him by the deputy checking him in past his station. The doors were made of thick steel with thick windows and eighth the size of the door.

He scanned the room and sat on the steel seat affixed to the pipe coming out of the brick wall before him. There was a counter made of concrete below the mesh screen that divided him from the inmate side. It was dirty with years of human contact and less than respectful treatment from the visitors on that side. There was a small opening at the bottom of the mesh to allow documents to be transferred from either side. The room on the other side of the mesh was approximately eight feet square, with a recessed light in the ceiling. Rex waited.

At least fifteen minutes passed while he watched the room below, called the MP (multi-purpose) Room. There was a stairway to the left. Men entering the room to visit had to climb the stairs to get to the attorney room, or for the public visiting through thick glass which they could see their visitors and speak with them on phones connected in each side.

A clanging of a door showed Billy coming through and making his way up the stairs. He looked the same as always, long hair, a beard and fear crossing his face. Rex felt guilty that his client looked so badly and so afraid. He knew that were he to have been handling the case as he should, Billy would feel differently. Today was the test. Would Billy trust him?

Billy made it to the top of the stairs and waited outside the visiting room door until the lock buzzed. He pulled the handle and entered the room.

"Hi, Rex."

"Good morning, Billy."

Billy moved forward and sat on the round seat of brushed steel and did his best to look at Rex through the mesh. It took some adjusting to find each other's eyes. When they connected, Rex's first impression was that Billy was looking for Rex to give him something, perhaps some encouragement.

"Billy, I'm here today to begin with an apology."

"What for?" Billy looked a bit baffled. He waited for Rex to respond.

"I've been so caught up in my own troubles, that I have not given my time to you, and you've been locked away, probably scared to death about what is coming."

Rex let that hang in the air while Billy processed it. Billy responded.

"Thank you, Rex. My brother told me you'd be here before trial. He told me you're the best, and that I can count on you. So, I'm okay." Billy looked at Rex with anticipation.

"I'm humbled by Doug's faith in me. I'm hoping that you will find yourself able to feel the same way. I should have been here sooner, and for that I am sincerely sorry, Billy. I ask you to forgive me, please."

Billy laughed, but it seemed like a cover. He had feelings, but probably wasn't used to sharing them with anyone.

"I can't remember anyone ever apologizing to me," Billy said, and it rang true. He'd been alone within himself far too long.

"I mean it, Billy. Will you forgive me?"

"Yes, of course."

Billy went quiet, and Rex took the stage.

"Thank you, Billy. We have a lot to cover this morning, and I think the best place to start is with what I expect will happen during trial, and how we will present you to the jury."

"I can't testify. I can't." Billy showed signs of panic.

"Easy, Billy, that's not part of my plan."

Billy relaxed a bit, then took a deep breath and sighed as he released it.

"What I want us to do today is share some feelings, and I need to go first. I am not only sorry for not being here sooner, but I'm also scared for you that I haven't prepared you for what's coming." Rex paused, and asked Billy if he was with him. Billy only nodded.

"Okay, let's talk about what that jury is probably going to be thinking, a good part of which is directly related to what happened to me."

Billy's response was not what Rex had expected.

"There's been talk in here, Rex. One guy told me I should get another lawyer, that you made some kinda deal. Is it true?"

Rex paused, taken aback by Billy's words. He took a deep breath, expelled it, and said:

"Then that's where we'll begin, Billy."

For the next couple of hours Rex and Billy bared their souls to one another. When Rex left he knew so much more about his client. He didn't know whether Billy had shot or stabbed the deceased. He had not asked. That was never an issue they discussed. If Billy would have brought it up, Rex would have engaged him. But it was so far outside the scope of what they had talked about, that were Rex to have attempted to delve into that realm, and if Billy had resisted, then all that Rex was trying to accomplish might have been blocked, and it wasn't his place to try to pry that out. Rex knew him better now and was firmly convinced that he had the right approach planned. Even though he was not certain what had happened with the death of Steve Michaelson, he knew that Billy could never be compelled to take the stand and testify about it. Of that, Billy was not capable regardless of whether he had any direct involvement in the killing.

52.

WHEN REX CAME INTO THE PARKING LOT, Carey was waiting. Rex thanked him for waiting, then said: "I need to see Eddie."

"Doug said you would. Let's go." Rex wasn't surprised.

They drove to the Ranch with four other members on their motorcycles, two in front and two in back. When they got to the gate at the Ranch, it was already open. Rex followed the bikes through, and up to the Clubhouse.

Eddie was sitting on the front porch in a rocking chair. The air was cool, with that sweet forest smell. Looking at his best friend as he approached, Rex felt a jolt of Eddie's energy hit him. He looked so much better, he even seemed a few pounds heavier.

Eddie called out: "I know you're impressed, but everyone's gonna think we're going steady from that smile on your face."

"That's the truth, since we were kids," Rex said with a huge grin.

Eddie stood to greet him. There was no IV, and Eddie stood firm, waiting to hug his best friend. A manly hug was shared, and Rex felt the energy that Eddie always possessed and controlled, like the flow of the Universe.

"Ready to get back in the saddle?" Rex was grinning, happier than he had been in a very long time.

"Don't do the cowboy routine with me. My horse is made of iron." They laughed.

"Didn't you get invited to the party?" Eddie laughed.

"Party? Nope, I guess I don't qualify for an invite." Rex wasn't sure whether Eddie was joking, but as he scanned his environment he realized that there was a lot of activity around him. Was there a party in preparation? And then he saw her coming his way.

His stomach jumped as she approached. She was smiling, and he drank in her beauty. She was dressed in jeans and work boots, and a long-sleeved flannel shirt. She looked like a mountain woman, with no makeup and her hair clipped on the top of her head.

"Hi, Rex. Can I talk you into staying for lunch and the party?"

He was slow to respond. It wasn't whether he wanted to be there, but she had taken his breath, and he was trying too hard to be cool. It wasn't working. He managed to squeak out:

"Definitely," and Eddie laughed at his effort. Then Rex laughed, then Melina. She said:

"Nobody rides for free around here. I could use some help," and she turned toward the barn and began walking. He followed her, quickening his pace to catch up. He looked over his shoulder at Eddie, who was smiling at him. Eddie offered thumbs up, and Rex turned back and increased his pace again to stay with Melina.

Once by her side, he didn't know what to say, so he got in step with her and did as she did. They began assisting in the construction of what began to look like a stage. All the wood was cut, and it appeared to have been used in the past. Everything was screwed together, with the pieces numbered on the back side. It was like putting a very simple puzzle together. A couple of the Club members were doing most of the lifting, so Rex fell in with them and they all quietly pieced it together. It took little more than an hour until a forty-foot square stage was laid out in front of the barn. It was set up for the band and dancing.

"Do you dance, Rex?" Melina was gazing into him. He felt her searching for the real Rex. He was surprisingly comfortable meeting her eyes.

"I've got some moves," he said, "but you'll probably have to teach me."

"Oh, I think you'll know exactly what to do. I'll see you in a while. I need to shower." And she walked off toward Doug's cabin. Rex found himself watching her every move as she walked away.

One of the members, Art, said: "Another beautiful day on the Ranch, eh, Rex?" Everyone within hearing range laughed lightly.

"Oh, yeah," Rex replied.

Rex drew in a deep breath of the forest air. It smelled clean. On the Ranch, it seemed as though the pollution of the world was barred from entering. A party at the Club House was like no other Rex had attended. No one got drunk; no one got stoned, except maybe some pot smoking; no one used drugs, and rarely a curse word was spoken. People laughed and danced and celebrated the good times; they shared their love for one another. There was always a feast of beef, and plenty of chicken. Fresh fruits and vegetables were abundant. All the food was raised or grown on the Ranch.

One of the major reasons Club members were so close was their riding together. They rode hard and fast, with their pack two by two, side by side, with the two behind the President and Vice President, and the others followed the same way. After years of riding together, there was a psychic connection between them that was born of needing to know what the pack was thinking and feeling always. Although technology had provided sophisticated methods of communication, the decades of being so very close, especially in a time of potential crisis—like being under attack—bound them at the soul.

There was an incident a couple of years before while coming home from a run. Traveling at 90 miles per hour, with the pack of twenty-two riding side-by-side, two-by-two—front wheels of those behind only a few feet apart from the back wheels of those ahead them—no room for error.

When three members and one prospect of the Saints of Fire M.C. came from behind on motorcycles, everyone knew. As the attackers drew near and began attempting an assault, the pack slowed and split in the back, surrounding the invaders and swallowing them inside the pack, driving them to the off ramp. As they sped up the Main Street off ramp, shots were fired, and all four of the attackers went down, three dead, one severely wounded—he did not survive surgery.

The pack went through the light at the intersection and drove back onto the freeway, heading east on the I10 toward the Cole Street off ramp in Danbrier one mile away. No one saw a thing.

They left the freeway on Cole Street and made their way across the northern boundaries of Danbrier, heading west on their way to Forest Mountain Road.

As they arrived at the entrance, the huge steel gates opened, and the pack rode under the stone archway, safely on Blood Oath property. There was an investigation, but no one saw anything, and the were no arrests, not even accusations. Some said it was because Saints of Fire came out of L.A. and were in sacred territory—even to the cops who wanted no gang wars in Danbrier. They viewed what happened as a quick and speedy resolution to what might have become a serious problem. Word had gone out about it, but there was little discussion in the community, and no one from the Club said a word about it.

As time passed Rex wandered about asking if he could be of assistance to anyone. He was trying to act cool, but he thought everyone knew he was waiting for Melina. He greeted the men and their wives; he made it a point to say hello to Richard West, father of Doug and Billy, and grandfather to Melina. Rex had known him since he first started doing work for the Club; they were friends. Richard rarely left the Ranch after he'd had a severe motorcycle accident when a truck cut him off the roadway. Fortunately, there were witnesses, and the trucking company was a large one. Rex represented Richard and got the policy maximum of two million dollars. Less Rex's one third Richard had plenty of money in the bank.

He sat with Richard on the front porch for a while, still looking casually for Melina. "It seems my granddaughter has taken an interest in you, Rex."

"Taken an interest? Really? I didn't think she even noticed me."

They both laughed, and Richard said:

"Turn around and find out."

He did and there she was, smiling at him. She extended her hand, and he stood and let her take him away.

"See you later, Richard," said Rex over his shoulder.

"Not tonight you won't. You kids go have some fun now."

Melina was pulling him to the side of the house where all the food was being served.

"Let's eat, okay?"

Like her dad, it really wasn't a question.

"Let's do. I'm starved. Food is all I could think about all day long."

She looked at him with an impish grin; then faked a sad face.

"Really?"

"No, not really."

They both laughed and got in line to get some food. Their eyes were locked on each other. Time was moving very slowly, and to Rex there was silence around them even though everyone was talking. It was like they were in a bubble all their own, and they understand each other without words. No one interrupted them.

When they got to the long table full of food, there was so much, and it smelled so good it was difficult to choose what to eat. Rex scooped chicken and some vegetables and potatoes onto his plate. There was a bowl full of watermelon, which he stacked on top of the meat.

Melina was picking her food more carefully. He watched her; he had never seen anything so beautiful. He was captivated. She watched Rex out of the corner of her eye. She smiled and told him to follow her.

They found a place for the two of them at a huge picnic table. They sat side by side as they began eating. They were talking with their mouths full and laughing. She moved her hand across his mouth, as though she was wiping off food. Her touch was so gentle and soft. An electrical charge raced through him. He stopped chewing. He couldn't seem to do anything but stare at her. She looked back and smiled. She leaned over and whispered: "You might want to finish chewing that food."

He snapped out of it, swallowed his food, and they both laughed.

She asked: "Where were you?"

"In that vast region called your heart, where I want to stay forever."

She smiled and leaned over and kissed him; gentle lips on lips. He heard an "ahhh" from across the table. It was a woman. Rex didn't look to see who, as he did not seem to be able to take his eyes off Melina, but he tried so he could get through his meal and perhaps find some place that was less inhabited. He wanted to have some up close and personal time with her, but the thought dawned upon him that there was no private place on the Ranch.

He also remembered there were no secrets in the Club. If a member had a problem, he was obliged to take it to his brothers. It was discussed as Club business, and a resolution of the problem was a group effort. The closeness of the Club was maintained by open and honest relationships, with no secrets. If someone had a problem, it became everyone's problem until resolved.

As they sat, he realized there was a band setting up about a hundred yards away on the stage he had helped assemble in front of the barn. He recognized a few of the musicians. They played rock and blues.

Melina said there would be dancing soon, so they had better not fill up. They took their plates and cleared their area of the table. She reached up and grabbed his face with her delicate hands and kissed him again. He sighed afterward. They stood together for a moment then started walking toward the barn. He reached over and put his arm around her, and she snuggled him.

They greeted the band members just as they began to tune up. Within minutes they hit it hard. Most of their music were covers of old rock 'n roll and blues songs. There was simply too much good music to need to write another song. The lead guitar player, Buddy, had it down.

Melina grabbed Rex's hand and they started dancing. She moved in ways he had never seen. She was *with* the music, as though it was being played just for her, and she was guiding Rex to her rhythm. He had never felt so good dancing—especially without any liquor in him. Back in the day, as the expression goes, he would drink and dance. With enough alcohol in him he didn't care how he looked, and always thought he was doing well. With Melina, it was different. His movement was in sync with her, and she was leading.

Melina let the sounds enter her and move her, the arrangements from the Universe. Her raven black hair was flowing with her every motion; and then another song, and another.

When the band took a break, so did they. Rex was dazed. They'd been dancing together for some time, but he had no idea how long. They were sweating heavily.

They hugged and stood there holding each other, glowing. He heard the applause. It was about the music, and the way it had made everyone feel—the oneness of all—not just about Rex and Melina. They joined in the acclamation.

Suddenly, Rex could feel Eddie Logan somewhere. Then he saw him. He'd been watching them dance. He was with Sally, and they were with a group. Rex asked Melina to come with him, and she held his hand as they walked over to the group. They hugged everyone, including Eddie. He was glad to hug them back. He smiled but did not speak. There was no need for words.

The night went on forever—or so it seemed. When things began to slow down, Rex and Melina took a role in helping clean up after the fun. They worked side by side so naturally; Rex smiling the entire time, goofy with love.

It was four in the morning before all the festivities were over, and everything was returned to its original tidy state. The Ranch was always left in order before the day was over. Everything on the Ranch had its place, and there it would be found the next day.

Rex wanted to stay the rest of the night but knew he should go home. He could feel that Melina wanted to be with him, but he knew she wanted them to be more than lovers. He wanted that too; he respected her feelings. However, he was not leaving without a kiss. He pulled her around the side of the house after everyone had either gone inside, or to bed. He put his hands on her hips, they moved toward each other very slowly. He bent to meet her. When their lips touched, he almost jumped at the sparks that flew. Their mouths opened slightly, and their tongues met and touched. They teased a bit, and then passion took over—joined together in a kiss, a fire burning between them. She moved closer, and they held each other tightly feeling and sharing the electric energy, and the sensations of their arousal.

When they pulled back Rex was on fire. He wanted more but knew he would have to wait. He was certain that whatever Melina might want would not include some quick action and a wave goodbye until later.

They were smiling at each other, and Rex was ready to leave. She turned and walked toward Doug's cabin. Rex thought she looked like a goddess in the nighttime with the moonlight shining off her hair and her light step, obviously the way of a dancer. She turned and smiled. She waved. Rex waved back at her.

"Are you ready to go, Rex?"

He knew the voice. It was his dear friend Carey Sorenson. Still looking after Melina, Rex said:

"I'm always ready, Carey. You know that."

They laughed. There were three other brothers with him, including Art.

He looked back at the road for a glimpse of Melina. He didn't see her, but felt her, and breathed in her scent that was all over him. He took another deep breath and sighed.

"Ain't love grand," said Art.

"Oh yeah," Rex replied.

Once home he found his way into his bed and fell asleep immediately.

53.

PEOPLE CAME AND WENT, BUT LIFE CONTINUED. Hearts changed, yet people stayed the same. Lies were told, but the truth was eventually thrown on the stage for all to see. It was always a question of whether at any given time people wanted to see the truth, for it was often painful, disturbing. Why must we hear it now, they asked—or simply, must we? That's what he told the troops whenever it was necessary.

Men went to war over lies told, and treasures to be taken. He had stolen all that he could, and developed a team that was willing, to the death. No man had ever started with less yet had accomplished so much—his core belief.

For Samuel James Ellifson, the only truth was what he said and did. He was a warrior, and his world involved violence and death, and taking what he wanted, killing to get it. That was what he had always known. He enjoyed being the hunter.

Since his early years when he stabbed the man who beat his mother, he was a killer. He was fourteen then, and other than sensing that it had a calming effect on his mother, he had no real feelings about it. He disposed of the body by cutting it up with a hatchet and an electric knife. He wrapped it in trash bags and got rid of it in the alleys near his building. In his neighborhood in L.A. there were plenty of trash dumpsters. Then he and his mother found housing in another building. No one would connect him to anything. That was his first kill, and there had been many since, always easier, and with purpose.

Even in the early days, his eyes seemed devoid of emotion. Some thought they looked like marbles, lifeless and empty. There was life in him, but he was different from others. He saw the way to power was through being willing, then acting without hesitation. The military mindset found home in him.

Although his service records were classified, his time in the Middle East was pure enjoyment for him. Charging into buildings, taking out the enemy, and seizing whatever he could, even the smallest of treasures. That had been the ultimate thrill. When he transitioned home, he still had that fire burning, and taking what he wanted required only a willing crew.

A profitable venture had been working very well until they hit the wrong house. The intended target, a drug dealer of some consequence, was nowhere to be found, but he had close ties with law enforcement, and the silent alarm was answered quickly.

Ellifson and his crew were run into the prison system almost as hastily. They were newcomers, but they stuck together. In time, they grew in number. All former military, all willing to follow his command.

He liked the military, and his command made prison a good home. His time in the service was good training. His time with his brothers, the Point Men, was the ultimate reward. He commanded, and they obeyed. They had a good thing going, until a failure to take out a target, the one called Eddie Logan—an important man who was getting too close. If he had died, it would have been a different story, but he didn't—and now Ellifson was the hunted.

He had done his time, and had skills, but there was a man waiting to take him out, and it wouldn't be pretty. He had already caught the marksman, and Ellifson suspected that he had told it all.

The one hunting him scared everyone. Although he had never known fear, he had become wary, and was preparing to leave the area.

54.

IT WAS MID-MORNING SUNDAY, and Rex was puttering around his house. He was anxiously awaiting Monday. He felt good that he and Billy had had some time together.

The doorbell rang. He went to the door, and there stood Doug, Ron and a somewhat healthier version of Eddie—as though he had hit the gym and gained back some size.

Doug spoke: "Can we come in and talk?"

"Of course. Why'd you ring the doorbell?" Rex inquired. No one spoke. "Let's go into my study." Rex scanned Eddie for signs of anything, but his best friend was not breaking character.

Once in the study, Rex sat at his desk, and with open hands offered the seats in the room. The three men sat, but not before Eddie laid an electronic device on the bookcase. Then, as always, Doug took the lead:

"This is what you need to know." He paused for a moment, as though picking his words, then began:

"It seems that Mr. Ellifson drove himself to a rest stop in Banning, down in Riverside County, turned off his engine, lit a cigarette, and blew his brains out." Doug showed no emotion when he spoke. Rex was visibly startled.

"When did this happen?"

"Last night while we were all partying," said Doug with a flat tone.

They were silent for a while. Then Rex spoke.

"Okay. I know this is no great loss to the world, much less to us. Why tell me? Why do I need to know?"

Eddie responded:

"It's simple, Rex. If you're gonna impeach Russ Walden, who, by the way is now Captain Walden, then you'll want to be able to ask whether that man is available, and if not, why. You'll also want to already have the answers."

Rex thought he detected remorse or even a sense of loss from Eddie. He didn't understand why he might be upset about the suicide of a man who engineered his attempted assassination. Apparently reading Rex's thoughts, Eddie further explained.

"Give it some thought, Brother. The first thing they'll think is it was me, or one of us," he nodded at Doug and Ron. "Then they'll try to take it somewhere that will help them."

"I don't see anything but trouble," said Rex showing signs of confusion.

"C'mon Rex," said Doug. He seemed impatient, so Ron intervened.

"Alright, let's say that this guy can be brought in as part of this case, which we know he can. They know he can but have no idea what we know. How do they get him in?"

Rex thought for a minute. Finally, the light went on.

"*They* don't; they can't. And when I do it's while I cross-examine Walden." Rex felt a return of his anger; he was feeling as though he had been left out of an important decision. Then he realized if it were a decision, it was his to make during trial, they had only offered the idea.

There was silence from the others as they carefully watched him. Nothing more needed to be said.

55.

IT WAS MONDAY MORNING, and Rex felt like an important part of a team walking toward the elevator in the courthouse. People stopped and looked, some moved out of the way. Doug was always mindful of how submissive people were when they saw him, especially when Ron was with him. Some stopped and stared quite openly. Blood Oath members were not wearing their patches. Rex had not inquired, but thought it was probably because Billy's case had nothing to do with the Club. Were it about a Club member, it might have been different. They had all worn their patches during the Carey Sorenson trial, and even got a ruling on that issue by the Court, favoring the First Amendment and their right to display their colors.

Doug was polite to everyone. His good manners and kind words always took people by surprise. With Doug people were just happy that he didn't break them into pieces and eat them. Although Ron was the quiet one, his size alone was imposing. He usually didn't offer much, other than an occasional "excuse me," or "pardon me, please," when people got in the way. When someone, particularly a small person or a child looked him in the eyes, he was always friendly. His smile could light up a room. Kids seemed to love him and were drawn to him. Rex once saw a child run to him in the hallways of the courthouse, and he bent down and picked him up and hugged him gently. The mother stood by and watched with a smile on her face. When Ron set the toddler on the ground he was disoriented. He had just been hugged by a giant.

Tommy was silent and pulled one of Rex's briefcases while he walked ahead of the group. He was doing double duty, Rex knew. He was scanning the environment for the presence of the enemy. Tommy knew the cop game as well as anyone. He would give Rex a briefing on his observations before they went on the record. There would always be observers on behalf of the prosecution team, and Tommy would scope them out.

They got off the elevator and walked the carpeted hallway to D-9. They entered, with Tommy pulling the one briefcase to the counsel table. He spoke to Rex in a hushed voice, and then sat in the public section. Doug and Ron had taken seats, each on opposite sides of the courtroom. All the other members who had come to court for Billy's case, which seemed about ten, took up positions in the hallway.

Because jury selection would begin soon, Judge Dorsemann would want all the extra seats available for prospective jurors. Doug and Ron would be given latitude because Doug was Billy West's brother, a fact known by few, and not yet public knowledge. Ron stayed because he was Ron, and no one wanted to ask him to leave.

The rest of the members waiting in the hallway would be enjoying themselves, holding open doors for ladies, extending greetings to the men. The courthouse was as much theirs as anybody's. However, if all the Club members waiting in the hall were to come in during jury selection Rick Turner might have a legitimate complaint. No one could exclude them from the hallway. Once a jury was selected or impaneled, there was nothing meritorious Rick Turner could say about their presence in the courtroom, especially since none of them were wearing their patch.

Department 9 of the Danbrier County Courthouse was one of the larger courtrooms in the building. The seating capacity was one hundred five, counting courtroom personnel and the lawyers. The usual jury pool was from 70 to 90 people in serious felony cases.

Rex greeted the Bailiff, Deputy Rita Alcazar, and was a bit friendlier toward her than the last time when he was the defendant. She smiled and told him that she was glad to see him back in the action. She reached out and hugged him. He hugged her back. It felt good, even though her Kevlar vest was between them.

He greeted the Clerk, Karin Kornder. She smiled and said:

"I'm really glad to see you, Rex." She was beaming.

"Thank you, Karin. Would you file these for me, please?"

"Of course. Judge Dorsemann usually likes to read them before we begin, so it may be a while before he takes the Bench."

She stamped the copies and returned them to Rex. He thanked her, returned to the counsel table then slid a copy to Rick Turner who had just come in and was setting up at the counsel table. Russ Walden was not yet present.

"Any motions, Rick?"

"Good morning, Rex. My only motion was about Blood Oath wearing their colors in the courthouse, but it appears to be a moot point. I'm still going to ask for a ruling on it."

Rick Turner exuded personal power. He was dressed in a black suit with a red tie and white shirt. His hair was freshly cut and combed in place. He was fit and looked exceptionally well. Rex felt a twinge of fear and choked it down.

"I don't think it will be an issue, either, Rick, but I will oppose it."

He walked back to his side of the counsel table, and he and Rick Turner both took their seats. Mark Mundo joined them a few minutes later. Once again, Rex had completely forgotten about him.

"Good morning, Mark. How are you?"

"I'm fine, Rex. You look good."

Rex thought it was Mark's way of saying he was glad Rex was okay, with all signs of his beating gone.

"Thanks, Mark. Are you ready?"

"You bet."

Rex lowered his voice and said to Mark: "Here is a copy of my *In Limine* motions. Just go with it, please."

"Will do."

Mark turned slightly toward the gallery. He nodded as he looked at Doug. Doug's reply was an almost imperceptible nod. Rex watched with amusement, knowing that Doug had given Mark a sermon about how to behave, which included following Rex's lead.

They sat quietly for a while until Rex saw Rita Alcazar coming toward them from the front of the courtroom. She spoke:

"Gentlemen, his Honor is ready. Mr. McKinley and Mr. Mundo, I'll have your clients brought in."

She went to her desk and made a call on her phone. Moments later Billy and Erich Trotter were brought in from the back.

Billy looked good. His hair was cut, his beard was gone. He was wearing a coat and tie, and slacks. Rex was very pleased and thanked Deputy Crownes "on behalf of Mr. West and his family." Deputy Crownes accepted the gratitude with a nod and a smile.

Erich Trotter looked good, too. He was acting like a soldier. He walked erect to the counsel table, then sat and looked straight ahead.

Judge Dorsemann came out of chambers and stepped up to the Bench.

"Gentlemen, I have read the motions *in Limine* from Mr. McKinley, and from Mr. Turner. Mr. Mundo, did you intend to file any motions?"

"I join Mr. McKinley."

"Very well. Then let's discuss Mr. Turner's motion first. We have dealt with this issue in the past, and when a member of Blood Oath Motorcycle Club was on trial in this courthouse, Judge Strobel had allowed the members to wear their so-called patch. I have not seen anyone wearing that item of clothing, and don't know whether it is an issue in this case. I propose to put the motion aside unless and until it becomes an issue. How do you feel about that Mr. Turner?"

"Your honor, I'm fine with that. I don't see we're going to have a problem in that area."

"Very well, that motion is moot at this point, but is can be reopened should the issue arise."

"Let's discuss Mr. McKinley's unopposed motions.

"First, Mr. Turner, did you want to argue against anything in particular?"

"No, your Honor. I submit."

"Very well, counsel. The Court agrees that the deceased shall not be called the victim or any derivative thereof. When I was a prosecutor I used that term for the very reason about which Mr. McKinley objects. I agree that it is a conclusion of fact that is for the jury to decide, and that by repeating it over and over it has the effect of playing to the sympathy of the jury, exactly the opposite of what the law dictates. Had someone objected when I was a prosecutor, and did this very thing, I would have been compelled to agree. That was my intent, unless restrained. Wouldn't you agree, Mr. Turner?"

"No, I do not, your Honor, but submit."

"Second, there being no objection, the defense expert, Mr. Farlow from Human Tech will be permitted to testify regarding the preservation of evidence, and on issues related to blood.

"Finally, the case of Izazaga has been cited by counsel, and I do believe that your office has had some recent experience with the use of that authority, Mr. Turner. Anything you care to add on that subject?"

"No, your Honor. Submit on that issue."

"Very well. That being settled, counsel, I have some rules that I expect all of you to follow.

"First, and foremost, there will be no rude behavior in this courtroom. Second, I expect counsel to be punctual, and ready each day. If you have witness problems, that is your problem, and you must fix it. If you cannot proceed, I will expect you to rest.

"Third, we are here to try a criminal case. It is perhaps the most important American tradition that we must be concerned that the defendants have a fair trial. I expect that we will all be mindful of that maxim as our number one priority.

"Finally, for now, I have no time limits on *voir dire if* you are doing your job. If you become repetitive or argumentative with prospective jurors, or, God forbid, boring, I will cut you off. I will try not to embarrass you in front of the prospective jurors. So, if I tell you that your time is up, please don't argue, but simply thank the Court and take your seat.

"I want you here at 8:15 every morning. We will begin with jury selection this morning, and will continue until we have a jury, unless some other issue in this case has arisen that requires my intervention.

"Are we clear, gentlemen?"

"Yes, your Honor," Rex said, followed by Mark, then Rick Turner.

"Excellent. Madam Clerk do we have a jury pool?"

Karin Kornder reported that they were ready in the Jury Assembly room. They had a pool of seventy-five prospective jurors. Rita Alcazar was sent to bring them to the courtroom. She left quickly.

Lists of prospective jurors had been handed to counsel by Rita before she left. They came in two forms; alphabetical, and random computer-generated. Rex began busily reviewing the alphabetical list for familiar names. He saw none. He put post-it labels on his juror sheet provided by the court, with six squares per line, and a separate line for alternates.

Russ Walden came in at that time and was in uniform. That was another psychological advantage that cop's play, and a very smooth way to make his appearance—just before the prospective jurors were brought in—but there was nothing wrong with it. He earned the right to wear that uniform. Good cops are always needed. He was wearing Captain's bars. Rex could feel his intense energy. He was a man of tremendous personal power. He looked fit in his uniform, and very comfortable in his surroundings.

Within a few minutes, Rita returned with a large group following her. Rex stood and reminded Billy and Erich that they always stood for the jury. Mark Mundo stood, too. Both men on the prosecution side stood.

Tommy, Doug and Ron moved to various locations in the back of the courtroom, blending in as though they were part of the crowd.

Karin Kornder conducted roll call, and all were present.

Rita Alcazar proclaimed: "Before the flag of the United States of America and the State of California, this court is now in session. The Honorable Gregory J. Dorsemann, Judge Presiding. Please be seated and come to order."

Judge Dorsemann was standing for the announcement, and then sat.

"Good morning, ladies and gentlemen."

"Good morning, your Honor," Rex said, and heard it from the back of the courtroom. Mark forgot to respond, and Rex looked at him. He responded,
"Good morning."
Rick Turner responded, as well.

56.

THE INTENSITY OF THE ENERGY was almost overwhelming. Rex realized that it was always that way, and he was going to blend into it and go with the flow, become an essential part of it. It was not about him, but the process.

Everyone that entered that courtroom was nervous and full of questions. They wanted to know what was going to happen. Many of them showed signs of recognition when they looked toward Rex.

Judge Dorsemann began his speech about the trial, during which he told the jury about the presumption of innocence. He asked that the lawyers stand and introduce themselves, and for the defense to also introduce their clients. Rick Turner stood first, and with his deep and powerful voice said:

"Good morning, ladies and gentlemen. I am Deputy District Attorney Rick Turner, and this gentleman in uniform standing beside me is Captain Russ Walden with the Danbrier County Sheriff's Department." They both sat.

Rex stood and looked out over the audience, then encouraged Billy to stand. He said:

"Good morning ladies and gentlemen. I am Rex McKinley, and this is my client, Mr. Billy West." They both bowed and sat.

Mark Mundo did the same. It was then that Rex got an idea of the size of Erich Trotter. He looked formidable.

Afterward, Judge Dorsemann read the witness lists for both sides and asked whether anyone knew any of the witnesses, parties or lawyers, and it happened. Several people raised their hands. Rex looked at Judge Dorsemann, keeping a straight face.

"Let's begin in the very back row, on my far left. Sir, would you please stand and tell the Court your name?"

"I'm Jason Latterman."

"Good morning, sir. You have raised your hand, and I assume that means that you know someone involved in this case. Please tell us who you know. And for the rest of you who have raised your hands, please pay attention, and do as I have asked Mr. Latterman."

"I don't really know him, but I read all about what happened to Mr. McKinley."

"And has that in any way influenced your thinking in this case?"

"I don't know. I thought it was wrong what they did to him."

"And who is 'they' Mr. Latterman?"

"I guess the Sheriff and the District Attorney."

Judge Dorsemann paused while scanning the courtroom before he replied.

"Do you understand that this case is not about Mr. McKinley, but instead whether his client and Mr. Mundo's client can receive a fair trial?"

"Yes, I do."

"Do you believe that you can overcome whatever feelings you might have about what happened to Mr. McKinley, and be a fair juror in this case?

Mr. Latterman paused and looked at Rex who was turned in his seat looking out at Mr. Latterman. He stared for a moment, giving no indication how he felt. There appeared to be a silent communication between them.

"I think I can be fair."

"Thank you, sir. You may be seated."

"Ma'am, sitting two seats to the right of Mr. Latterman. Please stand and state your name."

"Betty Wortham."

"Good morning, Ms. Wortham. Do you know one of the parties or lawyers?"

"I'm pretty much the same as this other man."

She pointed to Mr. Latterman.

"I also feel like I can be fair."

"Very well, Ms. Wortham. Ladies and gentlemen, we have more than half of you who have raised your hands. May I ask whether you are doing so for the same reasons as the first two people? If so, please lower your hands, unless for some reason related to what happened to Mr. McKinley you feel that you cannot be a fair and impartial juror."

Only one person, a woman, kept her hand up.

"The woman sitting in the second row, on my right side. Please stand and tell the Court your name.

"Penelope Rhingold."

"Good morning, Ms. Rhingold."

"Good morning. Should I speak?"

"Please do."

"I read about what happened with Mr. McKinley. I'm sorry, but I don't think I can be fair."

Would you care to elaborate?"

"Well, I am a Christian woman, and what Mr. McKinley did with that young woman was just horrible. I cannot find it in myself to understand or accept his behavior. I could not be fair to Mr. McKinley in the case."

Again, this woman was looking at Rex as she spoke. Rex smiled at her, but she only stared back.

"Gentlemen, will you stipulate that Ms. Rhingold can be excused?"

Both Rick Turner and Mark Mundo said they would. Rex did not break eye contact with Ms. Rhingold. Instead he said:

"I thank Ms. Rhingold for her honesty, your Honor. I will so stipulate."

Everyone was watching the non-verbal communication between them. It settled across the room that people had strong feelings for and against Rex, and that had what happened was going to play an important part in jury selection, and he appeared to be willing to face it, good or bad.

This kind of honesty with prospective jurors had never happened so quickly with Rex, and never without some lively questioning and sharing.

Judge Dorsemann began a speech about what happened to Rex, and that he was in fact the Judge who dismissed the charges against him. He reminded them that he was intimately familiar with the details of that case, and that were he to believe that it was somehow relevant to the case at bar, he would have recused himself. He told them that the trial was about whether the prosecution could overcome its burden in *this* case, and no other, and that burden was based upon the presumption of innocence.

"Does everyone understand?" Most answered "yes."

"Thank you all. Let's discuss hardships. Are there any of you here who do not believe that you can stay for the estimated three weeks this trial will take to complete? If you are not paid for part of that time, or if you have some other hardship, please raise your hand."

Two people raised their hands. It was usually at least half the group, Rex reflected.

The judge dealt with those two people, and counsel stipulated that they could be excused.

The judge read a few of the introductory jury instructions, then asked the Clerk to call names from the random list. Karin slowly and carefully called eighteen names. Rex wrote each of them, one through eighteen, on the yellow post-its he had already placed in order in the boxes on the form, left to right, two rows of six, and the bottom of the page where prospective alternates would later be placed.

When the time to exercise peremptory challenges arrived, which were used to excuse jurors without cause, Rex would make all the decisions, although he would make it appear that he was consulting with Mark. Because it was a life case—a potential sentence of life in prison—each side would have twenty peremptory challenges, split ten apiece for the two defendants.

After the eighteen people were seated and had the personal information check list, Judge Dorsemann began asking questions, including their marital status; prior jury service; whether they or any a family member had ever been convicted of a crime; whether they or a family member had ever been a victim of a crime; and, ultimately, whether they believed they could be fair.

It was just before the mid-morning break when Rex realized that no one had even tried to get off the jury, other than the two who just could not afford to stay. A few had family members with trouble of various kinds. One man admitted to a DUI conviction a few years back in Los Angeles County. But no one claimed anything that might prevent them from becoming a fair and impartial juror.

During the process, Rex seemed to be the focus of attention from most of these folks. He smiled at them, nodding when they answered a question posed by the Court. Some looked at him when they gave their answers. Judge Dorsemann looked at the clock. It was 10:15 a.m. He declared a fifteen-minute recess. He reminded them that they could not speak with the lawyers, and the lawyers were admonished not to communicate with them.

When the jurors had gone, Rex stepped over to Mark and said:

"Mark, you are going to need to do some *voir dire*. How are you in this area?"

"I can do it, Rex. Tell me what you want me to cover."

Good question. Mark might be helpful after all.

"How about you cover the area of being falsely accused? You know, ladies and gentlemen, do you think it is possible that Mr. Trotter may be falsely accused, and so on. How's that gel with you?"

"Whatever you want, Rex. I want you to know that I am not an idiot. I do have some skills."

"Okay, Mark. I'll go first, then you show us what you've got."

56.

THE INTENSITY OF THE ENERGY WAS ALMOST OVERWHELMING.
Rex realized that it was always that way, and he was going to blend into it and go with the flow, become an essential part of it. It was not about him, but the process. Everyone that entered that courtroom was undoubtedly nervous and full of questions. They wanted to know what was going to happen. Many of them showed signs of recognition when they looked toward Rex.

Judge Dorsemann began his speech about the trial, during which he told the jury about the presumption of innocence. He asked that the lawyers stand and introduce themselves, and for the defense to also introduce their clients. Rick Turner stood first, and with his deep and powerful voice said:

"Good morning, ladies and gentlemen. I am Deputy District Attorney Rick Turner, and this gentleman in uniform standing beside me is Captain Russ Walden with the Danbrier County Sheriff's Department." They both sat.

Rex stood and looked out over the audience, then encouraged Billy to stand. He said:

"Good morning ladies and gentlemen. I am Rex McKinley, and this is my client, Mr. Billy West." They both bowed and sat.

Mark Mundo did the same. It was then that Rex got an idea of the size of Erich Trotter. He looked formidable.

Afterward, Judge Dorsemann read the witness lists for both sides and asked whether anyone knew any of the witnesses, parties or lawyers, it happened. Several people raised their hands. Rex looked at Judge Dorsemann, keeping a straight face.

"Let's begin in the very back row, on my far left. Sir, would you please stand and tell the Court your name?"

"I'm Jason Latterman."

"Good morning, sir. You have raised your hand, and I assume that means that you know someone involved in this case. Please tell us who you know. And for the rest of you who have raised your hands, please pay attention, and do as I have asked Mr. Latterman."

"I don't really know him, but I read all about what happened to Mr. McKinley."

"And has that in any way influenced your thinking in this case?"

"I don't know. I thought it was wrong what they did to him."

"And who is 'they' Mr. Latterman?"

"I guess the Sheriff and the District Attorney."

Judge Dorsemann paused while scanning the courtroom before he replied.

"Do you understand that this case is not about Mr. McKinley, but instead whether his client and Mr. Mundo's client can receive a fair trial?"

"Yes, I do."

"Do you believe that you can overcome whatever feelings you might have about what happened to Mr. McKinley, and be a fair juror in this case?

Mr. Latterman paused and looked at Rex who was turned in his seat looking out at Mr. Latterman. He stared for a moment, giving no indication how he felt. There appeared to be a silent communication between them.

"I think I can be fair."

"Thank you, sir. You may be seated."

"Ma'am, sitting two seats to the right of Mr. Latterman. Please stand and state your name."

"Betty Wortham."

"Good morning, Ms. Wortham. Do you know one of the parties or lawyers?"

"I'm pretty much the same as this other man."

She pointed to Mr. Latterman.

"I also feel like I can be fair."

"Very well, Ms. Wortham. Ladies and gentlemen, we have more than half of you who have raised your hands. May I ask whether you are doing so for the same reasons as the first two people? If so, please lower your hands, unless for some reason related to what happened to Mr. McKinley you feel that you cannot be a fair and impartial juror."

Only one person, a woman, kept her hand up.

"The woman sitting in the second row, on my right side. Please stand and state your name.

"Penelope Rhingold."

"Good morning, Ms. Rhingold."

"Good morning. Should I speak?"

"Please do."

"I read about what happened with Mr. McKinley. I'm sorry, but I don't think I can be fair."

"Would you care to elaborate?"

"Well, I am a Christian woman, and what Mr. McKinley did with that young woman was just horrible. I cannot find it in myself to understand or accept his behavior. I could not be fair to Mr. McKinley in the case."

Again, this woman was looking at Rex as she spoke. Rex smiled at her, but she only stared back.

"Gentlemen, will you stipulate that Ms. Rhingold can be excused?"

Both Rick Turner and Mark Mundo said they would. Rex did not break eye contact with Ms. Rhingold. Instead he said:

"I thank Ms. Rhingold for her honesty, your Honor. I will so stipulate."

Everyone was watching the non-verbal communication between them. It seemed settled across the room that people had strong feelings for and against Rex, and that had what happened was going to play an important part in jury selection, and he appeared to be willing to face it, good or bad.

Judge Dorsemann began a speech about what happened to Rex, and that he was in fact the Judge who dismissed the charges against him. He reminded them that he was intimately familiar with the details of that case, and that were he to believe that it was somehow relevant to the case at bar, he would have recused himself. He told them that the trial was about whether the prosecution could overcome its burden in *this* case, and no other, and that burden was based upon the presumption of innocence.

"Does everyone understand?" Most answered "yes."

"Thank you all. We are going to move along. Let's discuss hardships. Are there any of you here who do not believe that you can stay for the estimated three weeks this trial will take to complete? If you are not paid for part of that time, or if you have some other hardship, please raise your hand."

Two people raised their hands. It was usually at least half the group, Rex reflected. The judge dealt with those two people, and counsel stipulated that they could be excused.

The judge read a few of the introductory jury instructions, then asked the Clerk to call names from the random list. Karin slowly and carefully called eighteen names. Rex wrote each of them, one through eighteen, on the yellow post-its he had already placed in order in the boxes on the form, left to right, three rows of six.

When the time to exercise peremptory challenges arrived, which were used to excuse jurors without cause, Rex would make all the decisions, although he would make it appear that he was consulting with Mark. Because it was a life case—a potential sentence of life in prison—each side would have twenty peremptory challenges, split ten apiece for the two defendants.

After the eighteen people were seated and had the personal information check list, Judge Dorsemann began asking questions, including their marital status; prior jury service; whether they or any a family member had ever been convicted of a crime; whether they or a family member had ever been a victim of a crime; and, ultimately, whether they believed they could be fair.

It was just before the mid-morning break when Rex realized that no one had even tried to get off the jury, other than the two who just could not afford to stay. A few had family members with trouble of various kinds. One man admitted to a DUI conviction a few years back in Los Angeles County. But no one claimed anything that might prevent them from becoming a fair and impartial juror.

During the process, Rex seemed to be the focus of attention from most of those folks. He smiled at them, nodding when they answered a question posed by the Court. Some looked at him when they gave their answers. Judge Dorsemann looked at the clock. It was 10:15 a.m. He declared a fifteen-minute recess. He reminded them that they could not speak with the lawyers, and the lawyers were admonished not to communicate with them.

When the jurors had gone, Rex stepped over to Mark and said:

"Mark, you are going to need to do some *voir dire*. How are you in this area?"

"I can do it, Rex. Tell me what you want me to cover."

"How about you cover the area of being falsely accused? You know, ladies and gentlemen, do you think it is possible that Mr. Trotter may be falsely accused, and so on. How's that gel with you?"

"Whatever you want, Rex. I want you to know that I am not an idiot. I do have some skills."

"Okay, Mark. I'll go first, then you show us what you've got."

57.

REX TOOK A BATHROOM BREAK, and Tommy caught up with him. He said:

"Eddie's trying to get us to let him come to court. He's looking pretty good. Do you need him yet?"

Rex would need Eddie when Mary Jane Rankin testified. He had interviewed her, and it was on video.

"He should be here when Turner calls Mary Jane Rankin. Are you sure he's ready?"

"He'll make himself ready. That much I know."

They looked at one another and smiled, then walked back toward the courtroom and made their way inside.

Billy and Erich were brought back in and seated. As they waited for Rita Alcazar to bring the prospective jurors back in, Rex spoke with Mark.

"Mark, I apologize if I have offended you. That was not my intention. I don't think you are stupid."

He smiled a big smile and showed a mouthful of yellow teeth. He was a smoker. Rex could smell it on him.

"Thanks, Rex. I really appreciate it. I'm still with you. You lead, and I will follow."

Rita Alcazar headed toward the back of the courtroom, and everyone at the counsel table stood.

The courtroom quickly filled, and the eighteen prospective jurors found their seats. There were groupings already, and they were talking to one another.

Judge Dorsemann stepped up to the Bench while Rita, with a very powerful voice, reminded everyone to "Remain seated and come to order. Court is now in session." It did appear she was enjoying herself.

"Mr. McKinley, you may inquire."

Rex stood and smiled, and then he said: "Thank you, your Honor."

Billy had zoned out that morning, but at least he looked clean. Erich had been sitting upright, looking straight ahead, just like a soldier. Something about him was nagging at Rex, but he let it pass.

Rex began with a smooth transition from it being about him to it being about fairness and the presumption of innocence. He was generally warmly received and engaged all the eighteen prospective jurors. It was productive, and he felt he had done all that was necessary to open the door to them being fair and seeing the case from the perspective of their responsibility as jurors. Just minutes before noon he announced: "I pass for cause, your Honor."

Judge Dorsemann looked at the clock and announced they would break for lunch.

Before Mark left Rex asked him what he was doing for lunch.

"Nothing, Rex."

"How about you join us, Mark?"

Fear crossed his face, but he responded cheerfully.

"Sure, Rex. Let's go."

"Meet us at Johnny's Café. We will have lunch catered for us throughout the trial."

"Okay," said Mark.

Rex looked at Doug who heard had him. Doug handed the car keys to Ron, said something, and got up and followed Mark out of the courtroom.

58.

THE ENTIRE DEFENSE ENTOURAGE HEADED over to Johnny's Café. Once there, they parked and went in to find that J.D. "Johnny" Dumas was waiting for them. He was proud to have the group in his place. He had made certain they had privacy in the back room, which was maintained primarily for musical events. But that day he had it set up for lunch at three private tables. Club members sat together. Doug and Mark Mundo took one table, while Tommy, Ron and Rex sat at the third table.

Rex glanced toward the table where Doug was with Mark Mundo. He seemed like he was being kind and patient with Mark; he had turned on the charm. Rex reflected that it was hard to teach someone who was afraid, and Doug of all people knew that to be true. Still, there was something nagging Rex about Mark Mundo; something he couldn't put his finger on.

Tommy shared some interesting information with Ron and Rex. Mary Jane Rankin was in custody. The word was she had been talking about running, and the guy who was supposedly going to testify about the gun gave her up—but Tommy said that was untrue propaganda to keep the defense confused. She was in jail because they wanted to make her tell the story they were pitching, or at least the story from Russ Walden. Maybe Rick Turner did not know. Tommy offered some specifics.

Also, Ron Porter fled the jurisdiction. Because he was a fool, he left a forwarding address. He had gone to stay with relatives in Arley, Alabama, a small town of less than three hundred people. Rex saw no need to bring him back, but he did inquire about Cheryl Porter. Tommy reported that she apparently had snuggled up to Captain Walden before the recently departed Mr. Ellifson became the deceased. The relationship between Cheryl Porter and the Captain was a complex and confusing relationship, Tommy said, with the most intricate delicacies. Rex asked what that meant. Tommy replied:

"She's attached to him at the hip. The message I got was that she was afraid of Ellifson since they missed killing Eddie. Apparently, he was on a rampage before he—or someone else—decided to end it."

"Or someone else?" Rex inquired.

Tommy smiled at him, said that he would be around keeping his eye on things. He left without eating.

59.

THEY WERE BACK AT THE COURTHOUSE by 1:15, all of them—Rex, Mark, Doug and Ron—and they were in the courtroom when Rick Turner and Russ Walden arrived at 1:25. Russ acknowledged Rex, but Rick Turner did not.

Deputy Crownes brought in Billy and Erich. Rex spoke briefly with Billy, and he responded with a nod of his head. He was listening. Rex could feel him coming to life since their meeting on Saturday. The morning had been a bit rough for him. Being in custody and awakened very early and fed very little, then chained for hours, had a wearing effect on a man. Although each man learned to tough it out, it was an exhausting process.

At 1:28 Rita Alcazar brought in the jurors. They found their way to their seats; all were present.

His Honor took the Bench as soon as the head count was completed. He greeted everyone, and deferred to Mark.

He looked at the jurors, and said: "Mr. Mundo?"

It was not uncommon for a prospective juror to admit bias that just could not be changed, resulting in him or her being less than fair to one side or the other—like Penelope Rhingold, who stood and told the Court she could not be fair because of what she perceived was Rex's bad behavior. That was considered cause.

Mark stood, and adjusted his pants, and left his coat unbuttoned. He greeted the jurors, and they responded in kind. He appeared to be a little shaky, so he told them:

"I'm a little nervous here today. I ask you to forgive me, but Mr. McKinley here is a hard act to follow."

There was some laughter. The jurors liked what he had just done; a good start.

"But you know, folks, this case isn't about the lawyers, it's about whether we can all pitch in and make sure the defendants get a fair trial. Agreed?"

People were nodding their heads with him and his country gentleman approach.

"For example, if I were my client, Mr. Trotter over there," and he started walking toward Erich Trotter, pointing at him, then he stopped, and turned back to the jury, "I would want people on the jury who believe that it is possible for a man to be falsely accused. Do you folks believe that is possible?"

He was doing much better than Rex had expected. The jurors liked him. People were nodding in agreement.

"Juror Number 3, do you think it is possible for a person to be falsely accused?"

"I sure do. I guess we've all seen that recently," she said. Juror Number 3 was a bit of a surprise. She was a Nun who did not wear a habit. Number 3 worked at the Catholic Church in east Danbrier, Our Lady of the Sacred Rose, which also housed a parochial school, grades 1 through 8. She did not live in the Convent. Rex had expected that she would be more conservative, maybe even somewhat aloof. Instead, she seemed angry about what happened to Rex; at least the unfairness of it all.

"Are you speaking of something specific?" Rick Turner jumped out of his seat. "Objection," he shouted.

Rex looked at Mark and he was smiling. That was slick. He didn't offer to withdraw that question, either. He wanted Rick Turner to cause a scene.

"Overruled, Mr. Turner. I think we need to get this out of the way, don't you?"

Rick Turner sat without responding.

"Thank you, your Honor," said Mark. "It's alright to answer that question, Ma'am."

She offered: "Well, I watch the news fairly regularly. I saw what happened to Mr. McKinley. Certainly, he was falsely accused. So, yes, Mr. Mundo, I do believe that can happen."

Mark's *voir dire* was excellent. He stayed on his feet and on target for an hour. When he was through, it appeared he had made his way into the hearts of the jurors. He paused, and looked at Rex, and smiled; then he said:

"Thank you, ladies and gentlemen. Your Honor, I pass for cause."

"Mr. Turner?"

60.

RICK TURNER STOOD, A TALL AND HANDSOME MAN, obviously physically fit; with a voice that was truly exceptional, his presence compelling.

"Good afternoon, ladies and gentlemen. I'm Rick Turner, and I represent the People of the State of California."

They all responded with nods or verbal greetings.

"I recall Mr. Mundo telling you that this case is not about the lawyers. Do you all remember that?"

None of the jurors responded verbally, although there was movement by some. Undaunted, he went at it again.

"I mean we all know what happened to Mr. McKinley here, don't we?"

Still no response.

"What I am trying to ask is whether you are going to give a fair trial to the prosecution. Anyone?"

Number 3 raised her hand.

"Yes?"

Judge Dorsemann intervened,

"For the record, that is juror Number 3."

Rick did not acknowledge his Honor; instead he stared at Number 3. He was standing near the jury box. Rex had turned his chair toward the jury.

"Number 3?"

"Well, sir, I am a bit surprised by your question."

"Ma'am?"

"I would think that after all of the bad press your office got from the prosecution of Mr. McKinley that your biggest concern should be whether the accused can get a fair trial in Danbrier County."

There was a murmuring in the courtroom that seemed to be in sync with what juror Number 3 had just said.

Rick Turner turned red, then said:

"You do understand that the prosecution is entitled to a fair trial, don't you? How about you, Number 1?"

"I agree with what the lady just said."

"And you, Number 2?"

Number 2 was a shy woman, a day care worker at a local children's program. Her anxiety was apparent in her response.

"What did I do?"

The courtroom went silent. Rick Turner took a deep breath. Rex felt anger in the courtroom. He had picked on the weakest one of them all.

"You didn't do anything. I'm just trying to find out if you people are going to be fair to the prosecution in this case. With all this conversation about Mr. McKinley, I want to know if you are all on his side."

Rick Turner had just jumped off the cliff and into the abyss.

Number 2 did not respond. Her eyes filled with tears. Rita Alcazar took the box of tissues to her, and Number 2 thanked her. Rita looked at Rick Turner with obvious anger. The men in the group of eighteen were visibly angry. The women were in varying stages of anger and compassion toward Number 2.

Rick Turner asked for a minute. He walked to the counsel table and grabbed his bottle of water. After taking a long drink, he walked stiffly toward the jurors.

"Ladies and gentlemen, I'm going to have to ask for you to accept my apology. Juror Number 2, especially you. I have been rude."

There was silence.

"Number 2, will you forgive me?"

"Yes."

"Thank you. Let me try to start again with you; with all of you. We are going to have some witnesses for the prosecution who are not law enforcement. In fact, a couple of them are probably not your average upstanding citizens, but we don't get to pick our witnesses. Is everyone with me so far?"

There was some nodding, but nothing verbal.

"For example, we have one woman who has a criminal history who will testify about certain things regarding one of the defendants. Will you disbelieve what she says just because she has been convicted of a crime? How about you, juror Number 8?"

Number 8 was a retired railroad engineer. The railroad companies in Danbrier County had employed a significant part of the population. Railroad employees who made a career of it were traditionally conservative politically, which also meant they tended to be pro law enforcement.

"I guess it depends."

"What if I were to tell you that she has been convicted of some drug crimes?"

"I guess I'd have to listen to her testify. I'd want to know if she's still using drugs."

"Thank you, sir."

Number 8 nodded.

"Anyone else?"

Number 6 raised his hand. He was a plumber who worked for Danbrier County. He was getting paid to be there. He told Rex he wanted to be on the jury. He was young, maybe thirty, wearing short sleeves, and had some tattoos on his left arm. He told Rex that he had served honorably for six years in the Army. Rex watched to see whether Rick Turner had seen him look toward Doug West when he said so.

"I imagine we've all had a drink or two at one time or another. I wouldn't fault her for getting high, so long as she doesn't come in here that way."

The way he said it made most of the crowd laugh. He rolled his eyes when he said getting high. Rick Turner seemed to like him. He thanked him for his response.

It went on like that for another forty minutes until Rick seemed to feel that he had been redeemed. He looked at them and smiled. He turned to Judge Dorsemann and said:

"The People pass for cause, your Honor."

"Thank you, Mr. Turner. The first peremptory is with the People. Mr. Turner?"

61.

"THE PEOPLE THANK AND EXCUSE JUROR NUMBER 2."

Number 2 began to tear up again. There was a murmur through the courtroom. "Juror Number 2, you are excused. Please go to the jury room. You will not be called for another year. Thank you for your service."

Number 2 looked at his Honor and smiled, but she did not speak. She was close to crying. Everyone saw it, except Rick Turner, who had his head buried in his notes.

"Juror Number 13, will you please take the seat left empty by juror Number 2?"

When she was seated, Judge Dorsemann referred to her as juror Number 2. Earlier, when Judge Dorsemann had asked her to answer the questions on the questionnaire, she had reported that she was married, had two sons, ages fourteen and sixteen, and they attended Cesar Chavez Middle School and Danbrier High School, respectively. Her husband was a physician with a local medical group, specializing in orthopedic surgery.

"Mr. McKinley?"

"Good morning, Ma'am."

"Good morning, Mr. McKinley."

Rex liked her and the answers she had given to Judge Dorsemann. He didn't want to seem to be repeating himself, so he simply asked:

"Number 2, is there anything you would care to add to any of the answers already given? "

"No, I think it has all been said."

"And do you believe in your heart of hearts that you can be fair in this case?"

"Yes, I can."

"Thank you, your Honor. I pass for cause."

He was still looking at her when he sat. She smiled glowing from within.

She was a very attractive woman.

"Mr. Mundo?"

Mark looked at Rex with a don't worry look, then stood.

"Good morning, juror Number 2."

"Good morning, sir."

"How are you today?"

"Very well, thank you. And you?"

"I am well, also." He smiled at her.

"Your Honor, I also pass for cause."

There was a bit of laughter, and a lot of smiling.

"Mr. Turner?"

Rick Turner stood and walked toward the jury. Rex turned his chair to watch. At that point, without prior approval of the Court the lawyers were prohibited from asking questions of the remaining eleven who had already been available for questioning.

"Good morning," he said while looking at Number 2. He had lowered his voice to a baritone; it seemed he was trying to be sexy with her.

Number 2 was not responsive to that gesture. Rick Turner appeared to be under the proverbial microscope, yet he seemed to have forgotten he had not started well. The new Number 2 did not reply.

"Ma'am, Number 2, is there something about me that makes you feel like you may not be able to be a fair and impartial juror?"

"No, Mr. Turner. Like you said, I don't think this is about lawyers."

Several people in the courtroom and jury box laughed a bit too loud. Number 2 kept a straight face. She was just giving him back some of his own medicine.

"Okay. Do you feel that you can be a fair and impartial juror?"

"Absolutely."

He stood there too long without another question. Finally, he thanked Number 2, and told the Court that he passed for cause. He returned to his seat. Once seated, his Honor addressed Rex:

"Mr. McKinley, the next peremptory challenge is with you."

Rex stood and looked at all the prospective jurors and said: "Your honor, on behalf of Mr. West, I will accept the jury as presently composed."

He looked at Mark, who clearly got the message.

"Mr. Mundo?"

Mark stood and walked toward the jury. He was just behind Rick Turner when he said: "On behalf of Mr. Trotter, I accept the jury as presently composed."

He bowed slightly and returned to his seat.

62.

"MR. TURNER, THE NEXT PEREMPTORY IS AGAIN WITH THE PEOPLE."

"The People thank and excuse juror Number 2."

"Thank you, juror Number 2. Please report to the jury assembly room. Your service is appreciated."

"Juror Number 14, will you please move to the position of juror Number 2. Thank you."

The new Number 2 had reported to Judge Dorsemann that he was married. He had retired from the Railroad. He had three children and two grandchildren. His youngest daughter was a Bailiff there in the courthouse. He had reported that "No one in my family has been accused of a crime; my son had somebody break into his car once. And, no, I cannot think of any reason why I cannot be a fair and impartial juror."

"Mr. McKinley," his Honor said.

Rex stood and stretched a bit as he gazed at all the jurors and began to focus his attention on the new Number 2.

"Good afternoon, sir. How are you today?"

"I am fine, Mr. McKinley. How about you?"

"I am well. I appreciate you asking."

He nodded with a smile.

"I wonder whether there is anything that you might like to add to the conversation I had earlier with the other jurors."

"No, sir. I think it was very clear. This is America. If we don't have fair trials, we will no longer be free. I can and will be fair."

Rex shared eye contact with him for a bit before saying: "Thank you, sir. Your Honor, I pass for cause."

Number 2 nodded with appreciations, seemingly acknowledging that Rex was taking him at his word.

"Mr. Mundo?"

Mark stayed in his chair. He said hello to Number 2. He asked how he was doing. After Number 2 replied "just fine," Mark stood and said:

"Your Honor, I pass for cause." He sat.

"Mr. Turner?"

Rick Turner stayed in his chair.

"Good morning, sir."

"Good morning, sir."

"Pass for cause, your Honor."

Rick Turner did not look at that man, which did not go unnoticed.

"Mr. McKinley, the peremptory is with the defense."

Rex looked at Mark, and they nodded to one another. Rex stood again and looked at the prospective jurors.

"Thank you, your Honor. Once again, and on behalf of Mr. West, we will accept the jury as presently composed."

He looked at each one before he sat. Judge Dorsemann asked Mark, who did exactly as Rex did, walking to the jury box before so stating.

"Mr. Turner, I do believe the peremptory is with the People."

"The People thank and excuse juror Number 3."

Again, he did not look up. Rex looked at Number 3 as she stood. She was the Nun. She looked at Rex and smiled; he smiled back at her. When she made her way out of the jury box she looked across the room to Rex and said in a hushed voice: "Bye for now."

Rex could only smile as he watched her leave. They continued jury selection until they had arrived at the afternoon break.

63.

"LET'S TAKE OUR AFTERNOON RECESS. Please return in fifteen minutes."

Billy, Erich, Mark and Rex stood. Rick Turner and Russ Walden missed the cue. They seemed to be arguing, and it did not go unnoticed by the jurors.

When the courtroom was cleared, except for Doug and Ron, Judge Dorsemann asked whether there was anything they needed to put on the record.

"No, thank you, your Honor," said Rex. He was wondering where Tommy may have gone.

"No, your Honor," said Mark.

Rick Turner did not seem to have heard him.

"Mr. Turner?"

Although apparently not angry, Judge Dorsemann did raise his voice a bit. Rick looked as though he had been completely oblivious to what had happened, including the clearing of the courtroom.

"Uh, no, your Honor."

Rex told Billy to do as the Bailiff said. He added:

"We're getting close to having a jury, so just do what you've been doing," which was being quiet and sitting still. Billy seemed completely traumatized by what was happening and was turning inward again. He had learned from him on Saturday that when things got tense for him, he simply hid inside himself, avoiding what was going on around him. Billy had shared his extensive history of drug addiction, too. He told Rex that he was still in a fog, but he was trying to find his way out of it. The feeling emanating from him that morning seemed like he shut down, but Rex wasn't about to let him crawl inside again. He would prod him, and touch him, and remind him of their conversation, and perhaps most importantly, his brother's love for him.

64.

REX AND MARK LEFT THE COURTROOM together and walked to the elevator. They rode up to the fourth floor. With little to say they got out of the elevator. There stood Michael Carter.

Rex stepped out and spoke to him: "Michael, how are you?"

"Fine, Rex." He rushed into the elevator. Rex felt pity for him. He had been given a bad case, and while he hadn't made it a personal assault on Rex, it had been taken personally by Rex at the time; but he was the defendant.

Mark and Rex used the men's room, then returned to the courtroom and waited for the jury. Rex remained standing with his hand on Billy's shoulder, just to let him know he was there with him. He squeezed a bit and told him that he was doing just fine. Billy acknowledged him; Rex knew he felt him. He was warming to human contact. Billy had yet to make any kind of eye contact, and Rex took that moment to ask him to look at him. Billy did so, very slowly. When their eyes met, Rex said: "We're doing well here, Billy. Please, we made some progress Saturday, and you can see it's going well. I'm not asking you to be anything other than yourself, okay?" Billy held Rex's gaze, and then he smiled. That was enough for Rex.

Rita Alcazar headed toward the door. The jurors came in and found their seats, and the others returned to the general location of where they had been sitting before the break.

Karin Kornder called roll, and everyone was present. She picked up her phone and whispered into it. Judge Dorsemann came out of chambers and stepped up to the Bench after everyone was seated. He acknowledged for the record that all parties and prospective jurors were present.

65.

"MR. TURNER, I DO BELIEVE THAT the peremptory challenge is with the People."

He stood and looked at the jurors and smiled. He said:

"The People accept the jury." He sat.

"Very well. Will those of you in seats one through twelve please stand and raise your right hands so the clerk can administer the oath."

They immediately began the process of picking alternate jurors, which was done in preparation for any of the sworn jurors who might have become ill or have some other issue intervene that would prevent them from completing their duty. To do so, they needed to fill the vacant seats in the row in front of the jury box. The clerk, Karin, called three names, and they were asked to sit in seats sixteen through eighteen. The people already in those seats were instructed to move over to seats thirteen through fifteen. Additional *voir dire* was permitted with each of them, and it did not take long to pick the alternates. Both Rex and Mark accepted the first three. Rick Turner exercised peremptory challenges on two of them, the second of which only after Rex and Mark had again stated they would accept the first three.

Finally, they had a jury, and alternates, who were sworn by Karin Kornder. It was 4:21 p.m. on the first day of trial.

Judge Dorsemann announced that they would begin tomorrow with opening statements. He thanked the remaining prospective jurors on behalf of all the parties and told them they were free to go. But only a few of them got up to leave. It seemed that they wanted to see what was going to happen. One man raised his hand.

"Sir, did you have a question for the Court," Judge Dorsemann asked.

"Yes, I was wondering if I can come back and watch this trial."

"Absolutely. This is a public forum, and you have every right to be here."

"Thank you," he said, and he remained where he was sitting.

"Ladies and gentlemen of the jury, I want you back here at 8:15 tomorrow morning. We will begin at 8:30, so please don't be late." After they had all gone, Judge Dorsemann asked if there was anything that needed to be resolved before they called it a day. Rex stood.

"No, your Honor," he said, and Mark immediately chimed in after him.

Rick Turner said, "No thank you, your Honor." He got up and left with Russ Walden following him. Neither of them looked at anyone.

Rex whispered to Billy that it had been a good day. Billy nodded. Rex added that it was a good jury, and Billy nodded again. Rex told him he would see him in the morning and squeezed on his shoulder. Billy tried to smile. He looked at Rex as he stood to go with the Bailiff.

As they were leaving the courtroom some of the left over prospective jurors were still sitting. They wanted to speak with Rex. He told them he needed to go but encouraged them to come back tomorrow.

"Please exercise that right and come and watch. I really can't discuss the case with you. I hope you will understand."

One came forward and extended his hand. They shook hands. He said,

"I saw what they tried to do to you, Mr. McKinley."

Mark Mundo left the courtroom. When Rex got into the hallway, Mark was in the process of receiving praise from Doug and Ron.

"Really good job, Mark," Rex said, and handed him his business card.

"My cell number is on there, also. Feel free to call me tonight. Let's talk about our Openings."

"Will do, Rex." He started walking down the hallway. They all watched him go. Mark had performed very well. Yet, to Rex, something about him still seemed hidden, murky. He had a feeling there was something not right inside that man. He had become a charmer, and a force to be reckoned with, a real courtroom dancer; yet there was something Rex could not explain, just a vague feeling at that time, like a light turned on, but the dimmer switch was used.

Mark called Rex that evening, and they spoke for about an hour. Mark had some great ideas and they agreed on a plan.

66.

IT WAS THE SECOND DAY OF TRIAL, and there was enthusiasm and excitement in the air when they drove up to the courthouse. Rex and his entourage were greeted by other members of Blood Oath. Rex felt the power of the group and the response of the people to them. It was about respect, and although he knew it was always there, he considered that he had unable to see the depths of it because of his own shortcomings.

No one wore their patch inside the courthouse; they removed them and left them with those who remained in the parking lot. It didn't matter, because the people knew they were a tight group with something special about them—true brotherhood.

The media was waiting. Some claimed that they would be in the courtroom, "so why not make a statement now?" Some of the Club members carefully and gently scooted the crowd out of their way so that the defense team could make entry into the building.

When they arrived outside Department D-9 Mark was waiting for them. He stepped forward and approached Doug first. Rex heard him say that he was grateful for his wisdom, and that he felt like a new man. He sure seemed that way. Rex allowed a contrary thought to cross his mind, but stuffed it back, not wanting any negative energy to enter. Something *was* different about Mark that day—he had taken some time to update his appearance; his teeth were much cleaner looking, a petty thing, Rex considered, but an effort at looking good, which he always thought important.

They all walked in the courtroom together. Rex began his hellos to the various courtroom personnel, and Mark was right there with him. Rex asked if they could have their clients out a bit early that morning. Rita Alcazar said she would take care of it. It was 8:02 a.m.

By 8:07 both Billy and Erich were brought into the courtroom, and they both looked good, especially Erich. Billy still carried remnants of an empty look in his eyes, but Rex could see something trying to emerge. So long as he looked straight ahead, no one could read anything from him. Rex and Mark spoke with their clients privately. Rex offered Billy words of encouragement. He told him that Doug said that he loved him and was proud of him. Billy stirred from the netherworld and smiled, making a crack in the mask of sorrow and loneliness he wore.

Rick Turner and Russ Walden arrived at 8:20, carrying poster boards, which Rex knew would have photographs of the deceased and the gory mess in the living room where Steve Michaelson was killed. A usual prosecution approach was to show as much blood and brains, and other things that would rouse the anger of the jury, or at least make them feel the horror of murder so that they would want to do something about it with swift and certain action. If it was murder, and if the defendants were responsible, it was an appropriate response by any jury. However, it was, at least technically, against rules. Neither party was to attempt to play to the passions of the jurors—but reality was always different. Rex knew that people didn't really presume anyone to be innocent. The horror of murder made that even more difficult.

At 8:28 Rita headed for the back door. She went into the hallway for a couple of minutes. When she opened the doors and the fifteen jurors followed her lead to the jury box. Rex, Billy, Erich and Mark stood. Russ Walden was standing erect and true. Interestingly, Rick Turner ignored the jury while nervously shuffling papers.

At 8:30 his Honor took the Bench.

"Good morning, ladies and gentlemen."

There was a resounding good morning from many.

The courtroom had filled up with Club members, the media, and some of the left over prospective jurors. A couple of them made it a point to sit by Club members. There were citizens, too, who undoubtedly had seen the news or read about it and wanted to get in on the action.

Judge Dorsemann made a statement to the people in the public section, also known as the gallery.

"Ladies and gentlemen, I am addressing all of you who are sitting as members of the public or the media. We have rules in this courtroom, the most important of which is that you will always show respect for these proceedings. There will be no talking, no shuffling in and out, and for those of you using electronic devices, they must have the sound turned off. Am I clear?"

There were nods from the crowd, and each of the Blood Oath members spoke with full voices and said:

"Yes, your Honor," again setting the example.

"Very well. This morning we are going to begin this trial with opening statements. Mr. Turner will go first. Then, Mr. McKinley and Mr. Mundo may give their opening statements, or they may choose to wait until the prosecution rests. They need not offer an opening statement at this time. First, I will read you some basic instructions, which he did. Afterward, he offered:

"Mr. Turner?"

67.

RICK TURNER STOOD. HE WAS DRESSED in a dark blue suit, with a white shirt and a red tie, just like every politician Rex had ever seen; red, white and blue. He was wearing his D.A. badge on his lapel. He nodded to Captain Russ Walden, who was wearing his Danbrier County Sheriff's uniform with his shiny new Captain's bars on the collars.

As Rick Turner got to the middle of the jury box, Russ Walden placed a two by three-foot poster on the easel.

There was a gasp from a couple of the jurors. Rex observed that it excited Rick Turner. Russ Walden sat just before Rick Turner bellowed: "Murder!"

He said it loud and firmly. His powerful and resounding voice echoed off the walls of the courtroom. Some people jerked in their seats. He might have been a bit too forceful, but he certainly had everyone's attention.

"That man lying there on the floor has a bullet hole in his forehead. His brains are blown out the back of his head and all over the wall behind him. And if that wasn't enough, he was stabbed twice in the neck by a large knife, after he was shot. That is what Dr. Melanie Chang of the Danbrier County Coroner's office will tell you.

"Ladies and gentlemen, this is a very simple case. And, please, don't expect a team to come in here and tell you all exactly what happened like they do on CSI. CSI is not a real-life situation. What we have here is real life," he paused for a moment, "and death." He exaggerated the word. Rex thought it sounded corny, but he knew he was biased.

"These two defendants went to the home of Mary Jane Rankin after dark, broke all of the outside lights, broke into her home, and woke her lover, Steve Michaelson. They dragged him out of bed, and they murdered him by shooting him in the head then stabbing him in the neck. They left his body behind as evidence of their evil deed.

"Ms. Rankin will testify that she knows Mr. West, and that he was very familiar with her home, as he stayed there on occasion. She will tell you that Steve Michaelson did not like Mr. West, and that they had some negative encounters in the past. She will tell you that neither Mr. West nor Mr. Trotter was given permission to be at her home that night.

"A second witness, Ms. Cheryl Porter will testify that she is the next-door neighbor of Mary Jane Rankin, and that on the night in question, Mr. West and Mr. Trotter drove to her home in Mr. West's old black pick-up truck around nine p.m. She will tell you that if you are coming from the end of the road where Mary Jane Rankin's house is located, her house must be passed before driving onto Highway 26. She will tell you that they parked the truck in front of her house, got out, and came into her home and asked for a beer and some money. She did not know what they had done, but she will say they were acting strange. Then Mr. West boasted about what they had done. They drank their beers, thanked her, and left. Mr. West was driving, and Mr. Trotter was the passenger. They raced away from her home.

"After speaking with Ms. Porter, Captain Walden here sent out a BOLO, which is the modern version of an all-points bulletin, to be on the lookout for the old black pickup driven by Mr. West. That truck was found within hours, and both Mr. West and Mr. Trotter were inside the vehicle when it was stopped.

"Captain Walden will also tell you of his crime scene examination, and that he has extensive experience in following tire tracks and making comparisons. He will tell you that he tracked the tires of a vehicle from the scene of the crime to the home of Cheryl Porter, and that he could read that those tracks stopped at Ms. Porter's house, and afterward raced out of that area, leaving a pull tire mark, meaning the tire on the truck that pulls the vehicle, such that it was digging in and throwing dirt behind the vehicle.

"He will tell you that he immediately set up evidence tape around the area to preserve this part of the crime scene which had spread to the Porter residence.

"You will see a series of photographs of the crime scene, all of them taken by Captain Walden. You will hear him tell you that the murderers attempted to make this look like a robbery gone bad rather than the cold-blooded murder that it was—cold-blooded murder!"

Certainly, Rick Turner was arguing there, but Rex didn't object. He didn't want the jury to think he was afraid of anything Rick Turner had to say. He and Mark had discussed whether they would object. They agreed that Rex would only do so should Rick's behavior become outrageous.

INSIDE THE LIE   195

"You will hear from Highway Patrol Officer Dale Rider that he and his partner, Jim Fairfield, were on patrol and were aware of the BOLO regarding Mr. West's pick-up truck. He will tell you they spotted the vehicle and his partner initiated a traffic stop, at which time both defendants surrendered. During a search of the vehicle, he found a black t-shirt in the bed of the truck. It had a substance that he believed to be blood.

"You are going to hear from Ms. Emily Grotto from the Danbrier County Sheriff's Forensic Science's Division. We call her place of work the lab. Ms. Grotto will explain the process of examination of evidence for the presence of DNA. She will also tell you that she determined that it was blood on the shirt found Officer Rider, and it was the blood of Steve Michaelson."

Rick Turner was on a roll. He was a very fine speaker, not to mention that his thunderous voice had the entire courtroom tuned into him. He paused and took a drink of water. Then he resumed, pointing his finger at Billy. Rex moved so that he was blocking his view of Billy. Rick Turner simply looked away. He continued:

"We will offer you the testimony of a man who was in a jail cell with Mr. West. He will tell you that Mr. West confessed to murdering Steve Michaelson. That he was told details only the killer would know; details that were not disclosed at the time this man spoke with Mr. West.

"Ladies and gentlemen, this is a simple case of murder. These two men, Billy West and Erich Trotter, broke into that home for the cowardly act of murdering a man who was sleeping. And they did murder him by blowing his brains out and stabbing the life out of him." He paused, looking at each of the jurors, then with a voice at first full of silk and cream, he said

"At the conclusion of the evidence I will be asking you to come back with the only logical verdict: GUILTY!"

He had raised his evocative voice for that last part, and his eyes were ablaze. He had begun glaring at the jurors, rather than sharing his outrage.

"Thank you, ladies and gentlemen." He took his exhibit off the easel and set it against his side of the counsel table.

The jurors seemed a bit dazed. They had just heard something about this case, and it sounded bad. They had seen the photograph of the body of a man who had in fact been murdered. He was naked on the floor of a room, with a huge pool of blood around him. There was a black hole in his forehead, and you could see where the blood had oozed out of the back of his head, and from the stab wounds on his neck. His clouded eyes were looking at nothing. He was dead. It was not a pretty sight.

"Thank you, Mr. Turner. Mr. McKinley, do you wish to give an opening statement now, or will you reserve?"

68.

REX STOOD.

"Thank you, your Honor. I will proceed now."

He walked to the center of the jury box. He drew in a deep breath.

"Good morning, ladies and gentlemen."

They all responded, some with more enthusiasm than others. A presentation of anticipated facts, gruesome evidence, always tended to change things, and they had now seen the brutality of murder with allegations that it was the defendants who committed the crime.

"As our judge has told you, this is called an opening statement. It is not an argument, but a discussion of what each of the lawyers believes the facts will show, not our personal opinions. For example, when Mr. Turner told you what happened inside that house, he said it as though it were fact. Yet, the evidence will show that there are no witnesses to the killing of Steve Michaelson, much less whether either of these men committed any specific act." He pointed at Billy and Erich as he said it.

"I'm not suggesting that Mr. Michaelson's death was not a homicide. The question here is not whether that man was murdered, but whether Mr. Turner has enough evidence to prove that it was a specific person or persons who murdered Mr. Michaelson, and if so, who did it.

"The evidence will show that Mary Jane Rankin initially reported that Steve Michaelson was not supposed to be in her house, and that she had broken off their relationship a couple of weeks before the killing. She was not there when he was killed.

"The evidence will show that Ms. Porter claims that these two men, my client, Mr. West, and another man, came to her home on the night in question, apparently after the killing of Steve Michaelson. And before I go too far, I want to make it clear that I do not speak for Mr. Trotter. That is Mr. Mundo's client, and he is very capable of defending his own client.

"Mrs. Porter will not tell you anything about bloody clothing. In fact, you will hear some things during the cross-examination of Ms. Porter that will directly contradict what Mr. Turner claimed she will say.

"Captain Walden will claim that he tracked the tires of the defendant's vehicle from the scene of the murder to Ms. Porter's home and that he surrounded that area with evidence tape to protect the integrity of the crime scene. That is a term you will hear frequently throughout this trial for the simple reason that if evidence is not properly preserved, then the Court will explain that the law allows you to disbelieve it.

"What the evidence will *not* show is that Captain Walden employed any kind of established scientific method of preservation of the tire tracks at the scene to compare them with the tires on Mr. West's truck."

Jurors were beginning to get back into the swing of things. The photographs were already fading into the background. But Rex knew they would be used over and again by the prosecution. A potential hazard of overuse of such a horrifying exhibit was that it might well serve to de-sensitize the jury to the savagery of the deed.

"Mr. Turner mentioned that he has a man who will come in and claim that he was in a jail cell with Mr. West, and that Mr. West confessed to murdering Mr. Michaelson, and was very specific with the details."

Rex was looking at Billy as he said it, and Billy looked back at him. He wanted to say it wasn't so, and the jury could see it. Rex smiled and nodded and put his hand up to make sure he didn't speak, and to make sure that the jury knew that he wanted to deny it.

"What Mr. Turner did not tell you is that the evidence will show that the man who claims my client confessed to him is a convicted felon, who has been in prison on more than one occasion, and who was not prosecuted for his own alleged criminal behavior after he reported his claim about Mr. West. In the legal profession, we call a man like Mr. Maddux a jail house rat."

"Objection. Argument."

"Overruled."

It was a foolish move by Rick Turner. It looked like he was trying to protect that man.

"You will see that there has been a manipulation of the evidence at the crime scene. There has been a significant change in the scene during the crime scene investigation.

"There is evidence at the scene that was not processed. There is likely DNA evidence that was not retrieved. There are footprints that were not examined. The list goes on and on, ladies and gentlemen.

"There will not be one single piece of evidence introduced that ties my client to the crime scene, and thus the murder of Steve Michaelson, other than the testimony of a jail house rat, and the neighbor, Cheryl Porter, both of whom I will question carefully. I ask you to please wait to hear *all* the questioning of all the witnesses.

"Now we have a lot of testimony, and that means direct examination *and* cross-examination of these witnesses. So, please, settle in for the long haul.

"At the conclusion of the evidence both sides will offer you closing arguments, telling you what we believe the evidence has shown, or what it has not shown.

"Following the close of evidence, I will ask you to find my client, Billy West, not guilty.

"Thank you very much."

He looked at each of them before he walked to his seat. As he sat, his Honor asked Mark if he wished to give an opening statement.

Mark stood and said:

"Yes, I do. Thank you, your Honor.

"Good morning, ladies and gentlemen."

He spoke as he was walking toward them. They all responded favorably. He stopped in front of them. He began pacing. Finally, he looked at them and smiled.

"I don't mind telling you good people, once again, that Mr. McKinley is a hard act to follow. So, I am not going to repeat what he has said, but I will join him in his presentation.

"I must, however," and he wiggled his right index finger in the air for dramatic effect while he smiled again, and looked at each of them, one by one,

"...tell you good folks a few more things that you will not be shown by the prosecution.

"First, I am certain that most of you watch CSI or one of those crime scene investigation programs, and I suspect that contrary to what Mr. Turner has said, you expect a great deal from the prosecution and their investigative arm, the Sheriff's Department. I'm certain that you do, and you should. It is Mr. Turner's burden to prove something happened to the deceased, and that someone here is responsible.

"Here, on this crime scene, you would probably expect to hear about fingerprints lifted from any given object. Even if none match the defendants, you might want to know who has been in that house. But you won't ever hear about that because there was no finger print evidence retrieved. In fact, there was no attempt made to find any, not even from the empty beer bottles you will see on the nightstand.

"You might expect to see if there was any DNA left behind on the pile of cigarette butts found in an ashtray beside the bed in the room where the deceased was found. But you won't hear about that either because no one tried to recover any such evidence.

"You might expect to hear that the clothing worn by the defendants when they were arrested was examined by the crime lab for a determination that there may be evidence, such as fibers or other evidence that might tie them to the scene of the crime or even gunshot residue, but you won't. There will be no such testimony offered because they didn't even try.

"What you are going to hear about blood on a shirt found in the back of the pick-up truck, is just that: a shirt found in the back of the pick-up truck. You might expect to hear about some other evidence that ties either my client or Mr. West to that shirt. Other than the claim that it was found in the *back* of that truck, a place that was accessible to anyone and everyone who came near that truck, you will not hear any evidence that connects that shirt to anyone. You won't hear Cheryl Porter say that either of the defendants was wearing that shirt that night. No, ladies and gentlemen, this is not the simple case that Mr. Turner has promised. On the contrary, this is a much more complex situation than he wants you to believe, because, simply put, the Sheriff's Department bungled their job."

"Objection."

"Mr. Mundo, that certainly borders on argument."

"Forgive me, your Honor, said Mark with a tiny smile spreading across his lips.

"I thank you ladies and gentlemen. I must ask for your indulgence for a few more days while you hear all of the evidence."

He smiled at each of them and returned to his seat.

The judge then advised the jurors: "Ladies and gentlemen, it is just about time for our morning recess. Let's take twenty minutes this morning. I want you back in your seats at 10:30 sharp. Thank you."

The lawyers and defendants all stood, and when the jury had left the courtroom, his Honor inquired whether they had any issues to resolve. They all told him they did not. He left the Bench.

Rex told Billy to go with the Bailiff and wash his face and freshen up. He had a comb and was using it. Billy nodded at Rex. He got up as the Bailiff instructed.

70.

REX LEFT THE COURTROOM THINKING OF EDDIE. Soon, he would ask him to make an appearance just before his cross-examination of Mary Jane Rankin got heavy. Rex was certain that Ms. Rankin would be up right after Dr. Chang. Most prosecutors cooperated with opposing counsel, as Rex did with them, sharing with each other who they expected to call each day. That way the other side could be prepared for any given witness. However, Rick Turner had not offered to share with Rex, instead he had told him that Dr. Chang would be up, and when Rex inquired about others, Turner had said: "You'll see." Rex responded with a glib remark of "I guess so, Rick. I was hoping for more from you." Rick had tensed a bit but did not respond.

When Rex returned from the men's room, Mark was standing with Doug and some of the Club members. As they entered the courtroom, Rex saw Dr. Chang standing near Rick Turner, speaking quietly with him. She and Rex had met on several occasions. Rex walked to her far side, the opposite side of Rick, and said hello to her.

"Oh, hello, Rex. How are you?"

"I am well, Dr. Chang. It is good to see you."

"You too, Rex."

He then left and walked over to the defense side of the counsel table and sat down. Billy and Erich were brought in, and they both sat at the counsel table. Rex told Billy about Dr. Chang, and that she would not offer anything that wasn't appropriate, like an opinion on who did it, but that he did have a surprise for Rick Turner. Billy looked at him, waiting, and Rex said: "It's a surprise, but a very good one." He chuckled, but Billy tensed. Rex leaned in and said: "I promise you'll enjoy it." Billy's body relaxed a bit.

Dr. Melanie Chang had been a pathologist with the Danbrier County Coroner for many years. She was a true professional; she simply did her job and did it well. She didn't care who won any given case. She was a doctor and a scientist, and she stayed abreast of all the current developments in her field. She was well versed on toxicology. She made it a routine to run a toxicology report on every suspicious death, which under California law compelled an autopsy. She did not know that Rick Turner had not turned over the toxicology report to the defense. Rick Turner did not know Rex already had a copy of it. Eddie Logan never let anything get by him.

Rita Alcazar walked to the back of the courtroom and exited into the hallway. They all stood. She brought the jury in, and they waited for them to be seated. Judge Dorsemann came in and stepped up to the Bench. Everyone sat. His Honor noted the presence of everyone, and said:

"Mr. Turner, please call your first witness."

"The People call Dr. Melanie Chang."

Dr. Chang stood in the front row, and Rita Alcazar led her to the witness stand. Once there, Dr. Chang stepped up, and continued to stand. She was a professional witness who knew what to do. After being read the oath by Karin Kornder, she confirmed it and sat down. She then stated her name for the record and spelled it.

Judge Dorsemann told Rick Turner to proceed.

"Good morning, doctor. Would you please tell the jury what you do for a living?"

Melanie Chang turned her chair to face the jury. She slowly and carefully explained her job duties as a Pathologist for the County of Danbrier.

"Would you please tell the jury about your training and education?"

She recited her curriculum vitae, or resume, by heart. It was a long and very impressive recitation of her many years of training and experience, including performing literally hundreds of autopsies.

"Did you examine the body of a man named Steve Michaelson, and if so, please tell the jury why and what you discovered."

"I did. Mr. Michaelson's body was brought to the morgue following his death on the night of August 25th this year. I was assigned to perform an autopsy to determine the cause of death."

"Were you able to do so, and if so, what was the cause of death?"

"I was, and the cause of death was a gunshot wound to the forehead, and two stab wounds to the neck."

"Were you able to determine whether Mr. Michaelson shot first, or stabbed first?"

"I concluded that he was shot, and then stabbed."

"Please explain."

"According to the report on the trajectory of the bullet, which included my examination of the photos of the crime scene, Mr. Michaelson had apparently been on his knees when he was shot. The report also indicated that there were blood spatters and brain tissue on the wall behind where he was undoubtedly kneeling. The stab wounds were inflicted when he was lying on the floor."

"How are you so certain that he was on the floor when he was stabbed?"

"Well, if he was he stabbed first, he would have collapsed to the floor. He could not have been stabbed in a kneeling position and then shot while he was on the floor or the blood and brain matter would not have been found on the wall. Second, the stab wounds are of a nature that the blood from them does not appear to have drained from him at any other location in the room but the floor where he was found."

"Were you able to determine whether he was alive when he was stabbed?"

"Yes, he was, which is evidenced by the fact that a significant amount of blood drained from the wounds to his neck indicating that his heart was still pumping when he was stabbed. For our purposes, until the heart stops, there is life."

"So, doctor, is it your testimony that Mr. Michaelson died from both wounds?"

"It is, and the wounds inflicted from either of the weapons would have resulted in his death."

"Thank you, doctor. I have nothing further."

It was short and sweet. Rex was uncertain whether Rick Turner chose that approach because he wanted to be able to object if Rex got into the toxicology report, or that he thought that anything beyond that testimony was unnecessary. If it was the latter, and if there were no toxicology results, Rex would have had to agree.

71.

"MR. MCKINLEY, DO YOU WISH to cross-examine the witness?"

"Thank you, your Honor. May I stand?"

"You may." Rex stood and started moving toward the prosecution side, and in front of the jury. He faced Dr. Chang.

"Good morning, doctor. How are you today?"

"Good morning, Mr. McKinley. I am fine. And you?"

"I am well, doctor, thank you.

"If I understand your testimony correctly, did you offer that Mr. Michaelson was still alive when he was stabbed?"

"I did."

"And you explained that it would be difficult to reconstruct a scene where he was shot, with blood and brain matter leaving the back of his skull and hitting the wall, if he were stabbed first, correct?"

"Correct, sir."

"Were you able to determine whether Mr. Michaelson might have been drugged before he was killed?"

Rick Turner jumped out of his seat and shouted: "Objection. Exceeds the scope of direct."

"Counsel," said Judge Dorsemann as he looked at Rex.

"I suppose it does, your Honor, and I can just call this witness in the defense case in chief, and ask the same question, so I am thinking about judicial economy."

"Mr. Turner, you do realize that Mr. McKinley can call doctor Chang and ask this question later, which, of course, will only lengthen this trial."

"Withdraw the objection, your Honor." Rick Turner had been ready to object, so he clearly had anticipated that Rex had the toxicology report. With

Eddie Logan as his investigator that would be a fair assumption. Rex thought that Judge Dorsemann nodded ever so slightly when he said, "You may proceed, Mr. McKinley."

"Doctor?"

"Well, as you know, I have a policy of running a tox screen on all questionable deaths."

"Please tell the jury what you mean by a 'tox screen,' Doctor."

"It is a toxicological examination of a blood sample of the deceased taken from heart blood, which means it is examined for the presence of a spectrum of drugs, both licit and illicit, as well as alcohol."

"And did you get some results?"

"I did."

"What did you discover?"

"Objection, hearsay?" Rick Turner sounded as though he were testing the idea of the grounds for the objection.

"Lay a foundation, Mr. McKinley."

Judge Dorsemann had a look of annoyance on his face. It was basic stuff, and Rick Turner was looking foolish.

"Doctor, the toxicology report that you received in this case, did you receive it from a source you consider reliable?"

"Absolutely. It is the same laboratory that is used for all drug cases, and all autopsy screenings performed in Danbrier County."

Rick Turner should have been embarrassed. The jury just got it. His office used that lab and its results to prosecute every drug case in the county.

"And did you rely upon that source for a report that you used in the ordinary course of business?"

"Yes, I did."

"And is that a business record that you are preparing when you dictate your autopsy protocol, using the results of the toxicology report from that lab?"

"Absolutely."

"Would you please tell the jury the name of that laboratory?"

"The Danbrier County Sheriff's Forensic Sciences Division Laboratory."

Rex paused for effect. He had been looking at the jury and not Dr. Chang since his second question of her. The effect of that was for them to look at him for the question, and then Dr. Chang for the answer. It looked a little bit like watching the audience at a tennis match.

Rex turned toward Rick Turner. He was slumped over his desk, concentrating on his pen or some other inanimate object. Russ Walden was facing forward, still as a tree stump.

"So, doctor, what did you find in Mr. Michaelson's blood?"

"He had a very significant amount of Rohypnol. There was some methamphetamine, too, but a much lesser amount."

"Let's talk about the Rohypnol first, Doctor. Would you tell the jury what that is, please?"

"Rohypnol is often called Roofies. It is the date rape drug we have all heard so much about these days."

"Please tell the jury more about this drug."

"Gladly. Rohypnol is the brand name of Flunitrazepam. I didn't name it." There was light laughter from the jury and the gallery. "It is a Benzodiazepine, a prescription pill like Valium, only much more powerful. It is tasteless and odorless, so it is easy to use without detection. It has been illegal to bring this drug into the U.S. since 1996, but, it is easily purchased on the streets. These Roofies come in 0.5 mg or 1.0 mg tablets, which are usually ground up and mixed into drinks of an unsuspecting victim."

"What do Roofies do, doctor?"

"Roofies cause sedation, a feeling of extreme intoxication, and amnesia. The powdered pills are generally dropped into the drink of a woman, or I suppose a man, by someone who wants to take sexual advantage of the person he or she is drugging. It takes only about ten minutes after ingestion for the victim to start to feel very drunk-like and have difficulty speaking and moving; eventually they may pass out.

"The amnesiac effect of the drug can last at least eight hours. And, even if you are not passed out, you may have no memory of anything that occurred while you were under the influence. Besides making you vulnerable to sexual assault, Roofies have other side effects, which can include seizures, coma, liver failure, and possibly death from respiratory depression."

"So, what you are telling this jury is that Mr. Michaelson had this drug in his system when he was killed?"

"As I said, previously, he had a very significant amount in his blood at the time of his death. Enough to possibly kill him were he not such a large man."

"How big was Mr. Michaelson?"

"His body was seventy-seven inches in length, or six feet five inches when standing."

"And how much did he weigh?"

She quickly glanced at her notes, but Rex did not take issue with it.

"He weighed three hundred seventy-four pounds."

"Big guy," Rex offered.

"He was a large man."

"From your review of the photographs, doctor, were you able to determine whether Mr. Michaelson was in bed prior to being killed?"

"Objection. Calls for a conclusion."

"Counsel?"

"I do believe that Dr. Chang testified on direct that she had reviewed the report on the trajectory of the bullet and the evidence of blood spatters and brain matter on the wall as well as the photographs of the scene to offer an opinion about where Mr. Michaelson was prior to being shot."

"Overruled. You may answer doctor."

"Well, it certainly seemed so; he was naked, and the bed does look like it had been slept in recently. The report I reviewed said his pants were found on the floor, which was an indication that he was either walking around naked, which was highly unlikely considering the amount of Rohypnol in his system, or he was in bed before he was killed."

"Are you telling the jury that Mr. Michaelson could not have been up and walking with that amount of Rohypnol in his system?"

"I am. Yes."

"Was there anything that you saw or discovered during your review of the photos of the scene, any of the evidence, or anything you discovered during the autopsy that led you to believe that my client, Mr. West, was in any way responsible for the death of Mr. Michaelson."

She paused, as that kind of question clearly was not anticipated by her.

"I would have to say no, Mr. McKinley."

"Thank you, doctor. Nothing further, your Honor."

72.

"MR. MUNDO?"

Mark took his time getting out of his chair. He was writing something rather rapidly, completing it as he stood, carrying the notepad with him.

"Good morning, doctor."

"Good morning."

"Based upon your review of the crime scene, as well as the toxicology report, is it your testimony that Mr. Michaelson had to have been drugged prior to his death?"

"Yes, that is my testimony."

"And that it would have had to have been administered sometime prior, say at least ten minutes before he was asleep?"

"I would say with the amount of the dose, he would have become unconscious very quickly."

"If he was unconscious, how would he get out of bed?"

"Good question. I would suggest that he had been unconscious for some time before he was roused from his sleep."

"Are you telling the jury that he had been drugged some time earlier, and then someone came in and, I think you used the term 'roused' him out of bed. Is that what you are telling this jury?"

"Yes. That is the only thing that makes sense."

"Do you wonder why anyone would have to break the outside lights if they knew he had been drugged?"

"Objection. Calls for speculation."

"I'll withdraw the question, your Honor. Nothing further of this witness, your Honor."

That was an excellent rhetorical question for the jury to ponder until they returned from lunch.

"Any re-direct, Mr. Turner?"

"No…your Honor."

Rick Turner sounded weak and feeble in his reply, keeping his head down.

As Rex was about to tell Billy he would see him after lunch, his Honor said:

"Ladies and gentlemen, we are going to break for the day. I apologize for any inconvenience. Something has come up that requires my attention elsewhere, and I will be otherwise engaged for the better part of the afternoon. I want you back here at 8:15 again tomorrow, and we will begin at 8:30. Thank you and have an excellent remainder of the day."

They all stood and waited for the jury to file out. The courtroom was full. Rex saw that Doug had a curious look on his face. Once the jury was out of the courtroom, his Honor inquired whether they had anything that needed to be resolved before they called it a day.

"I have nothing, your Honor."

"Nor do I, your Honor," said Mark.

Rick Turner did not respond immediately. He was speaking with Russ Walden. They looked like they were arguing again.

"Nothing now your Honor," he looked up and offered.

"Then I will see you all in the morning. I apologize about the abruptness of my need to put this over until tomorrow. I have had a personal emergency, and I must tend to it."

"We understand, your Honor," Rex said.

He sat back down and spoke with Billy. "It's actually a good time to break, Billy. Now they know he was drugged long before he was killed. Certainly, the killers didn't do that."

As Rex started pulling his file together, he observed that Mark was having a quiet conversation with Erich Trotter. Mark had redeemed himself in everyone's eyes.

Rex and the guys left the courtroom. Still no Tommy. Mark was leaving as they approached the hallway. His wife was apparently waiting for him outside the courtroom, and they watched them walk off arm in arm.

Rex heard Doug on his cell calling Johnny's to cancel lunch.

73.

AS THEY DROVE OFF REX FELT A BIT LIGHT-HEARTED.
Doug had the look, so Rex asked:

"What's up, Doug?"

"I think things are going well so far, how about you?"

"I do, but we're still a long way from home."

"I'm glad you're thinking that way," Doug replied from the front seat. He was always the grounded one. If Rex were to get excited by anything during the trial, Doug would find a way to bring him back to earth until they had a verdict. Doug was still pessimistic about the outcome of the trial, even after seeing the enthusiasm by some the jurors toward Rex, and how surprisingly well Mark presented. And he was right, as could be seen from the reaction of the jury to the photo of Steve Michaelson, as well as the testimony of Dr. Chang. Rex had to be careful with every moment of the trial.

"Coming up is Mary Jane Rankin. No doubt about it. She's been in custody for about eight days. She's got to be at the breaking point," Doug offered with a non-committal expression.

"Yep, she'll be hurtin'. I do intend to play nice, but not too much. She's got to give it up."

Rex watched Doug nod in the mirror.

"Hey, where's Tommy," Rex asked.

"He'll meet us at the house. He has a surprise for you."

As they arrived at the house and got out of the car, Rex was thinking about how to spend the rest of the day. Were it to be the end of the day, he would last only so long before going to bed. He always wrote notes from the day, ate, and fell asleep at his desk if he didn't go to bed. But that day he felt surprisingly refreshed, and there was time left in the day. When they got inside, there was Eddie Logan standing with Tommy in the kitchen. Rex almost ran to him. He gave him a hug. He looked good for a man who had been at death's doorway for so long.

"Are you ready to get back into the action?" Rex was almost giddy. He looked at Tommy, who simply nodded and stepped back. He understood the bond. He shared something very much like it with Patrick Moynihan. He had done everything he could to help Rex without seeming like he was trying to take Eddie's place. Now, it was time for him to fade away. He spoke:

"I'm on my way back to Santa Monica. If you need me, I can be here."

"Tommy, it has been my honor. I thank you from my heart." Remembering that Tommy did not hug, Rex reached for his hand. They shook hands and Rex felt the power of Tommy as he seemed once again to be scanning Rex to his very core.

Before he left, Tommy spoke confidentially with Eddie, then left the house.

Rex turned to Eddie and asked him to come into his study. Eddie was walking well, but it was apparent that he was still not fully into the swing of things. He still looked lean, and the aura of power that always emanated from him was subdued.

As they sat, Rex said:

"Tomorrow I need you, if you're good with it. Mary Jane Rankin is the next witness, and she's going to come in dying for some drugs. They'll have done their best to make her look good, but at eight days she'll be about to pop. They'll ask her where she lives, and she'll give some bogus address. I'd like you to wait in the attorney room until my cross to make your entrance. That ought to set her off. She'll remember you. Who can forget you? Then I'll go into her being in custody, and why. Sound good?"

"Yep. That'll work."

"Oh, and the guy about the gun isn't coming in. Turner never gave me anything on him, so he can't call him."

Eddie nodded and smiled while he got up. They went into the kitchen and lunch was served. Gail had been helped by a couple of the women from the Ranch, and the food was good.

After lunch, Rex told Gail that if she needed to finish anything she could, or if she would like she could take the rest of the day off. Gail chose to continue working. Rex advised that he was going to be lazy at home.

Eddie said he had to go. He was still investigating the status of Cheryl Porter. He wanted to know where she was staying, and whether she had anyone staying with her. There was a story there, which would undoubtedly come out when she testified. Before he left, Eddie told Rex that he thought she may be closer to Captain Walden than they knew. Rex took that as a fact, and soon would know the full story. He watched his best friend leave with Doug and Ron. They kept close by his side these days.

Eddie looked like he needed more rest, but he had reclaimed his role, which meant he would be back on the hunt, and nothing, not even a bullet in the back, would stop him.

74.

REX WOKE AT 3:45 A.M. He had been dreaming about people with two faces. He was trying to get them to turn around so that he could see who they really were instead of the smiling face they were showing. It was the nature of his work, trying to find what was behind each smile; each story; each person's heart, and whether they were lying—because the truth was always inside the lie. People lied for reasons. It was the lies that imprisoned us, hence the saying, the truth shall set you free. Although Rex was no great philosopher, he did understand that concept, although that was not a truism in most of his cases.

He performed his usual morning rituals, and then made coffee. Doug, Ron and Eddie came in around 6:00. Doug cooked some eggs, and they all ate breakfast together. They spoke very little; they were in tune with one another.

The four of them left together for the third day of trial. They followed the same routine, with heightened security. It was clear to anyone watching that there was still a concern, but they were trying to keep it as quiet and peaceful as possible.

Blood Oath members did wear their patches on the ride over, and any who remained outside kept them on. They never rode their motorcycles without wearing their Blood Oath patches. It was a rule; their law.

Their entry into the courthouse was smooth. Blood Oath members had charmed everyone there, except maybe a couple of the deputies.

It was 8:29, and they were all back in the courtroom waiting to begin. Billy and Erich had been brought in a bit early, and Rex told Billy that he expected Mary Jane to testify next. He told him that he had, once again, withheld a surprise for him. Billy said:

"If it's as good as yesterday, I don't mind waiting." He smiled at Rex, a relaxed comfortable look Rex had not seen before. He put his hand on Billy's shoulder and told him he was proud of him, and to stay cool. It was going to be a good day, even if Mary Jane or Cheryl Porter lied about him. He urged Billy to continue wearing a poker face.

Billy felt different to Rex. He looked rested and had some focus to him. He was beginning to watch people, something he had not done before. He was emerging, and Rex felt strength from him, something that had previously been wasting away while he lived the life of a drug addict.

Erich Trotter was another story. That day, like each day, he remained still, staring straight ahead, shoulders squared, like a soldier.

Melanie Chang was present again. Maybe Rick Turner had something else up his sleeve.

His Honor stepped up to the Bench, said good morning to all, and made a record that all jurors, counsel and parties were present.

There was an air of anticipation. Rex knew it was a phenomenon with jurors that they kept waiting for the prosecution to bring in someone who would save the day—something from our deep-seated belief that the cops and prosecutors are the good guys, and the case wouldn't be there, in trial, if there wasn't some substance to it, something that would prove the defendant's guilt.

"Mr. Turner, did you have any re-direct of Dr. Chang?"

"No, your Honor, but I would ask that she remain on call as a witness."

"Dr. Chang, you are to remain available to testify in this case with appropriate notice. Are you planning on being in trial elsewhere?"

"Not now your Honor. I will be available when called." She turned and left the courtroom.

"Very well. Mr. Turner, please call you next witness."

75.

"PEOPLE CALL MARY JANE RANKIN."

There was silence in the courtroom, still a full house, with Club members, reporters, some of the prospective jurors, and the public.

Eddie Logan was sitting in the attorney room, listening, and waiting for the right moment to come in and let Ms. Rankin see him.

As she entered the courtroom from the area near the Bench, Mary Jane Rankin still looked bad, poor soul. She tried to look sexy as she wiggled herself a little as she walked to the witness stand behind Rita. She was smiling, acting somewhat giddy; maybe just the anxiety of being in front of a jury.

Rita was not amused with her antics. She told her to step up to the witness stand, remain standing and raise her right hand and look to the Clerk. Rita stayed with her, which was the first indication to Rex that something was wrong.

Instead of looking at the Clerk, Ms. Rankin was looking over the courtroom; she was inattentive. She seemed wired to Rex, but maybe it was just the nerves. She said yes when asked whether she would tell the truth.

She asked the Clerk "what?" when she was told to be seated and state and spell her name for the record. Rita spoke quietly to her, telling her to take a seat and then tell the Court her full name, and spell it.

"Oh, okay," she said with a bit of a drawl, and complied. The judge looked at Rick Turner and said:

"You may proceed Mr. Turner."

Rick Turner stood and looked at Mary Jane Rankin. He smiled and said good morning and asked how she was feeling. His voice was deep, rich and calculated.

"Good morning, Mr. Turner. I'm okay."

She giggled.

"Miss Rankin, did you know a man named Steve Michaelson?"

Her demeanor abruptly changed. Her smile turned to a frown. She answered almost defensively, as though she had just been accused of something.

"Yeah, he was my boyfriend until he was murdered."

"Let's take things one step at a time, Miss Rankin, okay?"

"Sure."

Tears began streaming down her face; she was sniffling, too. Rita Alcazar walked to her and handed her a box of tissues. Mary Jane Rankin pulled out a couple of tissues and started wiping her eyes and nose. Her make-up was already starting to smear, and her eyes were very red. It was her pupils that Rex found interesting. She had a bit of a twitch in her hands as she blotted her eyes again. Rex intended to find the cause during his cross-examination of her.

"On the night that Steve was murdered, where were you?"

"At work at the Steel Spur. I was tending bar, and waitressing. We were short on help."

"Did you know where Mr. Michaelson was at that time?"

"He was at my house."

"Was he there prior to your going to work?"

She drifted off and was looking at the audience, her face tensing. She seemed focused on someone, but Rex couldn't tell whom. Eddie was still in the attorney room. Rex had no information that she knew anyone in the Club, but she knew that Billy was Doug's brother.

"Miss Rankin, would you please answer the question?"

"What?" She snapped back to attention.

"Was Mr. Michaelson at your house prior to you going to work?"

"Oh, yeah, he was. We were in bed together for a while, and then I got up and went to work."

She giggled and looked at a couple of the men on the jury. Some of the women on the jury seemed to project various stages of discomfort, but it was still too early for them to form a solid opinion of her.

Rex assumed that Rick Turner had spent a good deal of time with her going over the questions he was going to ask.

"Let me see if I have this correct. You and Steve were together, and then you went to work. Correct?"

"Yeah."

Judge Dorsemann said: "Ms. Rankin, I am going to ask you to please answer yes or no. Do you understand?"

"Yeah, okay. I mean yes."

"Thank you. Proceed, Mr. Turner."

"Do you recall whether there was any kind of problem with Steve and anyone else the night prior to his death?"

"Well, he and Scooter Billy had a grudge going for a long time."

"Who is Scooter Billy?"

"He's sitting there by that handsome young fellow at the end of the table. He has the blond hair, used to have a mustache, but doesn't now."

Rex could object, but he didn't want the jury to think anything this woman said was troubling to the defense.

"Your Honor may the record reflect that the witness has identified Mr. West?"

"It shall."

"Miss Rankin, would you please explain the grudge that you mentioned between Mr. West and Mr. Michaelson?"

"Well, they were usually mad at each other over me."

"Please explain."

"Well, Billy has always been in love with me. He stayed at the house sometimes, and Steve was jealous about it. He did some mean stuff to Billy."

"Mean stuff?"

"You know, he said stuff. He was a bully. Billy isn't very tough, and he usually left the house, or sat outside when Steve was over."

"Did you see Billy and Steve the night before Steve was killed?"

"Yeah, something happened between them at the Spur, and Billy got mad."

Rex let that go, too. It was food for cross-examination. Rex looked at Mark who was waiting for a cue from him. Nothing had been said about his client, and he knew not to wade in unless something was said about Erich Trotter.

"What happened?"

"Well, I only saw the last part. Billy and some guy were sitting at one of the tables drinking some beers when Steve came in and walked over and stuck his finger in Billy's beer, then put it in his ear."

"He put his finger in Billy's ear?"

"Yeah. He was being rude like always with Billy."

"The fellow he was with, do you see him anywhere in this courtroom?"

She looked out at the audience. Her eyes squinted. She was showing no sign of recognition.

"No."

"You don't see the man he was with in this courtroom?"

Rick Turner looked at Erich Trotter. The jury saw Rick Turner look at Erich Trotter. Everyone in the courtroom was looking at Erich Trotter except Mary Jane Rankin.

"No, he's not here."

Rick Turner appeared to be stunned and needed a moment to regain his balance—but he was standing erect with what Rex thought was a tiny smile at the corners of his mouth.

"Miss Rankin, you said that Billy got angry with Steve the night before Steve was murdered, correct?"

"Yeah, he was mad."

"How did you know that he was mad?"

"I know Billy really well. He was red-faced and embarrassed. Steve was always doin' things to him."

"Did he say anything about it to you?"

"Yes, he said 'I'm gonna kill that fucker'."

"Those exact words?"

"Yes, just like that."

Rex said: "Objection, your Honor. May we approach?"

Judge Dorsemann told them to approach. When all counsel was at side bar, and Rex was ready to make a record, his Honor told the jury to chat among themselves, and stand and stretch if they would like.

While at the Bench, the judge's microphone was shut off, and the feed on his voice and that of counsel went directly to the Court Reporter so that she could report what was being said.

"Okay, we are on the record, and the jury is unable to hear us. Mr. McKinley?"

"Your Honor, I have never received any discovery indicating that my client made any such statement. I am claiming surprise. I move that this testimony be stricken. I would ask for a word to the jury about my objection, and for the record I will be requesting a jury instruction about it."

"Mr. Mundo, have you received any such discovery?"

"No, your Honor. Like Mr. McKinley, this is the first I have heard of it."

"Mr. Turner?"

"She just told me yesterday."

"Then you should have immediately notified counsel, Mr. Turner. You know that far too well for me to have to tell you at this juncture. Please be seated, gentlemen." They all returned to their seats.

"Ladies and gentlemen, we have had a discussion here at the Bench. What we discussed is that this last statement by Ms. Rankin about Mr. West saying that he was going to kill Mr. Michaelson is something new. Neither Mr. McKinley nor Mr. Mundo were aware of it. It is the law of this state that they be given such evidence before it is introduced at trial. Mr. McKinley has asked me to strike it, and it is hereby stricken, which means you will not consider that testimony for any purpose. You will receive a jury instruction about the failure to disclose such evidence.

"Proceed, Mr. Turner."

"Nothing further, your Honor."

"Mr. McKinley?"

"Thank you, your Honor.

"Good morning, Miss Rankin."

"Good morning."

"How are you today?"

"Just fine."

"Are you a little nervous today?"

"A little, yeah."

"Have you ever testified in a court of law before today?"

"I had a traffic ticket. He was wrong, so I fought it."

"Other than a traffic ticket, have you ever been sworn as a witness and taken the stand to testify in a case of any kind?"

"Nuthin' like this."

"Did you speak with Mr. Turner or Captain Walden about your testimony here today?"

"No."

"Not ever?"

"I'm confused."

She smiled at Rex, almost suggestively, so he toned down his approach.

"Let me see if I can clear it up for you. I am not trying to confuse you. Before testifying here today did you discuss this case with anyone?"

"Oh, yeah, I spoke with Rick and Russ there."

"Do you mean our prosecutor, Rick Turner, and Captain Russ Walden?"

"Yeah, Rick and Russ."

"That's what you call them?"

"Yeah, they told me to."

Judge Dorsemann intervened. "Miss Rankin, in this courtroom we conduct ourselves with formality. You will hereinafter refer to them as Mr. Turner and Captain Walden, or Mr. Walden. No first names. Understood?" His Honor was being polite but firm.

"Okay. I didn't know."

"Proceed, Mr. McKinley."

"Thank you, your Honor.

"Miss Rankin, when did you last speak with either one of them?"

"Prob'ly last night, I think."

"You're not certain when?"

"Well, not exactly, there's been so much goin' on, ya know."

"When you last spoke with either of them, where were you?"

"You mean where was I at?"

"Yes, Ma'am. Where were you located?"

She turned red and looked to Rick Turner. Rex was looking at her sideways, and watching the jury, but they all turned to Rick Turner, who clearly knew they are all watching, and he dropped his head. Russ Walden was playing soldier, just like the man beside him, Erich Trotter, and they were both looking straight ahead.

"Ma'am, did you need me to repeat the question?"'

"I don't know what I'm supposed to say."

She was still looking at Rick Turner. He was not going to help her with everyone watching.

"Did someone tell you what you were supposed to say in this case?"

She turned on the tears, even sobbed. Jurors began folding their arms in front of them.

Rex let her cry. He waited. He was looking at the jurors only, not Ms. Rankin. He knew that if she didn't straighten up soon the Judge would intervene. He would do one of two things: take a brief recess for her to compose herself, which Rex did not want because Rick Turner would have a chance to coach her on that question; or he would tell Rex to continue, but Rex didn't want to take the chance. So, he decided to intervene.

"Miss Rankin did someone tell you what you were supposed to say in this case?"

"What do you mean?" Her tears dried. Her face was turning red; her breathing was coming in short gasps; her eyes became glazed, and she began gritting her teeth—all signs of methamphetamine use by Rex's analysis.

"I mean has anyone told you what to say while testifying?"

"I'm sure they haven't."

"Who is they?"

"I'm confused."

"Let's start over."

Rex paused and drew in a deep breath, all the while looking at the jury.

"Just a couple of minutes ago you said, and I quote you, 'I don't know what I'm supposed to say,' and then you looked to Mr. Turner and Captain Walden. I asked you whether someone had told you what you were supposed to say. That is where we left off. So, once again, has anyone told you what to say about any of your testimony in this case?"

"I still don't know what you mean."

"Okay. I do hope you understand that I am not going to give up on this question, Miss Rankin. Where were you located when you spoke with Mr. Turner and Captain Walden last night?"

"What do you mean located?"

"Where was your body at that time?"

"Oh, I was in a room."

"And what building was that room in?"

"I don't know, they drove me there."

"Were you in the county jail before they took you?"

Rick Turner looked like he had a spring on his butt when he jumped out of his seat and shouted: "Objection."

His Honor calmly reminded him that he must have some grounds.

"Irrelevant!" he shouted.

"Overruled, Mr. Turner. And, for future reference, you need not stand to object, nor do you need to shout. The Court can hear you very well from here.

"Miss Rankin, please answer the question, and Ma'am, please try to be more direct in your answers. Thank you." Judge Dorsemann looked at Rex, giving him back the stage.

"Miss Rankin were you in county jail?"

"Well, I guess I was in jail when they came and got me."

"And how long had you been there?"

"About a week, a little more maybe."

"Why were you in jail?"

"Objection, relevance."

Rex asked if they could approach. Once at side bar, and ready with the Court Reporter, Rex offered:

"Your Honor, this witness has been in jail for over a week, without charges pending, and without notice to the defense that she was being held against her will. I think this is a clear violation of the rules of discovery, and I do believe that I am entitled to inquire, and that the jury is entitled to know what has been done with this woman and how it may have impacted her testimony here. She thinks that she is supposed to be saying something but cannot remember what. This is the epitome of character evidence, not to mention bias and motive under Evidence Code, section 780."

"Mr. Turner?"

"How is any of this relevant?"

"Mr. Mundo forgive me for passing you by."

"I join with Mr. McKinley, word for word, your Honor."

"Very well, gentlemen. Please return to your seats."

They walked back to their seats in an orderly fashion, with Rex first, then Mark and finally, Rick Turner.

"Objection overruled. You may proceed Mr. McKinley."

"Thank you, your Honor.

"Miss Rankin, please tell the jury why you were in jail."

"I guess they wanted to make sure I showed up for this trial."

"What led you to believe that?"

"Because that's what they told me."

"And who is 'they'?"

"First it was some deputy. Then it was the Captain there, and then the Captain and the D.A."

"Are you being charged with a crime?"

"I think they found some speed in my purse."

"As in methamphetamine?"

"Yeah, meth."

"How much did you have?"

"Objection, irrelevant."

"Mr. McKinley?"

"I'll rephrase, your Honor.

"Miss Rankin was the speed in your purse for your personal use?"

"Yeah, it was some 'personal'."

She sneered when she used that term, common language among drug users, especially speed users, or tweakers. It was a denial that any amount of the drug found in their possession was for purposes of sales, as that charge carried a much more severe sentence.

"Is there a bail set for you?"

"I don't think so."

"Your Honor how is this relevant?" Rick Turner said as his face scrunched up. The standard for relevancy was whether the testimony proffered in some way tended to prove a fact in issue; but the character of a witness was always in issue. Thus, if a witness was a drug addict, presently addicted, then his or her testimony was subject to a good deal of speculation and doubt.

"Is that a serious question, Mr. Turner? If this witness is being held without bail for a simple possession of a controlled substance, then she is being held illegally, and Mr. McKinley will be allowed to develop that testimony."

"Thank you, your Honor," Rex said, and then continued.

"So, you have been in jail for several days without any speed, correct?"

"Yeah, several days."

"By now you must be in desperate need of the drug."

"Objection, irrelevant."

"Overruled!" Judge Dorsemann raised his voice.

"It hasn't been easy, ya know what I mean? Yeah, I'm hurtin' and they know it."

"So, you need the drug. Have you been told anything about when you might be able to get back to your life with drugs?"

There was no dig in his voice; instead he appeared calm, even kind.

"I testify, and I'll get out when this trial is over. No sooner."

"Who told you that?"

"Mr. Turner there."

And she pointed to him. He did not look up.

"When did he tell you that?"

"Last night when they took me to his office."

"You were at his office last night? Taken there from the jail?"

"Yeah, last night."

"Your Honor, I am claiming surprise, once again, for the record, but wish to proceed."

"Noted, counsel."

Rex looked at Rick Turner. That was State Bar reporting material. Rick Turner could find himself facing disciplinary proceedings for that kind of conduct.

"When you were first told that Mr. Michaelson had been killed in your home did you tell Detective Mosely that Mr. Michaelson was not supposed to be there. That you had broken up a couple of weeks before?"

Ms. Rankin's face changed to red; she appeared suddenly angry with the turn of questioning.

"I don't know what I said that night. I was drunk and high."

"You told the jury that you and he were intimate, and then you went to work. True?"

"I said that, yeah. That's how it was, the way I remember it."

"And what you told Detective Mosely, was that a lie?"

"Pro'bly."

"Why would you lie about a thing like that?"

"I was scared."

"Of what?"

"He told me that Steve had been killed in my house. Wouldn't you be scared?"

"Were you surprised to hear that?"

"What do you mean?"

"That the man you had slept with a few hours before was dead in your home."

"I was scared."

"And you ran, didn't you?"

"I left work. I didn't want to go home and see him."

"You stayed on the run for several days, didn't you?"

"I stayed with a friend."

"Who was that friend?"

"I don't know his real name. Just a guy from the bar I see sometimes. We call him Pappy."

"You didn't go back to work, either, did you?"

"Like I said, I was scared."

"Of who?"

"Them."

"Who?"

"I can't say. It's already bad enough. It'll get worse really quick."

"Okay, let's take this one step at a time. Do you realize that you have no right to refuse to answer any questions unless you are invoking your right to remain silent because you believe that you might be incriminating yourself?"

"I know all that stuff."

"You do?"

"Yeah, I know. They already told me."

"Who?"

"Them."

She pointed at Rick Turner and Captain Walden.

"The prosecutor and the Captain?"

"Yeah, them."

She pointed again with a shaky hand. Her face had flushed, and her eyes were squinted.

"You know that if you don't answer my questions that your testimony can be stricken?"

"I don't know what that means."

"It means that if you refuse to answer my questions, I can ask that the Court order your testimony to be stricken as though you never testified. How will that work out for your deal?"

"Objection! Assumes facts not in evidence."

Judge Dorsemann replied: "Quite the contrary, Mr. Turner. It appears to the Court that Miss Rankin is of the belief that she has a deal that she will be released after the trial is over if she testifies truthfully. Is that correct, Miss Rankin?"

"Yeah, that's the deal."

Mary Jane Rankin looked at Judge Dorsemann with eyes filled with tears.

"Counsel, please approach."

Once they were all there at side bar and ready to make a record, his Honor spoke.

"Mr. Turner, I don't want to hear about any more undisclosed discovery, especially where it is apparent that a witness has made a deal with you or law enforcement. Am I understood?"

"Yes."

"Yes, what?"

"Yes, your Honor."

"Please return to your seats, counsel.

They returned in the same order as before, but Rex remained standing.

"Mr. McKinley, please proceed."

"Miss Rankin, what time did Mr. Michaelson get to your house on the date of his death?"

"I don't know. It wasn't dark. I had to be at work at six, so pro'bly four."

"And you were home when he got there?"

"Yeah, he called and said he was coming over. I really didn't want to see him, but I couldn't tell him no."

"He came over and you two engaged in some sexual activities?"

"Yeah, we had sex."

"And did the two of you use drugs together?"

She hesitated, then said: "I don't think so."

"And when you left for work, what was Mr. Michaelson doing?"

"I think he was still in bed."

"Have you seen any of the photographs of the crime scene?"

"I saw them."

Her response appeared devoid of emotion; her voice hollow.

"Did you know that he was under the influence of roofies when he was killed?"

"What?"

"You do know what roofies are, don't you?"

"Yeah, I know."

"Did you put that stuff in his drink?"

Rex remained calm, getting ready for the kill. He watched her and the jury as they looked on at her.

"Please answer me, Miss Rankin. Did you drug Steve?"

"No. Never."

"I am showing you what has been marked as Exhibit 22, Miss Rankin. Would you please tell the jury whether that is a photograph of your bedroom?"

"Ya know it is."

"Is that a yes?"

"It's a yes."

"Would you look at that nightstand and tell the jury whether there appears to be three beer bottles on that nightstand?"

Rex put the photograph on the screen through the electronic projector. He had it connected to his laptop. Gail had numbered each of the photographs to match the list of exhibits that Rick Turner filed and which the Clerk prepared on the first day of trial.

"Yeah, three of 'em."

"If those bottles were tested for the presence of roofies would anyone of them test positive?"

She became red-faced again, her eyes glowing.

Rick Turner objected.

"Calls for speculation."

And it did, if she didn't know.

"Maybe I can rephrase, your Honor."

"Miss Rankin, you drugged Mr. Michaelson by putting roofies in his beer, didn't you?"

"No. Never."

Rex rubbed the back of his head with his right hand, and then with his left hand. A moment later the courtroom doors opened.

Mary Jane Rankin looked to the back of the courtroom and gasped.

"I take it you remember that man."

She nodded.

"You have to give an audible response, Miss Rankin," his Honor reminded her.

"I remember him."

As did the jury. Everyone knew that Eddie Logan had been shot. The media had been speculating about his health, and now everyone knew that he might have been severely wounded, and down for a while, but he was back, and wore a very grim demeanor.

"Do you remember his name?"

"Yeah, it's Eddie. I know who he is."

"Your Honor may the record reflect that Miss Rankin has just acknowledged the presence of Mr. Eddie Logan, my private investigator?"

"It may, counsel."

Eddie sat down in the front row next to Doug West.

"You hated Steve, didn't you?"

"No. I loved him."

"Did you tell Eddie that you hated him?"

"No. Never."

"Did you agree to be video-taped by Eddie while the two of you spoke?"

"He put the words in my mouth."

"Did you agree to be video-taped while you spoke with him?"

"I guess."

"Is that a yes?"

"Yeah, it's a yes."

"Did you tell him that Steve got what he had coming to him?"

"No, never."

She had not looked up even once during that discourse.

"How was Steve when you left to go to work?"

She paused now, her face was showing red again, her breathing choppy.

"Miss Rankin, please answer Mr. McKinley's question," Judge Dorsemann ordered.

"I don't remember it."

"Mr. McKinley, maybe you can repeat the question."

"Might I ask the Court Reporter read my question to Miss Rankin?"

"Certainly. Madam Reporter?"

And she read the question. It was a technique to give the jury a bit more time to watch her squirm and show them how obvious it was that Miss Rankin was being difficult.

"Ya know, I think he was asleep. You know how men get afterward."

She giggled, and jurors began crossing their arms in front again.

Rex let that hang in the air for a few seconds. He walked back to his position in front of the jury.

"Did Billy ever discuss with you what happened to Steve?"

"No."

"Are you telling the jury that you don't have any idea who killed Steve?"

"I think Billy did it."

"Why?"

"I was told."

"By whom?"

"Just around, ya know."

"So, you just heard it around?"

"Yeah, just gossip."

"But Billy never said a thing about killing Steve?"

"No, I never saw him again until today."

"Your Honor, I move to strike any testimony by Miss Rankin that my client killed Mr. Michaelson, as it is based upon hearsay, and not her personal knowledge."

Technically, that was what was called a speaking objection, where the lawyer explained the grounds for the objection. It was a good technique so that the jury understood what was happening. Most Judges do not allow speaking objections. Most often they didn't explain to jurors what was happening, which could be very frustrating for jurors. The better judges explained things as the trial progressed.

"Motion granted. All testimony from Miss Rankin about what someone told her about Mr. West is hereby stricken, and the jury is ordered to disregard it, and it must not be considered as evidence in this case."

"Thank you, your Honor."

"What did you tell the prosecutor and the Captain about what you believe Billy did?"

"That Billy killed Steve because he was jealous. That Steve used to come over and have sex with me, and that he made Billy sit on the porch and listen. I told him that Billy had a gun."

"Was any of that true?"

"Yeah, some of it."

"Which part?"

"About the sex stuff."

"Are you telling the jury that Billy was your boyfriend?"

"No, never."

She spoke with finality, and glanced at the jury.

"Who did you tell that Billy had a gun?"

"Him."

She was clearly pointing to Russ Walden.

"Captain Walden?"

"Yeah, the Captain. Him."

She was still pointing at Russ Walden, and he was looking at her with a very cool gaze. Rex wondered what the jury thought about that. He watched them, and could see some of them were confused, but seemed to be scrutinizing the prosecution side for any tells about whether anything Miss Rankin was saying might be true.

"But Billy never had a gun, did he?"

"I don't know."

"You just made that up?"

"Yeah."

"Did you end up with a gun that you thought might have been used to kill Steve?"

"Yes."

"What kind of gun?"

"I don't know. A pistol."

"A revolver?"

"Yeah."

"A .38 caliber revolver?"

"Yeah."

"Where did it come from?"

"This new guy around, calls himself Stinger."

"How is it that he gave you a gun?"

"He brought it into the bar and told me that 'there'll be peace in the valley now'."

"Is that the truth?"

"Which part?"

"That this guy Stinger gave you a gun and said that to you."

"Yeah, the truth, all of it."

"Is it as true as everything else you have told the jury?"

She paused, sucking in air as though she had been running.

"It's the truth."

"Did you tell Eddie Logan that it wasn't true?"

"He got me drunk."

"Who got you drunk?"

"Eddie."

"When?"

"The night I videoed for him. It's some pretty nasty stuff, but he got me drunk."

"My question was whether you told Eddie that the story about the gun and the statement about peace in the valley was a lie?"

"I don't remember. He got me drunk."

"Did he force liquor down your throat?"

"No, he just bought me some drinks. Ya know how it goes."

"You cannot say whether you told him it was a lie because you don't remember?"

"Yeah, he got me drunk."

"But you do remember the video?"

"Yeah, some nasty stuff. He wanted to see it, so I showed it."

"Are you suggesting that you made a video with Eddie Logan where you were being sexual on video?"

"That's what I said."

"But you cannot remember what you said on the video?"

"No, just what he had me do."

Judge Dorsemann intervened.

"Mr. McKinley, we are going to take our morning recess. Ladies and gentlemen of the jury, I want you back here in a half hour. We have some things to discuss before we bring you back in. Thank you."

Everyone at the counsel table stood.

"Gentlemen, you have five minutes to use the rest rooms. Be back here by 10:17. Thank you."

Rex nodded at Eddie and they left the courtroom together. They stepped into the elevator and made it to the fourth floor. They almost ran into the men's room, although Eddie did not seem his old able self.

"What's the judge going to do?"

"I don't know. Something just happened with him. Did you see it?"

"Yep, he changed."

They didn't speak another word.

76.

WHEN THEY RETURNED TO THE COURTROOM Judge Dorsemann was
on the Bench. Rick Turner and Russ Walden walked in behind them. Mark
Mundo was already waiting. Billy and Erich were brought in and seated.

Judge Dorsemann said: "Gentlemen, this case is unraveling at the seams.
Not my problem. What I do consider to be a problem is the non-disclosure by
the prosecution, and now the issue of a video where the witness claims that she
performed as she put it, nasty stuff on video. I don't think that is going to move
this case along. If that is what this video is about, I am not going to allow it. As
for you, Mr. Turner, I don't want to hear another word about deals, or evidence
that has not been disclosed. Is there more, sir?"

"No, your Honor."

"And for the record, your reason for failing to disclose?"

"No excuse, your Honor, except I didn't think it would become an issue."

"You mean you didn't think it would be discovered?"

"I just didn't think it would become an issue."

"It had better not happen again, Mr. Turner."

"Mr. McKinley, what about this video?"

"There is no sex of any kind on this video. I'm not sure why she said that,
but I do have copies for the Court and counsel."

"Are you telling the Court that this witness is lying about the nasty stuff she
claims is in the video?"

"I hope no one is surprised at this point, but yes, your Honor, she is lying."

"Very well. Please provide counsel with the transcript and video before you
use it.

"Anything further, gentlemen?"

They all said no, then remained standing for the jury to return. Mary Jane Rankin was brought back in and seated on the witness stand.

The jury was brought back in, and when everyone was seated, his Honor told Rex to continue.

"Miss Rankin, did you speak with anyone during our break?"

"Yeah, the witness lady."

"The witness' advocate, Miss Contreras there in the back?"

"Yeah, her."

"Did you discuss your testimony with her?"

"No."

"Miss Rankin, do you see this DVD in my hand?"

"Yeah."

"It is the video we discussed earlier. Are you sure you want to continue with your story about performing sex acts at Mr. Logan's request?"

"I thought I did."

"You thought you did what, perform sex acts, or that you wanted to continue telling that story?"

"I'm confused."

"Do you remember taking an oath when you first came in to testify?"

"Yeah."

"You promised to tell the whole truth and nothing but the truth. Remember?"

"Yeah."

"Have you been lying to the jury?"

Rex was looking at the jury. Whenever he stopped looking at Miss Rankin, she would turn red and her breathing would change. She even began twisting a strand of hair.

"No. Not ever," she said raising her voice.

"Okay, do you understand what perjury is?"

"Yeah."

"What is perjury?"

"It's when you get up here and lie."

"Last chance, Miss Rankin."

"Objection, argumentative."

"Sustained. Move on Mr. McKinley."

"I apologize, your Honor. At this point the defense would like to play Defense Exhibit A, and I ask that Court's Bailiff be permitted to give the transcripts marked as Defense Exhibit A1, to each of the jurors."

Rex stood and handed Rita Alcazar a stack of transcripts.

Judge Dorsemann did not respond. He accepted a transcript by Karin Kornder. Rex watched him carefully, waiting for his instruction.

"Proceed, counsel."

"Thank you, your Honor.

"Miss Rankin, please watch the video and read the transcript. I will have some questions afterward."

The screen opposite the jury lit up. Judge Dorsemann had it on his computer monitor, and monitors on both sides of the counsel table showed it.

The video began; it appeared to be a very shabby motel room. The only person on the video was Mary Jane Rankin. She appeared glassy eyed, her demeanor giddy.

"So, what do you want, handsome. A show?"

"No. I told you before that I do not want to have sex with you. I just want to speak with you."

"Okay, hon."

"You understand that this conversation is being video recorded?"

"Yeah, hon."

"My name is Eddie Logan and I work for Attorney Rex McKinley, who is representing Billy West."

"Yeah, you said that. Got anything to drink?"

"No, ma'am, I don't. Can you wait until we are through to start drinking?"

"Oh, I already started a long time ago."

"Are you presently under the influence of drugs or alcohol?"

"Yeah, both. And I feel good. And I can make you feel good, too."

"No thank you. Did you have anything to do with the murder of Steve Michaelson?"

"No. But he got what he deserved."

"Did you want him dead?"

"Sometimes."

"Why was he in your house that night?"

"I don't know. He wasn't welcome there."

"Why have you been hiding from law enforcement?"

"Because I don't wanna be in trouble for what happened."

"Why would you be in trouble?"

"They might think I had something to do with him being drugged."

"He was drugged?"

"Everybody knows that, silly." She slurred the last part.

"Everybody?"

"Yeah, they all know."

"Who are they?"

She started rolling around on the bed. She blew a kiss at the camera, then started to unbutton her blouse.

"Ma'am, if you do that I am going to shut off the camera and leave."

"You're no fun."

"This isn't about fun. Billy is being charged with murder. What do you know about it?"

"I heard Billy shot him, and his friend stabbed him, but I don't know. Steve was shitty to Billy all the time. He was a fuckin' bully. He got what he had coming."

"So, you *are* glad that he is dead?"

"Fuck him."

"Wow. He must have made you really angry."

"Yeah, he was a pig."

"Did you know that he was going to be killed in your house?"

"No. Not ever."

"Did you know that he was at your house?"

"No. He wasn't 'sposed ta be there, I told you."

"I heard that you were given the gun that killed him. Is that true?"

"Yeah, some guy gave it to me, and then he said there'll be peace in the valley, or some shit."

"Really? Where is that gun?"

She started rolling around on the bed fondling her body.

"Miss Rankin, last warning. I will shut off the video and leave if you do that again."

"You a fag or something?"

"No, I'm here on business. I'm trying to help a man who has been accused of murdering Steve. Is that story about the gun true?"

"Nah, it's bullshit. Something Ron and Cheryl started just for laughs. I got no gun."

"Ron and Cheryl Porter, your neighbors?"

"Yeah."

"Was Steve a tough guy?"

"Yeah, very tough. Big guy. Liked to hurt people."

"How do you suppose someone got to him?"

"I ain't one of them mind readers."

"How do you suppose he got into your house?"

"He had a key."

"Do you know why he was naked?"

"He was? I dunno. He was such a pig; he pro'bly had another bitch in there."

"Are you denying that you saw him before he was killed?"

"I was at work, hon. You can check that out."

Rex stopped the video when he knew that the jury had seen enough.

"Miss Rankin were you able to see all of that video?"

"Yeah."

"Was that the video you were thinking of where you claim that you performed sex acts for Mr. Logan?"

"No, not that one."

"Are you telling the jury that there is another video of you with Mr. Logan?"

"No."

"No there wasn't another video with Mr. Logan?"

"Yeah, there wasn't any other video."

"You told him that you were glad that Steve was dead, true?"

"Yeah. I was glad. He was a pig, and a rapist."

"A rapist?"

"Yeah, he used to make me have sex with him whenever he wanted."

"Did you kill him for it?"

"No."

"Did you have someone kill him?"

"No."

"Did you know that he was going to be killed?"

She became red-faced, her eyes glowing, then tried to turn on the tears. They wouldn't come. Instead, she covered her face, and moved in her chair, pushing up as though about to stand.

Rex walked past her so that his body did not block the jury's view of her. He was standing just behind her so that she had to turn to look at him, and the jury got a good straight on view of her.

"Please answer me. Did you know that he was going to be killed?"

She looked at Walden and Turner. Walden was looking at her with an icy stare.

Rick Turner, on the other hand, was still pretending to be surprised at her statements in the video.

"I didn't know."

"But you knew he was drugged. How?"

"How what?"

"How did you know he was drugged?"

"Like I said on the video, everyone knew."

"Who is everyone?"

"Objection. Vague."

"Overruled. That's what she said."

"Who is everyone, Miss Rankin?"

"I don't know. People just said it, and I heard it."

"You put the roofies in his beer, didn't you?"

She paused, and then she glared at Rex before speaking.

"I did what I had to," she said, her voice sounding raw, even bitter.

Rex paused for a full minute. Standing before the jury he looked at each of them before he asked:

"Is that a yes?"

"No."

"Well then, what did you mean when you said you did what you had to?"

"Forget that. I don't know why I said it."

"I think we're entitled to know what you mean by that statement."

She didn't answer. She tried to speak but words did not come. Then, with a huge effort she blurted: "I don't know what I meant. It just came out. I'm upset."

"Okay. Were you lying to Mr. Logan when you said that you didn't know that Steve was at your house?"

She froze, and didn't answer the question, so Rex rephrased it.

"Have you lied to the jury?"

"No. Not ever."

"So, Miss Rankin, were you told to put drugs in Steve's drink so that he could be killed?"

"I think I'm gonna need a lawyer."

"Didn't the deal you made cover this?"

"I don't know."

"Did you tell either Mr. Turner or Captain Walden that you drugged Steve?"

She looked to them for help. Everyone in the courtroom could see it, no matter where they were sitting.

"No. I never told them anything like that."

"Did you wash out the beer bottle?"

"What?"

"You did put roofies in his beer, didn't you?"

"No."

"Were you surprised that neither Mr. Turner nor Captain Walden knew there was roofies in Steve's drink?"

What was Rick Turner going to do? Everyone was waiting for her answer. Mary Jane was looking at Turner and Walden again.

"Ma'am?"

"I never thought about it."

"You never thought about what?"

"About the beer bottle."

"You never thought that there might be some evidence left in the beer bottle?"

She threw her hands up. "I don't know," she said with resignation.

"Miss Rankin are you telling the jury that you never considered that evidence of Steve being drugged before he was killed might come back at you?"

"I never thought about it. I didn't do it."

"You never thought about someone finding out that Steve was drugged before he was killed?"

"Never thought about it."

"Objection. Asked and answered."

"Sustained. The answer is stricken."

Rex continued.

"Did you tell Eddie Logan," and he turned and looked at him in the front row. The jury could see him, and Mary Jane Rankin had a clear view of him.

"Tell him what?!" She snapped at Rex.

"MISS RANKIN!" He shouted at her. "Do you think this is a joke?"

He stopped and waited, standing in front of the jury. She burst into tears. The entire jury had their arms folded across their chests—a group response.

"Waddaya wanna to know?" She said in anger, as she was looking to the floor.

"Have you been given immunity for your part in the death of Steve Michaelson?"

"What?"

"Were you promised that you would not be prosecuted for anything you did if you came in and testified?"

"Yeah, I get out as soon as this case is over."

"Did you tell either Captain Walden or Mr. Turner, or anyone in law enforcement that you drugged Steve?"

"No, no one."

"No one? Not ever?"

"What?"

"Did you discuss this with any of your friends, or any of those people who told you what to do?"

"I'm confused."

"Aren't we all?"

"Mr. McKinley!"

Rex stopped and looked at Judge Dorsemann. "I apologize, your Honor."

"Miss Rankin, you put roofies in the beer you gave to Steve, correct?"

"Objection. Asked and answered several times now," said Rick Turner with righteous indignation.

"Sustained. Counsel, it has been asked and answered several times. Do not ask again!"

"Yes, your Honor," said Rex.

"You told the jury that Steve called and then he came over, correct?"

"Yeah."

"You have told the jury that you and Steve were intimate, and then you went to work, correct?"

"Yeah."

"What did he drive to get there?"

"Huh?" She was clearly stunned by the question.

"Isn't it in fact true that you brought him home with you the night before from the bar, and he left his car at the bar?"

Mary Jane Rankin turned white. There was no vehicle belonging to Steve Michaelson found at the scene of the crime.

"I guess."

"Is that a yes?"

"Y'yeah, she stuttered."

"Is that a yes, Miss Rankin?" His Honor intervened.

"Yeah, it's a yes," her voice strained and gravelly.

Rex looked hard at Judge Dorsemann. Judge Dorsemann said:

"I'm sorry, Mr. McKinley."

"Thank you, your Honor," Rex replied, and continued:

"Then the part about him calling and coming over wasn't true, was it?"

"No."

"You were lying to the jury?"

"I didn't mean to."

"When you left him that next day to go to work, was he conscious?"

"You mean like awake?"

"Yes, Ma'am."

"Yeah, I think so. But you know how men are. He mighta been asleep."

"Will you please try to remember the last words you ever spoke to him?"

She burst into tears. Rex let it go, and she began to sob.

Rex was standing in front of the jury, and they were looking at him, not Miss Rankin. He paused while she cried some more, then said:

"Thank you, Miss Rankin. I have nothing further of this witness, your Honor."

"Mr. Mundo."

Mark stood and looked at the jury.

"Thank you, your Honor. No questions."

"Mr. Turner, re-direct?"

"Just briefly." He stood.

"Miss Rankin was everything you told the jury true to the best of your knowledge?"

She looked up, still crying.

"Yes," she whimpered.

"Nothing further," said Rick Turner, and he sat back in his chair.

"May this witness be excused?"

"No, your Honor," said Rex. "She may be needed for the defense case."

"Very well. Miss Rankin, even if you are released from custody, you will make yourself available to this court on one-hour notice. Do you understand?"

"I'm not going anywhere."

"Ladies and gentlemen, we are going to break a bit early for our lunch recess. I want all of you back here at 1:30. Thank you."

They all stood as the jury left. When they were gone, his Honor inquired:

"Who are you calling next, Mr. Turner?"

"Cheryl Porter."

"Will she take the rest of the day?"

"No. I intend to call Captain Walden afterward. He will take at least two hours for direct."

"Very well, gentlemen, please be back at 1:15."

"Thank you, your Honor," said Rex, as did Mark, and then Rick Turner. Rick shoved a document across the table. It stopped at Mark, who looked at it, and said:

"I think he wants you to have this, Rex."

Rex accepted the document. It was a conformed—court stamped—copy of the criminal complaint filed against Rex. The defendant's copy rarely had what that one had on the second page: it was signed by Rick Turner. He filed the case against Rex and had chosen that moment to let him know.

77.

EDDIE AND REX WALKED OUT of the courtroom together. When they were in the hallway, Rex spoke in anger:

"Why didn't you tell me it was Rick?"

Eddie stopped walking. Rex did the same as Eddie calmly said:

"Would it have helped you get through it?"

They didn't speak as they resumed walking toward the doorway to the world outside the courthouse. It was then the magnitude of it hit Rex. They were protecting him, not just from some additional pain at the time, but from acting like an angry asshole during the trial. A jury would not have understood it, and it would have hurt Billy.

"You're right," Rex said. Eddie nodded.

Once out of the courthouse, Ron and Doug joined them. Rex took a moment to appreciate his world. It was a beautiful day in Danbrier, and the power of it was generating through nature, and his amazing friends. The sun was shining, the sky had a few wispy clouds. He looked off at the mountains, embracing the beauty, momentarily escaping into the forest.

They got into his car, with the usual seating, and went to Johnny's for lunch. When they arrived, and got out of the car, Ron put his hand on Rex's shoulder and said:

"The jury thinks the D.A. is a real jerk. Don't sweat the small stuff."

They were unusually quiet during lunch. Mark had not joined them, which somehow felt right. Each time Rex thought about the behavior of Erich Trotter, the more a feeling crept upon him—Erich Trotter and Mark Mundo, something was being hidden from Rex, and he was becoming certain that his friends already knew. He would wait and watch.

When they finished eating, Doug pulled Rex aside.

"Smooth work, counselor. The jury thinks she drugged him, which she did."

"You know this to be true?"

"Doesn't everyone?" He smiled and patted Rex on the shoulder. He turned and stood next to Ron, who was smiling at Rex, also.

"Then let's get back and kick some ass," Rex replied, and he meant it.

"That's the attitude," said Doug. He was so imposing, yet his smile was completely encouraging. Rex felt like he could carry it with him anywhere and it would light the way. They drove back slowly with their usual entourage, Blood Oath, front and back. The sound of Harley's and the feeling of the brotherhood washed over Rex. He smiled.

They made their way into the courthouse and up to Department 9. They entered and waited for everyone to arrive.

Billy and Erich were brought in, and while they waited for the jury, Rick Turner stepped back, turned to Rex and with a very snide grin on his face said:

"How did you like that, Rex?"

Rex didn't respond, and didn't feel much, either. He saw Rick Turner as a petty person, small and ugly. The shame he had experienced was not completely gone, but it had turned into a teacher for him. He had something in common with the people he represented—that which no one would ever understand unless they had experienced it. Rex reflected that perhaps he should be grateful to Rick Turner at some level; because of what he did, Rex was trying to be a better man. But he had just told Rex that he filed false charges against him, and now he was gloating. Woe unto him. Forgiveness didn't seem like a viable option at that time.

Billy seemed upset by what Rick Turner had said. He asked Rex: "What'd he mean, Rex?"

"Don't sweat it, Billy. He's just an unhappy man."

Billy didn't seem to understand, but he nodded his head anyway. It had upset him, and Rex decided to explain.

"He's the one who filed the bogus charges against me. He's upset about how things are going. So, he tried to slap me in the face. You know what, Billy? That makes him a punk." Rex realized he was angry as he squeezed Billy's shoulder.

"Like your brother always says, don't sweat the small stuff. Eh?"

"How can that guy call himself one of the good guys, Rex?"

"Exactly, Billy." They smiled, but both were troubled.

Next up was Cheryl Porter.

Rex suspected that she would not be able to identify Erich Trotter, and that Eddie, Doug and Ron already knew that. Their way of dealing with things that had worked very well in the past was to wait it out, without explaining. If she didn't identify him, Erich Trotter would probably walk out at the end of the prosecution's case. If that was the situation, Mark and Rex would discuss Penal Code, section 1118.1, which allowed the court to direct an acquittal of a defendant, and that decision could not be appealed. Erich Trotter would be free forever. What manner of possibilities might that bring?

His Honor took the Bench and inquired whether there was anything they needed to discuss. They all said they did not. He instructed Rita Alcazar to bring in the jury.

As they were seated, the courtroom filled with media and observers. There were at least fifteen Club members, including Richard West, Doug and Billy's father, and Melina's grandfather. Rex acknowledged him and mouthed 'how are you,' and he smiled back. Rex told Billy his grandfather was there, and Billy looked out over the crowd and saw him. Rex felt him perk up. He smiled without stress in his face. When everyone was seated, his Honor said:

"Mr. Turner, please call your next witness."

78.

"PEOPLE CALL CHERYL PORTER."

Rex was watching to see which way she entered, whether from the back of the courtroom, or the hallway behind the Bench. She entered from behind the Bench; she was either in custody or was being protected. Rex suspected the latter. He looked to Eddie for an answer. He nodded, and approached Rex, who stood and met him at the bar, the railing that divided the public from the counsel tables and attorney area. All attention had shifted to them for the moment.

When he was near he whispered that she was being protected. They were afraid to bring her in through the hallway because she was testifying against the brother of the President of Blood Oath. Eddie said they didn't know that he and the others knew about Cheryl Porter and Ellifson. Rex nodded and returned to the counsel table. Russ Walden had been watching. Eddie looked hard at him, so the Captain looked away. Rex realized some of the jurors saw the way Eddie looked at Russ Walden.

Cheryl Porter was walked to the witness stand by Rita Alcazar, and led through the oath. She sat, stated her full name and spelled it. She did not look well. Rex recalled the early photos of her. She looked good on the morning of her interview, but that day in court she looked several years older.

"Mr. Turner, you may inquire."

"Thank you, your Honor."

He had his magnificent voice turned on again. Rex sensed a bit of happiness in him, and thought it was because he had shown him something that would hurt him. He also surmised that he believed that Cheryl Porter would leave the witness stand unscathed.

"Good morning, Miss Porter. Or is that Missus?"

"Well, I was married, but I am in the process of a divorce."

"I am sorry to hear that, Ma'am. You came in through the back door, behind the Bench. Are you presently in custody?"

"No."

"Do you know a man named Billy West?"

"I know that man there," pointing at Billy, "but I don't know his last name. His name is Billy. Some people call him Scooter Billy."

"May the record reflect that the witness has identified the defendant?"

"It may."

"How do you know Mr. West?"

"He was friends with my neighbor, Mary Jane."

"Miss Rankin?"

"Yes."

"Did you know Steve Michaelson?"

"Yes."

"How did you know him?"

"He was over at Mary Jane's house a lot. I think he claimed her as his property."

"You spoke with Captain Walden about this case, did you not?"

"I did."

So far, the woman had the jury's attention. She was polite, responsive, and the more she spoke, the more pleasant she appeared. She was looking at the jury appropriately, but not like a professional witness, only during her answers. She was engaging them.

"Did you see Mr. West the night that Mr. Michaelson was murdered?"

"Yes."

"Did he have anyone with him?"

"Yes."

"Do you see that person in this courtroom?"

She did exactly what Mary Jane Rankin did. It was a bit too obvious—it appeared staged. Rick Turner would have told her that Erich Trotter was sitting at the counsel table, and what he was wearing, or at least where he was sitting. Still uncertain what was going on, Rex looked to Eddie, who had his poker face on. He looked at Doug, who wore a very subtle smile, but underneath it all, Rex could feel his anger.

"No, he's not here."

Rex watched Rick Turner pretend to be concerned, but at least two of the jurors, a woman and a man, crossed their arms, another turned to stone.

"He's not?"

"No, he's not here."

Without a pause for dramatic effect, Rick Turner pushed on, and the flow of energy in the courtroom changed. The jurors looked puzzled.

"When was it that you encountered these two men?"

"Around nine on the night Steve was killed."

"Do you remember the date?"

"Not really, but I remember the night it happened. We've discussed it so many times."

"What happened with Billy and the man with him that night?"

"I remember them coming to the house. They drove up and stopped out front of the house. Billy knocked on the door. My husband opened the door and told them to come in."

"Did they come in?"

"Yes."

"Did you speak with Mr. West?"

"No, but I listened. He was talking to my husband."

"What did he say?"

"He said 'We just killed Steve. Got any beer?'"

"Just like that?"

"Something like that. I was pretty shocked."

"What happened next?"

"My husband got them each a beer."

"Then what?"

"Then Billy asked my husband for some money. He said they had to go on the run."

"Did your husband give them any money?"

"I think he gave them some, but I don't know how much."

"Do you remember what Mr. West was wearing that night?"

"Not really. Probably a t-shirt and jeans."

"How about the other man? How was he dressed?"

"Same thing, I think."

"Thank you, Ma'am. Nothing further, your Honor."

Judge Dorsemann said: "Mr. McKinley?"

"Thank you, your Honor. May I stand?"

"You may."

"Good afternoon Ms. Porter."

"Good afternoon."

"Have we spoken before?"

"Not that I recall."

"You say you know my client, Mr. West?"

"Yes, I've met him a few times at Mary Jane's."

"And you knew Steve Michaelson?"

"Yes."

"I think you said that he claimed Miss Rankin as his property, correct?"

"Yes, that was my impression."

"What gave you that impression?"

"Oh, the way he acted, I guess. He was always ordering her around, throwing her friends out when he came over."

"Friends like you?"

"Me, too, sometimes."

"Did you see him often?"

"Enough."

"Didn't like him?"

"Not much."

"Did you use speed with Mary Jane?"

"Objection. Exceeds the scope; irrelevant."

"Well, it does exceed the scope, but it is not irrelevant. Since this witness testified that she had never spoken with Mr. McKinley, I am going to give him some latitude.

"Ma'am?"

"I don't use drugs."

"Did you back then?"

"I might have gotten high a few times. So what?" Her face hardened; her eyes boring in on Rex. He was facing the jury.

"When you saw my client drive up to your house on the night that Steve was killed, what kind of vehicle was he driving?"

"It was the same one as always—a beat up old black pick-up, full of dents, with bald tires; a real junker."

"His tires were bald that night?"

She hesitated. She was smart. She glanced at Russ Walden. Just a quick glance. He sent a message by moving his head to the right, and then the left; very subtle, but Rex and the jury were all watching him.

"May I approach the witness, your Honor?"

Generally, there must be a reason to do so, and Rex had none.

"You may, Mr. McKinley."

Rex walked toward her and stood so that she could not see Russ Walden. Some of the jurors got it.

"Ma'am?"

"I didn't see his tires that night. He might have changed them."

"When he parked his truck, which way was it heading?"

"Toward Highway 26."

"Away from Miss Rankin's house?"

"Yes."

"Did you watch him drive away?"

"I looked through the window."

"Did he race out of there?"

"What do you mean?"

"Did he peel out, throwing dirt behind him?"

She tried to look at Russ Walden, but Rex moved with her so that she could not connect with either Russ Walden or Rick Turner.

"I don't recall."

Her faced stiffened, her eyes became bright, her face flushed. Her breathing seemed strained.

"Was there anyone at your home at that time other than you and your husband?"

"No. We were there alone."

"Did you call 911?"

There was an audio file, with a transcript prepared by Gail for Rex.

"Yes. After they left."

"What did you tell the 911 operator?"

"I don't recall."

"You told Mr. Turner that you remembered that night so well, and I quote, 'we have discussed it so many times.' Do you remember that testimony?"

"Yes."

"How many is 'so many'?"

"I don't know. Several. A half dozen maybe."

"You spoke with Mr. Turner maybe a half of a dozen times before you testified here?"

She was trying to see Rick Turner, but Rex was blocking her. The jury was perking up again.

"Yes."

"Did you ever discuss your 911 call?"

"I don't recall."

"Did you tell the 911 operator that you heard a gunshot next door?"

"I might have."

"Was that true?"

"We heard something."

"Did you tell the 911 operator that the killers were just in your house, and that they admitted to murdering Steve?"

"I don't recall."

"Did you tell the 911 operator that the killers had come to your home, admitted to murdering Steve Michaelson, and then asked you for beer?"

"I don't recall."

"Did you tell the 911 operator that your husband gave them money?"

"I don't recall."

"You don't recall what you told the 911 operator?"

"Not really, I was pretty shook-up."

"Are you telling the jury that you don't recall anything about the 911 call?"

"Not really."

"We have that recording here, Ma'am. Would listening to it help you refresh your recollection?"

"Maybe." She attempted to look at Rick Turner or Russ Walden, and Rex moved again to block her.

"Your Honor, I had not anticipated the need to play this audio file. May we take a short recess?"

"Ladies and gentlemen, we will take our afternoon recess now. Please be back in fifteen minutes."

After the jury left, Cheryl Porter was told she could leave. Russ Walden stood and moved in her direction, obviously to escort her out the back way.

The Judge asked if anyone needed to discuss anything.

"Yes, two things, your Honor," Rex said.

"First, I don't want Captain Walden speaking with this witness while I am still cross-examining her. It certainly seemed to me that she was trying to look either at him, or Mr. Turner to assist her during my cross."

"Deputy Alcazar, please escort the witness out through the back, and see to it that she is assisted by the witness advocate."

"Thank you, your Honor. Second, I'm afraid we have the same issue creeping up with Mr. Turner failing to disclose his conversations with this witness. Miss Porter says there were about six conversations with Mr. Turner. She said there were conversations on direct, and he didn't correct her. Now she is saying there were about a half dozen. Where are the reports?"

"Mr. Turner?" The Court inquired.

"I didn't prepare any reports. I was preparing the witness. I don't think I have to report preparation of a witness."

"Mr. McKinley?"

"He knows he has to report it if he is speaking with a witness. She is not his client. She's his witness. She says they spoke a half of a dozen times. Is Mr. Turner telling the court that he conducts his witness preparation without any discussion of the evidence?"

"I think you should explore that with her on further cross-examination before I make a ruling."

Rex was looking at Rick Turner. He had a very smug look on his face. He thought he just won something. Rex was wondering whether he ever listened to the 911 call.

Eddie came over to Rex and helped him with setting it up the audio for the 911 call. They got the transcripts ready to be distributed to the jury.

"You know this will be her breaking point? Take your time with her. It's obvious she's been coached, but she can't figure out what to do when you block her."

"I hope so. She's not as easily shaken as Miss Rankin."

"Yeah, but she's too confident," said Eddie with a smile.

79.

REX AND EDDIE AGREED THEY NEEDED a quick bathroom break. They made their way out of the courtroom and their usual run to the fourth floor, but this time when they stepped out of the elevator, there was Rick Turner and Russ Walden with Cheryl Porter, and they were berating her with raised voices. She had tears in her eyes. When they saw Rex and Eddie, pure venom and hatred was sent their way. Rick Turner had lost the smug look.

Rex and Eddie used the bathroom, and came back down the stairway, getting out just on the other side of the courtroom.

As they did, Rick Turner tried to come at Rex. Carey Sorenson intervened. He stood between Rick and Rex, and simply blocked Rick Turner's path. He did not speak. Some of the jurors saw it. They could see that Rick Turner was looking to start a fight. He was so angry he didn't realize what he was doing.

Rex had walked around Carey who kept Rick from following him. Eddie had moved forward and opened the door for Rex and they walked back into the courtroom.

Rex told Rita Alcazar they we are going to need a few minutes with his Honor before the jury was brought in.

Rick Turner came in with Russ Walden following. Cheryl Porter was right behind them. She looked shook up.

When his Honor resumed the Bench, he looked out at everyone. He could see that Rick Turner was angry. Everyone saw it.

"Counsel?"

"Your Honor, as Mr. Logan and I exited the elevator on the fourth floor, we saw Mr. Turner and Captain Walden speaking with the witness, Ms. Porter— clearly in contradiction to your order. She had tears in her eyes, and both men, particularly Mr. Turner seemed angry. In fact, Mr. Turner tried to get to me just outside this courtroom, with a very angry look on his face. I want to know what he was telling Ms. Porter, and I also want him to stay away from me."

"Mr. Turner?"

"Not true, Judge," he said with a very red face.

"Well, let's get Ms. Porter back on the witness stand, and bring in the jury, and you can ask her about it, Mr. McKinley. Ms. Porter, please resume the witness stand. Mr. Turner and Captain Walden, later we will deal with your apparent violation of my order that the witness not be contacted while she was on cross-examination." The look on Judge Dorsemann's face was one of obvious anger; there was fire in his eyes.

"Thank you, your Honor," Rex offered.

They all remained standing while the jury came in, and then the public. When everyone was seated, his Honor said:

"We are back on the record. All jurors are present, all counsel and the defendants are present. You may proceed, Mr. McKinley."

Rex was still standing and looking at the jury as he began walking toward them. He drew in a deep breath.

"Thank you, your Honor.

"Miss Porter, have you had a chance to think about what you said on that 911 call."

"I remember making the call. I remember being so terribly upset at what Billy had said about murdering Steve that I knew I had to call it in. I might have said something about hearing a shot fired. I don't remember what I said after that."

"Might playing this call help refresh your recollection?"

"Maybe."

"Before I do, during our recess Mr. Logan and I saw you in what appeared to be a heated conversation with Mr. Turner and Captain Walden on the fourth floor. You had tears in your eyes. What was that about?"

"Objection. Vague."

"Overruled."

"Nothing."

"Ma'am, I saw it, remember? What was Mr. Turner saying to you?"

"He thought I was lying about not remembering the call, and he was upset about it."

"Oh, did he tell you what he thought you should have said?"

"No, just the truth."

"Why were you crying?"

"I get that way sometimes."

She was much smarter and much tougher that Mary Jane Rankin. The jury saw how angry Rick Turner was with Rex in the hallway, so he decided to let it go for the time being.

"Let's see if playing the 911 call helps your recollection. For the record, this is defense Exhibit B, and the Transcript is B1."

"So noted, Mr. McKinley. May the Court Reporter be relieved of her duties to report this recording?"

"Yes, your Honor. Once again, your Honor, I ask that the Court's Bailiff be permitted to deliver copies of the transcript of the 911 call to the jurors, and a copy for the Court and the Reporter."

"She may do so, counsel."

Rex waited until everyone was settled and had a copy of the transcript in their hands. Cheryl Porter wore a blank expression. A cold looking woman; aggrieved, Rex thought.

The recording began. The 911 operator asked about the emergency.

"I want to report a shooting. I heard a gunshot from my neighbor's house. I think something bad has happened." Cheryl Porter's voice seemed devoid of emotion.

The operator responded:

"Can you see anything from your location?"

"No, the house is too far away."

"Are there any vehicles at the residence?"

"Nothing I can see." Still, Cheryl Porter was surprisingly aloof for someone who claimed to the jury that the killers had just been in her home.

"Stay where you are; I have deputies on the way."

Cheryl Porter could be heard saying that she thought that her neighbor's boyfriend might be in the residence where she thought she heard the shot. She did not mention Billy, or any person who she thought might have been involved.

The 911 call lasted until after deputies arrived on the scene. The jury could hear their sirens in the background, and then a pounding on the front door. The 911 operator told Cheryl Porter to have her husband look out and make sure it was law enforcement, and if so, to do as they said. Everyone could hear a man's voice in the background saying: "It's the cops." She told the 911 operator that the cops had arrived. The operator told to do as they said. The 911 operator hung up.

"Miss Porter was that your voice on the recording?"

"Yes."

"You reported a gun shot, correct?"

"Yes."

"Did you report speaking with Mr. West?"

"No. You heard it."

Rex looked to Judge Dorsemann, who nodded.

"Miss Porter, did you tell the 911 operator that two men had just been in your home, and admitted to murdering Steve Michaelson?"

"No."

"Did you tell the 911 operator that you knew who might have killed the man in the house down the road?"

"No."

"Did you tell the 911 operator that you helped the killers escape?"

"No. And I didn't do that, my husband did. My ex-husband."

"But you didn't see fit to tell the 911 operator that you knew who killed the man next door?"

"I wasn't sure he was dead."

"But you did suggest that Mr. Michaelson was probably there, true?"

"Yes."

"Why?"

"Because I thought he was."

"According to your testimony, you had information that Mr. Michaelson had just been murdered, true?"

"Yes."

"But you neglected to mention that in your phone call. Why?"

"I was pretty shook-up. I think I was afraid they might come back and kill me."

"Who might come back and kill you?"

"Billy and that guy."

Rex was looking at the jury while standing in front of them. He was trying to block out the feelings of hatred coming from Rick Turner behind his back. His hackles were going up on his neck. He drew in a deep breath and tuned out Rick Turner.

"Are you telling the jury that you didn't say anything about Mr. West and his unidentified friend out of fear that they might come back and kill you?"

"Something like that."

"Is it that, or something else?" Rex raised his voice, but his body showed no stress.

"I don't know what you mean."

"Was there someone else telling you what to say?"

Her face flushed. She appeared shocked that Rex asked that question.

"I have no idea what you mean."

"At any time prior to the Sheriff's men arriving, was anyone else at your home?"

"No."

"You spoke with Captain Walden that night?"

"No, it was in the morning."

"About what time?"

"It was still dark. Around three or four."

"Between the time that the deputies arrived, and the time that you spoke with the Captain, did anyone come by and visit with you?"

"You mean like deputies?"

"No, not law enforcement persons."

"No. Just the deputies and the Captain."

"Did the Captain or any of his deputies' park in front of your house?"

"No."

"When was the evidence tape put in place?"

"You mean in front of my house?"

"Yes."

"I don't really know."

"Did you discuss with anyone why it was put there?"

"I think it was Captain Walden who said it was to protect evidence of tire tracks, and we were not to walk through it."

"It was taped by the Captain, and he told you that it was to preserve those tire tracks?"

"Yes, that's what he told us."

"Nobody drove through there before he taped it?"

"No, you don't have to come that close to our house to get to Mary Jane's."

"And no one other than law enforcement told you to do anything?"

"No, there was no one else there."

"How about Sam Ellifson?"

She sharply inhaled and held her breath. Rex walked past her so that she had to turn her neck to answer his questions and was facing the jury. She stopped looking at them the way she had during direct examination. She would not turn and look at Rex. She looked to Rick Turner, then at Russ Walden, who was looking straight ahead, just like Erich Trotter. And then Rex saw it.

"Miss Porter?"

"What?"

"Was Sam Ellifson at your house that night?"

"Who?"

"You do know him, don't you?"

"The name doesn't ring a bell."

Rex let her hang there for a minute then said:

"Your Honor, may I have a minute?"

"Of course."

Rex signaled Eddie to come over to him. The entire courtroom watched him. Rex spoke with him while they both looked at Cheryl Porter, with Eddie doing a bit of an animated nod of his head. It was then that Cheryl got a good look at Eddie. She gasped and appeared to mumble something under her breath.

Rex asked Eddie: "Think I should show her the photo now?"

"Nah, just keep her on call."

Rex left Eddie and walked toward the jury. Eddie slowly returned to his seat in the front row behind Rex. He continued to stare at Cheryl Porter. She had tried to get either Rick Turner or Russ Walden to connect with her, but both were ignoring her.

"Miss Porter, do you recognize that man I was speaking with?"

"I've seen him."

"Do you recall when?"

"Actually, a couple of times. He came into the Spur one night. He left with Mary Jane. Then I saw him again, somewhere, but I don't remember where."

"He's kind of hard to forget, isn't he?"

"Yes."

"Was it that night when you were with Sam Ellifson?"

"I don't know what you are talking about."

"Do you know Sam Ellifson?"'

"No."

"You have never been with him?"

"No. I told you I don't know him."

"And no one was at your house the night of, or morning after the murder of Steve Michaelson other than law enforcement?"

"Objection! Asked and answered.

"Sustained. Move along, Mr. McKinley."

"Miss Porter, do you recall the clothing that Mr. West and his unidentified friend were wearing?"

"Like I said, jeans and t-shirts."

"Do you remember the colors of any of the clothing?"

"No."

"Do you recall seeing any blood on any of the clothing?"

She paused and looked to Rick Turner and Russ Walden. Rex moved forward and stood in her way, and he turned slightly and glanced at Turner and Walden. Rick Turner showed his hatred. The jury saw it.

"I don't remember seeing anything like that."

"Do you remember any strange smells?"

"No," she said, her voice almost a growl.

"You saw nothing on either man that might confirm that something violent had happened, and that blood was shed?"

"No!"

"Thank you, Miss Porter. You Honor I have no further questions now. However, I do not want this witness excused. I may wish to call her as an adverse witness in the defense case-in-chief. I would ask that the Court order her to remain available."

"Miss Porter, you are under order of this Court that you will remain available upon one hour's notice for further testimony. Your failure to be available could result in your testimony being stricken. Do you understand?"

"Yes."

"Mr. Mundo, any cross-examination of this witness?"

"No thank you, your Honor."

"Mr. Turner, any re-direct?"

"No, your Honor. Thank you, Miss Porter."

She walked off the witness stand, escorted into the back by the witness advocate. Rex looked behind him toward the media section. None of the reporters were using their electronic devices. The courtroom was quiet, almost silent; no one was moving.

80.

"MR. TURNER CALL YOUR NEXT WITNESS."

Rex detected a bit of disdain in Judge Dorsemann's voice. He seemed tired.

"People call Captain Russ Walden."

Russ Walden stood. He was one very impressive man in his Sheriff's uniform with Captain's bars on the collars. His shirt was short-sleeved so that his muscular forearms were visible. He looked at the jurors as he walked to the witness stand. He stepped up and remained standing. He looked to Karin Kornder and raised his hand.

She administered the oath. He answered, "Yes, so help me God."

He sat and recited his full name, then spelled it for the record. He turned in his seat and faced the jury. He smiled at them. Most of them smiled back. It was almost impossible not to fall under his spell, and he hadn't even begun.

"You may proceed, counsel."

"Thank you, your Honor," Rick Turner said with his rich, clear voice.

He had switched on his power; he was compelling. He had the attention of everyone in the courtroom. This was *his* time—he and Captain Russ Walden, cop *extraordinaire* would settle all concerns.

"Good morning, Captain."

"Good morning, sir."

"Captain, would you please tell the jury what you do for a living."

"I am a deputy Sheriff for the County of Danbrier."

"And your rank."

"I am a Captain."

Rick Turner then walked Russ Walden through his time with the department, his various assignments, the number of arrests he had made; the number of murder cases he had investigated, and finally, they arrived back at the scene of the murder of Steve Michaelson. It took about forty minutes to get to that point; very well done by Rick Turner and Russ Walden. It was seemingly effortless to invoke hero worship from the jurors. They each looked on with smiles and nods, and undisguised adoration.

"What did you observe when you first arrived at the scene?"

"After a briefing from one of the deputies on scene, laid out a plan to collect evidence."

"Did you find anything of significance?"

"I did."

"Please tell the jury what you observed."

"First, I realized that we were going to have a problem with some of the physical evidence. The area is desert, the Basin, and it is composed mostly of sand. The road to the house is sand, which made me focus first on evidence outside of the residence."

"Did you find any?"

"Yes."

"Please explain."

"I needed to preserve the integrity of the crime scene, so I took the necessary steps to do so."

"Please explain that phrase, preserve the integrity of the crime scene. Tell the jury what that means."

"To make certain that we can come into court and show that the evidence collected at any crime scene is credible, we must preserve it in its original state. Otherwise, defense lawyers, like Mr. McKinley there, will try to show that the evidence is not to be believed."

He pointed at Rex, and the jury gave a bit of a chuckle. Rex looked at the jury and raised his eyebrows and smiled at them.

The Captain continued.

"So, we need to make certain that everything we discover is kept as we found it until we can either photograph it, or collect it, or in some way preserve it so that we can offer it as evidence in a court of law."

He engaged the jury during all his answers. They responded with nods, smiles and even a flurry of note taking from a couple.

"And what specifically did you find at the scene?"

"Well, the first things I considered were tire tracks and foot prints."

"Why?"

"Because we had information that the killers had driven to the scene, and they had to have walked into the house."

"Objection, your Honor. Assumes facts not in evidence that there were 'killers', plural," offered Mark Mundo.

"Overruled. You may cross-examine on that issue."

"What did you do to try to find evidence of the killers?"

He emphasized the "S", looking sideways at Mark with a smirk on his face.

"First, because some of the deputies had driven to the scene, I had to determine which tire tracks were theirs, and exclude them from what I was seeing. I did the same with the footprints."

"Please explain to the jury how you did that."

He went into a detailed explanation about how he examined the tires on each of the Sheriff's units, and then found a set of tracks that did not match any of them.

He testified that he used the same technique with the footprints as he did with the tire tracks, but it was more difficult to find any prints that could be compared with anything, except a couple of boot prints that belonged to the first deputy on the scene.

He explained that because of the weight of a vehicle, and that the road was packed hard from the years of driving over it, it was much easier to read tire tracks.

The jury seemed totally engaged.

"Captain, were you able to preserve any of those tire tracks?"

"I was."

"How did you do that?"

He explained that he had light shined on them while he photographed them. He said that he preserved them that way because he had many years of experience taking photos of tire tracks and comparing them with known treads, and with the use of magnification he had been able to make accurate comparisons.

"We will hold off on that for a bit later, Captain. What else did you do to preserve evidence?"

Judge Dorsemann intervened.

"Mr. Turner, this looks like a good place to stop. Ladies and gentlemen, we are going to take our noon recess. Please remember the admonishment. Do not discuss this case among yourselves, or with anyone. I will see you back here at 1:30. Thank you."

They all stood and waited for the jury to leave the courtroom.

No one had anything to discuss with the Court. Rick Turner and Russ Walden stayed in the courtroom as Rex, Mark, Eddie and all the Club members walked into the hallway. The plan was to go to Johnny's for lunch, but Mark begged off. He said he had plans with his wife.

81.

WHEN THEY ARRIVED AT HIS RESTAURANT, they greeted J. D. Dumas. As always, he was happy to see them, and told them lunch would be served soon. They filed into the back room but didn't discuss the case. It is just a nice quiet lunch with good friends.

An hour later they returned to the courthouse. After parking they stood as a group before they made their way through security. There was a good deal of attention paid to them by the public and members of the media, but no one tried to intervene and ask questions.

As he got near the courtroom, Rex reflected that he could hardly wait until it was his turn. He was becoming restless. He knew that he probably wouldn't begin his cross-examination until the next morning. Russ Walden was the most important witness in the prosecution's case.

When they entered the courtroom, Rick Turner and Russ Walden were already inside. They had set up three easels with huge blow ups of Steve Michaelson in death. Mark came in after them.

The first was Exhibit 1, which Rick Turner had shown the jury during his opening statement. Exhibit 2, the one Rex had hoped Rick Turner would show; the one with which Rex would begin his questions about the crime scene. Then there was Exhibit 3: a close-up of Steve Michaelson's head and neck showing the bullet wound on the left frontal lobe and the two knife wounds on the left side of his neck. It was ugly and gory. A large amount of blood had drained out of those wounds, and Rick Turner undoubtedly expected to score big with each of the photos, the collective impact of them.

Billy and Erich were brought in just before Rita Alcazar went to get the jury. Rick Turner and Russ Walden were standing together near the witness stand, but they did not acknowledge the jury. Rex had seen this as a technique by lawyers and cops who wanted the jury to think that they were more important than the jurors themselves. Rex was taught early on that you never turn your back to the jury, except when walking to your seat at the counsel table.

When they were all seated, Judge Dorsemann resumed the Bench and made a record that everyone was present, and then directed Rick Turner to proceed.

"Thank you, your Honor," he said triumphantly. As he stood, Russ Walden returned to the witness stand. Judge Dorsemann reminded him that he was still under oath.

"Captain, before we discuss the rather large photographs in front of the jury, can we look at the photos taken outside of the residence again?"

"Certainly."

"Earlier we discussed tire tracks. You told the jury that you excluded those of the Sheriff's vehicles but found a single set that could not be explained. Correct?"

"Yes. When I was briefed, I was told that the killers drove from the crime scene to the residence at the beginning of the road—there are only two houses on the road—and that they had stopped there and spoke with the residents of that house. So, I walked the tracks that were clearly not any of ours. I followed them to the house. I had evidence tape placed around the scene in front of the house where the vehicle had obviously stopped, and later raced away."

Rex did not object to those conclusions.

"Was there any problem following those tire tracks?"

"Some. There were tire tracks from our units crossing over them in a couple of places, but I picked them back up easily enough."

"So, you are the one who put the evidence tape at the Porter's residence?"'

"Yes."

"To preserve that evidence?"

"Exactly."

"Then what did you do?"

"I took photographs of that area."

"May I approach, your Honor?" Rick Turner was walking toward the witness stand as he asked.

"You may."

"Captain, I am handing you what has been marked as People's Exhibit number 26. Would you please examine that photo and tell the jury whether that is the area you just described?" He did not put it on the screen for the jury to see.

"It is."

"Did you take that photograph?"

"Yes, that and many others."

"I am showing you Exhibit 27, would you please tell the jury what that depicts."

"When Mr. West was arrested, he was driving a black Chevrolet pick-up, I believe a 1978, and that is a shot of his right rear tire." Again, the exhibit was not shown to the jury.

"Were you able to make a comparison between the tire tracks at the scene, and this tire on Mr. West's truck?"

"I was."

"And your conclusion?"

"The tire on the truck is the exact same tire as the one that I found to have left that track at the scene of the crime. This photo was taken of the right rear tire track that I followed to the Porter residence. This is from just outside the evidence tape, there." Russ Walden was pointing to the photograph, which was still not visible to the jury. That was another conclusion to which Rex did not object.

"Did you take all of the crime scene photos?"

"Yes, all of them."

"How many were taken."

"Almost three hundred."

"Did they all turn out clear?"

"Unfortunately, not all of them, but most."

Rick Turner moved away from the Captain, taking the exhibits with him. He set them on the counsel table, and returned his attention to Russ Walden.

"After photographing the outside area, did you enter into the residence?"

"I did."

"What did you see?"

"I saw a Caucasian male lying on the floor. He was deceased. There was a pool of blood around him, beginning at his head, and stopping at a towel and what appeared to be a terry cloth robe, that was lying on the floor near the body."

"What did you do?"

"I scanned the scene to get an overview of the evidence."

"Other than the deceased, what did you observe?"

"I saw blood spatters and what appeared to be brain matter on the wall. I saw a small hole in the wall, which was later determined to contain a .38 caliber bullet."

"Did you find a gun at the scene?"

"No. Apparently, the killers took it with them."

"What else did you observe?"

"It appeared to me that the crime scene had been staged to look like there had been a robbery."

"Please explain this to the jury."

"Well, there was a wallet on the floor. It was later determined to belong to the deceased. It had been gone through, and some of the items were not in place, which made it impossible to close the wallet and put it into a pocket."

"Was there any money in the wallet?"

"No, and I think if there was any, the killers took it." That speculation was objectionable, but Rex remained silent.

"Captain Walden, we all see the photographs on the easels. I am pointing with the laser pointer to the first, which for the record is Exhibit 1. Would you please tell the jury about this exhibit?"

"I took this photo from inside the residence, looking down on the body of the victim."

"Objection. We have dealt with this issue," Rex said a bit too loud.

"Sustained. Captain, you will refrain from calling the deceased 'the victim'. Do you understand?"

Russ Walden responded: "Yes, your Honor."

Rex wasn't sure that the jury understood, but he knew that if they heard the word repeatedly, it would impact their thinking—exactly why the order.

Rick Turner ignored the objection and continued:

"In looking at Exhibit 1, Captain, do you see anything of evidentiary value?"

"Yes, the man received trauma to his forehead, which, although it does not show, resulted in the destruction of his skull on the backside of his head. Also, you can see the two stab wounds on his neck. These were obviously made by a large blade, and when viewed during his autopsy showed that they had penetrated his neck bone with the blade hitting the floor beneath him with both strokes. The assailant had to be very strong. Some of the jurors looked at Billy. Although he had gained a few pounds since his arrest, he did not look strong. Erich Trotter did, but no one had identified him, so he was just a wall of mist.

"Directing your attention to Exhibit number 2, Captain, what does this photograph show?"

"Well, I took this photograph to show where Mr. Michaelson's body was laid out in the general scheme of the room. He is found on the floor closest to the north wall, about six feet from the bed. You can see the west and north sides of the room."

"And Exhibit 3, Captain, what does it tell the jury?"

"Exhibit 3 shows the room from the north, looking to the south and east. You can see the windows on the south side, and the book case and other items on the east side."

The jury was being given a very close view of the deceased. The large pool of blood, the brains on the wall, and the messy place where Steve Michaelson died.

"Captain, let's talk about preservation of evidence, and the integrity of the crime scene. You took many photos for what purpose?"

"To show them to you to assist you in determining whether to file criminal charges; and to show the jury the evidence as it was discovered."

"And do you move things around during the investigation?"

"Not on my crime scene!" He said it with such righteous indignation Rex knew that few, if any, doubted him.

"Please explain that statement."

"If people start moving things then there is no integrity to the crime scene. We cannot say how and where we found evidence, and therefore cannot make conclusions about what we found. If I may give an example?"

"Please do."

"Let's say that we walk into a crime scene. We find a dead person on the floor, and there is a gun nearby. We pick up the gun to make certain it is not loaded, then take it into the kitchen and set it on the counter. Then we start taking photographs of the crime scene. We have information that leads us to believe that the gun was used by John Doe, and that after he shot the deceased, he dropped the gun and ran out of the house. The problem now is that we have contaminated the crime scene by moving the gun. We cannot show what happened by the photographs of the location of the physical evidence. On my crime scene, everything remains where it was found until all photographs have been taken, and the forensics team has completed their job."

It was a very well-practiced answer, and the jury was fully engaged, smiling, nodding and note taking.

"Captain, I am showing you People's Exhibits 12 and 13. Would you tell the jury whether you took those photographs, and what they depict, please?" Those photographs were shown on the screen for the jury.

"Yes, I took those. Twelve shows the wallet on the floor. You can see how it is not closed. That is because it cannot close with the items in it moved out of place, as though someone had gone through it. Thirteen is a photo of his jeans thrown across the room."

And it went for another hour of Rick Turner presenting Exhibits 1 through thirty-seven, which covered the inside of the house and the tire tracks.

"Ladies and gentlemen, we are going to take our afternoon recess. Please be back by 3:15. Thank you."

When the jury was gone, his Honor inquired, and they all reported that there is nothing to discuss.

82.

REX LOOKED TO EDDIE AND THEY walked out of the courtroom. They rode the elevator up to the third floor. They used the men's room, then returned. They did not speak, but they were feeling the same anticipation and excitement they had to suppress for the rest of the day.

When they returned there were three new photos: Exhibits 1a, 2a and 3a. They had the colored cone markers at each location that was determined to have evidence.

When they were back on the record, Rick Turner had Russ Walden carefully explain each photo, and why the colored cones were placed in each location, and if and why he directed the placing of the cones.

There were dozens of other photos that had the little cones, and those cones also had numbers on them which were markers for various pieces of evidence, which were included in this second set of photos. The presentation carried the case through the afternoon. The jury had been shown sixty-eight photographs, and three were discussed, but not shown to the jury. There had been a repetition of the blood and gore. Close-ups of brain matter and blood spatters on the wall and the floor behind the body, indicating that Steve Michaelson was in fact on his knees when he was shot, which was also an indication that the shooter was squatting down at his level. It all made sense, except certain specific things were not mentioned about which Rex would inquire.

Russ Walden had been an awesome witness. He had been forthcoming. He had been responsive, and he was engaging with the jury. But, he had yet to point a finger at anyone.

At the end of the day Rick Turner wore a victorious grin. He had scored big with a masterful performance. As a team, he and Russ Walden were the very best.

Those were subjects discussed with Doug, Ron and Eddie on their way back to Rex's house. He was starving and crawling out of his skin. He wanted blood; and was having issues with patience. He needed some straight talk before he popped.

When they went into the house, the air was filled with the smell of food cooking. In the kitchen, they found Gail. When she served them dinner, they ate in silence. After finishing, Rex commented on how great the food was, and how grateful he was for Gail who kept them going. All the others chimed in, and after they ate, Doug and Ron started helping clean the kitchen. Eddie and Rex excused themselves and went into the study.

"They sure are overlooking a bunch of stuff." Rex was attempting to be cute.

"Watch Juror Number 8. He's taking notes on everything. I think he's seen the briefcase. I also think there's something going wrong with him. I'm gettin' a feeling about him."

Eddie turned very serious. When Eddie Logan became that kind of serious, it was as though his entire body was turning into a powerful electrical charge. Rex could feel it.

"He is definitely attentive. It's hard for me to tell right now. I'm getting a feeling too, but it's confusing to me. He seems to want to please me, but I don't trust it."

He paused, looked at Eddie who was staring off through the windows; a look as though staring into another dimension. Rex knew he was divining some secret truth and would share his thoughts when he was ready—it could never be rushed. Eddie offered:

"Turner and Walden are doing such a great job. I wonder when the knockout punch is coming. They only have Cheryl Porter saying anything, and only about Billy. And, how odd that no one identified Erich Trotter. They'll bring in the cops who arrested them together, but I'm laying odds no one ever ID's Trotter."

"Do you know something I don't?"

"Maybe. More later." And his face turned blank and he looked off into the distance again. He had disappeared into another time.

Rex changed the subject.

"I am about to start pulling my own hair. I'm losing patience with this new me."

Eddie turned to his best friend, with a smile, and said:

"I know. Change doesn't come easy. Try to remember when I came and got you at the jail."

"Fucker!"

They both laughed, but not happily. It was a bitter feeling Rex embraced, and he knew he needed to get back into the zone of the new role he'd been growing into. It was not about him, and he was not going to allow himself to get caught in it—old behavior died hard.

As if on cue, Doug and Ron asked if they could join.

"Sure, please do."

"You know, Rex, I can see you starting to get antsy. What's going on?"

It was Doug with his usual serious analysis of everything.

"We were just talking about that. I'm feeling impatient. I want to reach up there and strangle them both."

"If I can see it, so can the jury," he paused, "and they won't understand. These two guys are in their hearts, and if you aren't cool with it, they're going to miss what it is you do later because you haven't gone with the flow. What you had in the beginning can be lost by your failure to honor their feelings. They have a hero up there, and you can only take him apart with a whole lotta cool, man. Get it?"

Rex paused. He'd just been told, once again, from a man he respected, who pulled no punches. It was a blast to the ribs, and it hurt. Enough to knock the wind out of his sails long enough for him to become introspective. He got it, and it was exactly what he needed all afternoon. He let it settle for a bit.

"I've had this old feeling creeping up in me all day that truly enjoys being an asshole with cops and other liars."

"There's nothing wrong with that equation, except the asshole part."

"I know. Thanks, Doug."

"Just bein' me," he laughed, and the room vibrated.

And then she entered. Rex felt her beforehand.

"Is this guy's only?"

Eddie, Doug and Ron all stood and left quietly, smiling at her on their way out.

Rex was awestruck. Melina Garza, the woman who had taken his heart. He thought about her day and night; she was a feeling residing deep inside him.

He stood, and she walked to him. Rex didn't know if he could move. She seemed a bit shy as she approached.

"Can I get a hug?"

And they embraced. Rex held her close and felt her body so close to his they were blending together. They both turned hot all over. He couldn't help becoming aroused. She felt him against her and began pulling him closer. They stood there for what seemed like an eternity.

When they drew back, they continued to hold hands. They whispered back and forth about what they had been doing. She took his hand in hers and held him. He asked her if she would like to sit for a while. They went into the living room and sat on the couch, where they began a quiet conversation. Rex felt himself drifting off.

He had no idea what time it was when he woke. Melina was still holding his hand. She leaned over and kissed him gently.

"I have to go."

"I'm sorry I fell asleep."

"Not me. It was a blessing to be able to watch you sleep so peacefully."

He walked her to the door, and a couple of the guys were out there. Her beautiful black hair was blowing in the breeze as she disappeared into the nighttime. He couldn't stop looking, even after she was gone.

83.

THEY WERE BACK IN THE COURTROOM at 8:30, with all the jurors present. After yesterday, if the jury was the voting population, Rick Turner and Russ Walden could be elected President and Vice President of the United States.

His Honor stepped up to the Bench and greeted everyone, and then made a record that everyone was present. Not one juror had been late, which was very unusual. The courtroom was packed, once again.

Other than Cheryl Porter's testimony that Billy told her he killed Steve, there very little to tie him to the scene, other than the tire tracks.

"Mr. Turner, you may proceed. Captain, please resume the stand, and you are still under oath, sir."

Russ Walden was standing by the witness stand, and he stepped up and said:

"Yes, your Honor."

"Good morning, Captain."

"Good morning, sir."

"How are you today?"

"Excellent, and yourself?"

"Excellent, as well. Your Honor, I have nothing further of this witness."

The jury laughed and chuckled.

"Mr. McKinley?"

Rex stood after asking permission to do so.

"Thank you, your Honor. Good morning, Captain."

"Good morning, counselor."

"Captain, at the time of your investigation of the scene of this alleged crime you were a Lieutenant, correct?"

"Correct."

"And you were recently elevated to Captain, correct?"

"Correct."

"Congratulations on your promotion."

"Thank you."

"And you have been the Captain in charge of the Danbrier County Detention Center since that promotion, correct?"

"Correct."

"How long have you been at the jail?"

"About three months."

Rex had been arrested and beaten less than two months past.

"Was this the last case you investigated before your promotion?"

"Correct."

"Sir, when did you discover that the deceased, Steve Michaelson, was the younger brother of Detective Donny Michaelson?"

"Objection!" Rick Turner shouted. "Irrelevant."

"Mr. McKinley?"

Calmly, Rex said:

"Motive and bias, 780 your Honor."

"Overruled."

"Sir?"

"I think I was told that at the briefing before I even saw the body."

"So, you knew that a family member of one of your own was lying dead on the floor in that house?"

"Yes."

"And did you feel any special sense of obligation to the investigation because of it?"

"I just went about doing my job, as always."

"You have explained to the jury how you go about your job, and that part of that process is to photograph everything, correct?"

"Correct."

"And your photographs of the crime scene were the only photographs of the crime scene?"

"Correct." His body tensed slightly as he answered.

"No other deputy took any photographs?"

"No. That was my job." Russ Walden tensed in his shoulders, his eyes narrowed as though squinting to examine something.

"Isn't photography of a crime scene part of the work of the forensics team?"

"Usually, but I am a photographer by hobby, and I like to do all of the photography work on my crime scenes."

"Your crime scenes?"

"Yes, *mine*." His words were harsh; seemed like a challenge.

"When you take charge of a crime scene, you always do the photography work, and the forensics team does not, correct?"

"Correct."

"Did you bring in a forensics team in this case?"

"Not exactly, no."

"What does that mean?"

"It means that we did not find any need for the team."

"Why?"

"Because we had the obvious evidence I have explained, and we had an admission. We knew who we were looking for, so we got to finding them."

"Isn't that contrary to all standard procedures?"

"No, not at all."

"Well, sir, would you tell the jury what standard procedure is for investigating a homicide scene?"

"Well, you have to preserve the evidence, as I have stated. That means we keep everyone out of the scene."

"Are you telling the jury that this was such a clear-cut case that you did not need to do a thorough investigation?"

"Of course not! This was my crime scene. We did a thorough investigation. We covered everything, as always."

Walden's face began turning red. He clinched his fists and his eyes were hard.

"And these tire tracks that you followed, and found to have stopped at the Porter home, other than photographing them did you employ any other method of preserving them for a scientific examination?"

"That was unnecessary, counselor. They were very distinct, and when the photos were compared with the tires on Mr. West's truck, they were a perfect match."

"Sir, isn't it true that the established procedure for preserving tire track evidence is to plaster cast them so that you have an exact impression to match with the tires, should you find the vehicle?"

"That was not necessary here."

"Sir, how does plaster casting work?"

"Objection. Irrelevant."

"Overruled."

"Captain, how does plaster casting work?" Rex pushed.

"You pour plaster into the impression, let it dry, and then remove it so that you have a hardened image of the impression."

"Actually, it's an exact image, isn't it?"

"Yes."

"And then an impression can be made of the actual tire, if it is found or believed to have been found, and a comparison can be made, true?"

"Yes."

"And isn't it true that the study of plaster casts is work for a forensic scientist?"

"I suppose."

"Because a scientist can use various pieces of scientific equipment, such as microscopes, laser measuring devices and the like to compare the impressions. True?"

"Yes."

"And they can compare markings on tires, such as gouges, cuts, nail marks, gravel marks, and other imperfections to determine, scientifically, whether the impression matches the tire exactly, true?"

"That's often the case, counselor." His remark seemed snide, and there was enmity in his voice.

"Captain, please tell the jury why you did not follow standard procedures and bring in your forensic sciences division to process the crime scene."

"I thought I already had, counselor. It was unnecessary. I made that call."

"Can you tell the jury whether that authority is granted to you by any written procedure, or did you just make that rule up?"

"Objection!"

"Counsel?"

"Me, or him, your Honor? Rex asked with all sincerity since he heard no grounds.

"Mr. Turner, the grounds?"

"Argumentative," Turner said.

"Overruled."

Rex continued: "Captain, please answer the question. Did you just make up that policy on the scene?"

"I told you, counselor, there was no need. We had the perps ID'd."

"My God Captain are you telling the jury that when you decide that the alleged perpetrator of a crime has been identified, that you do nothing further with the scene of the crime, but instead rely upon what one person has told you?"

"I know what I'm doing. I know how to catch a perp."

"By the way, Captain, how was it you excluded the tire tracks of Mary Jane Rankins' vehicle? She did have a car, didn't she?"

"I saw no evidence of any other tracks but ours and the defendant's vehicle."

"You did know that Miss Rankin lived there and drove to and from her residence somewhat regularly, didn't you?"

"And your point, counselor?"

"You don't understand the question, Captain?"

"Please repeat it."

"Captain, if Miss Rankin drove her car on that same dirt road shouldn't her tire tracks have been there, too?"

Rex paused, the let him go after a pregnant silence.

"Let's move on to something else for a minute while you think about an answer to that question."

"Objection! Argumentative."

"Overruled, counsel."

"Sir, may I direct your attention to People's Exhibit 2. Where did that go? Oh, here it is by Mr. Turner. Your Honor, may I ask that the Court's Bailiff assist me with the photographs and the easel, or may I have my investigator do it?"

"Mr. Logan may assist you, Mr. McKinley."

His Honor seemed to be anticipating what Rex was going to do. It was becoming apparent that Russ Walden did not do a thorough job. Where was the forensics team? No one thought about that the day before because they were mesmerized by the two titans.

Eddie joined Rex and stole all the attention from the jury. He knew it and smiled at them as he passed by to assist Rex near the witness stand. It became necessary for Rex to give it a minute so that they could get a closer look at the legend himself. Everyone knew that he was shot a little more than month ago, through the back and out his sternum. Most men would have died. None other than Eddie Logan would be standing in a courtroom, moving about without any apparent pain. In any event, the team of McKinley and Logan was taking over where Turner and Walden left off.

They set up the photo, and Eddie sat in Rex's seat at the counsel table. Rex explained to his Honor that Eddie would be assisting him by showing photos via the projector. He asked for permission. Judge Dorsemann said "absolutely."

"Thank you, your Honor, and thank you, Mr. Logan."

"You are welcome, Mr. McKinley," Eddie said with the tiniest of smiles.

The women jurors were still looking at Eddie; some of the men, too. Rex realized he had better get their attention back, so he walked to the middle of the jury box and stood. He looked at them and asked:

"Captain was anything found in Mr. Michaelson's hand?"

"Say again?"

"You didn't hear me?"

"I didn't quite get the question. Did we find something in his hand?"

"You got the question, sir."

The jury was watching him very carefully. He seemed to be playing dumb, and that was something he was not.

"I don't think so, counselor."

"Would you look closely at Exhibit 2 and tell the jury if you can see that he has his left hand squeezed closed, and if there is something reflecting light in his hand?"

He froze for a brief second, and then he regained his cool, but not before some of the jurors had seen it.

"I can't see anything there, but I do see that his hand is squeezed tight. Probably a reaction to his violent death."

It was a good answer. It took the focus off him and put it back on the horror of murder.

"Do you see that shiny item in his hand?"

"No."

"Wasn't it a key?"

"I don't recall any such item being found."

"And you would have made certain that everything on *your* crime scene was listed and catalogued, true?"

"You bet."

"So, there is nothing that was not accounted for on *your* crime scene, true, Captain?"

"That is true."

"As true as everything else you have said?"

"You bet."

"Is that a yes, Captain. Is it as true as everything else you have told the jury?"

"That is a yes, counselor."

"I am showing you an exhibit we have already seen, People's Exhibit 14."
Eddie put it up on the screen.

"Sir, will you please tell the jury whether there is a briefcase in that photo?"
Russ Walden sucked in a breath, then squinted his eyes as he looked at it.

"Do you see that, sir?"

"I guess that is what I am seeing, yes."

"And can you show me where that item is referenced or catalogued as part of *your* crime scene, Captain?"

"I don't recall seeing anything about it in my report, or any other report."

"What was in that briefcase, Captain?"

"I cannot say at the moment."

"You cannot say what was in a briefcase on *your* crime scene, Captain? How about People's Exhibit 32. Doesn't it appear that the briefcase is gone?"

Russ Walden paused, drew in a breath, and squinted his eyes again. "I cannot see it."

"Where did it go, Captain?"

"I don't know."

"You don't know what happened to a briefcase on *your* crime scene?"

"I just can't say at this time."

"If you were given some time might you be able to gather some information about that briefcase?"

"I don't know."

"Really?"

Rex lowered his voice.

"What about those beer bottles on that nightstand just above the briefcase?"

"What about them?"

"For starters, were they fingerprinted?"

"I don't think so."

"Why not?"

"It seems like an oversight."

"What might you have been able to determine if you did fingerprint them?"

"What do you mean?"

"Why do you fingerprint a crime scene, Captain?"

Russ Walden went silent. He looked up before he spoke.

"Would you repeat the question, please?"

"Why do you fingerprint a crime scene, Captain?"

"To find evidence of who might have been there at any given time."

"So, once again, Captain, you did not bother to try to find whether people other than who you thought had killed Mr. Michaelson had been on *your* crime scene, and what they may have done?"

"I don't like the way you phrased that question, counselor."

Rex paused, his face a blank. Then, while looking at the jury he said:

"Your Honor, may I ask that the Court instruct the witness?"

"You may. Captain Walden, you know better than to try to tell counsel how to inquire of you. Any objections are to come from Mr. Turner, and I did not hear any. So, sir, please answer the questions posed to you, and do not attempt to direct this process again. Do you understand?"

"Yes."

"Yes, what?"

"Yes, your Honor."

There was a tense silence in the courtroom.

"Back to those bottles on *your* crime scene, had they been fingerprinted it might tell you who touched them. True?"

"Maybe."

"Maybe? If there were not prints, what might that have told you?"

Russ Walden did not answer, but glared at Rex, his face red, eyes shining hot.

"Wouldn't that tell you someone may have attempted to destroy evidence, Captain? And if you did find prints, might that tell you who had handled the bottles, sir? Basic stuff isn't it?"

"Objection. Argumentative and compound."

"Sustained."

"If either of the Defendant's fingerprints were found at the crime scene would have been significant, true?"

"I suppose."

"And were cigarette butts in the ashtray sampled for DNA?"

"No."

"What might you have been able to find had they been examined?"

"You tell me, counselor."

"Oh, you are going to be glib?" Rex raised his voice. "How about who smoked them? How about whether there was anyone in that home that was not accounted for? That kind of thing, Captain?"

"No need."

"And would that be the same about DNA testing for the bottles?"

"Yes."

"What about testing those beer bottles for Rohypnol, roofies?"

"No need."

"But you heard the testimony by Dr. Chang, didn't you?"

"Yes."

"And you have known since her toxicology report that Steve Michaelson was drugged the night that he was murdered, true?"

"I knew."

"Yet you now tell the jury that there was no need to examine those bottles?"

"I didn't know at the time."

"Well isn't that exactly why you examine everything on *your* crime scene, Captain?"

Again, the courtroom was silent. Russ Walden was visibly shaken. He was red and hot looking. He drew in a breath and said: "Sometimes we don't need to do that."

"Can you direct us to that part of your procedures manual where is says 'sometimes you don't need to do that,' Captain?"

"Objection."

"Grounds, counsel?"

Rick Turner responded: "Argumentative."

"Overruled. You can answer, Captain."

"It's an internal thing," offered Walden.

"What does that mean?"

"That sometimes the case agent can step out of procedure if he thinks standards can be followed later."

"What?!"

Rex shouted the question, but then spoke softly.

"Are you telling the jury that you have the option not to follow standard investigative procedures?"

"No."

"Were there any non-law enforcement persons on *your* crime scene?"

"Can you be more specific?"

"Was that unclear? Let me rephrase. Was there anyone on *your* crime scene who was not accounted for in the incident reports?"

"No. Everyone was covered."

"You heard me ask Ms. Porter about Sam Ellifson. You know him, don't you?"

"No, I do not know him."

"Do you know who he was?"

"I keyed in on the name when you first mentioned it, but I'm not certain I can give you more than that."

"Was there any vehicle on *your* crime scene that was not a law enforcement vehicle?"

He glared at Rex before he answered. Although only seconds passed, it seemed longer. "Not on *my* crime scene," he said with dripping sarcasm, but the anger exuding from him was not masked by the attempt at derision.

"There was no vehicle belonging to Steve Michaelson?"

"Negative."

"Did you discuss with Miss Rankin whether she brought him home the night before he was killed?"

"We had a couple of conversations about it, yes."

"Captain, I am showing you People's Exhibit 26. Mr. Logan has put it on the screen. You have previously identified it as depicting the area where you believe that the pick-up truck owned by Mr. West was driven by him to the Porter residence, but it was not shown to the jury. Is that correct?"

"Correct."

"Is that the only photograph you took of this particular scene?"

"I think so."

"And we can see that the area is almost completely in the dark, except for a very small part of the corner of the house. Correct?"

"Correct."

"So really all that we can see is the yellow of the black and yellow evidence tape, correct?"

"Correct."

"I guess that is why the yellow, eh?"

"Yes."

Rex paused for a few seconds.

"Why no other photos with the little cones, showing where the specific tire tracks are located?"

"I thought I had enough."

"Enough photos of that area? Enough with that one?"

"Yes."

"From what I have been able to determine, this is the only part of the crime scene where the defense did not get at least three photos of the area depicted. Is that your understanding, too?"

"I don't know. I would have to look at my report."

"Would that refresh your recollection?"

"Probably."

"Your Honor, I have no objection to Captain Walden refreshing his recollection by way of his report."

"You may, Captain."

He didn't even look at his report book in the murder book, as it was called by law enforcement.

"I recall now that it was a tough spot to get a good shot, so I only took one. You are correct, counselor."

Rex looked at the jury when he asked:

"So, for the record, you only took this one photo of the area where you claim you determined that Mr. West's pick-up truck had been parked following the murder of Steve Michaelson?

"Yes."

"And that was because it was a difficult place to get a good photograph?"

"Yes."

"Because it was so dark?"

"Yes."

Rex slowly waked to his side of the counsel table and Eddie handed him an 8 x 10 photo. He stopped at Rick Turner's side of the table and offered it to him. He glanced at it and waived Rex away. It was an abrupt and rude gesture, with almost a grimace on his face.

"For the record, your Honor, I have shown what is marked as Defense Exhibit C to Mr. Turner." At that moment Eddie put Exhibit C on the screen.

"The record shall so reflect."

"Captain, would you please look at what has been marked as Defense Exhibit C?" He handed the photo the Russ Walden. As he had done with Mary Jane Rankin, Rex moved to the right and back a bit so that the Captain would have to look at him, and the jury would see his face.

"Does this appear to be an enlargement of Exhibit 26?"

Russ Walden's hands were steady as he held Exhibit C, taking time as he examined it.

"It appears to be."

"It is the same photograph as 26, except larger, correct?"

"Yes."

"Thank you. Would you please focus on what appears to be a red dot in the lower right-hand quarter of that photograph? Then, would you please tell the jury whether there is a shiny black pick-up truck parked inside the evidence tape?"

Russ Walden jerked his head around and glared at Rex. The jury was looking at him, and then at the photo on the screen. There were sounds uttered by jurors, even the public, and one "oh, my God," came from the jury box.

Russ Walden hung his head.

"Captain?"

There was utter stillness in the courtroom until he quietly said: "Yes."

"Did you say YES Captain?" Rex shouted the yes. Rex looked at the jury, waiting; he stood before them. They were looking at each other.

"Captain, how do you explain this?"

He did not speak and did not look up.

Rex waited for a full minute.

"Captain?"

He did not answer.

Rex waited again, that time even longer. He was looking over each of the jurors faces.

"Your Honor, will you please instruct the witness to answer the question?"

"Captain, please answer the question."

"It…uh, it wasn't there."

"That's your answer? It wasn't there? This is your photo of *your* crime scene, Captain. Mr. Logan, would you please show the jury Exhibit 26 again?"

"It's on," said Eddie, and all the jurors looked at the screen.

"Captain, looking at People's Exhibit 26, and focusing on that red dot in the lower right-hand corner, we can all see that a truck is there, it just wasn't clearly visible in that small photograph, true Captain."

Russ Walden did not respond.

"Who owns that vehicle, Captain?"

"I don't know."

"Really, well we can all see the license plate in Defense Exhibit C." Rex looked at Eddie, and he put Exhibit C back on the screen. And it was clearly visible.

"I am now showing you Defense Exhibit D, Captain. Do you recognize this document?"

"I've never seen that before."

"Does that appear to be a DMV printout showing that the vehicle bearing that license number is owned by Samuel James Ellifson?"

"Objection, hearsay."

"Sustained."

"We had that license plate run, Captain, and I'll bet you're not surprised to learn that the truck is owned by none other than Samuel James Ellifson. You did know that, didn't you, Captain?"

His Honor intervened.

"This might be a good time to take a recess."

Rex replied angrily: "I'm not through with him yet. We can wait."

"Very well," said his Honor.

"Please tell the jury how did Samuel James Ellifson's shiny black pick-up truck end up inside the evidence tape facing Mary Jane Rankin's house?"

"I don't know."

"You must have seen it, Captain. It was inside the evidence tape."

Russ Walden did not answer.

"Do you remember who Sam Ellifson is now, Captain?"

"I have a vague recollection."

"His truck is on *your* crime scene, and you have a vague recollection of him?"

"I just cannot place him right now, counselor."

"You do know, of course, that he was recently found with a bullet through his head and his brains splattered all over the interior of that pick-up truck, don't you, Captain?"

"I heard about it."

"It was in all of the papers, wasn't it?"

"I don't read all of the papers."

"You know that he was the founder of a very violent and notorious prison gang called the Point Men, don't you Captain?"

"I heard."

"And that the Point Men are all ex-military men. True."

"I might have heard that."

"Did his gang have anything to do with the attempted murder of Eddie Logan, Captain?"

There was a murmuring throughout the courtroom, and in the jury box. The sound grew loud, but Rita Alcazar said nothing. Russ Walden responded.

"That case is still under investigation."

"Sir, I am showing you what has been marked as Defense Exhibit E. Would you tell the jury whether you recognize either of those people?"

Eddie showed a copy up on the screen.

"We all know Miss Porter. That might be Ellifson."

"Might be?" Rex whispered to the jury.

Then with his voice just above a whisper, he said:

"You know very well who that man is Captain."

Judge Dorsemann intervened.

"This seems like a good time to recess. Ladies and gentlemen be back in the hallway in fifteen minutes.

"Gentlemen, do we have anything to discuss?"

"No, your Honor," said Rex.

"No, your Honor," said Mark.

"No, your Honor," said Rick Turner.

Eddie and Rex went into the hallway and hurried to the men's room on the fourth floor. When they were finished there, Eddie said:

"This is perfect. Go with the robbery."

"That's where I am heading."

"Do you think our judge is going to help him?"

"No."

"Neither do I."

84.

WHEN THEY RETURNED TO THE HALLWAY in front of the courtroom, Melina Garza was standing next to Doug. Rex walked to her and stopped, then reached for her and hugged her. He drew in a deep breath. He said: "I am so happy to see you, Melina. Can you stay a while?"

"Yes. I've been here, but you've been busy. Don't worry about me. Do what you have to do." She smiled and hugged him again. Rex gazed off into the distance while he held her, then he and Eddie went back into the courtroom. Rex could still smell her luscious scent on him. He smiled to himself. Her energy was within him.

Rick Turner and Russ Walden were huddled together in front of the witness stand, whispering to each other.

Billy and Erich Trotter were brought back in by Deputy Crownes.

Billy sat and tugged on Rex's coat. Rex leaned in toward him.

"My God, Rex," was all Billy said. He smiled.

Once the jury was seated, Judge Dorsemann came back out and took the Bench and made a record of their presence, then gave Rex the green light.

"Captain, I believe we left off with Defense Exhibit E. You said you thought that the man in the photograph might be Samuel Ellifson. Did you have a chance to think about it on our break?"

"It's him."

"Do you realize that Miss Porter was lying when she told the jury that she did not know him?"

"Maybe he was using a different name."

There were conversations and grumblings in the courtroom.

Rex paused before continuing, letting the noise die on its own. Rita Alcazar had made few efforts to contain the crowd. It hadn't been necessary.

"Captain isn't it true that since Mr. Ellifson's recent and gruesome death, Miss Porter has spent a good deal of time with you?"

"Define good deal."

"Like every day since she has been in your protective custody, going to lunch and staying at an apartment the Sheriff's Department uses for witness protection. True?"

"Where did you get that information?"

"Sir, you know how this works. I get to ask the questions. Are you keeping her in an apartment, and seeing her daily?"

Rick Turner stood and stated: "Objection. Your Honor this is confidential information protected by the Evidence Code."

"Counsel, please approach."

Once there, and ready to proceed, his Honor asked:

"Mr. Turner, what are you talking about?"

"Your Honor, this woman is a protected witness, and her whereabouts and the fact of her protected status are governed by the Evidence Code."

"Mr. McKinley?"

"What sections of the Evidence Code protect this information? I am not asking where she is being kept, but only if so, and whether the good Captain is the one doing the keeping."

"Mr. McKinley are you implying that Captain Walden is having an inappropriate affair with this woman?"

"No, your Honor, but I will not disclose my intended cross-examination. However, if Mr. Turner was paying attention to what was happening with his case, and with this witness, he might know that what I intend to ask is perfectly legitimate impeachment."

"I am going to give you some latitude, counsel, particularly in light of what has happened this morning. Overruled, Mr. Turner. Gentlemen, please take your seats."

They all returned to the counsel table, but Rex did not sit.

"Overruled. Mr. McKinley proceed."

"Thank you, your Honor," said Rex as he moved toward the jury again.

"Captain, can you see the date on that photograph, Defense Exhibit E?"

He looked at the photo again squinting his eyes again.

"Yes."

"And that date is just a week before the death of Mr. Ellifson, true."

"It appears to be."

"So, Miss Porter, whom you have been protecting and keeping in an apartment as a protected witness was dining with the leader of a very violent prison gang who is suspected of attempting to assassinate Eddie Logan, and she was under your protection at that time?"

"Objection, compound."

"Sustained."

"Captain, did you know that Miss Porter was seeing Mr. Ellifson?"

"I don't think so."

"Can you be more vague?"

The jury laughed, all of them except Number 8.

"Counsel."

"Sorry, your Honor. May I have a moment?"

"Of course."

Rex walked to the counsel table and whispered to Eddie.

"What has happened with Number 8?"

"I'm on it," Eddie whispered and left the counsel table, moving toward the back of the courtroom.

"Captain are you aware that Steve Michaelson's family owned Triple A Check Cashing and Loans here in Danbrier?"

"Objection. Irrelevant."

"Mr. McKinley?"

"I promise to connect it, your Honor."

"I will allow it subject to a renewed objection and a motion to strike."

"Sir?"

"Yes, of course I knew it."

"And you also know that the manager of the business reported a theft of at least fifty thousand dollars in cash the same morning that you investigated the murder of Steve Michaelson, true?"

"I recall that."

"Captain isn't it true that the briefcase we all saw on *your* crime scene was full of the cash stolen from the Michaelson family business?"

"I told you I don't know anything about that briefcase."

Rex lowered his voice, speaking only to the jury:

"That's right, I forgot. You don't know about an item of property on *your* crime scene."

Rick Turner bellowed: "Objection. Argumentative. Lacks foundation. Calls for speculation. Move to strike."

"Sustained on all grounds. That testimony is stricken."

Judge Dorsemann said: "Counsel, we are going to have a discussion in Chambers, now. Ladies and gentlemen of the jury, we will only be a few minutes. Please feel free to stand and stretch." With that, he left the Bench and Rex followed Mark, who followed Rick Turner to the Judge's Chambers.

"Gentlemen, I am coming down with the flu. I need to call it a day. I am deeply disturbed by what has happened in this case. I will be back here first thing in the morning. That is all. No comments requested or accepted."

Back on the record, his Honor announced that they would recess until the next day. He did not say why.

They all stood while the jury left.

When they had gone, his Honor apologized and told them to be ready to go in the morning.

"How much longer with the Captain, Mr. McKinley?"

"I don't know, your Honor."

"Very well. Mr. Turner have your next witness on deck. Understood?"

"Yes, your honor," Rick Turner replied.

Rex and Eddie waited for Rick Turner to stack his exhibits. Eddie took the defense exhibits to the clerk. Each exhibit had to be accounted for before they left the courtroom. When Karin Kornder gave the okay, Rex and Eddie waited for the prosecution team to leave. They would have to walk into the hallway, past the media and the Blood Oath members. Rex was certain Carey Sorenson would be out there.

Rex had a brief discussion with Mark. He suggested that he have his 1118.1 motion ready. He replied that he already had it done, which made Rex curious.

"Are you aware of something I am not, Mark?"

He smiled but did not answer, other than to say: "See you tomorrow, Rex."

Turner and Walden left the courtroom.

Rex and Eddie followed behind them, at a safe distance.

Once in the hallway, the members of the media could not restrain themselves, and attacked Rick Turner and Russ Walden. There were some less than complimentary remarks within the questions.

When Turner and Walden refused to comment, they turned to Rex, and one held the microphone toward Rex and asked:

"Is it over, Rex?"

"No, this trial is far from over. I know you have a job to do, but please be careful with your reporting. We have a trial in progress. Thank you."

He was immediately surrounded by Club members as they walked out of the courthouse. Melina was nowhere in sight. Rex wanted to see her again.

85.

"LET'S HAVE A CONFERENCE AT THE HOUSE, gentlemen. I have something to discuss with all of you," Rex suggested.

When they arrived and parked, they all went straight to the study. Gail was there working. She got up and greeted them all before she excused herself. Rex followed her into the kitchen. He told her that her work day was over. He needed to deal with business related to something outside the trial, and she was better off going home.

Gail grabbed her purse. She went into the study first, shutting down her computer. She smiled at the guys and said good day. Rex returned to his study after walking Gail to the front of the house. He told her how much he appreciated her. She turned and hugged him without another word.

Rex returned to the study, and once they were all seated, and the door closed, Eddie turned on a device that Tommy left behind, which Rex had been told was a signal jammer. Rex began:

"Okay, this is going very well. But it's not over. They'll bring in the rat next. I'm not too worried about him."

"Then what are you worried about, Rex?" Doug inquired.

"Erich Trotter."

"Ahhhh," Doug murmured.

"What is his connection to the Point Men?"

"We were sure you would figure that out in due time." Doug said.

"I'm guessing he has a relative in that gang. I'm also guessing that he set up Billy for the kill, and he's going to walk."

"He'll walk, but not before he completes his obligation to this trial." Doug looked like a giant made of roughly hewn stone.

"This Erich Trotter thing: I don't like it, Doug."

They all nodded quietly. Doug offered an intel briefing about the real Erich Trotter. The truth was disturbing.

They ate a quiet and peaceful lunch. Rex was thinking of Melina. He wanted to see her. He couldn't stay in the house the rest of the day; he didn't want to work. He wanted to see the woman with whom he wanted to share love—real sweet to the core love.

They finished their meal, and Rex stood to excuse himself to get his phone and call Melina when she walked in through the kitchen doorway.

He rose to greet her, then asked that the others excuse him. He walked Melina into the living room and sat with her.

"I was thinking about you just before you walked in the doorway."

"What were you thinking about?" She said it with a smile and a look that tore away any façade he might have tried to maintain.

"The truth?"

"Nothing but."

"I want to make love with you, Melina. It's a bit confusing, since I've been so screwed up, but you have taken me from it all, and I want to share my feelings with you. When I saw you at the courthouse today I realized that I love you."

She smiled and snuggled him.

"Me too." She said. "But, I'd like to wait until my dad is gone." She giggled, and Rex joined her. He grabbed her and began tickling her. She shrieked with joy and laughter. They were beside themselves when they heard motorcycles starting. They looked at each other, and Rex stood holding out his hand to her. She took his hand, and they found their way to his bedroom. He closed the door and drew her to him.

As he held her by her waist, he bent to kiss her. She put her hands on his cheeks and pulled his face to hers. Their lips met, and the heat of their passion was intense and welcome. Their tongues met, and the fire began. There was nothing else in the world but the volcanic heat and eruption soon to come as they began stripping their clothes off, then falling onto the bed.

They stayed together, making love, talking, sharing secrets, and their dreams of the future. When late evening arrived, Melina told Rex she had to leave. She promised to return and make him breakfast the last day of trial. He begged her to stay. She kissed him again, then renewed her promise. She moved toward the door, and she was gone.

He slept deeply without dreams, only to wake in the morning with a smile and energy he had never felt. He also had an overpowering feeling. He was in love. What a day to be in love.

He was walking into a war zone, facing a giant of a man, who with little more than his personal power and some very crafty but deceitful testimony had been able to swoon the jury. But the giant had fallen, and Rex wanted to keep him down. As he prepared himself for the day he reflected that Russ Walden would be his to finish, a grand finale, but it could not be personal.

He was ready for breakfast when Doug, Ron and Eddie arrived. They ate quietly while Rex waited for Doug to inquire about him and Melina. But he never did.

They made their way to the courthouse afterward, Blood Oath leading the way.

86.

"WE ARE BACK ON THE RECORD, all of the jurors are present, all of the parties and counsel. The witness, Captain Walden is back on the stand. Captain, I remind you that you are still under oath, sir."

"Yes, your Honor."

"Mr. Turner, your objection is overruled."

"Mr. McKinley, you may proceed."

"Thank you, your Honor.

"Captain, have you had some time to think about how Mr. Ellifson's shiny black pick-up got inside the evidence tape that you placed around it?"

"No."

"You didn't think about it?"

"No."

"And the relationship between Miss Porter and Mr. Ellifson, did you have some time to think about that?"

"No."

"You didn't think about it?"

"No."

"And the missing briefcase, have you had some time to try to figure out what happened to it?"

"No."

"Are you telling the jury, sir, that you still cannot explain what happened to that briefcase?"

"I have nothing to add, *counselor*." The way he spoke was like a hissing snake. Rex tried not to recoil, but his skin was crawling. He looked at the jury as he moved away from the Captain.

"Is there any of your previous testimony that you want to change, Captain?"

"No."

"Is everything you told the jury the truth?"

"Absolutely."

"So help you God?"

"Objection!"

"Overruled, counsel. That is the way he swore to tell the truth. He offered what is no longer required."

"You can answer, Captain," Rex said softly.

"Yes, so help me God."

Rex asked: "May I have a moment, your Honor?"

"You may."

Rex signaled Eddie to come over by looking at him with a nod. He was back in the gallery, sitting in the front row.

"Have you got some info on Number 8?"

"Yep. Let this lying bastard go and ask for a chambers conference. Ask that I be permitted to join."

"Cool."

Rex walked back over to the jury, and looking only at Number 8, he said: "Your honor, I have nothing further of this witness."

Still looking at Number 8, Rex said:

"However, your Honor, something has come up and I think it urgent enough to ask for a conference in Chambers."

"Very well, counsel. Ladies and gentlemen, please wait outside until you are brought back in. Thank you."

His Honor stood and stepped down and went into Chambers.

They waited for the courtroom to clear, and Rex gave the nod to Eddie to wait.

They all went to the Judge's Chambers door, and Rick Turner knocked. They walked in, but Rex stood closest to the door.

"Your Honor, I need Mr. Logan to be part of this."

"Bring him in."

When Eddie came in Judge Dorsemann walked around his desk and shook his hand.

"It's good to see you, Eddie."

"Same here, Greg."

"So, this is your request, Mr. McKinley. What's up?"

"Eddie?"

"Your Honor, I have been noticing some rather drastic changes in juror Number 8, his demeanor. So, being me, I decided to ask the court reporter to transcribe his voir dire so I could review the questions posed to him. He denied knowing anyone in law enforcement. He denied having any connection to law enforcement. So, I took a closer look yesterday. It seems that Number 8 was one of the main fundraisers for our former Sheriff in his last campaign. His behavior during Rex's cross of the Captain seemed to go from attentive to angry. I think it's grounds to inquire, your Honor."

"I cannot believe all the deceit and intrigue Mr. Turner. Did you know about this?"

"Of course not!" Although seemingly vehement, Rick Turner had turned red in the face, and his body language was tense..

Judge Dorsemann got on the phone and told Karin to tell Rita to bring juror Number 8 into Chambers; the court reporter, too.

In a few minutes there was a knock on the door. Rita Alcazar stepped in and reported:

"Your Honor, some of the jurors said they saw him leave the building. He is nowhere in sight. I got his cell number from Karin and tried calling him. He's not answering."

"Thank you, Rita. You are excused. Nothing is to be said about this to anyone."

"Yes, your Honor," said Rita as she left.

"Well, temporarily, that problem is solved. I am going to ask that the Danbrier City Police Department investigate this further and report to me. If I find any truth in what Mr. Logan reported, which I expect I will knowing Mr. Logan as I do, I am going to send that information to the Grand Jury. I would say that Number 8 has some explaining to do, but I will leave that up to the investigators."

Judge Dorsemann drew in a deep breath, releasing it with a sigh.

"Alright, let's go out and see if he shows. If not, we will replace him and continue with this trial. If he is present, we will recess again and make an inquiry."

"Mr. Turner, who is going to be your next witness?"

"Mr. Maddux, your Honor."

"Okay, let's get to it."

87.

THEY WERE BACK ON THE RECORD, and Number 8 was absent. Judge Dorsemann inquired whether any of the jurors knew what happened to him. No one had any information. Judge Dorsemann seated Alternate Number 1 as the new Number 8. He then gave the admonishment that there was to be no speculation about the former Number 8, and that they would proceed as though nothing had changed, and then said:

"Mr. Turner, please call your next witness."

"People call Ronald Paul Maddux."

The door behind the Bench was opened, and an obese man strutted in, wearing a t-shirt with short sleeves that barely fit his heavily tattooed arms. His head was bald and shiny. His eyes were small and close together, and his brow was furrowed. He looked around as he approached the witness stand. He glared at the jury. He looked at the counsel table and found Billy. He glared at him, and then smiled a crooked smile, with yellowed teeth showing as though he were ready to bite.

He stood and swore to tell the truth, then sat and stated his name and spelled it. He leaned forward in his seat and put his very large arms on the desk of the witness stand, but he did not look at the audience. He kept his gaze on Rick Turner.

"Mr. Turner, you may proceed."

Rick Turner stood, and began:

"Mr. Maddux, do you know Billy West?"

"Yeah, I know him. That guy over there; the skinny one with the blond hair."

"How do you know him?"

"I was in jail with him out at the Basin."

"How long were you in jail with him?"

"A couple of days."

"Did you speak with him about his case?"

"Yeah, he wouldn't stop yappin' about it."

"Please explain."

"Well, 'soon as I got in there with him he started tryin' to play badass with me. He was tellin' me all about this guy he just wasted."

"Did you respond?"

"Sure. I told him he ought not talk about his case. Somebody might be lisnin' and rat him out."

"What did he tell you?"

"He said this big guy was always messin' with him. He said the guy was bangin' his chick, and he couldn't take it no more, so he went over there and popped him in the head, and his homie stuck him a coupla times."

"He said it like that?"

"Yeah, just like that."

"What did you think he meant?"

"I knew what he meant. I asked him about the gun. He told me he had a six shooter, a thirty-eight. He said he capped him in the forehead. Blew his brains out, but the guy was still breathin', so his friend stabbed him…in the neck. Yeah, he said the neck."

"Did he tell you anything else?"

"Yeah, he said that they went next door and drank some beers and laughed about it. Then they hid out in the desert where they stashed the gun and the knife. Then some pigs…I mean cops caught 'em."

"Did he tell you anything else?"

"Nah, that was about it. He wasn't real thrilled with me tellin' him to shut up. I got tired of it, ya know?"

"Nothing further."

"Mr. McKinley?"

Rex stood slowly and began walking toward the jury. He faced them, and began: "Mr. Maddux isn't it true that you are a multiple-times convicted felon?"

Rick Turner turned red in the face and kept his gaze on the counsel table.

"Yeah, I got some bad history."

"Please, tell the jury how many felonies you have in your bad history."

"It might be four."

"How about six?"

"Could be."

"Well it is, and you know it, unless you have forgotten some of your felony convictions. For example, your first serious felony conviction was for robbery in 1987. You robbed an older gentleman of his wallet by threatening to beat him to death. I'm sure you remember that one."

"I didn't do that, I just pled out to get it over with." Maddux had become red-faced, his eyes hot and squinted, glaring at Rex.

"And your second serious felony, you were convicted of burglary of a residential dwelling. You broke into a family residence and stole some guns. You remember that one, don't you? That one resulted in your first trip to prison."

"I didn't really do that one. I took the beef for a friend." He seemed to try to laugh, but instead grunted.

The jury was not looking at Maddux; only at Rex as he stood before them.

"And your third conviction was for grand theft auto. I think today it would be called carjacking. You pulled a young man out of his car, slugged him in the face, and stole his car. You went back to prison for that one. Remember?"

"That guy owed me money. That's why I took his car." Maddux spoke as though angry; his voice lowered, his jaw clenched.

"And your fourth one was for possession of methamphetamine for sale, and felon in possession of a firearm. You do remember that one, don't you?"'

"I was havin' problems with drugs those days." He gestured with his hand in a dismissive fashion, palms up, arms moving as though he were throwing something over his shoulders.

"But, for some reason, you got probation in that case, with no further jail time. Would you please tell the jury why you didn't go to prison on that one?"

"It wasn't that biguva deal."

"No? A felon selling drugs while armed with a firearm. No big deal, eh?"

"They cut me some slack." He raised his voice.

"Is that when you started informing on people?"

"I ain't no rat!" He growled. He flexed his arms and started sweating. His eyes turned red and beady.

"Well, you said that you told Mr. West that he shouldn't talk about his case, because, and I quote 'somebody might be listening and rat him out.' That's what you are doing, right? You're ratting him out, right? You're a rat, aren't you?"

"Hey, mister, I just said I ain't no rat. You got that?"

"No, I don't. Maybe you can explain to the jury exactly what you are doing then?"

"Just doin' my duty."

"Oh, the good citizen thing, right?"

"Yeah. Is there some kinda problem with that?"

"Well, let's see, your fifth conviction was for another robbery. You robbed and beat an elderly woman. You pled guilty, but you didn't go to prison on that one, either. Remember?"

"That was a bullshit case, man. I didn't do none of that."

"But you still pled guilty?"

"Hey, you know how it goes when they got a hold on you."

"No, I don't. Care to tell us?"

Rex paused, but Maddux offered nothing.

"And your sixth felony conviction was for drugs again, and syringes, and another gun. Remember that case?"

"Hey, like I said, I've had a drug problem."

"But you didn't go to jail for that one, either. How many people have you ratted out to stay out of jail?"

"Man, I'm tellin' you for the last time, I ain't no rat."

"Right, just a good citizen."

"That's right. That guy's a killer." He pointed at Billy.

Surprisingly, Billy was looking back at him with a cool stare, maybe even a tone of disgust.

"So, you are just a good citizen with six felony convictions and two prior prison terms. You are a beater of old and helpless women, and you are a drug addict who will tell on anyone to beat a rap."

"Mister, you're crossin' the line with me."'

"Well, don't let me stop you from doing something about it."

Rex moved quickly toward him. When he got within a foot of the witness stand, he held his stare until Maddux looked down.

Rex turned and whispered to the jury:

"I didn't think so."

"Mr. Maddux, what were you in jail for when you met Mr. West?"

"Another bullshit case."

"Weren't you living with a woman and her child?"

"Yeah, I was stayin' with that bitch."

"And you slugged her in the face and yanked her baby out of her arms and threatened to, and I quote her words "break its fuckin' neck" if she didn't give you some money so you could go buy some drugs. True?"

"Where'd you come up with that?"

"That's what she reported, and that was why you were in jail, true?"

"She might've said it, but it was bullshit."

"And were you prosecuted for those felonies?"

"Man, I beat that beef."

"No one made you any promises that if you testified against Mr. West that you would have those charges dismissed?"

"I told you man, I ain't no rat."

"I'm sure we can all see that is exactly what you are, Mr. Maddux. You are the worst kind. You just rat on someone, and you go free. What is that saying, 'give up three, and go free?'"

He didn't answer, and Rick Turner remained silent.

Rex was standing in front of the jury and speaking only to them.

"Mr. Maddux, you are a robber, a thief, a burglar, a drug addict, a beater of women, and a jail house snitch! Why should anyone believe you?"

Maddux did not respond.

"There is no reason, is there Mr. Maddux? The truth is you are a very bad man, aren't you? Why should this jury believe a word you say?"

There was a long pause. Maddox did not answer.

Rex lowered his voice as he spoke directly to the jury.

"I guess we have the truth now, don't we?"

"Nothing further, your Honor."

"Mr. Mundo?"

"No questions, your Honor."

"Mr. Turner, any re-direct?"

"No, your Honor."

"May this witness be excused?"

"Yes, your Honor," Rick said rather quickly. Both Rex and Mark agreed.

Maddox stepped down without looking at anyone. He walked toward the back of the courtroom with Rita Alcazar behind him. He went through the doorway and was gone from sight. There was a collective sigh of relief in the courtroom, except from Blood Oath members. They remained still, faces showing nothing.

88.

"People call Highway Patrol Officer Dale Rider."

Rex knew Dale. He had been a couple of years ahead of him in school. He was always a cool guy. When he became a Highway Patrol Officer, he remained unaffected by his position of authority. He still had a hot rod that he showed in Berdoo at the Route 66 Car Show.

He was wearing his Highway Patrol uniform, and he looked good. He seemed in relatively good shape. His hair was still thick and curly and cut short. He was wearing short sleeves, and his arms looked muscular. He had on his Sam Brown belt, with a separate holster for his firearm, which looked to be a Smith & Wesson .40 caliber. He had handcuffs; mace or pepper spray; a hand-held radio; two ammo clips; and a clip-on microphone across his shoulder; the works. His leather creaked as he walked, and his uniform and leather were impeccably maintained.

He was walked to the witness and stood by Rita Alcazar. He knew the routine, and stepped up, faced the Clerk and raised his right hand. He said: "I do" at the appropriate time. He sat when instructed, then stated his name and spelled it.

He turned in his seat and faced the jury. He smiled at them and offered a hello. They were very happy to see him as was evident by their responsive greetings.

"Mr. Turner, you may proceed."

"Thank you, your Honor. Officer Rider, you are a California Highway Patrol Officer, correct?"

"Well, I'd better be wearing this uniform."

Everyone laughed with him. He smiled at the jury. He was in control.

"Were you on duty on August 27th this year?"

"I was; me and my partner, Jim Fairfield."

"Did you happen to make an arrest that day?"

"We did. Two men. There was a BOLO…" he looked at the jury, and explained:

"That means be on the lookout…for an older black pick-up truck with two men. They were wanted for a homicide."

"How was it you came about arresting them?"

"My partner spotted the truck. We lit 'em up—turned on our emergency lights—and the driver pulled to the side of the road. They complied with our demands, and we arrested them."

"Do you see those two men in this courtroom?"

He looked straight at Billy, and said:

"The fellow with the blond hair was driving. I know Mr. McKinley there, and I'm pretty sure he wasn't in that truck."

Everyone laughed again, Rex included.

"I don't see the other fellow. He was a big guy with a full head of hair and a full beard, kind of scraggly looking, like he had been living in the wilds for a very long time."

"May I approach the witness, your Honor?" Rick Turner asked.

"You may," said his Honor.

"Officer Rider, I am showing you what has been marked as People's Exhibit 127. Do you recognize that photo?"

While Rick Turner was walking toward the witness, Russ Walden had become useful, and was showing the photo on the screen. It was the booking photo of Erich Trotter. The photo showed a man with so much hair and beard all you could see were his eyes. He was squinting in the direct photo, so there was little that could be seen of his eyes.

His face was full of beard, and it was shooting out in all directions. He was very unkempt. No one had seen the man with Billy, not the one described in that manner—literally a wild man.

Dale Rider looked at the photo, and testified:

"That looks like the man alright. Like I said, and no offense intended, but he looked like he had been living in the wilds. But, no, that man is not in this courtroom."

A low grumbling noise passed through the courtroom.

Rick Turner sighed, then asked:

"Did you and your partner search the truck?"

"First, we patted them down, then cuffed the suspects, and put them in the back seat of our unit until the Sheriff's people arrived. While waiting, we decided to clear the truck for weapons."

"Did you find any weapons?"

"No, we did not."

"Did you find anything you considered might be of evidentiary value?"

"Well, in the bed of the truck, in plain sight, we saw what looked like a couple of black t-shirts. I put on gloves and retrieved them. They were in fact black t-shirts. One had what appeared to be dried blood on it. It was a size 2X. I bagged it. The other was a size medium, and it appeared to have some dried blood on it, so I bagged it also."

"What did you do with these items?"

"I held them until the Sheriff's people arrived. After I documented that I had found the items on each of the bags, I handed them over to one of the deputies."

"And what happened after that?"

"We finished our paperwork about the arrest, then went back out and finished our shift."

"Thank you, sir. Nothing further."

"Mr. McKinley?"

"Thank you, your Honor."

Rex stood and started walking toward the jury.

"Officer Rider, it's been a long time. How are you?"

"It has indeed. I am well, sir, and you?"

"I'm doing well, thank you. It is always good to see you."

Dale Rider smiled. "Likewise," he said.

"Officer Rider, on August 27th this year when you stopped the vehicle my client was driving, what was my client wearing?"

"As I recall it, he was wearing a white t-shirt and jeans."

"And there was nothing of evidentiary value in the cab of the truck?"

"No, sir."

"Did you speak with Mr. West?"

"I spoke *to* him, but not with him. I ordered him out the truck, and he complied."

"He did everything you told him?"

"Yes, sir."

"Sir, the t-shirts that you retrieved from the bed of the truck, one was 2X and the other was a medium?"

"Yes, sir."

"And you have no idea how they got there?"

"No, sir, I do not."

"And this stuff that you saw on those shirts, you are speculating what it was, are you not?"

"True."

"Your Honor, I move to strike any reference to blood in Officer Rider's testimony."

"It is stricken."

"Sir, how long had it been since the alleged homicide when you first spotted Mr. West's truck?"

"It was late afternoon of the following day."

"Thank you, Officer Rider. Nothing further, your Honor."

"Mr. Mundo?"

"No questions, your Honor."

"Mr. Turner, any re-direct?"

"No thank you, your Honor."

89.

"Yes, People call Emily Grotto."

Rita Alcazar walked to the back of the courtroom through the doors, and a minute later she returned guiding a woman. Emily Grotto appeared to be in her late forties or early fifties, tall and appropriately dressed for court, wearing a light pant suit with a pink silk blouse under her jacket. Her black hair was pulled into a braided pony tail, her face relaxed. She wore very little makeup, and her features were sharp. Her countenance exposed a certain beauty not measured from physical appearance alone. Her eyes were focused straight ahead as she walked with Rita toward the witness stand.

She was led through the initial phase, and finally sat.

"Mr. Turner, you may proceed."

"Miss Grotto, please tell the jury how you are employed."

"I am a Forensics Examiner, III, with the Danbrier County Sheriff's Department Forensic Sciences Laboratory."

"What does your work entail?"

"I examine items of evidence that have been delivered to the lab for analysis. I have special training in the discovery and examination of DNA."

"Please tell the jury about your education and training."

"Well, I have a bachelor's degree in…"

And she went through her lengthy curriculum vitae, at the end of which Rick Turner continued:

"Ms. Grotto, did you receive a t-shirt from the Sheriff's Department for examination?"

"I did. I examined it as a 'rush job' at your request, Mr. Turner."

"How did that item come to you?"

"We have a process where evidence is logged into the lab by the person delivering it, and the envelope in which it comes has a logging sheet so that there is a chain of evidence showing where the item was discovered, how it was packaged and by whom, and the various stages of possession of the item while it was in the custody of law enforcement."

She continued to explain the process in vivid detail.

"Did you receive some evidence that was logged as being part of this case?"

"I did."

"What was that item?"

"It was a black t-shirt, size 2X."

"What did your log sheet say about the discovery of this item?"

She looked at her notepad, and the sealed envelope sitting before her on the small desk portion of the witness stand.

"It was found by an Officer Rider, CHP, on August 27th this year."

"Just one item?"

"Yes. Only one."

Rex looked at the jury. Some returned his look with what appeared to be confusion.

"Did you do any testing on this shirt?"

Rex intervened: "Your Honor, may we approach?"

"You may, counsel. In fact, let's do this in Chambers."

They followed their little wagon train into Chambers, with Rick Turner going in first, and Mark and Rex waiting for the Reporter. Once inside and they were all seated, his Honor said to Rex:

"It's your request, Mr. McKinley."

"Your Honor took under submission my motion to exclude any testimony about the t-shirts found in the bed of the truck as not being sufficiently tied to the defendants. Now we have a witness who is going to offer testimony about a single t-shirt, size 2X, clearly not the size my client would wear. It is simply irrelevant to him.

"Also, I submit, the prosecution is not going to be able to introduce any evidence from the size medium t-shirt. Apparently, it has gone missing. Therefore, and because we have only one defendant who has been identified as having done or said anything, this 2X t-shirt becomes completely irrelevant."

"Interesting. Mr. Turner?"

"Your Honor, this is the piece of evidence that ties Mr. Trotter to the case. If it doesn't come in, we have no evidence against him."

"Mr. Mundo?"

"Your Honor, I am aware of the results attributed to this shirt. There is not one bit of evidence that ties this shirt to my client. I do believe that the prosecution is going to ask the jury to speculate that because this shirt is a 2X and my client is a larger man, then it must be his. The problem with that thinking is there is no evidence in this case to even suggest that my client was the second man at the Porter residence that night. No one, not even Officer Rider who arrested a second man, has been able to identify my client. I am also aware that there is no DNA evidence on that t-shirt to establish that my client ever wore it."

"Mr. Turner do you have any evidence to connect that shirt to Mr. Trotter?"

"Not exactly."

"If you cannot lay some foundation as to how this connects to either defendant, then I am going to have to sustain the objection. Can you do that, even minimally?"

"Not exactly."

Judge Dorsemann said curtly: "Everyone return to the courtroom, please. I will be out in a few moments."

They filed out of Chambers and returned to their seats. Rick Turner did something Rex hadn't ever seen before. He stopped at the witness stand and spoke to the witness.

His Honor returned to the Bench.

"Ladies and gentlemen, we had a conference in Chambers, and an objection was made to any further testimony of this witness. The Court is going to sustain that objection, and you are therefore to disregard any of the testimony by this witness. Ms. Grotto, you are excused."

"Thank you, your Honor," she said as she got up and walked out of the courtroom. Rex observed that one of the Club members, Vic Riddle, stood and walked to the door and held it open for her. She quietly thanked him, holding her gaze for a moment before she stepped out of the courtroom.

"Mr. Turner please call your next witness."

"People rest."

"Ladies and gentlemen, the prosecution has rested. What this means is that there will be no further evidence offered by the prosecution as part of its case in chief. Therefore, we are going to take our morning recess and lunch break together. The attorneys will probably have a couple of motions to argue before the defense proceeds. So, please be back at 2:00 p.m. I know that is a good deal of free time, so have a good lunch, and we will see you then."

The lawyers and defendants stood for the jury. All Club members stood. Two members were holding open the doors to the hallway.

90.

WHEN THE JURORS WERE OUT OF THE COURTROOM, the gallery was still full. Reporters had come *en masse*.

"Are there any motions?" Judge Dorsemann was looking at Mark, who stood and said:

"Yes, your Honor. I have filed a written motion for directed acquittal pursuant to Penal Code, section 1118.1. The essence of the motion is that the prosecution has been unable to produce even a shred of evidence to establish that my client did anything related to the killing of Steve Michaelson. I don't think that there is any standard by which this Court could find that Mr. Trotter might have done anything related to this crime." Mark looked at his brief and continued: "The standard for the court is: 'if the evidence then before the court is insufficient to sustain a conviction of such offense or offenses on appeal.' That, of course, is a direct quote from the Code. What possible evidence could there be that might establish that Mr. Trotter played any role whatsoever in the killing of Mr. Michaelson? Therefore, I ask this Court to enter a verdict of acquittal."

"Mr. Turner?"

"Well, since the Court has excluded the one piece of evidence that might have tied Mr. Trotter to this crime, I guess I'm left without any ammo."

"Mr. Turner, in Chambers you were asked directly whether you had any evidence to connect Mr. Trotter to that particular shirt. Your words were, and I quote, 'not exactly,' which was all that you said. Might you have something new on that subject?"

"No," he said with a low grumble in his voice. Judge Dorsemann looked at him hard for a moment before he said:

"Then I am compelled to grant the motion. I hereby find that there is insufficient evidence, in fact absolutely no evidence, to sustain a conviction for the offense of murder against Mr. Trotter on appeal, and therefore no cause to give the case to the jury. Mr. Trotter, you have been acquitted. Madam Bailiff, please remove Mr. Trotter from the courtroom and let it be understood that he is ordered to be released forthwith."

"Mr. McKinley, do you have a motion?"

"I do, your Honor. Although there have been two witnesses who have testified against my client, I urge the Court to make a factual finding as to their believability.

"First, Ms. Porter testified that my client drove to her home, parked outside in that place where the evidence tape was supposed to be preserving his tire tracks, and that he and some other man came in and asked for beer, boasted of the murder, got some money, and sped away. Then, of course, we find out what a liar she is, and therefore cannot be believed. We know that the evidence tape was protecting a vehicle, not tire tracks, and that vehicle did not belong to my client. Her testimony about the 911 call should be the final nail in her coffin, so-to-speak.

"Then, we heard Mr. Maddux who claimed that Mr. West confessed, in fact boasted about the killing, even played tough guy with him. Mr. Maddux is a convicted robber, burglar, thief, woman beater, drug addict, and obviously a long-term snitch. How can anyone believe him?

"Finally, the tire tracks that Captain Walden testified belonged to my client's vehicle is obviously untrue. There was another vehicle sitting inside the evidence tape. Thus, and even considering that his claim of identifying the tire tracks by other than acceptable methods, Captain Walden fabricated evidence and offered flat out lies to this Court." Rex turned to face Russ Walden as he spoke those words, but Russ Walden was staring straight ahead—a cold hard look to his features.

"Thus, I submit, your Honor, there is no credible evidence against my client, and I ask that the Court direct an acquittal as to my client. Thank you, Your Honor."

Before he spoke, Judge Dorsemann looked out at the parties, then into the courtroom. He sighed.

"Mr. McKinley, I will agree with you that Miss Porter and Mr. Maddux were impeached. I will agree with you that in my opinion, neither one is a credible person. I would not believe either of them if what they were claiming was true had happened before my very eyes. And the issue of the tire tracks is obvious."

Judge Dorsemann looked at Russ Walden who was still sitting rigid staring straight ahead—a hard man turned bitter.

"That having been said, it is not within the purview of the Court to make such a determination. Were this case to go to the jury, and were the jury to convict Mr. West, the Court of Appeal could find that the testimony of either Miss Porter or Mr. Maddux, or both, must have been believed to find Mr. West guilty, and therefore it is a finding by the trier of fact, the jury, and will not be disturbed on appeal. I do believe that is the standard, and therefore, the Court must deny your motion. This case must go to the jury."

Rex offered: "Thank you, your Honor."

"You are welcome.

"Anything further from anyone?"

"No, thank you, your Honor?"

"Nothing here, your Honor," said Mark.

"Nothing your Honor," said Rick.

"Very well, we will take a recess until after lunch. Mr. McKinley, do you intend to present a defense?"

"Can I let the Court know after lunch, your Honor?"

"Of course. I will see all of you, except Mr. Mundo and Mr. Trotter, after lunch."

91.

THEY WENT TO JOHNNY'S FOR LUNCH. Once seated, Doug initiated the discussion.

"This guy Trotter is getting out any time now. We have a ride available for him, if you think he might be a helpful witness."

Rex didn't think so. He said:

"If Erich Trotter is going to testify, the most that he can do is help the prosecution. We know he's connected to the Point Men, and he got a pass in this trial."

Doug frowned as he responded. "As we discussed, he's connected and if we're foolish enough to fall for their play, then Billy gets convicted by a man who has been acquitted. He can own the kill, and implicate Billy, and nothing can be done about it. If he owns it, Billy goes down." Doug said it with finality.

"Eddie?"

"Doug's right. We can't put him on. He's a wild card. What do we need him for?"

"Ron?"

"The case is over, Rex. There's nothing more to do. There's no evidence, other than the testimony of Cheryl Porter and Maddux. She's a liar, and the jury knows it. The jury hates Maddux. Even Maddux hates Maddux. You were careful and surgical in your dismemberment of him. Let it go."

"Is this a unanimous vote?"

All three men nodded.

"I guess it is a 4-0 vote. I feel good about it. There are no tricks left by Rick Turner. Closing Argument will be tomorrow morning. Judge Dorsemann will dismiss us for the rest of the day. Is there any chance the Sheriff can get to any of the jurors?"

Eddie said: "I think there is enough chicanery for you to ask the Court to sequester this jury. The question is, do you want to take the chance that the jury would resent the implication that you don't trust them. If this jury hangs there will never be a second fair trial in this county. People will be afraid, and the Sheriff will do whatever it takes to make sure you never get another chance like this one."

"That's serious stuff coming from the man who would not die," offered Rex, without a smile. "I'm going to miss having lunch at Johnny D's with everyone."

"Then let's have a barbeque at the Ranch," said Doug.

They laughed and ate and discussed anything but the case.

Back at the courthouse, one of the many reporters asked Rex whether he was going to put on a defense. Rex stopped in front of all of them. He was surrounded by Club members.

"Ladies and gentlemen, you know the rules. I cannot try this case in the media. Please, come in quietly, and you will get the story as it unfolds."

Rex and crew continued into the courthouse. He heard a remark about class act. He hoped it was about him.

92.

THEY ARRIVED OUTSIDE THE COURTROOM where Mark Mundo was waiting. "Mark, what's up?"

"May I speak with you privately?"

Rex directed him to the courtroom, and they went into the attorney room on the right. Rex closed the door, but not all the way, and stood blocking Mark's view of the door.

"What's troubling you, Mark? You did an excellent job. You were the sleeper. None of us knew you, and I was certainly a bit of an asshole with you. So, what's up?"

"Erich Trotter is gone. He was released almost immediately, which is very unusual. I tried to meet with him outside, and apparently he was picked up out back of the jail and driven out through the secured area in back."

"Why did you want to see him, Mark?"

Mark froze. Eddie was speaking as he stepped inside the door, followed by Doug and Ron, who closed the door. The room suddenly shrunk in size.

Rex told him:

"Mark, I've known for a while, and my friends have known all along. You did your job, and it didn't hurt Billy. It's good that Erich is gone. Were you thinking that he might do a turn-around for the prosecution?"

Mark was frozen. He appeared to have stopped breathing. His face was flushed, his hands began to shake, and he was looking down at the table.

"Here's how it's going to work, Mark," said Doug. "You know that I never trusted you. You did a good job, but you were thinking that you could engineer a deal that would free your guy, then send my little brother away forever. I hope they paid you well." Doug had an expression on his face that could easily have caused Mark to have a heart attack.

Mark still could did speak. Eddie said:

"Mark, in case you haven't gotten the picture by now, we've always known about your connection to Ellifson. Nothing is a secret with us. If we don't know, we find out. I took a bullet in the back, remember? I hope you made enough money on this deal to move out of Danbrier 'cause that's your only option at this point. Don't ever show your face here again. Ever!" Eddie raised his voice with the last word.

Ron stepped close to Mark and leaned down. "Mark, you never want to see me again," was all he said. From the look on Ron's face which Mark dared glace at, it was clear that Ron intended to invoke a fear that ran deep. Mark began shaking all over.

They all stood, except Mark. Eddie pulled him to his feet, and Ron patted him down for a wire. He checked his ears, too.

Doug bent down and looked in Mark's eyes for several seconds. Then they left and walked into the courtroom.

93.

RICK TURNER WAS THERE, but no Russ Walden. Rex could have made a scene about it but didn't.

Billy was brought in through the back and was directed to his seat. Rex spoke with him quietly, and Billy stiffened. Rex put his arm around his shoulder and pulled him close. He whispered some more. Billy surrendered and relaxed.

Rita walked to the back at 1:29 and out through the doors. In a minute, she was back with the jurors in tail.

Rex and Billy were standing when they entered and found their seats. Rick Turner stood a bit too slowly.

Rex had not moved over to take up the empty space left by Mark and Erich, leaving a seemingly vast open space between them. The absence of Russ Walden made it even wider.

Judge Dorsemann stepped up to the Bench. He gazed out over the courtroom and smiled as he said: "Good afternoon ladies and gentlemen." There was an enthusiastic response from the jury and the audience; an electricity of anticipation in the air. He then made a record about the presence of all who were necessary to continue with the trial. He did not mention the absence of Mark, Erich, or Captain Russ Walden.

"Mr. McKinley, you may call your first witness."

Rex stood and looked out over the courtroom, then began walking toward the jury. He stood directly behind Rick Turner.

"Your Honor, ladies and gentlemen, the defense rests."

He smiled at each of them, then returned to the counsel table. The courtroom was utterly silent as Rex sat next to Billy.

"Thank you, Mr. McKinley.

"Ladies and gentlemen, what this means is that the defense has chosen to rely on the state of the evidence, and not present any new evidence. I have previously instructed you that the law does not compel the defense to call any witnesses. Instead the law allows the defense to do what Mr. McKinley has done: to rely upon the state of the evidence without more.

"We will come back tomorrow morning and both sides will give their closing arguments. First, I give further instructions on the law. The prosecution will argue first, and then the defense. After the defense argues, the prosecution will be permitted to rebut any argument offered by the defense. Then I will give you final instructions about deliberation, and the case will be in your hands.

"You are excused until tomorrow morning at 8:30. I have not had to mention punctuality to you, which is rather unusual. So, I will simply say have a wonderful evening."

Rex and Billy immediately stood for the jury. Rick Turner stood slowly again. The jury filed out of the courtroom. It was Carey Sorenson who opened the door for them so that they passed by him single file. He smiled and nodded, but not a word was spoken. After the jury had gone, his Honor asked the routine question about any pending issues, and both Rex and Rick Turner told him: "No, your Honor."

"We need to deal with the exhibits, gentlemen. I have my list of what was introduced. Can we get through them quickly, or should we wait until the morning?"

Rex responded. "I have a list, as well, your Honor. Can we get this done now?"

Rick Turner joined in the request, and they went through the list of those exhibits that had been shown to the jury. They agreed which one's could be admitted. That settled, they were dismissed until the following morning.

94.

AT THE END OF THE DAY, Rex was home alone, and the house was quiet, although he still had security. He was writing the things he thought important. He would go over it several times and then again in the morning. When he delivered it, he would do so without his notes.

When he finally got to bed, he fell asleep as soon as his head hit the pillow.

He woke at 2:27 a.m. and made coffee. While it was brewing, he began practicing his closing to himself. He got into the shower later and was singing. It was a few minutes before five o'clock.

After his shower and as he left his bedroom to go to his study he heard something in the kitchen and assumed it was probably Gail. He changed his direction to say good morning.

Instead he found Melina. He stopped and stared. She turned and smiled. She seemed to glide toward him. He was trying to catch the breath.

"Are you glad to see me?"

She had an impish look on her face. She smiled, and he melted. For a split-second he tried to think of a smart remark. He didn't have one for the occasion.

"Yes, I am. Come to me, please," he said because he couldn't move. He couldn't pretend that he was not completely enthralled.

She took the last step and they embraced. He felt her love charging him up and filling him with hope and desire—and passion. They stayed that way for a while, then she whispered that she had come to make him breakfast for good luck.

"Having you in my life is more than good luck. I am blessed."

She smiled and kissed him; just a sweet touching of their lips. Rex felt fire inside. She stepped back and smiled.

"More coffee?"

"I better not. I'm plenty awake now." They both laughed.

They ate together. She made eggs, bacon, and potatoes. She served honeydew melon, also. "It's all organic," she boasted. They cleaned up together, side-by-side. Then she said:

"I know you're angry about what happened to you, and to my Uncle Billy. If you let your anger go, you will say all the right things."

Then she kissed him and said:

"I know that my Uncle Billy will go free today. I love you Rex McKinley. I'll see you in court."

And she walked out of the house through the living room and then the front door.

He felt the presence of Eddie behind him. Doug and Ron came into the kitchen after him. They had come through the back. He said good morning to them and walked off to get dressed, without another word.

95.

"LADIES AND GENTLEMEN, WE ARE BACK ON THE RECORD. This morning the lawyers are going to offer their closing arguments. They are admonished not to offer their personal opinions, but only what they believe the evidence has shown. It is argument, not statements of their belief in the truth of any given facts.

"I am now going to instruct you in the law. After argument, I will instruct you on how to proceed in your deliberations."

His Honor read jury instructions for about thirty minutes. When he was through, he said:

"Mr. Turner, you may proceed."

Rick Turner was wearing a dark suit with a white shirt and a red tie. His shoes were glossy black.

He walked to the easel and placed Exhibit 1 on it, the picture of Steve Michaelson, dead on the floor, blood pooled around him. His head had been destroyed, and he had bled from his neck also. It was a gruesome scene, the same one with which he started the trial.

He told the jury good morning. They politely responded. He explained that he had caught a cold, and that his voice was a bit strained. He seemed unable to turn on his magical voice.

"This case has had a lot of smoke and mirrors by the defense. An attempt has been made to disparage the character of each of the prosecution witnesses. But it has failed!"

He shouted the last part of the sentence, his voice gruff and raspy.

"That man there," he pointed at Billy—who was looking him in the eyes—"is a murderer. He plotted and burgled the house where an innocent man slept, and blew his brains out, without remorse, without mercy, and without cause.

"He is the worst kind of criminal. He is exactly the kind of man you must convict. He and his friend snuck in there under cover of darkness, then shot and stabbed this poor man to death." He pointed at the exhibit.

"There is nothing for you to do but declare him guilty, then let our justice system deal with him. That is your duty; your obligation; your code of honor.

"If you let this man slip through the cracks, we will have failed. We know better than to allow that to happen, don't we?

"This man is so cold-blooded that after he and his friend murdered Steve Michaelson they casually drove next door and drank some beer and boasted about their kill."

He began pacing. He raised his voice to a somewhat shrill note, and concluded:

"Now go into the jury room and do your duty. Do it for justice. Do it for Steve Michaelson. You must vote guilty! Guilty! Guilty!"

He started coughing as he sat.

"Mr. McKinley, please proceed."

"Thank you, your Honor."

Rex stood and put his hand on Billy's shoulder and whispered to him. Then he walked toward the jury. Once in front of them, he started to choke up. He tried to speak but could not. He looked at each of the jurors. He drew in a deep breath and said: "Good morning."

They all responded. He looked out over the courtroom and found Melina's eyes. He smiled at her, and held it for a few seconds, then turned back to the jury.

"Sometimes I get in the way of what needs to be said and done." He paused, drew another breath, and continued.

"Before I came here this morning I was planning to tell you about the things that we all saw, and I was going to make accusations, and ask you to be angry with the prosecutor and his witnesses. But as I left my house, the woman I love told me something. She said that if I let my anger go, I would say all the right things. At this moment, the truth of what she told me has washed over me, and I know she is right."

He smiled at each of them, his eyes glowing and wet. He looked at Melina and heard her in his mind saying that she loved him. He smiled to himself, then continued.

"This case is about whether the prosecution was able to overcome its burden of producing evidence that my client, William John West, is guilty of the crime of murdering Steve Michaelson.

"We viewed photographs, and we heard and saw people testify. What I ask of you is that you allow me to review what we have seen and heard. I will not go through all the details because I know that we have all seen the same things. However, on Mr. West's behalf, I believe that I must point out that the evidence does not show you who killed Steve Michaelson, and much less that there was any credible evidence that it was Mr. West.

"First, we heard from Dr. Melanie Chang who is a pathologist for the County of Danbrier. She confirmed that Mr. Michaelson was murdered and that he had been drugged. It was the powerful date rape drug Rohypnol, and that he could not have gotten out of bed if he had been drugged just prior to his death. Who drugged that man?

"The next witness was Miss Rankin. You saw her, you heard her. She told you two stories. The first was that Mr. Michaelson came to her house uninvited and forcefully imposed himself on her and then changed her story when confronted here in court about the absence of his vehicle at her house. Although she denied that she drugged him, she did say 'I did what I had to do.' She did not offer any testimony about Mr. West being at her home when Mr. Michaelson was murdered."

He paused, again taking a deep breath and looking at each of the jurors.

"Cheryl Porter told you that Mr. West admitted to murdering Mr. Michaelson. She said that happened at her home, and that he parked in front of her home in the spot where the evidence tape had been placed. Obviously, she did not know that we would all find out that there was a vehicle parked inside that evidence tape—a shiny black pickup." He paused again, looking at each of the jurors before he continued. "She called 911, and she didn't mention the admission by Mr. West. She could not identify the second man with him—no one could. Ms. Porter denied knowing Samuel James Ellifson, the leader of a violent prison gang that probably tried to assassinate Eddie Logan. But you saw a photo of her with him, which Captain Walden identified for you. What value was her testimony? Was she believable?

"Captain Walden told you about *his* crime scene, and how he preserved the integrity of the scene. Yet he could not explain the presence, and then later the absence of an item, that brief case, which may have contained some evidence of who murdered Steve Michaelson. He told you he did not know that brief case was on his crime scene.

"He did not bring in the forensics team to dust for fingerprints, or to check for DNA, or do any of the standard investigative procedures, and he told you that was because he already knew who it did, because of what Cheryl Porter told him, and nothing more.

"And then there were the tire tracks that he photographed, and swore they were a perfect match for the tires on Mr. West's truck—but he didn't follow any scientific procedure, and that wasn't his kind of work to perform anyway. The prosecution didn't even share those photos of the tire tracks with you. They are not exhibits in evidence for you to review because the prosecution never showed them.

"More importantly, we all learned that the tire tracks Captain Walden claimed to be protecting were not there inside that evidence tape because there was another vehicle carefully hidden inside that area surrounded by the evidence tape. How did he explain that to us? He asked us to disbelieve what we saw in the photograph taken by him. And that vehicle he was hiding inside that evidence tape belonged to Samuel James Ellifson, now deceased, a man the Captain pretended to know nothing about, but later acknowledged he knew or recognized. Can we rely upon the testimony of Captain Walden for anything? Did he help prove that anyone accused in this trial killed Steve Michaelson?"

"Perhaps we should believe Mr. Maddux, the jail house rat; the snitch. He's a robber, a burglar, a beater of elderly women, a gun-toting drug addict, and a jail house snitch. A rat who denied being exactly that—a man who would tell on anyone to keep from going to jail. And he got out of another case where he beat a woman and threatened to harm her baby. Why would the prosecution bring that kind of person before you?

"I had intended to come before you and rant about liars, and how horrible it was to see the attempt to con you into believing that which was not shown to you, or the audacity of the effort to convince you to disbelieve what you had seen with your own eyes. But now, somehow that seems crude, even demeaning to this process, this pursuit of justice. I don't need to tell you someone lied. You saw and heard all the evidence. You saw and felt it. You know the truth. But what you have seen does not offer even a hint that Mr. West did something to Mr. Michaelson."

He paused a moment and smiled at each of the jurors.

"I cannot tell you what you must do, for you have the power, not I. I can only plead with you on behalf of Mr. West. I can only ask you to go into that jury room and pick a foreperson, review the evidence, and vote your conscience.

"I pray that you vote not guilty. I ask you to find that there is reasonable doubt. In fact, I would suggest that this case is a classic example of reasonable doubt. There is no believable evidence against my client." He paused, and looked at the jury, smiling at each one, most returning the smile, some wearing serious expressions without smiles.

"Again, I thank you, each of you. You have taken this time out of your lives to be here. You have been punctual, engaged, and your hearts have been open. Because of you, my client has had a fair trial.

"I now ask you to give a bit more. Take all the time you need, and ask yourselves, do you have an abiding conviction that the charge of murder against my client is true? Did the prosecution prove to you beyond a reasonable doubt that Mr. West is guilty? Did you hear credible evidence of his guilt?

"I usually like to come up with some unique example of reasonable doubt to explain what it means in any given case because the law really doesn't give a specific definition. Proof beyond a reasonable doubt is proof that leaves you with an abiding conviction that the charge is true. An abiding conviction means that you will have a long-lasting feeling that the charge is true. You will be able to be at peace with such a decision. Ask yourselves whether you would be at peace with any decision other than not guilty.

"Thank you, ladies and gentlemen."

He continued to stand before them while drew in another deep breath. He sighed and smiled at them all. He turned his Honor, bowed and said: "Thank you, your Honor." Judge Dorsemann smiled and said: "You are welcome, Mr. McKinley."

Rex walked slowly to the counsel table and put his hand on Billy's shoulder, and sat. He put his arm around him and hugged him. Billy smiled.

"Mr. Turner, any rebuttal?"

Rick Turner stood and looked at Rex. He turned to the jury but looked out at the audience. Then he spoke:

"Don't be fooled by this silky slick defender of a murderer. Do your duty." He started to yell, but it came off as more of a growl. "Convict that criminal or we'll all be sorry." He paced back and forth, and then went to his seat. He sat, turned away from the jury, and began coughing again.

Judge Dorsemann then instructed the jury on how to proceed. It took about five minutes. Then the Bailiff was sworn, and she took charge of the jury. From thereafter, all messages, questions, needs for assistance of any kind would be funneled through her. She was their protector, there to serve them.

As the jury left, Billy and Rex stood, as did all the Club members, once again. Rick Turner did not stand, nor did he look toward the jury. He sat and stared at the counsel table and began coughing again.

The jury went through the door into the hallway behind the Judge. They were going to the jury deliberation room, where they would stay until they had arrived at a verdict, or if they had deliberated sufficiently and could not arrive at a verdict, which was called a hung jury, and grounds for a mistrial.

They would break for lunch, and at the end of the day they would go home.

After the public had made their way into the hall, with two members holding the doors open, Rick Turner left. The two members standing by the doors let them close before he got there. Neither said a word to him as he opened one and made his way into the hallway.

Rex asked the Bailiff who had come to take Billy back to the holding cell if he could have five minutes with him. He agreed and stepped back a few paces.

"Billy, I'm seeing something different in you, and I like it."

"It's the drugs, Rex. I've been clean a while now, and I've been praying. Something is changing in me. I like it, too. I can look people in the eyes."

They stood, and Rex hugged him again. "Okay, Billy. Go with the Bailiff. If you get brought back in that means something has happened."

"No matter what it is, I want to thank you Rex. You're a really good lawyer."

"Thanks, Billy. It has been my pleasure."

"I need to tell you something, Rex," he whispered. Billy looked deep into Rex' eyes.

"I'm not sure I want to hear it, Billy. Just go and wait, please." Rex felt a swarm of bees in his stomach. Billy persisted. He put his arm on Rex's shoulder, still looking in his eyes. He was being forceful, but respectful. Billy's eyes began to tear up and he started crying. Rex grabbed him and held him until he settled. Rex spoke calmly and quietly as he said: "It's okay, Billy. Just go with Deputy Crownes and wait, please."

Rex watched Billy go. He was standing tall. He looked his brother in the eyes and held his gaze. Rex turned toward Doug and saw something he'd never seen; his eyes were welled up with tears. The swarm of bees left Rex.

He checked his watch. It was 10:47 a.m. Now they would wait.

96.

THEY WENT OUT INTO THE HALLWAY and everyone was there. Doug and Ron were smiling, and other Club members came over and thanked Rex. Eddie gave him a hug.

"Nice job, Brother."

"Thanks, Eddie. I couldn't have done anything without you."

The hallway went quiet. Again, the Club members were setting the example. Some were standing, some sitting, but all were silent.

Eighteen minutes later Rita Alcazar came out and said in a much too excited voice: "They have a verdict."

Rex took a deep breath and looked at Doug who was almost smiling.

"Let's go," Rex said.

They all started walking into the courtroom. The public and media waited for two of the members to hold the doors open after their other brothers had gone inside. The two members stood holding the doors open until Rick Turner came into the courtroom. He did not thank them; did not acknowledge them. He walked to his seat at the counsel and sat.

Rex stood and waited for Billy to be brought out. In short order, he came through the back door. He wore a serious look on his face.

He sat as directed and smiled at the Bailiff. He said:

"Thank you, sir."

"You are welcome, Mr. West."

The door to the hallway where the jury had gone opened, and Rita escorted the jury in, and they each found their seats. Billy stood beside Rex. Rick Turner stood but did not look at the jury.

The judge came out of chambers and stepped up to the Bench. Rex and Billy sat, as did Rick Turner. Judge Dorsemann shuffled some papers out of the way, then looked up, and said:

"It is my understanding that juror Number 4 is our foreperson. Is that correct?"

"It is, your Honor," she said.

"It is also my understanding that the jury has reached a verdict."

"That is correct, your Honor."

"Would you please hand the verdict forms to the Bailiff?"

She stood and waited for Rita Alcazar to take them. Rita did not look at them, but instead walked to Karin Kornder and handed them to her. Karin did not examine them either. She handed them directly to the judge.

Judge Dorsemann wore his poker face while he went through the forms. He seemed satisfied, then handed the forms back to Karin.

"Madam Clerk, will you please read the verdict?"

Karin stood, and in her usual professional way she said:

"We, the jury, in the above-entitled action find the Defendant, William John West, not guilty of the crime of murder."

There was complete and total silence in the courtroom. The Club members remained very serious. They had manners; they showed respect.

His Honor looked at the jury, and said: "Is this your verdict?"

They all said yes.

His Honor looked at Rex, and then Rick Turner, and asked:

"Would counsel like the jury to be polled?"

"No thank you, your Honor," Rex said as he faced the jury and smiled.

"Mr. Turner?"

"No thank you, your Honor."

"Ladies and gentlemen, you have done your duty. I thank you on behalf of the parties and of the People of the State of California. You are now excused. If you would like to wait in the hallway, I am certain that the lawyers may have some questions for you."

The entire courtroom stood. The jurors filed out, and Rex said:

"I hope you can stay a while. I would love to speak with you."

Two members open the doors for them. Others followed them out into the hallway. Doug, Ron and Eddie continued standing. The media rushed to the hallway, and the Club members holding the doors whispered to each of them.

His Honor looked at Billy and said:

"Mr. West, you are a free man. I do believe that the Bailiff will need a thumb print on a document or two, but you will no longer walk into the back to be confined.

Billy said: "Thank you, your Honor."

"While I still have both attorneys, I want to say to you Mr. Turner, that your behavior during this trial has been less than professional. What you do and say now will have a significant impact on my continued respect for you."

Rick Turner looked up, and then he stood. He looked at Judge Dorsemann and began to cough. The he said with a very scratchy voice:

"This has been a tough trial, Judge. I may have been out of line at times. I did not know of some of the worst things, like the lies. I did not intend to sandbag. I ask the Court to forgive my conduct." He turned as though he were leaving.

"Mr. Turner do not leave. We are not through. You were out of line several times. There were lies told that I am still shaken by, and I want to accept your denial of complicity. I will not review your trial strategy. I will, however, warn you that you have lost respect in my eyes, and the word has undoubtedly spread like it does in any courthouse. You have some amends to make, and only time will tell.

"I am disturbed that Captain Walden did not return after you rested. His conduct was questionable, to say the least. I am uncertain what I might do considering the evidence of the truck on the scene. I think that issue is out of the hands of your office, Mr. Turner, but you should be forewarned that what happened before this jury has cast a shadow on your reputation." He paused, looking at Rick Turner, who was now hanging his head.

"I will accept your apology. I hope to never see or hear of that conduct on your part; never again!" He was very emphatic.

"I do believe we are through here," said Judge Dorsemann.

Rex remained silent as Rick Turner sat at the counsel table his head hanging. He looked defeated and deflated. The courtroom king had been deposed, and all because of his own behavior. He took himself down with a Sheriff's Captain who had crossed the line of decency; fabricated evidence.

"Thank you, your Honor," said Rex. "I thank all of your courtroom personnel, and Deputy Alcazar."

Billy chimed in beside him.

"Yes, Your Honor, and to Deputy Crownes, who has brought me in and out of this courtroom every day, I thank him, too. He treated me like a man, and I owe him a debt of gratitude."

Rex was impressed by those words from Billy West.

"Mr. West, on behalf of the court and personnel, we are grateful that we could be part of this trial."

Deputy Crownes came over to Billy with a couple of forms, and an ink pad for his thumb print. Billy complied with a smile.

Rex asked Billy if he was ready to face the world. He said he was, then asked if he could walk over to his brother. Rex told him he was a free man.

He walked straight to Doug. They began a quiet conversation. Soon, Doug grabbed Billy and hugged him. Billy hugged him back. He had tears in his eyes but was not crying. Then Richard West stepped up and tapped his son on the shoulder. Billy turned and sobbed. Richard hugged him and held him.

Melina waited her turn, and hugged Billy. Rex heard her tell him that she loved him.

97.

REX DECIDED THE LET THE BROTHERS and Richard West have their time together, but he couldn't take his eyes off Melina. She got through with hugging her uncle and turned to Rex like she knew he was watching and waiting. She smiled and walked toward him. As she drew near she said:

"You are the greatest lawyer on earth, Rex McKinley." He melted. She hugged him tight and held him until she felt him begin to get hot. She said: "There are people waiting for you. Go to them. I'll be waiting." She turned him gently toward the door. She left the courtroom and walked out into the hallway. He was met by lights and cameras, and his many dear friends. The media seemed more interested in the Club members and Eddie Logan than Rex. He was grateful to stand back and watch. Finally, one of them saw him and the madness began. Fortunately, the Club members came to his aid, and Rex asked the reporters to be gentle. They laughed.

Rex made his way through the reporters until he found the jurors. All fourteen were still there waiting for him. They had refused to speak with the media.

As Rex approached them, they surrounded him. They shook hands and shared hugs. Rex's eyes began to tear up. There wasn't a word spoken by any of them; words would have only spoiled the moment.

The media persons were standing and watching, some filming with cameras and phones, but no one asked questions.

When Billy and Doug finally walked out of the courtroom, the media attempted to get to Billy. He was quiet and solemn. He was free, and he was grateful. Those were the words that Ron gave to the media on Billy's behalf: "Free and grateful."

After a few more minutes, Rick Turner walked out of the courtroom. Everyone stopped what they are doing, even those in the media; the hallway fell silent. Rick Turner paused for a moment, as though he wanted to turn and say something, but he continued walking down the hallway.

Rex and the jury stayed together a while longer, until they started leaving, one at a time. Rex looked to his friends and saw Melina with her father and the guys. He walked over to them, and she moved to his side. They held hands so naturally. After a few minutes, Melina whispered to Rex that she needed to take care of some things and that she would see him soon at the Ranch.

As they rode back to Rex's house he asked his friends:

"Does anyone know what happened with Erich Trotter?"

He watched Doug in the rearview mirror as the carved-out-of-stone look settled across his face. He paused for effect, and said:

"He's gone," and there was finality in his words. Rex quietly reflected on what that meant. If he was gone forever, so be it.

"We're gonna drop you off and get things started for tonight. Carey will ride with you when you come up." Doug's expression had changed to the happiest Rex had ever seen.

Rex could hardly wait to get to the Ranch. He wanted Melina. He needed her. He wanted to spend the next month recuperating from the trial, and from what he had been through with his own case, and he wanted to spend that time with Melina.

98.

THE MEDIA HAD A FIELD DAY WITH THE VERDICT. "PROSECUTION SHOULD BE PROSECUTED" was the headline in the Danbrier Sentinel. Stanton Sensa was the only journalist courageous enough to make that kind of statement. There were news reports on the various television channels, with films of the hallway, of Rex and all the members of the Club, and Eddie Logan. A female reporter did her best to get next to Eddie and ask him about how he was healing. The look on her face was one of adoration; Rex thought she wanted to have his child—not the first such impression.

One writer told the world that Billy West was Doug's brother. It didn't take much to figure that part. He didn't know what else to say, other than explaining the presence of the Club, *sans* patches, which had always been reported as Rex's security force. Rex was grateful for the explanation. He knew how the Club felt about people thinking they, the Club, were at the beck and call of anyone outside their membership, Rex included.

The headlines went nationwide because of the underlying story of the Sheriff's Captain who clearly fabricated evidence, and a prosecutor who put on such a shameful display of lying witnesses. Rick Turner and Captain Walden had been convicted by the media. There were photos of Samuel James Ellifson, as well as discussion of his alleged suicide. He was said to be the leader of the assassination team sent to murder Eddie Logan, and boss of the violent prison gang, the Point Men.

It was rumored that the trial Judge, the Honorable Gregory J. Dorsemann, was going to file a complaint with the State Bar of California reporting continued professional misconduct on the part of Rick Turner during the Billy West trial, and that he was attaching transcripts of the relevant parts of the trial where Rick Turner had been rude, and worse, where he had clearly suborned perjury. He knew that the Captain was lying, and if he did not, then he failed in his duty to know.

That story was not true, and subsequently Judge Dorsemann made it a point to let the media know that he had no intentions of doing any such thing. He refused to comment on how he felt about the behavior of Rick Turner.

The arrest and promises to Mary Jane Rankin was repeated over and over. The missing briefcase got a lot of attention. There was quite a bit of speculation about whether there was a connection between Samuel Ellifson and Captain Russ Walden, as well as his blatant perjury about the tire tracks.

One news outlet suggested that Cheryl Porter should be arrested for perjury, and that an inquiry should be made into her relationship with Ellifson.

Most significant to Rex was the demand by the Sentinel that an investigation into the attempted murder of Eddie Logan be conducted. It had become apparent that the Sheriff's Department never made any effort to investigate that crime, and the Sentinel was beginning to call it a cover-up to protect someone or some persons within the Sheriff's Department. "It wouldn't be the first time they tried to sweep their dirt under the rug," was the allegation in the Sentinel.

Billy West had gone home. He was living in his own cabin on the ranch. It seemed he had quite a knack with tools and an excellent grasp of the operation of motorcycles. It seemed the nickname Scooter Billy wasn't just a joke.

He made peace with his brother, Doug, and with his father, who was overjoyed that his errant son had rejoined the family. Rex was told by Eddie there had been no discussion of Billy becoming a member of the Club. That might come in a few of years if Billy showed himself to have the quality of character required.

99.

THE CASE OF REX MCKINLEY v. the County of Danbrier, Henry John Martin, Sheriff, Donny Michaelson, an individual, Carlos Meza, an individual, and Does 1-10, inclusive, settled—sixty-two days after it was filed.

Patrick Moynihan rejected the initial proposal of settlement, but his counter-offer was accepted. Patrick wanted to go to trial. The county lawyers did not; they knew Rex's case was flawless. Mindy Thorn was a witness to so many crimes by their employees, and there were even a few Danbrier City police officers and two deputies who were willing to come forward, one of whom was Larry Wear, who wanted so badly to carve out his pound of flesh. Patrick and Rex did not want to expose him to the long-term trouble, and at that point no one knew of him—except Russ Walden. They kept him a secret witness who would somehow magically appear with information and photos should the need arise—but only then. Russ Walden had always known that Deputy Wear had taken his own set of photos of the crime scene, and although he had feared the revelation, it never became an issue; the Captain had more important things to worry about.

The County of Danbrier wrote a public apology, which was published on the front page of the Danbrier Sun Newspaper, and the Danbrier Sentinel. The Deputy County Counsel handling the defense personally delivered a check for five million dollars to the office of Patrick Moynihan. Rex split it with Patrick Moynihan, as agreed.

Rex gave half of his share to Eddie Logan. Eddie looked at the check and laughed. He said: "What the fuck, Rex!"

Rex and Melina had been together every day since the trial. Rex proposed marriage to her, and she accepted. They had not set a date for the wedding, but it would be at the Blood Oath Ranch. The mighty Doug West had given his blessing.

www.ingramcontent.com/pod-product-compliance
Lightning Source LLC
Chambersburg PA
CBHW021445240626
47153CB00001B/309